I0523603

DOUBT OF THE BENEFIT

RAY SCOTT

Publisher: Silverbird Publishing
Ray Scott
website: www.raycwscottwriting.com.au

First published in Australia 2023
This edition published 2023

Copyright © Ray Scott 2023

Cover design, typesetting: WorkingType (www.workingtype.com.au)

The right of Ray Scott to be identified as the Author of the Work has been asserted in accordance with the Copyright, Designs and Patents Act 1988.

This book is a work of fiction. Any similarities to that of people living or dead are purely coincidental.

All rights reserved. No part of this publication may be reproduced, stored in a retrieval system, or transmitted, in any form or by any means without the prior written permission of the publisher, nor be otherwise circulated in any form of binding or cover other than that in which it is published and without a similar condition being imposed on the subsequent purchaser.

Scott, Ray
Doubt of the Benefit
ISBN: 978-0-6486011-9-7
pp394

ABOUT THE AUTHOR

Ray Scott was born in Kent in England and lived and worked for over 30 years in the Midlands near Birmingham. After National service in the Royal Navy he joined the insurance industry and was employed for many years in Birmingham and Wolverhampton. He and his wife Mary and their two boys immigrated to Australia in 1970 and have lived since then near Melbourne where he again joined the insurance industry, while Mary rejoined the nursing profession.

Ray has been writing for many years. This is his sixth venture into publishing, the others being *The Fifth Identity, Cut to the Chase* (also a paperback) *The Wimmera Shoot, Double Dutch,* and *Line of Dissent,* all thrillers.

www.raycwscottwriting.com.au

To the regrettably late Tony Gelme,
a good friend and a skilled exponent of the written
and spoken word.

CHAPTER 1

Two Asian men knocked on the door of an hotel room in Jakarta, Indonesia and were admitted. Two Asians were already in the room, after greeting and embracing the newcomers they all seated themselves around the table.

'Our arrangements are nearly complete, we have a date, and believe we'll succeed where we failed last time,' said one of the room's original occupiers. His name was Julius Lebak, he had cropped black hair and a slight beard. His three companions all possessed similar beards, all four were casually dressed.

'How are matters in Taranga now?' asked Lebak. 'As you can appreciate, I'm not able to see for myself these days.'

This caused a ripple of amusement from his companions.

'Since our previous attempt at government failed,' said one of the new arrivals. 'De Souza has clamped down very hard, anyone suspected of complicity with the attempted coup is either under arrest, under observation or left Taranga altogether.'

'So, Hassan, you are saying any local attempt to kill De Souza…!'

'Would be extremely difficult, if not impossible,' said Hassan Qassim. 'This confirms the wisdom of attempting an assassination elsewhere, and this proposed state visit of De Souza to Australia a few months hence provides a good opportunity. Australian is security conscious, but may be unprepared to combat a long-range rifle shot in a public place.'

'You agree, Marid?' Lebak turned to the other new arrival.

'No doubt in my mind, we are ready to take advantage of this visit, much desired by both nations,' replied Marid Jaafar. 'We have obtained tenancy of an office overlooking the front entrance of the hotel where informants tell us De Souza will be resident during his visit. We are also searching for another city base, there is a vacancy in a serviced office block nearby which gives an excellent cross fire position.'

'We registered a legitimate business in Sydney some time ago,' said Qassim. 'This was at the time of our previous coup attempt, so we are well established there. We have also contacted and recruited many young Taranganese men studying at Australian universities, many are ready to assist your cause, Julius, and to establish the true faith in our country.'

'You have done well,' said Lebak. 'Meanwhile I've been in contact with Juan Rivera, who assisted us last time in Australia. He will return independently to Australia and make his way to Sydney. He charges much for his services, but is an excellent marksman. If he can get De Souza in his sights, he will not miss.'

'What of Javid here?' asked Qassim.

'I have already made arrangements to be shipped to Australia under cover,' replied Javid Sattar, the other original room resident, 'I cannot get there openly, my name is on their list of…' he smiled '…undesirables…therefore I shall avail myself of the services of a contact of ours who runs...er...an overseas immigration business.'

There was more laughter at that and Javid continued.

'I must leave soon, a Federal election in Australia is imminent and the present Opposition in Canberra have expressed their intention of curbing people smuggling and tightening immigration laws and procedures should they win government. I shall base myself initially in Sydney, I have a sister living there.'

'Is she one of us?'

'No, her husband is from Pakistan so neither have much interest in Taranganese politics. I have hopes of their son, my nephew, who I have sounded out over the phone and he seems very sympathetic to our cause.'

'Good, then we are well placed.,' said Lebak. 'This time, we should not fail, we have tightened security and strictly restricted our inner circle on a need-to-know basis...not like last time when by a combination of bungling and sheer bloody coincidence an interloper gained admittance to one of our final planning sessions...!'

He broke off and irritably hit the table with his clenched fist. There was a brief silence as they all recalled a planning meeting held by conspirators of the previous abortive coup in Taranga City. Two men had been despatched to collect Johannes Van Elderen, a co-conspirator from Indonesia, an expert in electronics who was to disable the electricity services of the public utility prior to the takeover. They had arrived at the designated hotel but Van Elderen's flight had been delayed, and the man they brought back with them was Douglas Van Ekeren, a visiting Australian businessman who coincidentally had been expecting a car to take him to a business meeting scheduled for the same time. After the meeting had run for 20 minutes Van Ekeren had realised he was not only at the wrong meeting, but also what he had got into. He feigned illness, made easy by being white as a sheet with fear, made a premature exit and left to thunderous applause. When the real conspirator, Van Elderen, materialised Van Ekeren was boarding a flight back to Australia. He was subsequently abducted to ensure his silence, but had escaped and blew the plot to ASIO in Canberra.[*]

Lebak leant forward and again hit his hand in exasperated fashion on the table.

'This time there will be no such mistakes. Once De Souza has been disposed of, I shall land on Taranga, take advantage of the confusion, establish a base, summon the faithful and march on Taranga City.'

'Like Napoleon from Elba,' commented Qassim.

'Indeed, like Napoleon, as you say,' Lebak joined in the general laughter, rose from his chair and raised the glass by his side. 'Comrades...I give you a toast ...to New Taranga.'

---

[*] *This incident and its aftermath were the subject of a previous novel entitled "Double Dutch" by the same author released in 2019.*

CHAPTER 2

A month later, at Avalon Airport, situated on the west side of Port Philip Bay near the city of Melbourne, Australia, passengers were collecting their cases from the carousel. Among them was a man of average height, mid-thirties, with a short beard, wearing a baseball cap and leather jacket. With other passengers he reached the Customs area, went through the normal procedures and presented his passport.

'What is the purpose of your trip, Mr Alvarez?'

'Strictly business,' was the response. 'I run an engineering business in Valparaiso and am meeting with representatives of your motor accessories industry in Melbourne.'

The Customs official scrutinised him, appeared satisfied, nodded and waved Alvarez through.

'Have a good trip, Mr Alvarez,' he said.

Alvarez left the airport building and was approached by a man waiting outside.

'Juan?' he asked.

'Yes,' responded Alvarez.

'I am Dawoud. I have a car waiting.'

'Good,' responded Alvarez. 'How are matters going?'

'According to plan,' replied Dawoud. 'The Presidential visit is due within a week and we are finalising arrangements. We are exploring locations overlooking his hotel.'

'Good,' responded Alvarez. 'Have you obtained the other items I requested?'

'We brought in some of the latest versions from Taranga, fresh from Moscow,' he gave a short laugh. 'We took delivery of a consignment this week.'

'I need time to become conversant with it,' said Alvarez, 'New weapons need to be properly calibrated. With a long shot we can't afford mistakes, there will be only be time for two attempts at the most.'

*

Robert Colbeck's phone rang; it was his receptionist, Angela Parish.

'Mr Colbeck, those gentlemen are here about the vacant office on the 11th floor.'

'Thanks Angela, send them in.'

Colbeck's company operated a serviced office block which provided offices for rent, plus common services, ground floor reception desk, the main telephone switchboard, office cleaning, secretarial services if required plus conference rooms for the use of clientele.

Serviced office blocks suited small businesses such as small insurance brokers or agents, private detectives, individual lawyers, architects, personnel agencies and the like who didn't require, or couldn't afford, large office spaces or street frontages but who needed a city address. If or when these businesses expanded and employed more personnel, they were then able to move to larger individual premises

Angela accompanied the newcomers into the room and introduced them. Colbeck rose to greet them, his paperwork indicated they were Hassan Qassim and Marid Jaafar, involved with experimental farming equipment.

As they chatted Colbeck studied them covertly. He approved of what he saw, both wore dark suits, were clearly of Asian origin while their English, although accented, was good. Their completed application form was already before him.

'You're interested in renting our vacant office, I understand?'

'That is so, may we see it?' asked Qassim.

'Indeed, you may,' Colbeck rose to his feet. 'Please follow me.'

He led the way to the elevators and they disembarked on the 11th floor. The vacant office was on the south side of the building.

Colbeck unlocked the office door and they entered. The taller of the two, Marid Jaafar, advanced to the window and peered out intently. Colbeck was puzzled to see him move his head from one side, up and down, then look at his companion. He said something in a language Colbeck didn't understand whereupon Qassim joined him.

'Is there a problem?' Colbeck asked curiously.

'What's that outside the window?' asked Qassim.

'What's what?' Colbeck went over, the object of their query was a pole sticking out horizontally from the next-door building. 'Oh, that building used to be a department store years ago. That's a flag pole, they used to hang their company banner from it.'

'It blocks the view,' said Jaafar.

'View?' Colbeck just stopped himself adding 'Of what?' to avoid saying anything to upset the transaction. He could see little to stimulate the casual viewer, merely tops and sides of buildings and the frontage of the Worthington Hotel several hundred metres away. The horizontal flag pole jutting from the neighbouring building merely interfered with the line of sight of the front steps of the Worthington Hotel.

'You have other offices on the same side of this building?'

'Several on various floors,' conceded Colbeck. 'None vacant at present, although one is to be vacated during the next two or three weeks, two floors down, roughly the same position as this one.'

'Two weeks or so,' the two men exchanged glances. 'May we see it please? We may be interested in it when it falls vacant.'

'Certainly,' agreed Colbeck. 'There should be nobody there at present; the occupants are on the road most weekdays.'

As he led the way downstairs, Colbeck was puzzled. He couldn't see how the flag pole could cause problems, unless they intended to sit and gaze out of the window all day.

He paused outside the offices of Hill & Berrett, who were shortly vacating. He had no qualms about allowing them to view the office, providing he accompanied them. Hill and Berrett were commercial travellers, their speciality was European spectacle frames, mainly French. They were rarely in their office, spending most of their working days on the road calling on optometrists throughout Australia. Colbeck knew they were both up country this week.

Colbeck unlocked the door, the two men entered and looked around with interest. Colbeck was not surprised when the smaller of the two promptly headed for the window. He re-joined his companion, they conversed and nodded.

'My friend and I are agreed. We shall take the office upstairs,' said Qassim. 'You say this will be vacant in two weeks?'

'Yes, about that,' said Colbeck.

'This view is good,' Jaafar said to Qassim. 'You can see the Harbour Bridge from here.'

Colbeck looked briefly at what little of the harbour bridge he could see, bewildered at their pre-occupation with views from the windows. He turned around and became aware Qassim was by the desk; just placing his hand in his jacket pocket. Colbeck cast his eyes over the desk, but all that could have been within Qassim's reach was a card holder for Eddie Hill's business cards. He began to feel uneasy and decided he'd done enough to accommodate these two.

'Shall we settle the paperwork?' he marched to the door, keeping a close eye on them. They exchanged glances and followed him into the corridor.

Downstairs in his office Colbeck dealt with the various forms.

'In the name of Qassim and Jaafar is it?' he asked.

'The company name is Agnarat Wen,' Qassim handed over a business card. 'That will be the name in which it will be leased.'

After negotiations were complete, it was agreed they would take over the office the following Monday. Colbeck escorted them to the street door, then returned to the foyer where he met Barry Rawlings, the building superintendent.

'Have you let the former Craig & West office on the 11th?' asked Rawlings.

'Yes,' Colbeck answered thoughtfully.

'You don't look too happy, Bob,' observed Rawlings. 'Everything OK?'

'I don't know, Barry,' answered Colbeck. 'There's something strange about them, nothing I could put my finger on, just bloody weird, if you ask me!'

*

As Robert Colbeck reflected on the strange behaviour of his recent visitors, two men were conversing in the building that housed ASIO, the Australian Security & Intelligence Organisation in Canberra. Francis Burton, the First Assistant Director-General of Security and Intelligence, was with Alan Kelsey, Director of Counter Terrorism Investigations.

'We may have a national security problem, Alan,' Francis Burton was saying.

'Don't we always,' Kelsey replied cynically. 'If we didn't, we wouldn't be here.'

Burton permitted himself a faint smile and flicked through the file before him.

'I'm referring to the imminent state visit by President De Souza of Taranga,' he said. 'The relationship between Taranga and Australia is more delicate than usual.'

Kelsey nodded; the problem was complex. Taranga was an island nation in the Timor Sea between East Timor, Australia and Sumba. President De Souza was a former Army colonel, who had recently deposed an oppressive Marxist dictatorship, which had called itself The Peoples Marxist Republic. This regime had originally swept aside a democratically elected government by coup d'état shortly after Taranga gained independence from the previous Dutch administration, and forcibly retained control over the island for twenty years by eliminating opposition.

With Taranga bankrupt, De Souza had led a successful military coup d'état and become the secular leader of the island nation whose population was a mixture of the Muslim majority, Christians and Hindus, plus many still disaffected Marxists. The religious factions lived in an uneasy alliance, presided over by De Souza and his thinly disguised military government, who ruled with a heavy hand but gave no preferment to any religious doctrine.

'How do you mean, more than usual?'

'I spoke with Colin Minton of ASIS this morning,' replied Burton. 'I want you to see him for a briefing. You'll also be seeing Gary Phillips, the resident ASIS operative at our embassy in Taranga, who'll give it you straight from the horse's mouth.'

'When?' asked Kelsey. ASIS was the Australian Secret Intelligence Service, the sister service of ASIO. Where ASIO dealt with counter intelligence and internal security, ASIS dealt with external overseas intelligence. They were similar to the American versions of FBI and CIA, or Britain's MI5 and MI6 respectively.

'Now,' was the reply.

*

Colin Minton advanced to meet Kelsey and warmly shook his hand. Minton was in his late thirties, and spoke with a trace of a Yorkshire accent although he had left England as a small boy. Another man, also present, roughly the same age as the two of them, raised a hand in salute to Kelsey.

'Good to see you again, Alan,' he said.

'You too, Gary,' Kelsey extended his hand. 'What brings you to Canberra?'

'First hand de-briefing,' commented Phillips. 'Plus, a family wedding in Adelaide that fortuitously arose at the same time, which enabled me to visit and report here without raising any eyebrows.'

'De-briefing?'

'There's something brewing in Taranga, Alan,' said Phillips. 'We're not fully au fait with what's going on, but have reason to believe it will affect you and internal security.'

'You mean another coup is on the cards in Taranga?'

'So our sources inform us.'

Kelsey turned to Minton.

'Here we go again, wasn't there an attempt to upend De Souza this time last year?'

'There was,' said Minton. 'It started to unravel when that visiting businessman, Van Ekeren, stumbled on it by accident and dissidents kidnapped him when he arrived back in Sydney to shut him up.'

'I remember, Van Ekeren escaped and blew the coup. He reached us after they pursued him through Victoria and New South Wales,' said Kelsey.

'Correct, De Souza crushed the coup but Julius Lebak, the main instigator, escaped and is still active.' said Phillips. 'He has a large following, if he takes over, he intends to seal an alliance with Indonesia with the intention of both nations exploiting that undersea oilfield jointly. He's ruthless and doesn't care what allies he attracts.'

'I remember Lebak,' Kelsey nodded. 'He eluded De Souza's security police when they arrested the coup leaders.'

'He did, he's resilient and resourceful. We believe he's formed cells within Australia, he has links with people smugglers and many Taranganese dissidents have entered Australia.'

'With what object?'

'We're currently negotiating a trade deal with Taranga. Lebak doesn't want that, he wants less connection with us and more with their northern neighbour and China. He wants to remove De Souza, that's no secret, he knows without De Souza at the helm the regime could collapse.'

'A characteristic of many totalitarian regimes,' commented Kelsey.

'Too bloody true. De Souza is visiting Australia shortly

to finalise the deal, we've heard whispers there could be an assassination attempt while he's here,' said Phillips. 'Security is tight in Taranga, particularly since that last coup attempt, maybe Lebak thinks we are less secure here.'

'He's probably right,' Minton turned to Kelsey. 'Do we know of any Taranganese expats likely to be a problem?'

'Yes, but none we'd describe as militants,' replied Kelsey. 'Anyone specific on your radar, Gary?'

'We have a contact within the Taranganese Security police, according to this source one of Lebak's lieutenants has disappeared and it's believed he re-surfaced in Australia, a man named Javid Sattar.'

'Javid Sattar,' pondered Kelsey. 'The name means nothing. Who or what is he?'

'A fanatical bastard, from Pakistan originally. He tried to reach Australia illegally but when Australia stopped the illegal boats he only reached Indonesia and then Taranga. While there he hitched himself onto Lebak's bandwagon and became his righthand man. Now he's vanished and we fear he's smuggled himself into Australia.'

'With what in mind?'

'We think to organise an attempt on De Souza when he arrives, that's the short term,' said Phillips. 'The long term, to lay foundations for a Taranganese undercover or subversive organisation within Australia. There's another point.'

'Bloody hell! What else?'

'When Van Ekeren was kidnapped, one of the participants was Juan Rivera, remember him? Marksman for hire and a damned good one. We've heard the intention could be to re-introduce Rivera here for this visit of De Souza to carry out what failed last time.'

'I remember now, when Van Ekeren escaped from them and

reached ASIO, he effectively scuppered that. Rivera had to get out of Australia quick, which he did,' said Kelsey. 'We've no idea how he did it or where he finished up.'

'South America,' said Minton. 'We think he did some island hopping across the Pacific. But now he's vanished from Chile and been sighted in the Philippines, we think on his way back here. Rivera is a hitman, as you know, if he's heading here there's a target in mind…I don't think it's kangaroos.'

'De Souza,' commented Kelsey. 'No prizes for guessing that.'

'Who will be with us sometime in the next few weeks, we're all primed up ready to provide top security,' said Minton. 'I had words with Stan Ellison of the Australian Federal Police about it this morning.'

'De Souza is always surrounded by a large security detail. They've thwarted several assassination attempts,' said Phillips.

'Just hope and pray it doesn't happen here,' commented Minton.

'There's also a faction that wants to merge with Indonesia.' said Kelsey.

'Like Tanganyika and Zanzibar. Well…some in Indonesia may welcome the idea after they failed with East Timor,' said Phillips. 'That attempted coup in Taranga last year damned nearly came off? It went pear shaped because Van Ekeren was mistaken for Van Elderen, one of the conspirators.'

'I remember,' said Minton. 'But why should anyone want to merge with Indonesia after the East Timor disaster? Would Indonesia want that?'

'The current Indonesian government doesn't! But some religious fanatics want a combined fundamentalist Taranga and Indonesia, they believe swallowing Taranga may be the start of a Pacific Caliphate.' Phillips shrugged. 'The present Indonesian government certainly isn't averse to controlling all that oil under the seabed either, but they're wary of any extreme fundamentalism that comes with it. We must be watchful, some fundamentalists are here now ready to cause trouble!'

'What could be the preferred mode of attack when De Souza arrives here? Suicide bomber or a long-range rifle shot?' asked Minton.

'Either, we'll have to guard against both,' said Kelsey. 'Also his entourage is always on the alert for possible poisoning.'

'When's he arriving?'

'Within weeks,' said Phillips.

'Do we know where the threat will come from?' asked Minton. 'Is it anything to do with that terror cell currently in court?'

'That looks like a separate grouping,' Kelsey shrugged. 'That's all we know.'

'Various groups may have common aims but tend to isolate themselves from each other,' said Phillips. 'What information we had about a possible Taranga coup emanated from a source in Taranga but it's gone silent. We fear the worst!'

CHAPTER 3

When Geoff Miller thought back over the whole affair, its proximate cause was that damned burglary claim. It instigated a chain of events that eventually involved Miller in Australian national security. The trigger action was the misplacement of a business card.

He arrived at the given address, knocked at the front door whose appearance confirmed a burglary had taken place. The middle panels were kicked in; plus, shreds of material on the shattered wood where the intruders had forced entry, together with a small blood smear on the step. The householder answered the door.

'Mr....er...' Miller began, referring to the file.

'Butler, Bert Butler,' Butler looked fiftyish, fit and active with greying hair. He was a self-employed carpenter and builder and very weather beaten, after years of toiling in the hot Australian sun.

'I'm Geoff Miller,' said Miller. 'Insurance loss adjuster, we've had a call from Jupiter Insurance. You've had a burglary?'

'You're quick off the mark! I've only just reported it.'

'I was in the area. I can see what they did to get in, what's it like inside?'

Butler grimaced and opened the front door.

'See for yourself!'

The living room was a shambles, newspapers and magazines scattered over the floor, furniture upended, other items plainly missing, indicated by indentations in the carpet.

The intruders' progress could be tracked through the house. They had exited through the rear laundry door with what items they could carry. There was a small, fenced backyard, with a rear gate which opened onto a laneway. Tyre marks outside indicated a vehicle had entered one end of the lane and exited the other, the laneway was open both ends and accessed different streets. The tyre indentations in the soft earth were deeper in one direction, indicating which way the thieves had departed.

'What time do you reckon it happened?' asked Miller.

'Morning before noon,' Butler replied. 'Both me and the missus work during the day. I came home lunch-time and found it.'

'Do you normally come home midday?'

'No, I left a set of tools behind.'

'Have the police been?'

'About 2 o'clock, they looked around, said they'd be back but they haven't yet. Something about sending someone to check for fingerprints and that blood sample on the step. One of the buggers cut himself!'

'OK,' Miller nodded. 'We've paperwork to complete.'

'How did you get here so soon?' Butler asked

'I had another job three streets away, rainwater damage.

They called me on my mobile so I came straight round. I'll need details from you, they've given me very little.'

They re-entered the house.

'How long before they pay out?'

'Difficult to say, but Jupiter Insurance are usually prompt,' Miller looked around the sitting room. 'There's some good furniture here, and good pieces...' he indicated a picture on the wall and various trophies and ornaments. 'You should have a monitored alarm system installed. The value of your contents must exceed the point where the company requires one.'

'Nah!' Butler shook his head. 'Pointless expense! Lightning doesn't strike twice.'

'They may insist on it,' said Miller, not for the first time astonished at the short sightedness of people. 'This suburb has recently become very burglary prone.'

'Insurers want it all their own way, don't they? Don't we pay enough in premiums?'

Miller didn't rise to that but continued jotting on his clipboard. The locks on the external doors were, in his view, quite inadequate. He wondered if there were any warranties on the householder's policy regarding installation of effective locks.

Miller returned to his company's offices in Melbourne. He worked for Winwood Walker & Co, a loss adjusting firm founded twenty years previously by Jack Winwood and Ross Walker, both former insurance company men. The firm was used by many insurers in the Melbourne market. They had twenty staff, with five outside investigators.

They dealt with insurance claims ranging from fire, burglary, water damage, public liability policies and workers' compensation surveillance, but not motor claims which needed specialised assessors. The claim for Albert William Butler was routine, although jarring to see the damage committed by the intruders.

Insurance companies delegated many claims investigations to independent firms of loss adjusters, except anything $1,000 or less as the adjusters' fees could exceed the claim. It was expedient and economic to dispose of small claims by issuing a cheque.

Miller was aged 26, unmarried and had formerly worked on the sales force of two insurance offices, Jupiter Insurance and Renown Fire Office, before moving into loss adjusting.

He dealt with the water damage claim, but before he started on Bert Butler's burglary claim he glanced at that morning's newspaper. It was coffee time and some office staff were gathered around the two drink machines.

On an inner page was the trial of alleged terrorists charged with planning to plant an explosive device in the diplomatic area of Canberra. The article was centred on whether the identity of an ASIO agent, who was to give evidence, should be publicised. The defence counsel was determined to identify this agent, hinting darkly at racial discrimination and conspiracy, while the security services were grimly defending their right to keep his identity under wraps.

This article was topical because of the impending visit of the President of the island nation of Taranga, with fears of incidents or demonstrations whilst he was in Australia. Although pursuing moderate and secular policies, he maintained a firm grip and was opposed by extremist religious groups who wanted the island state run on strict religious lines.

Miller read the article about ASIO with interest. He had considerable sympathy with undercover operatives and, after the attack on the twin towers in New York in 2001, very little sympathy with terrorists. He couldn't understand why emigrants to another country, such as the United States, Britain, Canada or Australia, because of problems in their own homeland, should then want to change the country that gave them sanctuary to one resembling the one they had left, it didn't make sense.

He heard the sound of high heels on the parquet floor. One of the female staff arrived and placed a file on his desk.

'What's this?'

'Surveillance.'

'That makes my day.'

'I thought you'd say that.'

Miller looked up in irritation, which dissipated as he perceived the messenger. Jacqueline Jameson had been with the company for a few months, and was always stylishly dressed. He found her not only physically attractive, but liked her manner, her cultured diction and her refusal to join the other girls in office gossip.

'You thought correctly,' he opened the file. 'What is it?'

'From the Compensation Board, man with a bad back,' said Jacqueline. 'He's been off for months. They suspect the worst. Name of Papadopoulis.'

'Where's he live?'

'Thomastown.'

'OK. Leave it with me, thanks.'

She smiled, turned and set off for her desk at the other end of the office. Miller watched her go; she walked well too. As she reached her desk, she suddenly swung around and her eyes met his, she was fully aware of the effect she was having. Miller hastily looked away and returned to Bert Butler's burglary.

The State Government, who ran Workers Compensation insurance, found themselves obliged to use surveillance to check on a minority of claimants who attempted to rort the system. There had been cases where claimants took second jobs whilst their injury allegedly rendered them unable to continue normal employment.

Miller was later accosted by Bill Clucas, the office manager. Clucas was in his mid-fifties and had been in the insurance industry since his late twenties, after spending time in the Australian Navy. He had formerly worked with various companies and insurance brokers, was very experienced and had been with Winwood & Walker for six years.

When Winwood & Walker wanted an office manager, they interviewed many, including Bill Clucas. In response to Winwood's question: 'Why should I offer a man of your age the job in preference to somebody much younger?' Clucas had replied: 'Because at my age it's unlikely anyone would try to lure me away with a higher salary. If you take me on you won't have to worry about re-hiring in a few years or months, I'll stay until I retire!' Winwood hired him on the spot.

In addition, his elder brother was a senior officer with Victoria Police, which often gave Clucas unofficial access to useful information.

'Did Jacqueline give you that file for Papadopoulis?' asked Clucas.

'I've got it here.'

'This man has been off before. I remember the name and the Thomastown address from when I was working elsewhere.' Clucas said slowly. 'Be very discreet, he may lock onto anyone watching him.'

*

Miller parked near the claimant's house at 7.00 am, but the first day was uneventful. On the second day a utility drove to the house and the claimant emerged dressed in working clothes. He boarded the utility which Miller followed discreetly. The utility turned into a small building site.

The claimant and the driver alighted and unloaded material from the utility. The claimant, despite his bad back, had no difficulty lifting floorboards. Miller obtained four minutes video footage. The claimant and his companion entered the building, carrying lengths of timber.

Miller drove to a vantage point further away; a site worker had cast glances in his direction so he decided to be less conspicuous. The claimant clearly had a second job that didn't prejudice his so-called bad back which allegedly prevented him doing his normal job.

The following day the claimant didn't stir from the house until 10 o'clock. When he did, he advanced to the front gate and gazed fixedly at Miller's vehicle 70 metres away. That was enough, he knew he was under surveillance, so Miller aborted. As he passed by, the man gave him the finger sign, Miller kept his eyes rigidly to the front as he passed.

'You did well on this one,' Jack Winwood viewed the video after his return. 'You were rumbled you say?'

'Yes, he knew,' commented Miller. 'Papadopoulos was looking fixedly at me and gave me the Melbourne tram driver's salute as I passed him. Bill Clucas warned me, he remembered him claiming benefit before in similar circumstances.'

Winwood chuckled.

'Yes, he warned me too. Well, there's enough here for their lawyers to bite on, humping those planks around gives the lie to his bad back. The Compensation Board won't appreciate him working elsewhere while he claims benefit. How did he lock onto you?'

'Possibly tipped off on the work site, I reckon two of his

workmates had cottoned on,' Miller said ruefully. 'I doubt if they knew who I was observing, but if it was a talking point at lunchtime Papadopoulos would put two and two together.'

'Not the first time we've been sprung, Don Atkinson was rumbled last week, the claimant ran up the road at him. Don nearly ran him over,' said Winwood. 'Hazards of the trade eh?'

*

Miller entered the Police station and asked for Detective Constable Peter Grace. When Grace fronted Miller referred to the Butler burglary file and Grace produced his own Butler file. They checked the two lists of stolen items, one given to the police and the other supplied to the insurers. If they didn't correspond, sometimes they didn't, the insurers list sometimes longer than the one supplied to police, the insurers would jump on any discrepancies. Miller considered there wouldn't be any problems, he liked Butler and thought he was straight. He was, the two lists tallied.

'Caught anyone yet?' asked Miller.

'Nah!' Grace shook his head. 'We had three in the same street that day, we think we know who did them, but no proof yet.'

They chatted for five minutes, swapped business cards, and Miller left.

*

'Not another one!'

Jacqueline laid the file on Miller's desk.

'You won the raffle,' she said gravely. 'If you succeed with this one you get another one free.'

'Where is it?'

'Up country, near Bacchus Marsh.'

'Another Greek?'

'No, a genuine Anglo-Saxon.'

She placed the file on his desk, gave him a flashing smile and returned to her desk. Again, Miller watched her go, ready for a sudden swing around to catch him admiring her posterior. When she did, his eyes were on the file.

He thumbed through the top sheets. The claimant was late 40's, name of Bryant, allegedly suffering from a knee injury and off work over a long period. He was shortly to attend the compensation board's doctor in Melbourne, a good opportunity to observe him.

Miller parked near the claimant's house in Bacchus Marsh in the early morning. Two days before he had successfully obtained footage of Bryant as he attended his medical appointment. He had walked normally until he neared the surgery, then adopted a limp.

Today was boring, very little occurred. He saw the claimant occasionally, he emptied his mailbox and later walked to the milk bar to get a newspaper. He returned and looked straight at Miller's car. He didn't seem to take much note of it and re-entered the house carrying his newspaper. There was little else to report so Miller called it off about 2.00 pm.

*

'What have you got on this one?' Winwood asked. 'They want surveillance for three days, don't they?'

'I've done two. I'll do the day's surveillance late morning and see what happens.'

When Miller thought over the alarming sequence of events that evolved, he reached the conclusion that was the day matters really went pear shaped. The first jarring note in the sequence of events which caused such an upheaval in his life came soon after he passed by the house at 9.30 am to park further down the road, some distance from the claimant's house to avoid being too obvious. Anyone claiming compensation benefits, especially if fraudulently, as seemed likely in this case, would check for possible observers.

The claimant came to his front gate around 10.30 am, apparently collecting mail although Miller couldn't recall seeing a mailman. He looked up and down the road and returned indoors. Miller added the excursion to his log.

Fifteen minutes later a police car moved in behind him. Miller was merely mildly curious when two constables alighted, but came to earth with a bump when a hand knocked on his driving side window.

'Could you step out of the car, please sir.'

Miller looked blank, whereupon the request was repeated, he opened the door and clambered out.

'Are you a parent, sir?' the constable was young, with an aggressive tilt to his chin.

'I'm sorry, parent of who...what?'

'Can you answer the question, sir.'

'What do you mean, parent?' Miller looked puzzled. 'How can I answer the question when I don't understand what you're asking.'

'We had reports you've been parked outside this kindergarten for over an hour, sir. Can you offer any explanation?'

'Kindergarten!' Miller was thunderstruck. 'What kindergarten?'

'That one there, sir,' the constable pointed to the corner property.

'Kindergarten?' Miller was still perplexed. 'Where does it say it's a kindergarten?'

'There's a big notice around the corner.'

'Kindergarten! I didn't know it was one,' Miller protested. 'I haven't been around the corner. I came straight up the road from the freeway. I've seen no sign. There isn't one on this road.'

'Can you identify yourself, sir?'

'Yes. Here's my card.'

He produced a business card from his wallet and handed it over.

'What are you doing here? Out of territory, aren't you?'

'I don't have a territory. I work all over Victoria and New South Wales.'

'In New South Wales?' the constable looked quizzical. 'But you're Detective Peter Grace of Victorian Police.'

'Detective Peter...Christ! That's the wrong card.'

'Can you come and sit in our car please sir.'

'Look, there's been a mistake, I'm a loss adjuster and enquiry agent, I'm investigating a claimant on behalf of the Workers Compensation Board.'

'Why are you impersonating a police officer?'

'I'm not impersonating a blasted...I mean a police...Oh bloody hell!'

The next hour was a nightmare, Miller was taken to the local police station where he endeavoured to explain his real identity and why he was there. A phone call to Jack Winwood clinched it eventually. Winwood wasn't overpleased at the tangle Miller was in, but then, neither was Miller. He had to walk back to his car and pass in front of the house he had been observing. He saw a face at the window and thought ...had he been put in the frame by the claimant who had rumbled him? If so, that was the second time in ten days.

After reaching his car, he took a turn around the corner, there was indeed a large sign indicating it was a kindergarten, not apparent from the street where he had parked or from the road he had arrived by that morning. He angrily climbed into his car and drove off.

*

'How the hell was I to know it was a bloody kindergarten?' Miller was in Jack Winwood's office as was Ross Walker. The meeting had been stormy, both Winwood and Walker were scathing because he hadn't checked the area before parking.

'If the sign was where you say, I can understand you not seeing it,' Winwood said soothingly. 'But in our line of business we have to be careful.'

'Giving the police a detective's card didn't help,' sniffed Ross Walker.

'I can't account for that,' Miller said. 'I place any cards I receive like that in the file that relates to them. How it got into my own card wallet I've no idea.'

'What happened about the card for Detective Grace?'

'They phoned him and asked if he knew me. Initially he didn't, he must see quite a few in the course of a week and maybe more than one loss adjuster. When I referred specifically to Butler's burglary case and his address, he remembered it. He said he'd given me one of his cards and confirmed he had one of mine.'

'What about the cameras?' asked Walker.

'They didn't help, a man parked outside a bloody kindergarten, armed with three cameras,' Miller said bitterly. 'I had to show my digital camera and they went through it. Luckily, I had previous cases on it. They also checked the video camera, but I hadn't used it. They confiscated the film from the third camera, there were shots of Butler's house on it, that burglary claim, but there was no workers' compensation footage. They're going to develop it and let me know when they're satisfied.'

'Who was Constable Lonsdale?'

'That officious prat!' Miller ground his teeth. 'He was the one who arrested me. For that bastard, I was the paedophile arrest of the decade, he didn't believe me and didn't want to. In fact, his last words to me were on the lines of: 'I know you're guilty…I'll get you mate…no worries!'

'I rather got that impression,' sighed Jack Winwood. 'He sounded very young and aggressive.'

'He was, straight out of the Police Academy I'd say,' Miller grated angrily.

'OK.' Walker said. 'We'll take you off this one, we'll put Don Atkinson on it for the final observations. Different man… different car. Do you reckon he rang the police?'

'I couldn't say, it could have been anybody, might even have been the kindergarten, their windows overlooked where I was,' Miller said and added bitterly. 'They're probably on the lookout for paedophiles like me!'

CHAPTER 4

Miller's escapade became the main conversational topic for the female staff which didn't help his temper. He wouldn't have minded if they'd approached him and asked questions or sympathised, but they clustered around and gossiped, accompanied by surreptitious glances in his direction. It was those sidelong glances that got to him; almost suggesting he was an outed pervert.

After he'd observed the tight group clustered around the coffee machine during their not so covert talkfest, he realised Jacqueline Jameson was not among them, she remained at her desk. She caught his eye, inclined her head at the chatterbox group, grimaced and smiled. That was the bright spot of his day.

Thereafter his routine proceeded normally, except Winwood tactfully directed Clucas to give Miller burglary and fire claims only, for over two weeks after that he was given no surveillance cases.

His colleague Don Atkinson took over Miller's last

surveillance job, compromising video footage indicated he too was engaged in a secondary occupation. Compensation payments were suspended, which gave Miller some satisfaction.

It was weeks before he received his next surveillance job. He couldn't be isolated indefinitely but appreciated the lay-off. One day he heard measured footsteps approaching, he knew who it was and when to look up for maximum visual effect.

Jacqueline was still five metres away as he took stock and experienced a thrill as she paused to exchange words with Peter Hallam, another assessor. Miller took advantage of her temporary preoccupation with Hallam to cast his eyes over her before she resumed her progress towards him. In the process, she delivered a beaming smile that hit him right between the eyes.

Over the past month they'd had occasional conversations and discussions on various claims, had struck a rapport and he was aware the gossip machine was including them in their tittle tattle. He had ascertained where she lived, and that they both supported the same Australian Rules football club, a reliable conversation piece.

As she occupied the chair on the other side of his desk, with a file no doubt intended for him, he cursed his underlying shyness that prevented him asking her questions about herself or, more important, whether she would fancy a date. He feared a rebuff.

By this time, Jacqueline Jameson had been at the company for several months, her employment background was similar to his, having formerly worked at an insurance company and subsequently in the broking market. Her age, at a guess, was 22-25, her status appeared to be single; there was no ring on her finger. He regarded her fixedly as these thoughts ran through his mind, which caused her some discomfort.

'Sorry,' he said. 'I was deep in thought.'

'That's all right,' she replied. 'A penny for 'em.'

'I was just wondering about something,' he said with perfect truth, but again his nerve failed him. 'Is that for me?'

He eyed the file she was clasping to her chest, realised her cleavage was also directly in line and hastily averted his eyes

'I'm afraid it's another surveillance job,' she said apologetically. 'I intended to give it to Don Atkinson but he's away this week, so is Jack Winwood.'

'It's not near a kindergarten, is it?' Miller asked bitterly.

'No, I've checked for kindergartens within a mile radius,' she gave a little giggle.

'What is it?'

'A bad shoulder and right arm, he claims he can't use them.'

'Another Greek?'

'Looks like it, his name's Smith,' she replied. 'Probably one of the Athens Smiths!'

Miller grinned and noted the address.

'Bugger it!' he said feelingly. 'It's in the same area as that last bloody fiasco.'

'Not quite,' she said. 'It's nearer Ballarat this time. If it had been the same town, I'd have given it someone else.'

'All right, leave it here,' said Miller. 'I suppose they want it done yesterday.'

'They usually do,' she looked over his desk. 'You have quite a few here.'

'Mostly evening calls,' said Miller. 'I have to ascertain proof of ownership of stolen items. Most of these clients are both working so can't be seen during the day.'

'You're doing some tonight, are you?'

'No. I'm going to the football. A friend gave me a couple of tickets.'

'You have some good friends,' she said. 'Hawthorn are playing, aren't they?'

Miller nodded. True, he had two tickets for the Hawthorn FC game, but nobody to go with. The friend who supplied the tickets was interstate this week, which was why he'd offloaded them to Miller. Any other friends he might have offered the second ticket to were either away or involved elsewhere.

'Who's the lucky girl?' she asked. 'I hope she supports Hawthorn.'

A wild thrill ran through him. He wondered if she would... hell...no! He couldn't stand the thought of a rejection. In any case, this woman must have a dozen boyfriends.

'No, that is, the other ticket's spare, none of my friends could make it tonight.'

She sat and regarded him, her mind obviously clicking over.

'Really!' her eyes bored into his. 'I know someone who'd be glad to make use of it.'

*

The following Monday morning Miller found a good surveillance position, but initially toured around the immediate vicinity looking for schools or kindergartens; he had no wish to renew acquaintance with Constable Lonsdale. Finally, he was satisfied and parked at about 7.30 am, switched on the radio to listen to the news and watched the claimant's house at the end of a cul de sac.

Miller still couldn't believe events of the previous Friday night. From the point when she had virtually invited herself to accompany him to the football, the rest of the Friday afternoon and evening had been a blur. She had returned to her desk after they had agreed he would pick her up from her home later that evening, and when he left the office at lunch-time he had received a smile and a 'See you later!' as he passed by her desk.

That evening he had arrived outside her house, still wondering if he was dreaming. He had been momentarily shattered when a young man his own age answered the door, and experienced intense relief when he discovered he was one of her four brothers.

He had waited in their living room for about five minutes and was taken aback when she had appeared stylishly dressed for a cold night in a leather jacket, wearing a team scarf and a beanie hat.

'Let's go,' she announced and led the way out to his car.

The game itself had been exciting, Hawthorn had scored a goal in the last half minute to win the game, whereupon Jacqueline had leapt to her feet and danced a jig. Miller had to admit she was a far from boring companion, her loyalties were certainly easy to discern. She was at odds with many umpiring decisions and frequently vented her displeasure!

'You hide your loyalties well, don't you' he observed wryly as they re-entered his car after the game, which caused her to crack up with laughter.

'I try.'

Later he spent an hour at her home, her brothers were similar football fanatics. He arrived home well past midnight.

*

Miller tensed as a four-wheel drive passed by and stopped at the end of the court. A man, matching the description of the claimant Smith, emerged from the vehicle and after a brief chat with the driver, entered the drive and the house. The vehicle departed and passed Miller on its way out.

For the rest of the day, that was it. Apart from Smith's wife driving off with a couple of children, presumably to school, and returning half an hour later, nothing happened.

The next morning Miller arrived an hour earlier, at 6.15am, and selected a slightly different position. After an hour, the same four-wheel drive appeared at the same time as the previous day, the same routine as the day before. He finally gave up at 10 o'clock, after the wife returned from her school trip, nothing else occurred.

He had words with Ross Walker the next morning.

'He could have a night shift job,' Miller said. 'He's coming back *from* somewhere. He can't be leaving in the morning. I was there at 6 o'clock yesterday.'

'He's doing something regular, and regularity denotes employment, maybe a night shift,' Walker commented. 'Try late-night surveillance.'

The following evening Miller eased the car into a convenient place to observe the house. He debated whether to have a coffee from his flask but decided against it. If the claimant was holding down a night shift he could move anytime, and he didn't want a full bladder if it became a long journey.

After fifteen minutes, the same four-wheel drive entered the court; its rear lights hit his mirror as it paused by the house behind him. He ducked down to avoid being seen. A light came on in the claimant's porch, he emerged and boarded the vehicle which accelerated towards the court exit, passing Miller who had parked facing the entrance to the court ready to follow.

Following a vehicle at night was more unobtrusive than during daytime, headlights in the mirror could be anonymous but in daylight the same car persistently following would eventually attract attention. He followed the other vehicle for ten kilometres, on main highways and a section of freeway, before it turned into a housing estate. It entered an open gateway, the entrance to the carpark of an all-night café. There was another entry at the far end of the carpark from a main highway. It plainly catered for truck drivers; a couple of rigs were in the forecourt. In the dim light he saw the claimant and driver disembark and enter the café.

There was a cul-de-sac opposite the carpark entrance, Miller parked there facing towards the transport café and, armed with a small digital camera that fitted easily into his pocket, crossed the carpark on foot and entered the café. The claimant had never seen him so he'd be no wiser if Miller appeared at the counter.

On entry he was assailed by tobacco smoke; the café and its clientele seemed to abide by their own rules and ignore anti-smoking regulations. He was wearing sweater and slacks so wasn't out of place, he thrust his way to the counter and faced Smith, the claimant.

'Coffee thanks, mate,' he said. 'White, no sugar.'

'Anything else, mate?'

'No thanks, that'll do.'

He looked around as he waited, several tables were occupied but three were vacant, about eight or nine truckdrivers were in there.

He observed Smith closely as he prepared the coffee, he didn't have problems moving his arm and shoulder. Miller considered manipulating his camera onto the counter so he could press the button, but thought it too risky. He took his coffee to an unattended table, drank it slowly and watched Smith closely as he worked. Another man appeared behind the counter occasionally, probably Smith's 'chauffeur'.

Miller took some surreptitious shots from the table, finished his coffee and wandered outside. Through the front window, he could see the counter clearly, the internal light was good. He put the digital camera onto zoom and pressed the button, took three or four shots, went to the side window and did the same without using the flash, which would attract attention. He returned to the court where his car was parked, climbed in and began to view what he had.

He was quite unprepared for what happened next. A youth suddenly emerged from a nearby garden gate and sprinted down the footpath. Miller heard a door open and light flooded out from the hallway of the house, a second man rushed down the same front path, through the front gate onto the pavement. He looked around, headed for Miller's car and hammered on the window.

Miller lowered it halfway; his camera still in his hand.

'Yes...hello,' he said.

'You bastard, give me that.'

'I...you what?'

'That! That fucking camera you bloody pervert!'

'What?' Miller was thunderstruck. 'What the hell?'

'You've been taking pictures through my daughter's bedroom window, you bastard.'

Miller pressed the locking switch for the car doors.

'Sorry. You've got the wrong man, mate,' he pointed towards the end of the court. 'The bloke you're after took off in that direction.'

'Don't talk crap you fucking liar, I can see your camera. Give it here!'

Miller saw no point in protesting his innocence. He started the car and moved off, with the householder in pursuit. Miller accelerated, turned right at the 'T' intersection and left his pursuer behind. Miller saw him in the mirror staring after him before running back into the house.

Miller was shaking as he attained the main highway, drove for about a mile then pulled in, until the shakes subsided.

After disposing of the shakes Miller pulled back onto the main road and was heading for Melbourne when he became aware of flashing lights in his mirror. The householder must have noted his registration.

'Oh God!' he said to himself. 'End to a perfect day.'

As the police left their vehicle and advanced towards him, Miller's heart sank.

'Oh bloody hell!' he groaned. 'It's Constable bloody Lonsdale.'

CHAPTER 5

There was a timid knock at the office door and Alan Kelsey looked up irritably.

'Yes, come in.'

Mike Duval, a younger member of his Counter Intelligence team, entered. Duval was an earnest young man in his early twenties, a computer whizz kid who spent most of his time at his computer terminal. He also spoke French fluently; his parents had emigrated from the Channel Islands when he was a child.

'We've found something, Chief,' he said. 'Bob Bramble says you should see it.'

Kelsey nearly responded on the lines of 'Can't it wait?' ... but realised it would be inappropriate to vent his ill humour on Duval.

'What is it?'

'Bob said he preferred you to see...!

'Yes...sorry...lead the way.'

Duval led the way to his computer terminal where Bramble was waiting. He stood up as Kelsey approached and pointed at the screen.

'You should see this.'

Kelsey peered at the image. It was an airport scene and depicted a man carrying a small overnight case.

'Recognise him?'

Kelsey leant forward, then nodded.

'That's Jose Rivera,' he said finally. 'Where's this?'

'Avalon Airport in Melbourne.'

'Was he apprehended?'

'The hell he was, nobody knew who he was at the time. We've ascertained he was travelling under a false passport as a Chilean businessman, and walked straight in.'

'How did we get onto this?'

'Mike and Marcus Templeton routinely run through arrivals at Sydney and Melbourne airports and carry out ID checks.' Bramble said. 'They ran this through the system, amongst several others, and came up with it early this morning.'

'When did he arrive?'

'Last Tuesday.'

'Shit! That means he's been loose in the country for three days!' snapped Kelsey. 'He could be anywhere. Come with me, Bob.'

He returned to his room and indicated a vacant chair.

'That bastard being here means trouble. Any suggestions?'

'He's an expert marksman. Who is he likely to shoot?'

'Who is visiting Australia? Who could be a possible target?'

'De Souza?' suggested Bramble.

'Bloody hell!'

Kelsey sprang to his feet and walked to the window. Rivera was well-known in international intelligence circles as a gun for hire. There had been many assassination attempts, some successful, that had borne his hallmark, but he had never been apprehended. He had sometimes taken refuge in Eastern European countries after the Communist collapse, but was now thought to be based in South America.

'Alert all field offices. Tell everyone to be on the lookout for this bastard,' Kelsey said. 'If he's on the loose we've got a problem. Have we informed the Feds?'

'I got on to Stan Ellison straight away. He nearly hit the roof; he's thinking of launching an enquiry into security at Avalon.'

'With good reason,' Kelsey commented drily. 'I hope to God he wasn't let in armed to the teeth!'

*

Miller was taken to the same police station where he and Constable Lonsdale had made their previous acquaintance, he had been within a short distance of it when apprehended. Lonsdale's demeanour was of an expert sleuth who had successfully cracked the case of the Northern Suburbs Pervert, as far as he was concerned Miller's guilt was cut and dried. He had triumphantly appropriated the camera when Miller was processed and incarcerated in a cell overnight. Miller's car remained at the roadside.

The next morning, in the interview room, despite the seriousness of the situation, Miller refused any offer of legal representation. He asked for Jack Winwood, but he was interstate and they contacted Ross Walker. This didn't suit Miller at all, he didn't get on too well with Walker. Further, when Walker finally arrived, being diverted from his journey to Albury where he was to adjust a large fire loss, he was not in a good temper. Nevertheless, his state of mind provided an unexpected bonus. Ross Walker was so short tempered and irritable on his arrival he didn't care what he said or to whom.

Miller was interviewed by Detective Sergeant Caslake aged probably in his 40s. Constable Lonsdale was present, still wearing his triumphant air and presumably mentally gauging his promotion prospects.

'What you were doing in Aysgarth Court at that time of night?' asked Caslake.

'Carrying out surveillance,' Miller answered sulkily.

'My oath you were!' Lonsdale snorted. 'A young girl aged 14 undressing in her bedroom and you were caught fair and...!'

Caslake gave a sidelong glance at Lonsdale, clearly irritated by the interruption. It seemed Caslake didn't like Lonsdale either.

'Who were you surveillancing...surveying...observing?' Caslake got into a tangle with his words.

'I was observing Andrew Smith, the subject of a compensation investigation.'

'This case here?' Caslake tapped the file lying on the desk. Miller nodded.

'But Smith lives about 10 kilometres away, according to the address on file,' said Caslake. 'What were you doing at Aysgarth Court?'

'He was leaving his house each evening and returning in the early morning. We suspected he was doing night shift work. Last night I followed him from his home address.'

'You expect us to believe that! Smith was nowhere near Aysgarth...!' but Caslake raised a hand and Lonsdale subsided. At this point Ross Walker entered the fray, hitherto he'd been jotting notes which he compared with another pad produced from his brief case.

'I can confirm that,' said Walker. 'Mr Miller and I discussed this case two days ago and this very point was mentioned. I sanctioned night surveillance as Andrew Smith's movements suggested he may have alternative night shift employment.'

'Where did you follow Smith?'

'To an all-night café on the main road to Sydney, he was serving behind the counter.'

'We called in that café after interviewing you last night, we've also checked with them over the phone, nobody named Smith works there,' snorted Lonsdale.

'How do you account for that?' Caslake turned to Miller.

Miller was momentarily at a loss, with no answer, but Walker stepped into the breach.

'That's hardly surprising. While claiming compensation benefits from his real employers, he was working there illegally, probably using a false name to avoid taxation complications. When police force members go moonlighting, do they use their real names?'

Caslake grunted and was about to say something then changed his mind. The thinly veiled counter accusation had come out of the blue. He glanced at Walker, but Walker's gaze never wavered and Caslake decided to let it go.

'You have photographs on your camera,' Caslake switched the subject.

'Yes.' Miller replied.

'Which you said were taken through a window.'

'Yes, the window of the café,' said Miller. 'I also took some inside.'

'These pictures could relate to anything, maybe a bedroom window?' said Caslake.

'The one I saw was obviously a bedroom window,' Lonsdale interjected angrily. 'This isn't the first time...!'

Caslake held up his hand. Again Lonsdale subsided.

'Why don't you run them through your computer,' snapped

Walker. 'You can hardly see what these photos are depicting when viewing them through a keyhole screen like this.'

'We can't,' said Caslake as if that settled the matter. 'Our computer is down'

'No matter,' Walker reached for his brief case. 'I've got my lap top here. Is there a point we can plug it in?'

Caslake didn't look too pleased while Lonsdale looked furious. Miller wondered if their computer really was out of action or whether they'd assumed he'd been caught red-handed and were hoping to elicit a confession by merely relying on relentless questioning and low magnification photographs on the small camera screen.

'That point is too far away from this table,' Caslake indicated a point on the opposite wall. 'We'll have to make do with what we have here.'

'No worries,' snapped Walker. 'I can use this on battery, I also have an extension cord.'

Caslake acquiesced with some reluctance. Walker extracted an extension cord from his case and ran it from the electric point on the opposite wall. He opened up his lap top, and plugged in Miller's camera.

'I'll do that, we don't want these pictures deleted, do we?' Caslake said pointedly.

'It might help your case if they were,' Walker responded coldly. 'But it certainly won't help ours, these prove Mr Miller observed this man working illegally. It would cause us considerable inconvenience to obtain them again, especially after it seems your constable tipped off Smith last night that he was being investigated. I'm hardly likely to erase them, any more than you would. Right, let's have a look.'

They ran through them. Miller had taken ten, some inside the café and others through windows. One was very fuzzy, it looked like a shot through any window, it could even have been a bedroom window, it was probably the only one the police, personified by Constable Lonsdale, had looked at before consigning Miller to the pervert class. Lonsdale sniffed as it appeared on screen, to him it was still an open and shut case.

'Not much doubt about this one,' he said.

But later ones were more definitive, the next was a more focused version of the same one and was clearly the inside of a transport café. The subject, Smith, could be seen behind the counter and showed up equally clearly on others Miller had taken inside the café. A cursory check confirmed it was the same scene as the first indistinct shot, better focused.

'By God! If this is a young girl's bedroom it's certainly crowded, it must have been an orgy! But I can't see any fourteen-year-old,' Walker commented sarcastically. 'Can anyone point her out, how about you, constable?'

Lonsdale flushed angrily. The latter four, taken through the side window, were clear. They showed the counter and tables occupied by beefy, tattooed truckies. They also showed Smith's features clearly as he prepared and served cups of coffee.

'It appears to me your young constable has difficulty discerning the difference between a transport café packed with truck drivers, and the bedroom of a 14-year-old girl,' Walker placed undue emphasis on the word 'young' as he rose to fresh heights of sarcasm. 'He must know some interesting teenagers,' he turned his head and looked pointedly at Lonsdale. 'Did you see this man at the counter when you went in there?'

'I ...um...' Lonsdale peered at the picture on screen but Caslake intervened.

'I'll ask the questions if you don't mind,' he said coldly, but Walker wasn't intimidated, he merely looked expectant. Caslake turned to Miller.

'When you returned to Aysgarth Court, you say you saw ...!' Caslake began, but Walker had the bit between his teeth and intervened.

'Did you see that man at the counter?' Walker turned again to Lonsdale. 'When you went into the café to confirm Mr Miller's story and to check the registration of the vehicle he said would be in the car park, did you see Smith in there and speak to him?'

'I said I'll ask the questions,' snapped Caslake.

'You haven't asked it,' Walker was equally terse. 'Did he or didn't he...see or speak to that man in there?'

Caslake looked exasperated, but decided to concede.

'Did you see this man, Reg?' he asked Lonsdale.

Lonsdale hesitated.

'Well, I'm not too sure but ...!'

'Can we take that as a yes?' asked Walker.

Caslake looked at Lonsdale who gnawed his lip, then finally, grudgingly, nodded.

'Well...we seem to have established something,' said Walker. 'If you check that file, you'll find a photograph of this man obtained from his employer's personnel file.'

Caslake riffled through for the photo. It was undoubtably the same man.

'Did you find any footprints outside the house?' asked Walker.

'Forensics haven't advised us yet.'

'Did you find any garden soil on Mr Miller's shoes?'

Caslake began to look irritable.

'None that was apparent, yet.'

'Hmmm!' Walker leaned forward. 'Then I take it Mr Miller is free to go.'

'I'm not so sure about that.'

'What are you holding him on? Taking photographs through the window of a 14-year-old girl's bedroom, or taking photos through the window of a transport café?'

'The girl's father thought he had been peering through her bedroom window.'

'He thought! Can he prove it was Mr Miller?'

'Can you prove it wasn't!'

'There's a clock on the wall in this photograph,' Walker pointed out. 'It says 10.44 or thereabouts, the time is also on these photographs and it coincides with the transport café clock and some are subsequent to it in time. What time was the Emergency call made?'

Caslake referred to his notes.

'22.54'

'How far away was the house in question from the café?' asked Walker

Caslake turned to Lonsdale.

'Well?'

Lonsdale flushed and pursed his lips.

'About 50 metres,' he said.

'It bloody well was *not*,' Miller snapped angrily. 'It was nearer 300 metres, probably more than that, nearer half a kilometre. The entrance to the carpark was about 300 metres, and the court where I'd parked my car was another 50, easily.'

'Well,' said Walker. 'Let's split the difference, say 180 metres, and assume a scenario. In less than 10 minutes, since we can see this shot here was the second one Mr Miller took in this first batch of four from outside and later he took two photos from this angle, went around and took four from the other side, making eight shots in all, all of which bear times on them. He then walked or ran over 200 metres back to his car, dodged around the back of the house, after isolating it from all the other houses, peered through the bedroom window after isolating it from all other bedroom windows, returned to his car and started checking the photographs he'd taken.'

'I reckon he did,' snorted Lonsdale.

'Bullshit!' snapped Walker. 'He'd have to be an Olympic sprinter to have done it in the time. And where are the pictures of the bedroom window and the 14-year-old? There aren't any.'

'We want to go through all the shots on the camera if you don't mind.'

'Very well, let's try some more shall we,' Walker pressed a key and more pictures appeared.

'Hold on, what's that?' Lonsdale pointed triumphantly. 'That's one of a young girl.'

Miller's heart thumped for a second, what had he got on his camera? Then he had a closer look at the shot on screen, it was Jacqueline Jameson. She was sitting on the couch in her house, with a beaming smile, which had not left her features since the football game ended. She was still wearing the plunging neck line she had worn at the office; she had removed her top coat but still wore her Hawthorn FC scarf around her shoulders. The shot showed plenty of cleavage, Miller had been standing up and she had been sitting down. She was also sitting with her legs crossed; showing more thigh than she should, to which Miller had offered no objections at the time.

Somebody was standing on the right-hand side of the shot; one of her brothers. Miller had been chatting to him about the game at the time; when Jacqueline had suggested a photo of herself wearing her team scarf to celebrate the last-minute victory. It was after he had brought her back home from the football.

'You like photographing young girls in football gear, do you?' Lonsdale sneered. 'Who's that?'

'That's the daughter of a friend of mine; she is also one of my employees,' Walker said coldly. 'I don't think she'd be very flattered that you mistook her for a 14-year-old since she is nearly twice that age.' His sarcasm was cutting.

Another shot appeared on screen. Miller remembered that one. She had been leaping about like a dervish when Hawthorn had scored the winning goal, waving her scarf over her head. This one had caused great amusement when he showed it to her in the car, her brothers had later been equally amused. Lonsdale had no comment to make about that one, although Caslake permitted a trace of a smile.

'We still want to retain this camera for the time being,' said Caslake although he sounded irritable.

'No objection at all, but I want to save all those café shots if you don't mind, we need them for our file; the report has to go in tomorrow,' said Walker and added cuttingly. 'They are very important to us and I don't want to risk them being lost by clumsy handling, if you don't mind! I'll save them onto my computer now, thank you.'

'This is all part of your duties?' Caslake asked Miller while Walker was downloading the photographs. There was a conciliatory note to his voice.

'Yes, we check some claimants if we suspect the system is being rorted.'

'You just go snooping on ordinary citizens, do you?' Lonsdale cut in nastily, he didn't sound pleased. Caslake turned to him, Miller thought he was going to shut him up but Walker was ahead of him.

'Snooping yes, but how would you describe it when you are hiding in bushes on freeways trying to catch people just over the speed limit,' he said acidly. 'While you are raising revenue for the state coffers, we stop wastage by preventing fraudulent payments being made from them. It all goes to pay your wages, and ours.'

That concluded the interview, Walker completed the downloading of Miller's shots onto his computer, as a concession to Miller he included the two of Jacqueline. He then disconnected it. Miller coiled up the extension cord and Walker replaced it in his bag. Walker also picked up the Andrew Smith file.

'One other point,' said Walker. 'When you went into the transport café, you did go in there didn't you?' he turned to Lonsdale, who looked grumpy and forbore to answer. 'From that I assume you did. Did you mention anything to this man Smith about him being under surveillance?'

Lonsdale didn't answer, so Walker turned to Caslake.

'I'd like a definite answer from your colleague, Detective Sergeant,' he said. 'As you can appreciate, this man was, and still is the subject of an investigation by the State Government; it could prejudice our inquiries if he has been tipped off and severely prejudice any reports we have to make.'

'Tell them, Reg,' Caslake turned to Lonsdale. Caslake didn't look pleased, nor was he. He was realising he had allowed himself to be carried along by Lonsdale's impetuosity.

'No!' said Lonsdale. 'I just went in and stood by the door and had a look around.'

'Well, I hope that's all you did,' said Walker. 'This man is suspected of being a serial rorter of the system and needs to be stopped. If he was tipped off, even inadvertently, it could cost the state of Victoria a lot of money. Incidentally, where is Mr Miller's car?'

'Where we left it, by the roadside.'

'Well, I hope it's still there. We'll need the keys, please.'

*

As they drove to Miller's car, Miller tried to apologise but Walker shook his head.

'Apologise for what?' asked Walker. 'You were a victim of circumstance. Although you were caught up in a situation, I can't fault your procedure on the night. I can understand the girl's father jumping to conclusions after chasing a Peeping Tom away from his premises. It was your bad luck he was peeping through the window on the same night you were there. The father sees a car parked outside and a man viewing camera shots on his digital. Did you see much of the man who ran from the house?'

'Not much,' confessed Miller. 'It was fairly dark, he passed under a street lamp while legging it, he was white, young, and wore a baseball cap.'

'Like half a million others!' Walker commented dryly. 'The chances of catching him are zilch unless he's caught doing it again. What gives with that bloody constable? He doesn't seem to like you.'

'He's the one who arrested me on that kindergarten caper,' said Miller. 'He's convinced I'm a pervert, he saw a link between my two arrests and must have seen me as a fast track to promotion.'

'I think you're right, he's young, impetuous and presumably ambitious.'

'And disappointed,' suggested Miller.

'Yes, disappointed and made to look foolish. We'd best keep you out of this area in future, hell hath no fury like a young constable scorned, he'll be on the lookout for you if only for speeding fines....! Ah here we are!' Walker pulled into the roadside. 'It looks OK, no damage.'

Walker opened the door and turned to Miller.

'How long have you been involved with Jacqui Jameson?'

'I haven't, what I mean is, this was the first time. I had two tickets for the Hawthorn football game and all my friends were away, not interested or, in one case, already going. It was when she gave me this case file for Smith. We were chatting and I mentioned I had a spare ticket. She invited herself.'

'That sounds like her, I've known her father for years, we used to work together at Commercial Union Assurance,' Walker handed Miller his keys. 'I'll see you when we're next in the office. Regarding Jaccqui, I don't like office liaisons, if this relationship develops, keep it low key in the office...all right?'

CHAPTER 6

Three immediate consequences resulted from the Andrew Smith case. Two followed on from Ross Walker's last comment as Miller prepared to motor back to Melbourne.

Firstly, when he entered the office a meeting of the Photocopier Mafia was clustered around the machine headed by Lucy Browning, the blue-eyed blonde; the usual head gossip. They all turned and regarded him as he entered, clearly his latest sexual escapade was the main topic. He wasn't sure how they got hold of it, Walker certainly wouldn't have spread it around so he deduced it must have been Walker's secretary, Margaret Greenwood, a married woman to whom gossip was second nature. She would have known of Ross Walker's hasty summons to bail Miller out and probably wasted no time propagating it.

Secondly, during ensuing weeks, his relationship with Jacqueline Jameson did develop into a liaison. They dated quite frequently and occasionally visited the stadium at Docklands to watch Hawthorn play. But within the office they kept it low key, he had no wish to fall out with Ross Walker. Their relationship within the office was strictly business apart from arranging assignations outside it.

Thirdly, he revised his previous estimation and wariness of Ross Walker, although Walker could be a hard man where his business and the welfare of the daughter of a friend and ex-colleague were concerned, he was also a fair one. Further, Walker's handling of the police interview had been masterly, he had given an experienced detective sergeant and an inexperienced and impetuous constable as good as he got.

Miller's investigative cases were, in the main, burglary and fire losses for the next few months. This suited him, after the scary happenings in his last two workers compensation surveillance jobs. Then, a month later, another surveillance job turned up, had he been able to foresee the consequences he would have turned it down flat.

At the time he was finalising a report that related to a claim arising from a teenage party, held without the knowledge of the parents who were away on a weekend, which resulted in gate-crashers and considerable damage to the house.

He became aware the chair opposite his desk was occupied, he looked up, it was Jacqueline Jameson. She had one leg draped over the other which exposed a distracting expanse of leg. His heart sank, she held what looked like a surveillance file.

'Don't tell me, it's a surveillance job,' he said.

'It's a surveillance job,' she replied brightly.

'I asked you not to tell me that,' whereupon she smiled and he was lost.

'What is it?' he asked gloomily. 'Tell me the worst.'

'You have to see Ross about it,' she said. 'He wants to discuss it with you.'

'Now? Or can I finish this?'

'Soon, someone's with him now, but when they've finished, he wants to see you. Keep an eye on his door.'

'It's not in the name of Bryant or Andrew Smith, is it?' he asked suspiciously.

'No, Asian at a guess.'

'What's his problem?

She glanced at the facing sheet.

'A bad back, he's been off work for several months. Don Atkinson did work on it, but he's just gone away for a month,' she turned as they heard a door open and close. 'I think he's free.'

Walker was on the phone when Miller entered. He stretched out his hand for the file, motioned Miller to sit, finished his call then opened the file.

'Funny one, this,' he said. 'He's been off for months and we've only just been asked to investigate. Don did the initial surveillance; the claimant left his house early Monday morning and Don followed him for bloody miles; they finished well up country. I'm not clear what he could be doing in the bush if he's working illicitly, I can't see anyone travelling vast distances to do farm labouring when there's plenty of opportunities in the suburbs where you can do moonlighting, like driving a cab or...' he smiled ruefully: '...serving coffee in a transport café.'

Walker riffled through the file and returned to the running sheet.

'Don did a couple more observations on the man's home but there was no sign of him. We staked it out, nothing. But after a week he returned, Friday night.'

'Maybe he took a holiday,' suggested Miller.

'Without his wife and kids?'

'Some blokes do.'

'Perhaps,' Walker shrugged. 'But there's something screwy here. Don followed him to Warracknabeal, but they struck off towards the desert areas in northern Victoria, last seen disappearing in the sunset in a cloud of dust. Missing over a week, then returned Friday. Same thing the following week, driven by the same bloke in the same four-wheel drive...shades of Andrew Smith, eh?'

'You want me to do the same?'

'No,' said Walker. 'We can't risk losing him again and that's no criticism of Don Atkinson. He did well to track them as far as he did.'

He paused to drink his coffee.

'I suggest Pete Hallam sets up outside the house and reports when he's picked up again. I want you at Warracknabeal, stay overnight if necessary and Pete will give you pointers to enable you to intercept when they reach there. Don gave details where they left the main road at the point where he lost them. The Compensation Board want to wrap this one up, they reckon he's rorting the system big time.'

'Good enough,'

Although recent events had curbed Miller's enthusiasm for surveillance jobs this didn't involve staking out houses.

'When you reach there, fill up with petrol immediately, if they do pass through, you'll need a full tank, if you have to stop to fill up, you'll lose them.'

'I'd never have thought of that...thanks!'

'All right...sorry! Point taken!' Walker smiled. 'But we must find what this bugger is up to, this case slipped through the Compensation Board's net and got stuck in a pending file or someone's in tray. They've paid out heaps, their top management have gone ballistic; somebody had a right bollocking. These regular trips up north indicate this man is up to something.'

'When do they want an answer?'

'Yesterday!' Walker thrust the file across the desk. 'It all depends on the claimant's next trip. He leaves Monday and returns Friday. The Compensation Board will carry the cost of a trip to northern Victoria and a night or nights in a motel; they reckon it's worth it. They think there's a rort here, I'm inclined to agree.'

So did Miller, it did look odd. Someone working a second job while on benefit could usually be traced to other employment nearby, to travel to the north of the state on a regular basis and be away a week at a time did seem strange.

*

The following Sunday Miller travelled north to Warracknabeal, and booked into a motel. The weather was good and he enjoyed the trip. He reached Warracknabeal then wandered around the town for an hour. He had a look at the main Post Office, one of the town's main architectural attractions, plus the log-built lock-up that dated from 1873, erected when the first police constable arrived in town. He visited the Warracknabeal Hotel, operational since 1891, had a couple of beers and made up an ad hoc darts four.

He returned to the motel for the evening meal and turned in for the night. He awoke at 7 o'clock next morning when Pete Hallam phoned.

'His transport has just arrived,' Hallam announced. 'Usual routine. I'll ring you again in about an hour.'

They exchanged a few pleasantries and Hallam rang off. Miller entered the restaurant and ordered breakfast, then drove to a nearby service station to fill up, grimacing at the price of fuel in the country town.

'Glad the comp board are paying for this lot,' he muttered as the pump clicked away. He returned to the motel and Hallam rang again.

'On the road to Ballarat, same direction they took when Don Atkinson tracked them. It's a grey Land Rover, with a large aerial,' said Hallam. 'It's not a conventional one so they may have a transmitter on board. I'm about 400 metres behind. Oh…the registration is…' he rattled it off.

'Ring me later,' said Miller and Hallam rang off.

He read the newspaper, slipped under his door by the motel staff. He scanned through it, checking on the sports news. The football codes were a big item, with the end of the season nearing, top teams jostling for finals places.

Other news was fairly mundane, a cabinet minister was suspected of having an affair with his secretary, the Prime Minister had recently returned from overseas, and there was news on the impending state visit by the President of Taranga, due in Australia within the next few days. He was to spend time in Canberra and several days in Sydney. There was a long article about the ongoing terrorist case in Sydney, the ASIO operative had finally been allowed to keep his identity under wraps. There had been a fire in a plastics factory in Melbourne.

'Somebody will pay for that,' Miller mused as he flicked through the pages. 'Wonder if we'll get the job.'

Hallam rang again an hour later.

'Avoca, they're filling up, so am I. I'm at a petrol station across the street. I'd say we're heading for the North Western Highway, if they do, that would confirm Don Atkinson's report so far. Then we should head for St Arnaud. I have to go; they're heading back onto the road. I'll ring again.'

Miller was stretching his legs around the motel car park when Hallam rang again.

'OK!' he reported. 'North Western Highway it is, heading for St Arnaud, and probably Donald after that. Make sure you're tanked up. Ross will never forgive you if you run out of fuel.'

Miller told him to do something unnatural, they exchanged a few similar pleasantries and Hallam rang off, promising to phone again when he reached St Arnaud. Miller returned to his unit and had another browse through the file.

The subject of the claim, Ali Hammoud, worked for an engineering firm in Fitzroy North, a northern Melbourne suburb. He had been off work with a bad back, allegedly caused by lifting something too heavy. He had been receiving compensation for several months, initially with a certificate from his own doctor and latterly one issued by the Compensation Board's doctor. The latter had said in his opinion Hammoud was fit for light duties, and wryly commented this type of injury was not easy to pinpoint.

Miller read that as a guarded comment, the doctor had reservations whether the injury was real or feigned but, in some cases, it was not easy to confirm one way or the other. A skilled rorter could reproduce all the symptoms, while in the current social climate the courts tended to give the benefit of every doubt to the claimant. Magistrates and tribunals were notoriously generous with insurers or taxpayers' funds. Further, facilities for light duties within many companies were limited. Despite the therapeutic value to the injured party, wages could be paid for work carried out which was of little or no value to them.

Hammoud had been allocated for surveillance to Don Atkinson, who had made a full report. Atkinson had parked outside the claimant's house for some days, seen him take off on a Monday morning and after that, during the week, had seen nothing. The process had been repeated the following

Monday and, acting on impulse, Atkinson had followed the vehicle as far as Warracknabeal before losing it. Being unprepared for a prolonged journey, he had had to fill up with fuel, then despite subsequently checking all the town's exits had had to concede defeat.

Atkinson's overseas holiday trip to Europe and Britain had intervened while surveillance was still proceeding. Normally cases would be completed by one operative but Atkinson's leave caught up with him with this one still incomplete.

Miller wondered whether the country chase was worth it, but agreed it was important to ascertain what the man was doing. If he was working the Compensation Board needed to know. If they found enough evidence of fraud to suspend payments, then two or three nights in a motel and a few tanks of petrol would be worth it. Hallam rang again.

'At St Arnaud, heading for Donald. I may have a problem, they circled an island twice and I had to continue on. They may have cottoned on; I've been behind them some time now. I waited up a side road in the town until they passed me, since then I've kept well back.'

'Are you still with them?'

'For the present, yes,' Hallam replied. 'But if I follow them through Donald, they may realise I'm tailing them.'

'Bugger it!' Miller pored over the map. 'Listen Pete, stay with them to Donald; see which road they take, Charlton or Warracknabeal. I'll head east from here to Litchfield. If they do head for Charlton you'll have to keep going after them and I'll follow. If they head for Warracknabeal I'll be waiting at Litchfield and then you can peel off. OK?'

'Sounds good to me, Geoff. I'll be in touch.'

Miller pondered whether to book another night at the motel but decided against it. There were several empty rooms so if he needed another night, he could book in on speck. He checked out, drove for Litchfield, reached Carron, a small settlement, then Hallam rang again.

'OK, they're heading for Litchfield, Geoff, on the Borung Highway. Buloke is in front of us, should be there soon. Where are you?'

'Carron, heading for Litchfield. I'm not far off, I'll put on the pace a bit and hope there are no cops around.'

'Don't,' cautioned Hallam. 'I've seen two patrol cars in the last half hour. Take it easy, if they reach Litchfield and head north for Birchip, I'll stick with them until you get round me and take over. Don't risk getting booked, it'll hold you up for half an hour and you'll lose them.'

Hallam had a point, by the time a conscientious constable checked licence details their quarry could be miles away and permanently lost.

'You're right, Pete. Heading for Litchfield now.'

*

Miller reached Litchfield ahead of Hallam and the Land Rover, but not by much. He parked by the roadside with the turn off for Birchip just ahead. His phone rang again.

'Just passed the Litchfield sign, the Land Rover should be with you any time soon.'

'I see it and the large aerial you mentioned, Pete,' Miller responded. 'Vehicle grey in colour, and...hold on a minute while they get closer...got it!' He read off the registration.

'All yours, Geoff...' responded Hallam. '...they're turning off to Birchip now.'

'Got them, about to follow. You'd best head for Warracknabeal.'

'Will do, could do with a cup of coffee...and a gents' toilet!'

Miller chuckled. This was the bugbear of the outside representative. What to do with a full bladder; stop by the roadside or wait until the next settlement. Always a risk to relieve your bladder on the roadside, a country policeman's eyes would light up at the thought of apprehending someone for alleged indecent exposure. Miller often wondered what policemen did with a full bladder on the road miles from anywhere.

'There's a pub in Litchfield,' he told Hallam. 'There's a urinal there.'

'Thanks Geoff, I'll remember you in my will.'

As Miller approached the turn to Birchip, Hallam's vehicle approached on the road from Donald. He flashed his headlights and waved as he went past. Miller waved back then turned onto the Birchip road.

'I'll report in to Ross Walker,' was Hallam's parting shot as Miller accelerated after the Land Rover. 'See you when I see you.'

Miller replied in like vein and headed north.

*

He kept the vehicle in front at arms-length, he hung back and where possible kept other vehicles in between. This route was a slight variation from when Atkinson tracked them, but could finish up at the same destination.

The Land Rover reached the settlement of Lascelles and filled up at the petrol station. Miller debated whether to follow suit, but his petrol gauge was well over the three-quarter mark. In addition, he could attract attention if he drew up at the same petrol station, he couldn't see another. He travelled on, took the Henty Highway to Ouyen, stopped, turned around and parked. He thought they would head for Hopetoun and was well placed to follow if they did; merely turn right onto the Hopetoun Road.

Ahead he saw flashing red and blue lights, a police car was following another car, the latter obediently drew into the roadside just in front of the service station where the Land Rover had completed filling up. The police car drew in behind the stationary car; a constable emerged and headed for it. Miller watched; his main emotion was: 'Sooner him than me!' He had sympathy for the miscreant driver, there was little or no traffic on the road and Lascelles was hardly a prolific built-up area. As the policeman approached his prey, Miller had a nasty shock.

'Shit! It's bloody Lonsdale.'

It was! There was no doubt. Constable Lonsdale strutted to the driver's window and addressed him. What on earth was Lonsdale doing here? Last seen he had been in the Ballarat and Bacchus Marsh area. Why was he here? Maybe he'd been packed off to a more remote country area after he'd made a complete ass of himself. Caslake, the detective sergeant, had become excessively irritable with him as the interview progressed. Or maybe Lonsdale had been on probation and was now permanently posted.

Miller huddled in his seat; if Lonsdale was in the vicinity Miller deemed it advisable not to be seen. He wound up his window, thankful for tinted windows. He hoped Lonsdale didn't have telescopic eyesight or a photographic memory to enable him to read and recall Miller's registration number.

The Land Rover left the service station and turned for Hopetoun, as Miller thought likely. He drew into the road with indicator flashing and turned onto the Hopetoun road. The Land Rover seemed to be heading for the same destination as when Atkinson tailed it; they'd just selected a different route. He looked behind as he drove on; Lonsdale was still addressing the driver.

'That's $165 down the pan!'

At Hopetoun the other vehicle turned right and headed north for Patchewollock. When they passed the turn off for Dattuck, Miller checked his petrol gauge; he still had over half a tank, but wondered how much further they were going.

He soon had his answer; the other vehicle's brake lights illuminated as it turned left onto a track. Miller came up slowly, halted at the end of the track and considered his next move. He disembarked and wandered over to a post with a few boards nailed on it, the signs named those who lived up the track. Lindsay, Parmenter and Agnarat Wen Pty Ltd, with the inevitable post boxes. In Parmenter's case it was a cut off milk churn with his name on it, while Lindsay had a post box on top of a three-foot post, similar to those in most suburbs. There was a cylindrical receptacle for Agnarat Wen which contained a copy of the Hopetoun Courier, a local newspaper.

If Miller went up the track, he needed a convincing reason for being there. He dialled the office number, but was in a dead zone. He drove a kilometre up the main road and dialled again, still no joy. He returned to Hopetoun and within the town boundary obtained a signal.

It was answered by Lucy Browning, one of the photocopier Mafia. He didn't ask for Jacqueline, it would be all over the office if he did, but asked for Bill Clucas.

'Hi there Geoff,' Clucas came through loud and clear. 'Where are you?'

'Not sure, somewhere north of Hopetoun. Can you look up and check the firm Agnarat Wen for me ...' he spelt it out: '... and let me know what or who they are.'

'Sure can, give me an hour or so, I'll do a credit check first if you like. I'm still waiting on the registration of that Land Rover'

'OK, is Jacqueline there?'

'Standing right beside me, Geoff,' Clucas gave a low chuckle. 'She was in here when you came through, now she's all ears. I'll hand you over, give me an hour and I'll have some information for you.'

Miller spoke with Jacqueline, she commented the Mafia were all agog and laughed when Miller made an appropriate comment. They had a brief chat, there was a film showing somewhere she wanted to see, she asked when he'd be back.

After finishing the call, he returned to the track and decided to enter it and explore. He travelled 100 metres and paused when he reached a gate bearing the sign 'Lindsay'.

The house was visible behind distant trees, a four-wheel drive vehicle was coming up the long driveway from the house towards the track he was on. He went further up the track, turned around, fell in behind the four-wheel drive when it reached the road and headed for Hopetoun.

It parked in the main street; a tall stylish looking blonde woman, probably late thirties, alighted from it with a young girl aged about 12 or 13 and they entered the newsagency. Miller did the same, a local newspaper might be useful and it also supplied an excuse for entering and having a closer look. The woman, presumably Mrs Lindsay, was chatting with the newsagent while her daughter was thumbing through magazines on the rack. Mrs Lindsay spoke with a refined accent, had an affluent look and had the aura of a businesswoman. From her mode of dress, smart though casual, Miller deduced she was well off, and that whatever she had she'd earned for herself. Miller considered it unlikely the Land Rover he had been following had come to roost at her residence. That left Agnarat Wen and the other one, what was the name…Parmenter?

He selected a local newspaper from the rack and approached the counter. As he was paying for it his phone rang, he scooped up his change and walked to the door.

'Miller!'

'Clucas,' was the response. 'Agnarat Wen are described as general dealers and seed merchants.'

'General dealers?'

'Yes, which covers anything you want it to,' commented Clucas. 'Ladies' underwear to drug dealing, you name it.'

'What about seed merchants?'

'Anything from watching grass grow to drug dealing,' Clucas remarked cynically.

'Oh! So…what the hell have we here?'

'Good question,' said Clucas. 'The company's directors or proprietors are Hassan Qassim and Marid Jaafar, obviously Asian. They have a registered office in Sydney.'

'Not Hopetoun or Patchewollock?'

'Apparently not.'

'Maybe they sell Persian carpets.'

'Maybe,' said Clucas. 'But I doubt it. There wouldn't be much of a market for Persian rugs in Hopetoun, maybe in Melbourne to fly over traffic jams!'

'If Hammoud was heading anywhere down that track it's likely to be there.'

'It does look that way,' said Clucas.

'All right, I'll see what I can find.'

CHAPTER 7

Miller continued to follow the lady he assumed was Mrs Lindsay. She made two or three stops in the town, collected groceries, visited a book shop where she spent time talking to the proprietor, and entered a computer store. He later followed her when she returned up the Patchewollock road, waited until she turned off onto the track, gave her enough time to reach her own driveway, then also drove onto the track. He passed the Lindsay gate, continued on and after a short distance reached another gate with "Parmenter" written across it. Behind it was a long winding driveway that curved down round a spinney of trees and vanished from view, presumably to a farmhouse behind the trees.

He kept going, and fifteen minutes later reached a gate across the track; with signs bearing the words "Private Property" and "Keep Out". Wheel marks on the track probably belonged to the four-wheel drive containing Hammoud and his chauffeur.

Miller sat with the engine running and considered. He could

serve no useful purpose sitting outside the gate, nor did he feel disposed to open it and drive through without a convincing reason for being there. He eyed the track beyond the gate, there was an abundance of trees; maybe it would be better explored on foot.

But if he did that, it would be unwise to leave the car where it was now. Currently Hammoud had little reason to suspect his workers' compensation status and payments were being investigated. A car parked outside the gate wouldn't necessarily cause Hammoud to suspect he was sprung, but the proprietors of Agnarat Wen would be curious if an empty car was parked outside their gate, wonder why it was there and…where was the driver?

Miller turned his car around and headed back. Outside Parmenter's gate he'd seen a lay-by, with a track leading into a clump of trees outside the boundary fence. He left the car to have a look at it, but it only extended for about 40 metres, with heavy tyre marks on it. He deduced it could be where Parmenter parked his tractor or ploughing gear during the early spring season. It was empty, partly hidden from the main track, with a curve in the short lay-by track so anyone coming up to or from Agnarat Wen's gate could drive past any vehicle parked there, without seeing it. They might see it on the way back from the main road, but if they did, it would be reasonable to assume it belonged to Parmenter.

That was probably the best bet. Miller checked his watch and considered the options. He heard popping noises which emanated from the Agnarat Wen direction. It sounded like gunfire; a large flock of cockatoos was rising upwards in the far distance. He thought these birds were protected, but knew farmers often disregarded the letter of the law, cockatoos could be a pest. He could remember his father, years ago, going into the garden banging a drum to discourage a flock of cockatoos attacking the lead on the roof.

He returned to his immediate problem. He'd be better off trying an incursion into Agnarat Wen on foot tomorrow After all the travelling carried out today by Peter Hallam and now Miller himself, time was getting on. If Hammoud *was* working, he would now be near the end of a working day. This could mean another night in a motel, he pondered whether to check whether Ross Walker would sanction another night, then dismissed it. After all, what was another $100 or so if Hammoud was dishonestly claiming benefit?

*

Miller arrived back in Hopetoun and selected the Hopetoun Community Hotel in Austin Street. He booked a room for the night then rang the office.

'What will you be able to do?' asked Clucas.

'Not entirely sure,' admitted Miller. 'I can explore on foot, there's good cover with plenty of trees lining the track, maybe I can spot anyone working there. I have my binoculars, but the zoom on the video camera is good. If he's working some distance away, I could possibly pick him up with some footage.'

'See what you can do, but don't do anything bloody silly,' cautioned Clucas. 'Keep your distance, if you're seen on the property, it will be difficult to explain. Incidentally, the owner of the Land Rover is named Ahmed Halim. He lives in Brunswick.'

'I wonder if he's rorting the system as well.'

'Good question!'

'His name doesn't help much. I wonder what work they're doing.'

68

'That's another question. See what you can find out, but don't overdo it. If you can discover what this company does up there, fair enough, but don't creep around peering into windows...Oh! Sorry Geoff.'

'OK, OK! I know what you mean. By the way, while we're on that subject, that blasted police constable...what was his bloody name?'

'Lonsdale?'

'That's him...that bastard is working up here, I saw him this morning.'

'Really? Maybe they booted him up there to get him out of their hair. Nice to have friends around!'

'Friend my arse! I'll keep in touch, Bill.'

*

Miller swung into the track again next morning but could see no activity, the Lindsay property showed no sign of any vehicle movement. He passed the Lindsay gate and reached the Parmenter gateway. There was still no sign of life and the small parking area Miller had earmarked for his temporary car park was vacant so he backed into it. When he was coming out, he might need a quick getaway, like the incident on his previous surveillance job.

He took his notebook, binoculars and the video camera, with his digital camera in his trouser pocket. He donned a sweater and left his jacket in the car. He walked the distance towards the Agnarat Wen gate, ready to dive into bushes if anyone appeared, but reached the gate without incident. At this point he realised he had no business cards, all still in his jacket pocket, but reflected it wouldn't be a good idea to broadcast he was an insurance investigator. If he had to explain his presence this could forewarn Hammoud and jeopardise the Compensation Board's investigation.

He examined the gate, checking for any trigger programmed to set off warnings in the house. There was no sign of one so he passed through the gate, closed it, entered the tree belt and walked parallel to the track, examining the ground closely for possible hazards should he have to exit in a hurry.

He walked nearly half a kilometre, the line of trees persisted, being mature conifer style trees that acted as a wind break. The track swung to the left, the trees on the left-hand side of the track ceased, so Miller crossed onto the other side where the trees continued on. On the left side of the track the ground fell away, the land became a saucer shaped valley with a hill on the far side. Then the trees recommenced as the track swung back again to the right and the trees on the right-hand side thinned out.

Miller emerged into a two-metre gap between the trees, on the right-hand side the land fell away into a much deeper valley. It was still saucer shaped; he could see tree covered hills on the far slopes several kilometres away. On the distant reverse slope was a farm buildings, surrounded by hedges and a line of trees ran from the boundary of the house garden. On the other side of these trees was a flat expanse of land, with small structures on it.

He sat on a rock to use his binoculars, elbows on knees. He concentrated on the markings or frameworks on the land, they looked like structures often placed on children's playgrounds. At the far end was a platform, with an object propped upright on it, but in the early morning haze he couldn't make it out. He moved closer and made a sweep with the binoculars but saw no movement anywhere. The track ran from the house and disappeared behind a slight rise in the land, but he assumed this track must eventually curve around and become the one he was presently on.

He tramped through the tree line, keeping a watchful eye on the distant farmhouse. The sun was now quite warm. Then the track, and the tree line, began to rise up as Miller reached the top of the rise, the track did indeed curl around to the right and descend to the farmhouse.

There was some activity at the house, figures emerged from the left-hand side of the building and approached the flat expanse to the left. He flung himself flat and used the binoculars. The figures came into sharp focus as he adjusted the lenses, he was surprised to see they wore battle fatigues and carried firearms.

He reached for the video camera, placed it on maximum zoom and focused on the distant activity. With the sunlight now full on them, they stood out clearly, he ran the video over four minutes. There were about twelve of them, some peeled off and began clambering up the wooden frameworks, jumping from the other end, others wriggled and crawled through pipes on their stomachs.

He heard popping sounds again, this time more pronounced and realised it was rifle fire, directed at the small stage or dais at the far end of the paddock. The small structure he hadn't been able to make out clearly before now stood out as the effigy of a man.

He took more footage then decided on a closer look. He collected his equipment and walked through the trees again, keeping a watchful eye on the distant activity. The trees thinned out and became a single line, cover was limited so again he lay on his stomach and operated the video. He disturbed some rabbits just in front of him, the bank he was resting on contained numerous rabbit holes; he was in the middle of a rabbit warren.

He focused on the flat paddock, now slightly closer, placed the video camera on maximum zoom and re-commenced filming. He discarded it and picked up the binoculars, he was now close enough to focus on the men in the distance and visibility was good enough to recognise Hammoud. He picked up the video camera again, the magnification wasn't as good as the binoculars but good enough to identify Hammoud as he scaled bars and mock walls. He took four more minutes of footage, concentrating on Hammoud.

But he concentrated too much, he heard voices. He turned to the right and saw two men armed with rifles approaching through the trees. They were dressed in fatigues like those in the distant paddock, with scarves or bands across their head, in Arabic fashion.

His mind clicked over, this was a security patrol, they hadn't spotted him yet but discovery was inevitable; he had no cover and couldn't run.

He snapped the video camera shut, slipped it into its case and bundled it up. He wrapped the shoulder strap around it and thrust it deep into the nearest rabbit hole. By the time he'd thought about the binoculars, there were shouts and sounds of running feet. He jumped to his feet, put a short distance between him and where he had stashed the video camera, but was looking down the barrels of two rifles as the two men ran up to him. They looked quite capable of using them, so Miller stood still.

CHAPTER 8

The two men motioned to Miller to raise his hands but he shook his head, whereupon one of them jabbed him in the gut with his rifle barrel and he jack-knifed, gasping with pain. He was jerked roughly to his feet, propped against a tree and his equipment confiscated, but his video camera lay undiscovered where he had left it.

'Who are you? What's going on?' he protested.

They said nothing, at least, not to him. One of them spoke into a shortwave radio, in a language Miller didn't understand. In the distance a Land Rover materialised behind the house, travelled up the track and pulled up nearby.

Miller was bundled into its rear with his two guards, and the Land Rover headed back to the farmhouse. He tried to converse and asked what the hell was going on, but they either didn't understand or didn't want to.

The Land Rover reached the farmhouse and he was ordered

out. He didn't understand the words but the sign language was enough.

He was hustled into the farmhouse, pushed into a hallway, thrust into a small room off the hall and left to his own devices. Apart from himself and his two captors, the house seemed deserted.

He was in the room nearly twenty minutes. He examined it but it possessed little of note. It hadn't been decorated for years and damp patches affected the plaster. Blankets and sheets were on a bedstead in the corner. A window overlooked a garden, through which the track passed before it wound back to where he had been apprehended.

The door was flung open, his two captors were accompanied by a man wearing battle fatigues and a scarf over his head. He beckoned and Miller was escorted down the hallway, into another room, which looked like an operations centre. A large chart was on the wall with red arrows pointing in from various directions and intersecting at a central point. He was prodded into another room beyond and pushed into a chair.

'Who are you?' snapped the man with the scarfed head.

'My name is Geoff Miller, who are you?'

The question was ignored. The scarf over his interrogator's head was similar to those Miller had seen worn by armed Palestinians and Arabs on television news screens. He had a black stubble around his cheeks and chin, his black hair nearly covered his ears. He had a small scar on his forehead and another on his left cheek.

'What were you doing on that ridge?'

Not an easy question. He discarded the first answer that came to mind, he was bird watching, and the second, that he had been observing Hammoud for workers compensation purposes. He wasn't going to admit that, not yet anyway, this could prejudice the Compensation Board's case and that of Winwood & Walker.

'What were you doing on that ridge?'

Inspiration came, he thought of a quite feasible and believable solution, even to a group of people who were, as now seemed likely, up to no good.

'I'm a reporter from the Hopetoun Courier,' he said finally. 'We had reports of gunfire and my editor sent me to investigate.'

The man at the desk thumbed through Miller's notebook, appropriated by his two original captors on the ridge. He flicked over a couple of pages. Miller had been making rough notes, for writing up later at the motel. He had merely noted movements and hadn't written Hammoud's name anywhere, ironically had the 'arrest' taken place minutes later he may well have done that. To the uninitiated, Miller's notes could easily be mistaken for a journalist's jottings.

'What did you see?'

'Not much,' Miller replied with some truth. 'I couldn't make out what was going on. My binoculars had fogged over and before I could clear them your two men were onto me.' He was about to lapse into silence, then remembered if he was posing as a journalist, he would be inordinately curious. 'What *is* going on here?'

The other didn't answer but sat with his brow puckered.

'How long were you on the ridge? Why were you investigating us?'

Miller had to think quickly, he didn't want to give the game away regarding Hammoud and his compensation rorting. This wasn't loyalty to his chosen profession or the Compensation Board; but because the unsuspecting Hammoud could be his link with the outside world. If he, Miller, disappeared...with difficulty he suppressed a shudder of fear...then Clucas's file would instigate a search and they'd have some idea where to start. If he exposed Hammoud, the latter may take steps to put an end to the compensation investigation, by coming clean and going off benefit, or disappearing. While the investigation remained open, Miller had hope.

'I've already told you, we had ...' Miller nearly uttered the word 'complaints', but decided it may bring forth a more specific question: '...reports of gunfire from people. I was asked to find out what it was.'

'Why?'

That question seemed strange, but maybe to some foreigners the repeated discharge of firearms could be considered a normal occurrence, as normal as an Australian or an Englishman playing cricket.

'Because it isn't usual.'

'Not usual?' the man looked quizzical. 'You mean people reported it, what people?'

'I've no idea,' realistic ignorance was the best card here. 'I merely acted on information received from my editor.'

'So...information came into your newspaper and you decided to investigate.'

'I didn't, my editor did,' Miller managed a convincing shrug. 'It sounded like an interesting news item so we followed it up.'

'Why?'

'I've just told you — because it was news. We are a news organisation, that is what we do...why we exist.'

'This is the first time you've been observing us?'

'Yes, I didn't really see anything, as I said before, my binoculars fogged up and I didn't...!'

'I think you are a government spy.'

'I tell you I am from the Hopetoun Courier, I've been...!'

'Lock him up again! I'll have to decide what to do,' Miller's interrogator snapped to the other two who dragged Miller to his feet.

'Wait a minute,' he protested angrily. 'You've no right to hold me here. Just what is going…!'

He hit the floor with his ears ringing and head splitting.

'Enough of that you fool!' the scarfed man shouted at the guard who had just felled Miller. 'Just take him back to the room, we'll deal with him later.'

Whether it had been a rifle butt or clenched fist Miller had no idea, but although the blow had nearly knocked him silly, the fall onto the floor went some way to clearing his head. His forearm hit the floorboards, a searing pain raced through his nervous system and hit his muzzy brain. He was dragged to his feet and ushered through the operations room, where he faced the wall chart full on as he went through. He was pushed violently by one of his captors, stumbled involuntarily and fell forward against the wall with his hands flat onto the wall map.

Despite the pain he had the presence of mind to have a good look at it. It was a map of Sydney, the inner city somewhere south of the Harbour Bridge. The red lines intersected at a point a few streets south of the bridge, from Miller's knowledge of the city it looked like the area of George Street, Hunter Street or maybe Martin Place. There was a red circle on the map a short distance south of the bridge, he couldn't see where exactly. Then he was manhandled into the hallway and into the room where he had been before.

His two guards departed and closed the door behind them, leaving Miller to his own devices, painful elbow and aching head. There was a fair-sized bump on the side of his head, which hurt to touch.

Miller sat on the bedstead, nursed his head and tried to think. What had he stumbled on? His initial reaction had been that he'd blundered onto a drug baron's private domain; he'd seen television and press reports of police raiding country properties with large tracts of land growing marijuana plants. But here there was no land under cultivation, apart from Parmenter's which had looked like wheat, plus a few sheep.

That eliminated a drug syndicate. What else? These men were armed to the teeth and resembled a private army, but a private army for what? Miller immediately guessed the answer. Fundamentalists? Terrorists? This was a guerrilla army in training. All the obstacles in the paddock, the target practice, the dress code, all indicated a training ground.

Miller thought back to recent newspaper articles about the terrorist court case in Sydney. The Opposition were insisting it was a scare campaign, a government stunt to persuade electors they had uncovered a plot, to stimulate votes in their favour. Miller had empathised with the Opposition's premise; but not now.

How long had this training ground been in operation and how had it escaped discovery? What about the near neighbours, Lindsay and Parmenter? The Lindsay property was well down the track, maybe three kilometres, with few reasons to wander up the track. Parmenter was closer, but if he was scratching a living from the land, he'd have little time to pry around his neighbours. The gunfire had sounded like popping noises from where Miller had parked his car, rising flocks of cockatoos would be a satisfactory explanation for any nearby farmer who also suffered transgressions from those aggressive and destructive birds.

More important, what were they intending to do with him? Taking into account his cover story, as far as his captors were concerned, they would worry because the editor of the Hopetoun Courier should know where his reporters were. If any journalist failed to report in for days, they'd have some idea where any missing reporter's last assignments would have been. His captors may consider they couldn't hold him indefinitely.

In Miller's real situation, Winwood & Walker knew Miller's whereabouts, his last report being from Hopetoun. He'd given Clucas a map reference where the Land Rover had turned off, the only question was whether it had been accurate enough to pinpoint it. Nevertheless, if he vanished without trace that would be where investigations would start.

Miller wondered if his captors were aware Hammoud was rorting the compensation system. Unlikely, they would hardly welcome anything that could cause a security breach … which was precisely what *had* happened by triggering Miller's investigation. If the compensation claim followed its natural course, and any subsequent investigation with regard to Miller's disappearance, Hammoud would have some explaining to do, to police and his fellow terrorists.

Miller recalled when the World Trade Centre in New York had been targeted in the early 1990's by terrorists who had placed a bomb in the basement inside a van, the van had blown up and wrecked the underground car park. One of the terrorists, presumably through parsimony, had foolishly tried to retrieve their rental or part thereof by claiming the van had been stolen. But by then the FBI had already traced the van and advised the hire firm, who reported it when the terrorists applied to have their deposit returned. The FBI jumped them which led to the terrorist organisation's arrest and that of several others. Hammoud had made a similar faux pas.

Miller was left to his own devices for hours; he heard footsteps nearby trooping in and out. The ringing in his head had subsided, but he still had a severe headache. Then the door opened and a plate was pushed in by a guard. He made no comment; left it on the floor and the door slammed shut.

Miller examined it cautiously. It was a small plate of soup, some bread, a piece of cheese, and a cup of tea with no milk. The tea was hot, and the soup lukewarm, but he was hungry and attacked it with relish. It occurred to him afterwards it could have been drugged or poisoned, he began to feel sweaty and lightheaded, but shook his head angrily which caused him to wince as his headache intensified, but the malaise cleared. Imagination can be a man's worst enemy.

An hour later the door re-opened, another man entered and collected the plate.

'How long are you going to keep me here?' but Miller's question was ignored.

He had another snack that evening, then as dusk closed in two men entered, one stood by the door and the other beckoned to him. Miller's hopes raised, were they going to release him? But his hopes were dashed, it was merely a toilet break, he was escorted to the end of the hall to a lavatory with a wash-hand basin. Having a full bladder, he was grateful for the excursion, but they gave him little time to loiter. When he'd run the tap and washed his hands, the door re-opened and he was escorted back down the hallway to the room.

That was it for the day, someone was posted outside the door, dusk merged into night and he had little recourse but to utilise the bed.

He awoke next morning to the clumping of feet in the hallway outside, and sounds of activity from the floor above. Again, a meal was pushed into the room on the floor, which he examined and decided to consume. He checked it for any taste peculiarities but it seemed normal, two pieces of toast, scrambled egg and a sliced apple. The tea was again without milk but refreshing. He had another toilet break; the hallway was empty but he could see activity outside through the open door at the hallway's rear end. Outside two men stood before a bench, with firearms before them in their component parts. He heard a barked command, and the two men began to re-assemble the guns. This much he saw before he was pushed into the toilet but no more.

He heard more activity some distance away, shouts and occasional gunfire. There was no guard outside the toilet door when he eased the door open to peer out. Sounds emanated from the operations room, any thought of trying to escape in that direction were nil. In the other direction lay the front door, but figures were moving around outside, if he tried to run, he wouldn't get far. He left the toilet and a guard materialised from the room at the rear who motioned him back into his bedroom and closed the door.

This routine continued for two days, meals were supplied by the guards, and he was escorted to the toilet. There was little or no conversation; except to tell him where to go, usually the toilet. This trip necessitated walking past the door of the operations room, sometimes closed, sometimes not. On one toilet trip another man entered the front door, he and the guard engaged in desultory conversation and left Miller standing near the operations room door. He concentrated on the map, the red lines were quite distinct, emanating from south west and south east of where they intersected, while the red cross he had seen before looked like Wynyard Station. They finished their conversation and Miller was re-escorted to his room, or cell.

During the days, frequent bursts of rifle fire occurred outside and once what sounded like a sub-machine gun. At night, he heard footsteps as they returned to the building, and a buzz of conversation from the operations room.

He knew he was sinking into a kind of torpor, acceptance of his fate, but slowly a feeling of rebellion took over. He remembered what had come to be known as the Stockholm Syndrome, where people on hi-jacked airliners began to empathise with and enter into a rapport with their captors.

'This won't do,' he muttered one day as he meekly walked in a set track to the toilet and back to his prison cell with one of his captors following.

He lay on the bed and nutted it out. His captors must be leasing the property; it was unlikely they owned it. A terrorist organisation planning a terror attack would hardly purchase a country property which was liable to be confiscated after the event. They would rent, use and leave the premises when they were ready to do whatever they were planning, to never return. The property looked run down and must have been leased for a set period.

The military training couldn't go on indefinitely, eventually even neighbours like Parmenter and Lindsay would wonder what was going on, and anyone else who lived within earshot. The property was near a National Park, there must be park rangers there who would lock onto it if it operated in this manner for long.

This indicated the lessees, or terrorists, Miller now assumed this was what they must be, had a definite object in mind which, according to the map on the wall, was in Sydney. Those red bands could indicate lines of fire and, if so, who was going to be in those lines of fire? There had also been explosions, either small ones or else a long way from the house, which indicated something else. It was not long since bombs had exploded on Madrid commuter trains, in Mumbai and the London Underground.

What would their intentions be for Miller himself? There

were two scenarios. One, they would release him when they had carried out their intention and vacated the premises. Two, they could kill him to stop him talking. What they didn't know was that he knew the identity of one of the terrorists, or a second one if he took into account Hammoud's chauffeur. Either way it was imperative he escaped.

CHAPTER 9

'Have we heard from Geoff Miller?' Winwood asked as he entered Clucas's room.

'No,' answered Clucas. 'We last heard two or three days ago when he rang from Hopetoun. He was entering a property to scout around, since then we've heard nothing, and we're not too sure where it is. He said it was on the road to Patchewollock.'

'Hmmm!' Winwood pursed his lips. 'That's odd. Not like him.'

'No. I'm wondering if anything has happened to him.'

'Like what?'

'An accident?'

'You mean a motor accident?'

'Not specifically, but that's possible,' Clucas responded.

'If he had, we'd have heard by now, if not on the news, then via the local hospital or police,' said Winwood. 'Could he have had an accident off the road somewhere?'

'That area is quite remote. If he has, it could take time to isolate where he is,' replied Clucas.

'Can we check anything about the locality, such as who owns land around there?'

'Should be possible, I'll make enquiries.'

Winwood paused by the door.

'What day does this Hammoud character usually return to Melbourne?'

'Friday nights.'

'Get Pete Hallam onto it, see if he returns as usual.'

'Then what?'

'I don't know, but if Geoff is missing for much longer, we'll have to start making enquiries, or get the police onto it.'

*

Miller prowled around the room looking for weak points. He found some, but wasn't sure whether they helped. The builders of the property hadn't catered for rooms being used as prison cells, there was no lock on the door, but a guard was stationed outside every night. The windows were similar; not barred but secured with screws. The walls were plaster, Miller scratched at them with his eating utensils and made inroads, but wasn't sure whether he'd get anywhere, he could merely emerge into another room.

Egress would have to be through the door, which spawned further questions, when and how? If he got out, where should he go and how far would he get?

The meal routine persisted but there was no conversation. He cautiously tasted each meal, suspecting it could be doped, but detected no unusual taste, while hunger was such the urge to wolf it down was irresistible.

He had noticed, although a guard was customarily stationed outside his door at night, during the day this routine was relaxed, but with so many milling around the hallway and operations room any chance of escape during daylight hours was impossible. He'd observed this by opening the door the merest crack and squinting through it. Even if he successfully escaped the house, he still had to evade armed men in the grounds.

*

'Anything from Geoff Miller?' Ross Walker asked Clucas later that day.

Clucas shook his head.

'Not a cracker!'

'There's something screwy going on here,' said Walker. 'Where's Jack?'

'In his office,' Clucas waved to Winwood. 'Jack! Still nothing from Geoff Miller.'

'Shit!' Winwood came over, entered Clucas's office pen and flung himself into the chair next to Walker. 'What happened with Pete Hallam, did Hammoud return?'

'Don't know yet, he usually returns Friday nights,' Clucas said. 'He may be on his way back now. Pete's going there this evening to check.'

'Is that a note of Miller's last phone message? Let me have a look.'

'He was investigating a track off the road. He said there were three homesteads or farms up there, Lindsay, Parmenter and this Agnarat Wen mob.'

'Did you find who owns the land this Agnarat mob occupy?'

'Not yet, I've asked a contact in Victorian Land Registry,' said Clucas.

'Any joy on Lindsay or Parmenter?'

'Harriet Lindsay is an author, or authoress.'

'They probably call them au-persons these days,' Winwood snorted. 'An author? What sort of stuff does she write?'

'Mainly historical fiction, my wife has some of her books at home. Historical and romantic stuff mainly, Roundheads and Cavaliers, Regency period and Napoleonic Wars, all boy meets girl, or soldier meets heiress! She's been living there for years with her young daughter. I believe she's divorced.'

'Then Hammoud is hardly heading *there* every week, unless he's a history student with a yen for romance! Where's her husband or ex-husband?'

'He's something in the film or television industry.'

'How did you find that out?'

Clucas grinned and tapped his nose.

'Entre nous!' he replied.

'Smart bastard! What about Parmenter?'

'No information...yet! Probably a farmer.'

'Well apart from worries about Geoff, we have to send off a report soon,' said Winwood. 'Both of you come into my room while we work out what to do next.'

*

On the fourth night Miller noticed a difference in the routine. Firstly, there were new arrivals. A vehicle arrived out front and headlights described a parabola across the front of the house. Miller heard his sentry leave his post, so he turned off the light in his room and opened the door a fraction. Arrivals entered the front door, trooped down the hallway, passed by his door and entered the operations room. He eased his door shut as they passed, re-opened it and peered out again. The door to the operations room was open and he heard voices. He wondered if there was any prospect of escape, crept into the hallway then realised he could make out what was being said.

'The time is approaching. We're nearly ready.'

'You say Juan is on his way?'

'He phoned a few minutes ago. He's left the main road and is on the track,' another voice said and added. 'Can we trust him?'

'He is known to us, he works for money, he is a dead shot with a rifle, that's why we're using him. He's a professional marksman and we need someone who won't miss. True he's European, not of the faith nor Taranganese, but if they arrest him afterwards this will confuse the authorities. Apart from his abilities, that's another reason for using him, if the authorities catch him, nothing will associate him with us.'

'Good. What about our target? When does De Souza arrive?'

'In three days, he meets the Australian Prime Minister in Canberra, then attends a dinner at that Sydney hotel. That's when we strike. We also plan a diversion on the railway system in the central city stations, starting from Wynyard Station and then we...!'

There were footsteps within the room, Miller scuttled back towards the safety of his room. Luckily, they were merely closing the door, possibly for secrecy or because of a draught. Probably the latter, if they'd done it for security purposes somebody would probably have peered out to check.

At this point, with nobody in the hall Miller decided he had a good chance of escape, there was no sentry, it seemed they were all engaged in the conference room. He re-opened the door of his room, peered out, then decided it was now or never. He closed the door behind him and crept up the hallway to the front door. A light was on in the porch, but no light in the hall, which was very dim.

Then he heard footsteps on the porch, two men entered through the front door. Miller backed into an alcove in the hallway and stood stock still. He waited for denouement but the two men paused and conversed in the entrance hall. Miller slowly sank onto his haunches, praying his knees wouldn't crack. There was a wooden chest in the alcove about a metre high, he was in the narrow space twixt the chest and the side wall of the alcove, it was a space less than a metre in width and depth; with a similar gap on the other side of the chest.

Somebody opened the operations room door and stood in the light of the open doorway. It looked like the Boss man, the scarf wearer who had interviewed Miller.

'Juan,' he called out. 'Is that you? Come this way.'

The two new arrivals advanced towards him and embraced. They passed the petrified Miller, on his haunches in the alcove between the chest and the panelled wall, in the dim light they failed to see him as they warmly greeted each other.

'Juan! Greetings! Any problems?'

'No,' said the newcomer. 'I had no trouble passing through Avalon Airport and was met outside.'

'No problems reaching here?'

'Si, no trouble.'

'Good. We've been discussing details of your mission, just a few days to go.'

'Is everything as planned?'

'Yes, but we have one small problem. We caught someone spying on us. He said he was a journalist but we checked with the local newspaper, they have no record of him. We don't know who he is, he could be a police spy or government intelligence. We're holding him in the house but he is a danger. When we leave here, we must be rid of him.'

Miller went cold with horror. His cover had been sprung, no real surprise, it merely needed a phone call and a request to speak to their reporter Geoff Miller. Geoff who? Miller? We have nobody here etc etc.

'No problem, leave that with me,' said Juan. 'I will deal with it tomorrow morning.'

'We also discovered a car parked up the track which must be his,' said the Scarfed Man. 'Victorian registration. We'll deal with that tomorrow as well.'

'We can arrange a convincing scene,' said Juan. 'An accident, maybe drink influenced...!' They walked into the kitchen area and their voices trailed away. Miller squatted, paralysed, desperately trying to stop fainting from sheer fright.

'No! No!' he hissed to himself. 'Don't pass out now you prat!'

His anger at his reaction bore fruit, it superseded his fear and the fainting sensation subsided. He was alone in the hallway again. It was now or never ...he had to get out... now! Delay would be fatal...literally! He must move from this dim hallway, if anyone else entered and reached for the light switch...he was gone. Juan and his companion must have been the new arrivals they expected, luckily for Miller they didn't know where the light switch was, current residents would have switched on the light.

The front door was ajar, Miller could see lights outside, apart from the porch, in the driveway to the gate, elsewhere all was darkness. Miller's first instinct was to rush out through the door and head for the darkness, but saner counsels prevailed.

His second and saner instinct was to behave as though he was one of them. There was an umbrella in the hallstand, he plucked it out, held it in the port arms position reminiscent of a rifle, and slowly walked out. He also appropriated a floppy hat from the hallstand before he went through the front door.

He stepped off the porch and into shadow. To walk along the relatively well-lit drive could result in him being recognised and reveal the status of the umbrella, whereas in shadow or semi-darkness it could be mistaken for a rifle. He walked around the side of the house, pulling up sharply when a man appeared from the shadows. He was about to flee, but the other raised a hand in salute followed by a muttered greeting. Miller mumbled something he hoped would be interpreted as an acceptable response. They passed each other and Miller headed for the boundary fence and trees.

He quelled the almost irresistible urge to scamper or run. Quite apart from attracting attention, it would be asking for trouble in the gloom with the attendant danger of tree roots and potholes. His object was to put as much distance as possible between himself and the house without falling headlong.

Up above, the Southern Cross was in view, he decided if he was to head for the main Patchewollock-Hopetoun Road he should retain the Southern Cross over his right shoulder and thus head east.

He reached the trees and a fence, which was no obstacle, he clambered over it and continued on. He had one worry, was he heading in an obvious direction? Or, would the obvious instinct of an escapee be to head in the direction from which he had originally approached the property, via the track and gate where he left his car.

He looked back and could just make out the light in the operations room; presumably the planning meeting was still in progress. With luck, they might be so pre-occupied nobody would think to check on him.

He must have reached a couple of kilometres, or a mile, from the house before he was aware of signs of activity and heard shouting borne on the wind. He could see pinpoints of light flashing in the general direction of the house away in the distance. His absence had been discovered.

CHAPTER 10

The night was cold and Miller was shivering. He headed east, guided by the Southern Cross, but trod carefully; a twisted ankle now could be fatal. His former captors wouldn't be certain which way he'd gone and may have divided their forces, which meant they could be spread thinly.

The full moon presented a problem. There was activity some distance behind him, with occasional torchlight flashes. He pointed the umbrella ahead of him to warn of any object in his path before he walked into it.

He followed a narrow track, not sure whether that was wise but thought if he blundered through undergrowth, he would make more noise and progress would be slower. He could hear rustling noises, which he assumed was wildlife, and occasional bird calls. This worried him, if his pursuers had any tracker instincts, they would head for noisy bird calls.

He was still heading east, occasional headlights flashed across the sky some distance ahead, which he assumed was the Patchewollock-Hopetoun Road. He looked back and was alarmed to see lights flashing through gaps in the trees. Had he left an obvious trail, or was this merely a search line they'd thrown out?

He reached a small shed by the side of the track, ran to it and peered in the window but saw nothing. Maybe it was a ranger post, he tried the door but it was padlocked. He looked ahead, in the dim moonlight he saw the track thread through the undergrowth ahead of him, but decided now was the time to break the routine. He struck off to the right, held the umbrella ahead of him and moved off the track. He had a rough idea of the direction he was travelling, the headlights in the distance were over his left shoulder, so he assumed he was now heading south as opposed to east.

He had travelled some distance when he heard voices. They were behind him, he assumed they had reached the shed. He kept going and with difficulty negotiated the thicker bushes in his path. It appeared they had no dogs with them, which would have proved his undoing. Then a torch appeared on his right, causing adrenalin to run and his heart to thump, he heard footsteps, and halted just before he stumbled out of the bushes onto another track where men were moving towards him. Miller froze, sank to the ground and wriggled under a thick bush. Clearly another search party travelling parallel to those near the shed, he was travelling at right angles to their mode of travel and had nearly blundered into them.

He lay flat, still holding the umbrella but realised the chrome tip on the end could reflect light. He hastily pulled the handle towards his feet, covered the chrome tip with his hand, then lay still. He turned his face into the leaves and mulch, a white face could show up in torch light.

The footsteps approached; to his horror they halted just after they passed by him. He thought he had been discovered, but they had stopped for a cigarette break. He heard the click of a cigarette lighter and a flame flared. He risked a glance upwards through the foliage of the bush he was sheltering under and saw three glowing cigarettes.

'Think we'll find him?'

'He could have gone in any direction. I think we're wasting our time,' another replied in a husky undertone.

'That bastard Juan won't be pleased, he'd made arrangements to dispose of him,' said a third voice.

'Who is this Juan?' asked the first speaker. 'I've never seen him before.'

'He's not one of our brothers, that's certain,' replied the third man. 'I was told he kills for a living, for money, not because he believes.'

'He kills at a distance, he can hit what he aims at, I've heard that of him,' added the second voice, Miller isolated this voice easily from the others, this man sounded husky as though he had a cold. Miller hoped he had…a bad one!

'Where is he now?'

'On the other track; heading for that main road. We should meet up with him soon.'

They moved on and Miller was able to track their glowing cigarettes until they finally disappeared. He stayed where he was for some minutes, his ears attuned, then crossed the track and continued in the same southerly direction, his ears cocked for any others who may be in the vicinity and likely to cross his path. This took him further from Juan, clearly not popular with the rank and file, being committed for money not ideals.

Miller kept moving but didn't rush it. He knew one rash move could either advertise his presence to anyone who stopped to listen, or incapacitate him if he sprained an ankle.

He paused briefly and considered. If he continued in a southerly direction, he should eventually reach the track leading off the main road by which he had reached the Agnarat Wen property. He may find his car but this would be of little value, since the Agnarat people had his ignition keys. Miller had heard that secret agents like James Bond started vehicles by reaching behind dashboards and pressing wires together, but had no idea how to do that. They'd probably stake it out anyway, deeming it likely he'd head for it.

Miller decided his best bet was the main road, if he turned to his left, he would head for it again, running parallel to pursuing groups using tracks through the trees. He decided to travel southwards another 100 metres or so, then bear left.

He reached his target, as far as he could tell in the half-light, then eased towards the left. He could see stars through the leafy foliage. He still had the umbrella and was loath to abandon it, although it was doubtful what use it would be in a struggle.

He moved forward, occasionally paused to listen, heard heavy trucks in the distance, bird calls, what sounded like a fox, and a passing aircraft. He wasn't sure of the time, they had removed his watch, now probably on the wrist of one of those bastards tracking him. He kept his eye on spasmodic headlights ahead, eased forward silently and brandished the umbrella before him to warn of any undulations in the terrain.

He continued on in this fashion, the sky ahead began to lighten and a cloud formation in the sky turned red as a result of diffused light from the rising sun.

He would have to move more quickly, he wanted to be near the main road before daylight. It was lighter now and he could make out outlines of trees before he walked into them, which had happened a few times. He stopped, listened and continued on.

*

The early morning sun hit the windows of Alan Kelsey's office in Canberra. Kelsey was an early starter as were his colleagues.

'What have you got?' Kelsey asked as Duval and Bramble entered. 'I hope to God it's good news.'

'We can't say whether it's good or bad, Alan,' Bramble motioned to Duval for a folder he was carrying. 'There's no doubt it was Juan Rivera who arrived through Avalon Airport, he used a passport in the name of Alvarez. We picked him up on another camera. He's grown a short beard but the features match. We've been in touch with the Chilean authorities, his passport was fake.'

'Fake or stolen?'

'They didn't elaborate,' answered Bramble. 'But it served its purpose and the bastard is here. CCTV picked him up entering a car which headed towards Melbourne.'

'And we've lost him?'

'Yes and no,' Bramble laid the folder on Kelsey's desk and riffled through it. 'We obtained the rego and Mike here contacted Inspector Alain Tyson of the Victorian Police Anti-Terror Squad last night. The plates were false, but we tracked the vehicle via CCTV, he was dropped off in the Melbourne CBD a couple of hours later.'

'Then what?'

'We've asked Alain Tyson to track CCTV coverage of the street where he was dropped, if there is any, to see where he went after that. That's going to be a big job. All we can do now is wait.'

*

It was nearly daylight when Miller breasted a rise and saw a farmhouse or residence before him with chimney smoke curling into the still air. Now it was lighter, he could move faster. His first thought was to find a phone so he could ring Bill Clucas or anyone else from Winwood & Walker. He was reticent about contacting the police; it would be just his luck to find himself speaking to Constable bloody Lonsdale. He skirted the house, deeming his pursuers could consider the Lindsay and Parmenter dwellings as priority destinations, saw nobody but did see Mrs Lindsay's vehicle, the one he'd previously followed into Hopetoun.

He crept through the garden, using bushes and undergrowth as cover, then after a lengthy reconnaissance, crossed the lawn and peered cautiously through windows, one of them looked like a laundry, the second was clearly a lounge room. He proceeded to a kitchen window and saw a woman moving around in there, dressed in a sweater and jeans, the same woman he'd followed into Hopetoun, presumably Mrs Lindsay. She looked out, caught sight of him and started back in alarm, so he spread out his hands and waved in what he hoped was a placatory gesture, then raised a hand to his ear as if speaking into a telephone.

After some hesitation, she opened the kitchen window about three inches.

'Who are you? What do you want?'

'My name is Geoff Miller,' he deemed giving his name first off could instil confidence. 'I need to use a telephone.'

'You're not coming in here,' she snapped. 'Go away, or I'll send for the police.'

'That's what I want you to do,' said Miller. 'Please do, please ring the police, they should know what's going on over the hill on the Agnarat property.'

That gained her attention.

'The Agnarat property, the one at the end of the track?'

'Yes,' Miller replied. 'There's something odd going on there.'

'That's the old Walters farm,' she said. 'What do you mean... odd?'

'There's a terrorist training camp there, there's gunfire and men in battle dress.'

She leant forward on the kitchen bench and eyed him thoughtfully through the slightly open window.

'It's probably one of those paint ball combat places.'

'It isn't! Whatever it is, it's real. They're using real guns and explosives.'

'Who did you say you were?'

'Geoff Miller,' he said. 'I'm a loss adjuster from Melbourne. I was investigating the property when I was jumped by men with rifles. I've been held prisoner for about four days, I've lost count. I escaped yesterday and they're looking for me ...please believe me.'

She opened the window wider.

'I'll ring the police now,' she said. 'I've often heard strange noises from over there too. Wait a minute.'

She made no attempt to invite him in, but Miller wasn't worried as long as she phoned the police. She was on the phone for about four minutes, then returned to the window.

'It's done,' she said.

'Can I call my employers in Melbourne. They'll be wondering where I am.'

She hesitated, then handed the phone instrument through the window. It was cordless with push buttons on the hand set, the phone's number was on a label adhered to it. Miller took it and dialled the Melbourne office number.

There was no reply. It rang and rang, then the answering

machine cut in so Miller left a message. He asked them to call him urgently as he had vital information and gave the number of the phone he was using. He asked them to respond urgently. Miller looked for his watch, but recalled one of the guards had removed it when he was 'arrested' and he'd never had it back.

'What's the time?' he asked.

'About 7 o'clock,' she replied. 'You look cold. All right, you can come in. The police should be here any minute.'

She admitted him through the kitchen door, and poured him a cup of coffee. After the insipid tea he'd been drinking for the past few days, it tasted like nectar. She replaced the phone on its rest and motioned him to a chair.

'I have to go and roust my daughter out, she's due at school shortly.'

She left the kitchen and Miller sipped his coffee. He could hear her moving somewhere in the house and voices as a recalcitrant teenager was rousted out of bed and hounded into a bathroom. He poured himself another cup from the pot, then the phone rang.

Miller started to his feet, it was possibly Jack Winwood, usually an early arrival in the office, responding to his call. Winwood's first reaction would very likely be to administer a rocket to Miller for not being in touch. He reached for the instrument from the wall, fumbled it, nearly dropped it and successfully fielded it. He placed it to his ear and was about to speak when he realised Mrs Lindsay had already answered an upstairs extension.

'Mrs Lindsay, you say you have a Mr Geoffrey Miller in your house?' said a voice which Miller promptly recognised as belonging to Constable Lonsdale.

'Yes,' he heard her reply. 'He said he was a loss adjuster from Melbourne.'

'A loss adjuster from Melbourne, is he?' Lonsdale's voice adopted an element of urgency. 'Listen! My name is Constable Lonsdale from the local police. We shall be with you very shortly.'

'Good! I hope it won't be too long, I have to get my daughter to school.'

'Your daughter...wait a minute ...you have a daughter...how old is your daughter?'

'Thirteen.'

There was a short silence before Lonsdale spoke again.

'Listen Mrs Lindsay, you may be in danger. Keep away from this man Miller. We have reason to believe he's a possible sex offender likely to commit sexual offences. You did say you have a 13-year-old daughter?'

'Yes.'

'Well, if you have a room where you can lock yourself in, do so. Where is he now?'

'I'm at one end of the house and he's at the far end.'

'Well we're not far away, don't be alarmed.'

'But I don't understand this. He asked me to ring you. He said he was alarmed about the property further up the track. He said there was a terrorist training ground there.'

'Really, he said that did he? I don't think so,' Miller heard Lonsdale give a deprecating laugh. 'I've had contact with this man before and he usually has a convincing story to justify himself. Just wait until we arrive.'

Miller heard Lonsdale ring off and hastily returned the phone to its rest. He stood there numb with shock. What the hell was the matter with bloody Lonsdale? It also raised another question, what should he do now? Should he wait for the police and try to explain about Agnarat Wen? What would happen if he did? Lonsdale's reaction of amused scorn and disbelief meant Miller would probably be manhandled, handcuffed, thrust into a divisional van and hustled off to the nearest lock-up despite protests or attempts to warn about an illegal guerrilla army. He had little doubt anything he said would be ignored or, even worse, treated with derision.

Lonsdale had been humiliated twice and made to look a complete fool by Ross Walker at their last meeting. He would have the urge to prove himself, and the idea of Miller, peering into windows and skulking around another house with a teenage girl in it would be proof enough to Lonsdale his hypothesis was correct, especially at such a time of day. Once could be explained as a mistake, twice could be coincidence, three times…!

Miller re-considered; he should be able to make nonsense of whatever Lonsdale tried to throw at him. But it wasn't certain he'd be able to and even if he succeeded it would take time, and during that time, what did the terrorists have planned? He had to impart his information to somebody who could act on it, and quickly.

Miller decided to get out before the police arrived, he didn't give much for his chances of convincing Lonsdale of his imprisonment at the Agnarat Wen property, he knew Lonsdale wouldn't listen to anything he didn't want to believe. He moved to the door then, as an afterthought, turned and seized hold of toast and marmalade from one of the plates on the table, probably the teenage daughter's breakfast. Miller decided his need was greater than hers, he crammed one piece into his mouth and, clutching the rest, opened the door and ran across the lawn, chewing with relish. It had been years since he'd had toast and marmalade for breakfast. As he headed into bushes on the east side of the property, he realised he'd left the umbrella behind.

CHAPTER 11

'Still nothing from Miller?'

Clucas looked up as Jack Winwood entered his office and shook his head. Winwood dumped his brief case onto a chair and occupied the other.

'I don't like this.'

'Pete Hallam rang last night, Hammoud hasn't returned,' Clucas replied. 'Pete left it until 10 o'clock, then decided to check the address we uncovered for the Land Rover, in Brunswick somewhere, to see if the other bloke was back. There was no sign of the vehicle.'

'So Geoff Miller disappears and these two don't return home either.'

'That's right, Pete's coming in shortly, we'll have a full report when he does.'

Winwood glanced at the reception desk through the glass partition of Clucas's office.

'Where's Lucy Browning this morning? There's nobody on reception.'

'She's off sick, or so she says,' Clucas said shortly.

'So...who's on reception?'

'Nobody yet. There's only one girl in; it's not 9 o'clock yet. Some will have been held up by that level crossing accident at Caulfield. I'll find someone, probably Jacqui Jameson.'

Winwood nodded.

'She'll do well there. We need someone with a bit of nous and personality on the front desk. OK, let me know when Pete Hallam arrives.'

*

Miller floundered through heavy undergrowth, he could hear police sirens in the distance and assumed Lonsdale and his cohorts were either approaching on the main road or were on the access track. He left the Lindsay residence in his wake, negotiated the hedge surrounding the property and headed into a wooded area.

He checked the direction from which he had originally approached the Lindsay property, on the alert for anyone in battle fatigues. His choices were to either cross the main road when he reached it, or alternatively head north for the National Park. Miller wasn't sure what was in the park, or whether it was patrolled. Since the terrorists had been making plenty of noise without any reaction, it seemed not.

He emerged into a clear area, looked around for cover but had to cross an open space to gain the next area of undergrowth and trees. He moved to his right, to place as much distance between himself and the location of the Agnarat Wen homestead, then took the plunge and sprinted across the open area, a paddock of about 100 metres. As he neared the trees, he heard shouting behind him and a whirring sound, followed by the sound of a shot.

'Oh God!' he exclaimed involuntarily and zig-zagged desperately to confuse further shots, then reached the trees on the other side. He risked a backward glance and saw others emerge from the previous belt of trees and head in pursuit.

'Bugger it!'

He headed right where he estimated the road was. Another shot hit a tree trunk in the area he had just left and screamed off into the ether. He continued running, beside himself with terror and expecting any minute to feel a smashing blow between the shoulder blades. He swung left, due north, out of sight of any pursuers and hoped his change of direction was unobserved.

He floundered through trees and bushes, heard shouts behind him but it seemed his ruse had worked, but for how long was questionable. He ran at a crouch to present a smaller target.

He wondered what Mrs Lindsay had told the police, had she told them about the training camp? He shook his head in despair, it was doubtful whether Lonsdale would listen anyway, he would have paedophile in his sights and nothing would shake it.

*

Jack Winwood re-entered Clucas's office, having asked Jacqueline Jameson to move to reception, she was moving across with files she was working on. He took a chair and directed a question at Peter Hallam who had followed him in.

'You say the Land Rover driver hasn't returned either?'

Hallam shook his head. Winwood was studying the Hammoud file.

'What sort of place was it?' asked Clucas.

'Multiple tenancy,' said Hallam. 'I viewed it about 7 o'clock this morning. A woman covered from head to toe in a hijab was putting something in one of the bins. Several blokes left in the early morning, probably for work, they looked Asian or Middle Eastern.'

'Hmm!' Clucas rested his elbows on his desk. 'Like our friend Hammoud.'

Clucas reached for the Hammoud file and Winwood pushed it over.

'What's up?' Winwood asked.

'Have you looked at the name of the company. I've just noticed it on the file. I was looking at it upside down. Look at it again, what does it spell backwards?'

'Agnarat Wen!' Winwood eyed the sheet on top of the file. 'New Taranga!'

'What the hell does that mean?' Hallam asked.

'It could indicate something or nothing, but something could represent trouble,' said Winwood. 'Or it could merely give their origins, remember that client we had last month who named his company Noxas Wen, which was New Saxon backwards. There was nothing sinister in that.'

'But this could be different,' said Clucas. 'Is Ross Walker in yet?'

'Can't see him,' Hallam leant back and craned his neck in the direction of Walker's office pen.

'Go and check him out, if he is, ask him to come in here.'

Hallam headed for Walker's office and passed Jacqueline Jameson, on her way to Clucas's office. She entered and handed Winwood a written note.

'What are these?'

'Messages from the answering machine, I've just played them back, there are three calls. One is from Geoff Miller.'

CHAPTER 12

Miller had no idea in which direction he was travelling, but hoped it was towards the main road. He could hitch a lift; with the risk he could flag down other members of the group who were searching for him, but couldn't worry about that now.

He could hear traffic not far ahead. He hit a track through the trees and broke into a steady jog trot, it forked so he selected a narrow path bounded by trees and bushes.

He stopped to listen, voices and sounds of movement were behind him. They didn't appear to have gained on him and he had one advantage, he could maintain a steady pace away from them, while they would be unsure which direction he had taken. On the other hand, they had guns and were prepared to use them. They only had to sight him at a distance, a lucky shot could wing him which would be the end of the chase.

Sunlight crossed his face; he was out of the trees with another 50 metres to the road. He glimpsed a heavy truck passing from right to left, heading for Patchewollock. He ran down the path which crossed the paddock, knowing he would be in full view when his pursuers emerged from the trees, but could do nothing about that. The path ran parallel to a hedge alongside the road, he sprinted along it and reached a gateway. It was open and he emerged onto the roadside. He looked back, they had seen him and three men were running across the open paddock in pursuit, rifles at the trail.

He ran along the roadside, risked a glance behind him, nobody had yet reached the gate. He ran on, looked back and saw the first of his pursuers emerge from the gateway, now 100 metres behind. He waved to his companions and set off in pursuit. Miller was astonished to see he still carried his sidearm which would be in full view of any passing motorist. That aspect obviously occurred to one of his wiser colleagues, Miller heard an authoritative shout, the gunman stopped and looked uncertainly at his sidearm, which enabled Miller to gain valuable ground.

Miller decided to cross the road and looked from left to right preparatory to crossing it, a vehicle appeared around the bend and bore down on him, he hastily stepped back. It pulled up with a scream of brakes and a cloud of dust. As he stood by the side of the road, he heard shouting back down the road, his pursuers ran back to the gateway and re-entered the paddock.

'Stand still, Miller,' a voice said. 'You're nicked.'

Miller stood numb with shock. Momentarily he was overjoyed to see Constable Lonsdale, it rendered him less likely to be shot, but the feeling of relief quickly dissipated. He was still in trouble. He had fallen out of the frying pan into the fire.

*

'Who am I speaking to?'

Winwood was in his own office pen with Clucas and Hallam, his phone to his ear, He leant forward, the others in the room could hear vestiges of chatter from the other end.

'Mrs Harriet Lindsay?' he said. 'Good morning, my name is Jack Winwood. We received a call from your phone nearly an hour ago, assuming we have the right number, from one of our colleagues, Geoff Miller. Is he there?'

The others could just hear a voice on the other end of the line, while Winwood's facial expression changed from inquiry to puzzlement.

'You what? Do you mind repeating that?'

She did, Winwood looked even more puzzled.

'The police said what?'

She told him again.

'Wait a minute. Can I just get this straight,' he looked at his audience and raised his other hand in a perplexed gesture. 'You say Geoff Miller appeared at your window, asked you to call the police, was very unkempt and wandering around your garden.'

There was more from the other end of the phone.

'Hold on...hold on! What's this about your daughter's bedroom window?'

Winwood saw it was frustrating for his colleagues who could only hear one side of the conversation. He placed a finger to his lips then switched his phone onto speaker.

'Who said he'd been peeping through the bedroom window, your daughter?'

'No, she didn't see anything,' Mrs Lindsay's voice came loud and clear through the speaker phone. 'The police constable insisted this man Miller had a history of molesting teenage girls...!'

'What policeman?'

'The policeman who came, he called me before he arrived and warned me about this man Miller.'

'Warned you? About what?'

Clucas scribbled a note and pushed it towards Winwood.

'He said he was a suspected sex offender.'

Winwood picked up Clucas's note.

'Was this police constable named Lonsdale?'

'Yes, I think that was his name. Four of them arrived at the house, but by the time they got here Mr Miller had gone, one of them stayed to search the garden and outhouses, the others drove to the main road. They told me to leave the house.'

'Leave the house? Good God! Why should they tell you to do that? Where are you now?'

'I diverted my phone to my mobile, I'm in Hopetoun outside my daughter's school.'

'You've no idea where Geoff Miller is now?'

'None at all. He escaped.'

'He...what? Escaped ...!' Winwood's voice went up an octave on the second syllable, he looked at his colleagues and raised his eyes skywards. 'What exactly did Geoff Miller say to you when he arrived?'

'He asked me to phone the police, he said something about men with rifles, he said he'd been held prisoner at the house at the end of the track for three days. I mentioned that to Constable Lonsdale but he seemed quite derisory.'

'Lonsdale seemed ...?' Winwood flapped his hand in frustrated fashion for the benefit of his audience. 'Never mind, Miller mentioned a house, which house?'

'It's further down the track, it's the old Walters' farm, or used to be. I'm not sure who occupies it now, old Mr Walters died months ago and his son took it over. I think he leased it out, but I don't know anything about that.'

'We understand it's occupied by a group called Agnarat Wen.'

'Oh...that does ring a bell, that's right, there's a sign at the end of the track on the main road. They're leasing it, I think. I've seen several vehicles coming and going on the track in recent weeks. But what about this man Miller, who are you?

'My name is Jack Winwood. I employ him.'

'Well, I understand he's dangerous and I found the whole experience very disturbing and frightening. You should be more careful who you choose for colleagues or employees.' There was a crunch as she disconnected.

Winwood put down the phone and looked around in disbelief.

'Well!' he said. 'You all heard that. I don't think she's a member of the Geoff Miller fan club.'

'There's something screwy here,' Ross Walker had entered and been listening to the verbal exchange. 'What was that about being held captive in a farmhouse for three days?'

'That's what he told Mrs Lindsay,' Clucas replied. 'She said she mentioned it to our friend Constable Lonsdale, who ignored it. Now she's convinced Geoff was lusting after her daughter.'

'I don't follow her reasoning,' Walker commented. 'She said herself that Geoff asked her to call the police. If, as she says, he's peering through bedroom windows with a view to perving at or assaulting teenage girls, that would be the last thing he'd ask her to do.'

Winwood thumped his hand on the desk, and conversation ceased.

'We have a decision to make, what do we do?'

'Contact the police?'

'The police are already involved, if we do that, we'll merely find ourselves diverted to those who've already tabbed and ticketed Geoff as a paedophile,' said Walker. 'That bloody Constable Lonsdale is a nut case, I came across him when we had that fiasco at the transport café, he tried to make out a photo of the inside of a transport café depicted a teenage girl's bedroom. He's a young upstart who wants to make a name for himself.'

'Sounds like a bit of a prat to me,' commented Winwood.

'But leaving that aside,' continued Walker. 'There's something odd about the property at the end of the track; Even Mrs Lindsay appears to have thoughts about that.'

'Maybe she thinks they're child molesters,' suggested Hallam.

There was some laughter, but Winwood held up his hand.

'What's our next course of action, I'm open to suggestions.'

'I could go up there and have a look around,' suggested Hallam.

'And do what?' grunted Walker. 'You could finish up the same as Geoff.'

'I've been thinking,' said Clucas. 'This could be more than a police matter. My brother's a superintendent in the Victorian Police, as you know. Can we leave it for an hour or so? I'll make enquiries.'

*

'Name'

'Geoffrey Miller,' Miller snapped angrily. He hadn't taken kindly to being handcuffed, bundled into the back of a police car and driven to the nearest police station with a smirking Lonsdale beside him in the back seat. On arrival, while emptying his pockets, he attempted to tell them about the farmhouse at the end of the track, but nobody listened.

'Suspected Peeping Tom and sex offender,' said Lonsdale. 'I

know this man. I've come across him before.'

'I am *not* a sex offender,' snapped Miller. 'Will you *listen* to me. I tell you I've been held prisoner in a farmhouse for three or four days, there's a terror group ...!'

'Don't tell me what to do, my friend,' said the desk sergeant. 'Can you offer any explanation for being in Mrs Lindsay's garden in the early hours of this morning?'

'Outside her teenage daughter's bedroom...!' interceded Lonsdale.

'I've just told you; I've been...!'

'Yes, held prisoner by a private army,' Lonsdale sneered. 'You'll have to do better than that, Miller. If there were paramilitary armies around here, we'd know about them.'

'Good Grief! One of them was in that gateway to the paddock when you arrested me, he was holding a bloody rifle! Didn't you see that?'

'Can't say I did.'

'Bloody hell!' Miller clasped his hands to his temples. 'Can I make a phone call?'

'No, you can't, take him down. We'll interview him later when somebody is in from CIB,' said the desk sergeant.

As the cell door slammed behind him, Miller was overwhelmed with despair and fury. He sat on the bench seat and beat his hands on his knees with frustration.

'Shit!' he ground out angrily. 'Hell and Damnation!'

*

'What did you find out from your brother?' Jack Winwood asked impatiently.

'He's making enquiries,' Clucas replied. 'He said he, or someone, will be in touch.'

'When?'

'Within the hour, he said,' replied Clucas. 'All we can do is wait, I'm afraid.'

'OK,' sighed Winwood. 'We'll wait. In the meantime, we've got other work to do.'

CHAPTER 13

Half an hour later Clucas's desk phone rang.

'Mr Clucas?'

'Yes.'

'My name is Alan Kelsey. I've had a call from Superintendent Nick Clucas, I understand you are related.'

'My brother. I phoned him this morning'

'Then you know what I'm talking about, I intend to call and see you, would this afternoon be convenient?'

'Yes, what time?'

'Can I be flexible, anytime between two and four? A case of when I get there.'

'I'll expect you when I see you,' said Clucas. 'Who are you?'

'Somebody who's been talking to your brother, concerned about the same thing you are!' Kelsey replied. 'I'll see you this afternoon.'

*

Miller was briefly interviewed, Lonsdale attended as the arresting officer, and a Detective Sergeant named Preston was present. Miller again tried to broach the subject of the Agnarat Wen property at the end of the Parmenter-Lindsay track, but the only subject under discussion was his sexual preferences and predatory tendencies, plus his predilection for standing on tiptoe and peering through bedroom windows.

'You were seen by Mrs Lindsay creeping around her garden in the small hours, were you not?' asked Preston.

'No, I was not, I don't know what constitutes small hours in your book, but 7 o'clock in the morning doesn't in mine.' Miller replied heatedly. 'Nor was I creeping. I went up to the kitchen window and attracted Mrs Lindsay's attention. If you call that creeping you must use a different dictionary from the one I do,' Miller hit his clenched fist on the table. 'Will you please listen to me! I keep telling you, I was held prisoner for three or four days by what seemed to be a terrorist group in a property up the same access track. I managed to escape and the Lindsay property was the first one I reached.'

'And she was so alarmed at your behaviour she rang the police,' interposed Lonsdale.

'Hell's Teeth!' Miller exclaimed furiously. 'I asked her to ring you.'

'All right, let's assume you asked her to ring us, why didn't you wait for us?'

That was not an easy question to answer, how could Miller say he had overheard a conversation between Mrs Lindsay and Lonsdale that was so wide of the mark he'd panicked and decided to run for it? Presented with the same set of circumstances he'd have done the same again, the course this interview was taking confirmed his decision to bolt had been correct, despite its disastrous result.

'I want to make a phone call,' Miller said in exasperation.

'Who to?'

'My employer,' as soon as he uttered it Miller knew this was a mistake. Lonsdale may be reluctant to renew his acquaintance with Ross Walker.

At this point the door to the interview room opened. A constable beckoned to the detective, there was a brief conversation before Preston returned.

'Sorry, we have to go, there's been an incident in the town,' Preston announced. 'We'll deal with you later, Mr Miller.'

*

It was about 3.00 pm when a fair-haired man, nearly 6 feet tall, presented himself at the reception desk of Winwood & Walker. He laid a small brief case on the counter.

'I have an appointment with Mr Clucas,' he said.

Jacqueline Jameson looked up, and saw a pair of blue eyes regarding her. The man inclined his head in a quizzical fashion and gave a half smile.

'Oh yes,' she said. 'Who shall I say?'

'Alan Kelsey.'

She rang through to Clucas, but he had seen the visitor arrive and was already approaching reception, realising this was the man he was expecting.

'Bill Clucas,' he extended his hand. 'You'll be Mr Kelsey?'

The other nodded and picked up his brief case, Clucas indicated his office pen.

'Come this way, Mr Kelsey,' Clucas turned to Jacqueline. 'Jacqui, can you tell Mr Winwood when he returns Mr Kelsey is here.'

He led Kelsey to his office pen.

'Where are you from?' Clucas asked.

'Just flown in from Canberra,' Kelsey sat down. 'You're Nick Clucas's brother? How come you never joined the police force?'

'I joined the Navy, he joined the police,' answered Clucas. 'Guess we both liked dark uniforms. I left the Navy when I was about 28, but he stayed in the police.'

'What branch were you in?'

'Signals and coding, in the days when we used the Morse Code.'

'Why did you leave?'

'My time expired and I didn't sign on again, I was a Petty Officer and been recommended to apply for a commission, but they were downsizing and prospects looked doubtful. I thought I may as well be an unemployed ex-Petty Officer as an unemployed ex-Warrant Officer. After demob I made a few false starts, then joined the insurance market.'

'A wise decision, I was in the navy too but stayed longer than you did, it helps when you're resident in the wardroom. I struck the same difficulty, downsizing and lack of opportunity. I became a public servant instead.'

'In ASIO?'

Kelsey raised an eyebrow.

'I didn't say that,' he said.

'No, I did! You're involved in intelligence and security?'

'OK, OK...you were right first time, but don't broadcast it,' Kelsey made a pretence of looking over his shoulder. 'As soon as anyone even hints we're in the vicinity it reaches the ears of the local press.'

'How do you know Nick?' asked Clucas.

'We've had contact over the years,' commented Kelsey. 'We've used each other as sounding boards and information sources more than once.'

Clucas rose and closed his office door.

'You have a problem?' Kelsey asked.

'Frankly, Mr Kelsey, I'm not altogether sure, but something screwy is going on.'

'The name's Alan', Kelsey said. 'Nick referred to you as Bill, so I'll use that if that's OK,' Clucas nodded and Kelsey continued. 'You were sure enough to have told Nick you were bothered, otherwise I wouldn't be here. I'm here to listen, if your suspicions or whatever they are, prove to be groundless, then so be it. Better follow a fruitless lead than ignore a vital one. It's my job to follow up anything that's ...well...screwy! So what is it?'

'OK, I'll tell you from the very beginning, starting with who we are and what we do.' Clucas said. 'We are loss adjusters and claims investigators. We deal with insurance claimants and all types of claims investigations...!'

'I know what a loss adjuster does, go on.'

Clucas gave a brief account of the sequence of events when dealing with workers compensation claimants, the often protracted and boring task of conducting surveillance on some claimants to check whether they were genuine; and the very small percentage who used their absence from work to take other jobs, rort the system, receive benefits and cash in hand from elsewhere.

'I get the picture, Bill, we do surveillance as well, not quite the same reasons, but by and large the job is similar. It can be boring, needs keen eyes and a strong bladder.' Kelsey commented. 'So?'

'We had this claimant named Hammoud, the Compensation Board stuffed up, they were paying benefit for some time before anyone locked onto it,' Clucas reached for the file and explained the sequence of events as he flicked through. He reached the point where Hallam and Miller carried out a joint exercise to follow Hammoud and his chauffeur.

'Miller was lying in wait in Warracknabeal?' asked Kelsey.

'Yes. They maintained touch all the way. They swapped short of Litchfield. Hallam signed off while Miller followed the Land Rover to Birchip and then Lascelles.'

'Expensive business for the Comp Board,' remarked Kelsey. 'I assume they're paying for all this?'

'Whatever they pay us for travel, motel and hourly rates, it's worth their while if we prove someone is swinging the lead,' Clucas responded and Kelsey smiled.

'I wasn't criticising,' he said. 'I'm fully aware many people rort the system, which means we all pay in the long run. Please continue.'

There was a knock at the office door, Ross Walker and Jack Winwood entered. Clucas made the introductions, merely introducing Kelsey as being from Canberra. Clucas gave the new arrivals a brief resumé of what he'd already told Kelsey.

'Carry on, Bill,' said Winwood.

Clucas continued with Miller's later tailing of the Land Rover until he reached the gateway beyond Hopetoun

'Any indication what lay beyond that gate?' Kelsey asked.

'I was coming to that, the name of the people who owned it, or rather who leased it, as we found out later, was Agnarat Wen.'

'Which spells New Taranga in reverse,' said Winwood.

'Does it indeed?' Kelsey raised an eyebrow. 'Yes, you're right, it does.'

'Miller said he was going to check it out, then vanished for three or four days,' Clucas continued. 'We didn't know what to make of it, there hadn't been reports of accidents in that area. Then today we found a message on our answering machine from Geoff Miller. He'd put it on in the early hours.'

'What did he say?'

'Not a lot, but said he'd been held prisoner for three or four days on the Agnarat property and he'd ring later. He never did,' said Clucas.

'What did he mean, held prisoner?'

'We don't know. We haven't heard from him since. But he left the number he was ringing from; it was another of the properties on the track, occupied by a Mrs Lindsay.'

'I spoke to Mrs Lindsay,' said Winwood. 'Apparently Miller appeared outside her kitchen window about 7.00 am, and asked her to ring the police. She did and presumably Miller then rang us, and left a message on our answering machine. Mrs Lindsay said he was dishevelled, as though he'd been ploughing through undergrowth.'

'What about the police? What did they do?'

'Ah!' Ross Walker entered the fray for the first time. 'There we struck a problem.'

'What sort of problem?'

Walker sat back and made a steeple with his fingers.

'We'll have to digress slightly here. Just let me say that the constable who dealt with Mrs Lindsay's 000 phone call was named Lonsdale, presumably attached to a local police station. Just bear with me, and I'll tell you another story, but it's relevant to what may have happened here.'

Walker embarked on Miller's kindergarten episode when apprehended with a car full of photographic equipment, the alleged Peeping Tom case involving photographs taken through the transport café windows, and the subsequent fracas with the indignant father.

'He thought Miller was the Peeping Tom and was checking his illicit shots,' said Walker. 'The police arrested Miller later, and again it was the same Constable Lonsdale. Miller was jailed overnight, he sent for me and I dealt with it next morning. I think I humiliated Lonsdale, the man is an absolute prat! His Detective Sergeant didn't seem over impressed with him either.'

'How is this relevant?'

'Mrs Lindsay said Lonsdale...presumably he's been packed off to the country shortly after his last brush with Miller... told her over the phone before he arrived that Miller was a suspected paedophile, and his intention must have been to spy on her teenage daughter.'

'Did she mention the property at the end of the track?'

'Only that the owner was named Walters, or used to be, he died months back and she thought his son had inherited it. We're chasing that up now,' said Walker

'What about the imprisonment angle, any mention of that?'

'The police, personified by Lonsdale, pooh poohed the whole idea and it seems lost in the wash. Apparently, Miller mentioned men armed with rifles to her.'

'Men armed with rifles? Did she tell the police that?'

'Maybe she did, but she became convinced Miller was lusting after her daughter and just ran with it.'

'Hmmm!' Kelsey sat back. 'One small point, you say Mrs Lindsay said Miller asked her to call the police?'

'That appears to be so,' said Winwood. 'She told me that when I spoke to her.'

'If he was peeping through windows spying on teenage girls, would he ask her to do that?' Kelsey queried. 'Surely that would be the last request any pervert or Peeping Tom would make.'

Winwood shrugged.

'Whether that point occurred to her or not I can't say. I didn't have time to put it to her, she hung up on me after castigating me for employing perverts.'

'I need to make a call,' said Kelsey. 'In addition, I need a look at your file, if that's OK with you. I'd also like to see your man Hallam if possible.'

'I'll fetch him,' said Walker. 'He's in now, we told him to hang on until you arrived.'

*

Kelsey later interviewed Hallam, who confirmed everything Clucas had told him. Hallam also added information regarding the northward journey and mentioned the Land Rover had circled a traffic island twice which indicated they could have cottoned onto him.

'Does that often happen when you're tailing people?' Kelsey asked.

'Not often,' answered Hallam. 'But yes...it happens. The few who rort the system realise someone will check on them if they're off for long periods. Eventually they develop eyes in the back of the head.'

'So, it's possible any suspicion could just be confined to the compensation angle.'

'Yes,' agreed Hallam. 'That's how I'd see it in the normal course of events.'

'OK!' Kelsey nodded. 'That's all I wanted to know, presumably they wouldn't consider anyone was following for any reason other than the Compensation Board?'

'Possible, I don't know for sure what's going on here, but yes...possible'

Kelsey used a vacant interview room to have a long conversation with Canberra. He returned to Clucas's room where the others were still sitting and conversing.

'OK,' he said. 'Leave it with us. I've briefed one of my colleagues. I'll return to Canberra tonight. We'll collate this information, then look at the location.'

'Good,' said Clucas. 'You don't think we've been wasting your time?'

'My Oath...you have not!' Kelsey shook his head. 'This has been most fruitful. It could relate to a development we're currently investigating which has caused us concern. There's also a current court case in Sydney which relates to a similar situation, so we can't afford to dismiss anything like this. I agree with you, Bill. Something isn't right! Just leave it with us and we'll be in touch.'

'If we need to contact you urgently, do you have an office in Melbourne?'

'We do, but contact me in Canberra, where I'm normally stationed. In any case the area we've been talking about is probably nearer the ACT geographically.'

CHAPTER 14

Kelsey sat in a conference room in the ASIO building in Canberra with two colleagues, Robert Bramble and Denis Shackleton. Bramble was early 30s, dark-haired with a tanned complexion. He was a tough looking individual, most of his bulk accumulated in the gym and playing second grade Rugby Union in Sydney. He was aggressive by nature and not popular with junior colleagues as he tended to be domineering. Shackleton was late twenties, fair haired, thin and wiry. Kelsey had a copy of Bill Clucas's file before him.

'I've brought you both in because this has connotations that could be serious. We'll call this Operation Dusty, make a note of that.'

'Dusty?' asked Bramble.

Kelsey looked around and gave a half smile.

'The guy who stumbled across this and is in deep trouble as a result, is named Miller.'

'Logical,' grunted Bramble.

'This compensation file is freely available to us, but nobody else, not in its entirety anyway. Winwood & Walker have given us considerable slack by supplying a full copy of it. If we leak anything out it could, quite apart from internal security concerns, prejudice a Workers Compensation investigation and a possible court case. Is that understood?'

The others nodded

'Both of you study this file, I promised I wouldn't make further copies, and intend to honour that. I'll leave it with you both to study then we'll discuss it. Cancel any arrangements you have for the next week or so, we'll be going to Patchewollock and could be there for a week or so, depending how fast we wrap this up. Any questions?'

'I gather this has Taranganese connotations,' said Bramble, more a statement than a question.

'It may have, nothing's certain yet, but it looks that way.'

'Any photographs?' Shackleton queried.

'One...the man who is the subject of this file, supplied by his employers. This is a reliable copy, Bill Clucas, the loss adjuster, had the photo scanned. After you've studied it, there's more. But get this into your heads first. I'll be back within the hour and fill you in on detail,' Kelsey rose to his feet. 'I'll leave you two with the file, have a good look at it. I have to arrange a car from the pool and other...essentials. OK?'

The other two were in no doubt what he meant by other essentials, a visit to the armoury. Kelsey departed, leaving Bramble and Shackleton studying Clucas's file.

Kelsey returned after half an hour and looked around. They both nodded.

'OK!' said Kelsey. 'To give a brief synopsis, Miller and his colleagues carried out a routine surveillance, as the file states. Now Miller has disappeared from the radar without trace somewhere in the Patchewollock area. This is the point where he followed this man Hammoud and his driver companion, whose name we now know is Ahmed Halim. I'm presently consulting Records to check if we know anything about either of them.'

'Is this a missing person investigation?' asked Shackleton.

'Partly, but Miller re-appeared briefly after he'd been missing three or four days, he turned up looking dishevelled outside the kitchen window of a lady named Harriet Lindsay and asked her to contact police. He alleged he'd been imprisoned for three days in a remote property at the end of the track and mentioned armed men and a training ground.'

'Where is he now?'

'We don't know because he's vanished again. It's hard to believe, but the local police have done nothing to check what he said. They believe he's a paedophile, because a constable apprehended him some weeks or months ago when he was parked for a long period outside a kindergarten in Bacchus Marsh with a car full of cameras. He was carrying out surveillance on a compensation claimant down the road, unaware he was parked by a kindergarten.'

'They think he's a paedophile on the strength of that?' Bramble was incredulous.

'There's more, a Peeping Tom was seen peering through the bedroom window of a teenage girl a few weeks later in the same area, by coincidence Miller was outside the house in his car checking shots on his digital camera of another claimant under investigation. He was later arrested by, would you believe, the same constable.'

'The long arm of coincidence,' commented Bramble.

'And the law,' Kelsey commented ruefully.

'So...what's the problem?'

'The problem, or part of it, appears to be a young constable named Lonsdale who refuses to believe Miller has just been in the wrong place twice at the wrong time.'

'Now three times!' interjected Bramble.

'You what...? Oh! Yes, I suppose you're right. Well on the strength of that he firmly believes Miller was at the Lindsay property for the purpose of peering through windows at Mrs Lindsay's teenage daughter.'

'Has he been arrested?' asked Bramble.

'We don't know. After Mrs Lindsay sent for the police, Miller rang his office on the same phone. Then inexplicably he took off and hasn't been seen since, possibly the police have arrested him. This is what we have to find out, we need to talk to him.'

'What's our course of action, Alan?'

'Firstly, see Mrs Lindsay to discover exactly what Miller said to her,' Kelsey looked at Shackleton. 'I want enquiries made of the police in that area. Do they know anything of Miller's whereabouts?'

'When do we start?'

'Now. We head for Patchewollock, take a motel room and operate from there. Pick up what you need and let's go.'

*

Miller was in his cell, another day had passed, Constable Lonsdale and Detective Sergeant Preston didn't return that day. Whatever it was that caused them to suspend the interview was serious. Finally, Miller lost patience, when the next meal was delivered, he demanded to see whoever was in charge.

'That may not be possible, I'll see what I can do,' the constable promised, but time dragged on and still nothing happened. Miller began to wonder about the legal ramifications of his confinement. Surely nobody could be confined this length of time without being charged or even properly interviewed. The next time the constable arrived with his meal, Miller demanded a lawyer. It was late in the day, presumably all the local lawyers were near their knocking off time and/or on their way to their respective homes. Miller, seething with anger, had to spend another night in the cell lying on an uncomfortable bed.

*

The next morning Kelsey & Co moved into a local motel room, Kelsey spread the files over the table.

'First stop, Mrs Lindsay,' he announced. 'I've arranged for Melanie Cassidy of Sydney office to join us at Patchewollock, she'll be attached briefly to the team, she should be here within the hour. I want her to interview Mrs Lindsay and the daughter. This is wholly our investigation, but we are under an obligation to Jack Winwood and Ross Walker. If we quash this Peeping Tom allegation it will do them and Miller a favour. I don't like the sound of Constable Lonsdale,' he turned to Bramble. 'You know Mel, don't you?'

'Too well. I worked with her in Sydney,' Bramble wasn't enthusiastic. 'She's a hard woman.'

Kelsey grinned.

'Her bark is worse than her bite but...!'

'No...it's not.'

'Well...yes...OK, but she's a good operator, and I'd prefer a woman to do the Lindsay interviews. Whatever did or didn't occur, Mel will sniff it out.'

Bramble nodded. Melanie Cassidy was a sharp featured woman in her mid- thirties, a forceful woman, of average height, fairly trim and with a prominent bust. Bramble had previously worked with her and knew her well. She had been married and divorced, on what grounds wasn't known, presumably infidelity but there was some speculation about her sexual leanings. It had also been suggested her husband probably couldn't cope with her skilful use of sarcasm and acid comments.

'We'll start with the local police. We've got to find Miller and quickly.'

*

Kelsey rang Mrs Lindsay and introduced himself as being from the police, he decided it would be desirable not to reveal intelligence agencies were interested or involved. He arranged to call that afternoon, in company with a female colleague. Quite aside from Mel's interviewing expertise, he considered Mrs Lindsay would probably relate better to a woman of mature manner and years. He left a Canberra number in case she wished to change the arrangement, deeming mention of Canberra should instil confidence.

'Worried she'll think you're a paedophile?' Bramble said.

'Too right,' commented Kelsey. 'She mentioned Miller twice in our conversation and you know how long I was talking to her …not very! She asked if he'd been arrested yet.'

'Understandable. But if he was, surely the police would have told her,' Shackleton suggested.

'You'd think so,' responded Kelsey. 'If only to put her mind at rest. But I'm not clear how the police mind works in this area.'

'But if Miller was imprisoned at that property, he must have told them about the private army,' said Bramble.

'If he did and they registered it, we in Canberra should have received a report by now,' said Kelsey. 'As it is we've heard bugger all, any information we do possess came from Bill Clucas in Melbourne, which came from Miller's brief message and what Mrs Lindsay said Miller told her. We've had no information from anywhere else, which means the local police, if they arrested Miller, could have ignored what he's been saying. We'll find out today, but we must find Geoff Miller.'

*

Shackleton brewed some coffee and soon a fragrant aroma filled the motel unit. They had just arranged the cups when they heard a car swish up outside. Kelsey moved to peer through the window.

'That's Mel,' he said.

'I gathered that from the skidding and squeal of brakes,' Bramble commented sourly and Kelsey chuckled.

'You're not pleased?' he said.

'She's all right,' Bramble conceded. 'But I'll bet her first words will be a critical comment.'

Kelsey opened the door to admit her.

'G' Day Alan. Long-time no see,' she stretched out her hand, then turned to Bramble. 'Hallo Bob, I like your moustache! Makes you look like a man!'

Shackleton broke up at that. Melanie Cassidy swung around and eyed him.

'Who's your friend?' she directed at Kelsey.

'He just works here,' responded Kelsey which caused grins all round.

'Now, what's all this about? Yes thanks! Milk and sugar.'

*

They set out for the Lindsay residence, in two cars. Melanie Cassidy had been around the motel unit like a cyclone, clearing up papers, re-adjusting positions of travelling bags, hitherto left all over the floor and in traffic areas, and putting paper wrappers, previously around cakes of soap, in the bins.

'Doesn't take long for three men to turn a motel room into a pigsty,' she had sniffed.

Kelsey and Cassidy were in her car, the other two trailed behind. It had been agreed, while the Lindsay interview was in progress, Bramble and Shackleton would explore further up the track to check it out. They had decided not to drive up to the Agnarat Wen gate, but drop the car along the track and walk the rest of the way.

Melanie had been briefed on the situation before they left, and was told she may have to do some astute questioning to ascertain exactly what had occurred when Miller had arrived at the Lindsay property.

'I think there's been a case of possibly leading the witness, where the situation as originally experienced was later distorted by what an overzealous police constable believes happened,' Kelsey explained as Melanie swung her car out of the motel and turned left onto the main road. 'We both know from experience this can happen, but I'm surprised Mrs Lindsay let herself be persuaded.'

'Unless Miller did peer in through the wrong window when he first arrived outside the house,' said Melanie. 'In his situation, alleged or otherwise, it would be logical to check the nearest one to see if he could attract attention.'

'Possible, but this Peeping Tom scenario could merely be part of Constable Lonsdale's enthusiasm and two twos making five.'

'I'm inclined to agree from what I've read so far,' said Melanie. 'But what if he did inadvertently find that window first?'

'That's what we have to find out,' said Kelsey. 'If the daughter saw nothing, then I'd say we approach the police, if they have Miller, and scotch that one. We need Miller with us, we must know what he saw and, if possible, get him back up that track.'

'And persuade the police, if they've got him, to release him.'

'I doubt if they've charged him yet, I imagine Winwood & Walker would have heard if they had.'

They located the track leading off to the right, or to the west of the main road. Kelsey asked Melanie to pause shortly after they entered. The other car drew up behind, Kelsey got out to have words with Bramble.

'There are the signs, they clearly give all three names, this confirms what Miller told his employers,' he said. 'Check the end of the track. We have nothing on Parmenter. He's worth a visit just to see if he's seen anything off line.'

'OK.' Bramble nodded. 'We'll see you later.'

'Be prepared for trouble, and be careful. OK?'

'Don't worry. I used to be in the Boy Scouts,' replied Bramble.

'Good job you didn't say that in front of Melanie, imagine what she'd have made of that!' said Kelsey which caused some amusement.

'What was that about?' Melanie asked as Kelsey re-entered her car.

'I told Bramble to be prepared, he said he used to be in the Boy Scouts,' explained Kelsey, knowing she would sniff out any evasions within seconds. 'He was glad you weren't around when he said it.'

Melanie cracked up with laughter.

'Bramble in the Boy Scouts...wish I'd seen it!'

They separated when they reached the gate to Mrs Lindsay's house. Bramble and Shackleton proceeded onwards, there had been rain overnight, the track was muddy and slippery.

Melanie Cassidy entered the track to the Lindsay house.

'Nice house and garden,' she commented.

'That's why,' Kelsey indicated a man with a wheel barrow working the flower beds.

'My gardening is limited to a window box,' said Melanie.

'My wife does ours,' said Kelsey.

They reached the house and Melanie parked the car so it faced back towards the track. The gardener eyed them curiously, but continued his labours. Mrs Lindsay saw them through the front room window and opened the front door as they arrived on the step. She was tall and graceful, late thirties, wearing slacks and a tight white seater, Kelsey cast his eye over her approvingly.

He introduced himself and Melanie and explained they were following up a police investigation, he said nothing initially about ASIO. She invited them into her sitting room. Kelsey looked around the room, it had flowered curtains, the lounge suite was of a floral pattern and there was a smell of floor polish. The incoming sun gave a pleasant homely feeling. Mrs Lindsay waved them to chairs.

'What's this about?' she asked. 'I've already given a full statement to police.'

'We're not the police,' said Kelsey.

Mrs Lindsay's eyes widened and she straightened up.

'Pardon?' she asked. 'You said you were.'

'Yes, I did, we're not members of the police but we are attached to them for this investigation,' said Kelsey. 'We are from the Federal Government in Canberra.'

'Federal Police?'

'We have affiliations with them,' said Kelsey.

'I don't think I quite understand.'

'We deal with intelligence and internal security,' said Kelsey.

'We are particularly interested about the contact you had with Geoff Miller, in the early morning a few days ago.'

'Security?' Mrs Lindsay became somewhat hostile. 'What has this to do with security, I was told the man was spying on my daughter.'

Kelsey glanced at Melanie. It had been agreed, after they gained entry to the house, she would lead the interview.

'Can we clarify that?' she asked. 'You were told he was doing what? Who actually said that?'

'Well,' Mrs Lindsay considered as she cast her mind back. 'I was told this man was known to the police...!'

'Who said that?'

'The constable, his name was Lonsdale,' Mrs Lindsay said. 'He was the one who took my statement.'

'Who actually said Miller had been spying on your daughter?' asked Melanie. 'Was it you or Lonsdale?'

'Well, Constable Lonsdale said this man had a history...!'

'Prior to that you were aware of nothing untoward about Miller,' Melanie persisted. 'Apart from his sudden appearance outside your window looking the worse for wear?'

'No.'

'Where did Miller first appear, where did you first see him?'

'I saw him outside my kitchen window, on this side of the house.'

'Where is your daughter's bedroom?'

'On the other side; the west side of the house.'

'Did your daughter say anything about seeing Miller?'

'I don't think she saw him at all, she got out of bed, then went to the bathroom.'

'Did she say anything about seeing Miller outside the house?'

'I've just explained that, she never saw him at all.'

'But she would have seen him if he'd been peering through

her window?'

'What's this all about? Why are you asking these questions?'

'We are trying to establish certain facts. We don't believe Miller had any interest in your daughter,' explained Kelsey. 'He said something else to you, where he'd come from.'

'Oh, something about being held prisoner in a house down the road, a highly improbable story. That's old Mr Walters' place. I didn't place much credence on that, so I rang the police.'

'That's another point we wish to clarify, Mrs Lindsay,' said Melanie. 'Whose idea was it to ring the police? Yours or Miller's?'

'I...well...now I think about it...he asked me to. I did that and then he asked if he could use my phone to call his office, somewhere in Melbourne,' said Mrs Lindsay. 'Then I let him into the house.'

'Why did you do that?'

'Because he'd asked me to ring the police, I assumed he was all right at the time.'

'If he was wanted by and known to the police, why would he ask you to ring them?' asked Melanie.

'I don't know...I can't answer that.'

'Did you tell Lonsdale that?'

'Yes, I did but he didn't take much note of it.'

'Let's go back to the beginning. What happened after you'd rung the police?'

'I had a call from Constable Lonsdale. He rang about ten minutes later. He said this man Miller was dangerous, and asked me if I had any teenage children.'

'He said what?' Kelsey looked surprised. 'Did you mention anything to him that Miller had told you?'

'About what?'

'About his being held prisoner.'

'Yes, I did mention it. I think I also mentioned I'd heard noises or activity from that direction myself over the past few months.'

'What sort of activity?'

'Well, I suppose it could have been gunfire, maybe they were shooting rabbits or cockatoos.'

'What was Lonsdale's reaction to that?' Melanie took over again.

'He didn't seem to react at all, although I remember he did make a joke about it. He just took my statement then left.'

'Did you mention gunfire when you dictated your statement?'

'I did mention it, yes. But the constable didn't include it.'

'Have you heard from the police since?'

'No, not yet.'

'Have you seen or heard any activity from the Walters property since that day?'

'No, why should I? Occasionally I see vehicles passing on that track, sometimes it's Mr Parmenter's truck, I know that one by sight. There has been considerable activity on that track the last few days, mainly outgoing.'

'Has there, by God!' Kelsey leant forward. 'Have you seen any movement around your own property?'

'No...oh yes. The other day, the same day Mr Miller and the police were here. I did see some men moving around in the trees on the west side. But I haven't seen them since. I assumed they were rangers from the national park.'

'Why did you assume that?'

'They were dressed in khaki, like battle dress, they were carrying weapons. I assumed they were rangers.'

'Where did Constable Lonsdale come from, what police station?'

'It's just down the road, in Alma Street after you've entered the town.'

'Is your daughter at home, Mrs Lindsay?'

'No, she's at school.'

'I may want to see her,' said Melanie. 'I want to know if she saw anything from her window that morning, not just Miller, anyone.'

'What is all this about?'

'We don't know yet, but we intend to find out. Thank you, Mrs Lindsay,' Kelsey stood up as did Melanie. Melanie cast her eye over the bookcase, then turned to Mrs Lindsay.

'Are you Harriet Lindsay, the author?'

'Yes.'

'You write books with a historical background, Regency period and Elizabethan?'

'Yes,' Mrs Lindsay began to melt visibly and become more receptive.

'I've read all your books. I find them fascinating. Your historical detail is so accurate. I enjoyed your last one, the one set just after the Battle of Waterloo.'

'Oh, The Angove Legacy,' Mrs Lindsay looked very pleased. 'It's very nice of you to say so, thank you.'

'It's part of a saga isn't it?'

'Yes, I'm working on the next book now.'

'Good. I'll look out for it. It's a pleasure to have met you.'

Kelsey led the way out, with Melanie in his wake still chatting to the lady of the house. He turned as they reached the porch.

'Can I see the window where you first saw Miller?'

'Certainly,' Mrs Lindsay led the way around the side of the house. Her demeanour had taken a turn for the better since Melanie's avowed enthusiasm for her fiction writings. Kelsey had a look around.

'Where was Miller?'

'Standing about here,' Mrs Lindsay indicated an area of lawn.

'I opened this window and we talked, then I rang the police and afterwards let him use the phone, I passed it through the window.'

'OK!' Kelsey shook hands with her. 'Thank you for your assistance, Mrs Lindsay.' They returned to Melanie's car.

Kelsey rang Shackleton's mobile when they reached the Lindsay track.

'Did you see anything beyond the Agnarat gate?' he asked

Melanie could hear the conversation as Shackleton's voice crackled in Kelsey's ear.

'Go and see Parmenter then, see if he knows anything,' ordered Kelsey. 'We'll deal with the police. We've ascertained the police station where Lonsdale is stationed.'

Again, Melanie heard the crackle of Shackleton's voice in the mobile phone, Kelsey nodded, 'OK. Follow up Parmenter, we'll see if we can find Miller.'

CHAPTER 15

A constable opened Miller's cell door and beckoned to him. Miller was escorted to the interview room, the constable stood near the door with arms folded. Constable Lonsdale and Detective Sergeant Preston entered and occupied the other side of the table.

'Can you please tell me precisely what is going on?' Miller asked coldly. His first reaction was to lose his temper but realised this would get him nowhere. 'How much longer do you intend to hold me here?'

'We have a statement from Mrs Lindsay,' Lonsdale said. 'She says you were seen outside her daughter's bedroom window.'

'By whom?'

'Mrs Lindsay.'

'Bullshit!' Miller snapped angrily. 'If she says that she's a bloody liar. She was in her kitchen when I saw her. Does her daughter sleep in the kitchen?'

'Mrs Lindsay rang us because she was alarmed …!'

'She rang you because I asked her to, I've already told you that,' Miller kept his temper with an effort. 'I assume she put *that* in her statement. Has anyone investigated the property at the end of the track, operated by Agnarat Wen?'

'Why should we do that?' Lonsdale said with an unpleasant smirk. 'Have they got any teenage daughters?'

'God Almighty!' Miller exclaimed in sheer frustration, but there was a strong reaction from elsewhere. Preston plainly felt Lonsdale was overstepping the mark and thumped his hand on the table. Miller sensed he was puzzled and irritated by Lonsdale's over zealousness, similar to Detective Sergeant Caslake's reaction at Miller's previous intrreview.

'I tell you there's a militaristic operation going on there, I saw it. They jumped me and I was taken to the house by men armed with rifles ...!'

The door opened and a uniformed constable beckoned to Preston.

'What is it?' Preston asked impatiently.

The constable leant over and whispered into Preston's ear. Preston raised an eyebrow, asked him to repeat it then stood.

'Interview suspended 2.14 pm,' Preston said for the benefit of the tape and departed.

'Why don't you just come clean and stop wasting our time, Miller,' Lonsdale said after the door closed. 'Do you seriously expect us to believe this cock and bull story about an army of men with guns and being held prisoner?'

'No!' Miller responded with some heat. 'Certainly, nobody as stupid as you.'

Lonsdale flushed angrily.

'That's enough of that!'

Two people awaited Preston at the reception desk, a fair-haired man and a woman. They both had a look about them which seemed to denote authority, particularly the male, what he'd heard some describe as Class "X". He'd seen that look with senior police officers.

'What is it?' he asked the desk sergeant brusquely, ignoring the two visitors.

'They are enquiring about the man in custody, Geoff Miller,' was the reply. 'They're from Canberra.'

'Canberra?' Preston sensed alarm bells ringing. 'Did you say Canberra?'

'Yes, he did,' the man responded. 'You have a man named Geoff Miller in custody?'

'We do, what is it to you?' replied Preston.

'We wish to see him, urgently,' was the reply. 'My name is Alan Kelsey, and this is Melanie Cassidy. Can we talk?'

'Go ahead,' said Preston.

'Not here, in private.'

'Why not here?'

'We don't normally deal with matters of national security in public.'

Preston was about to retort, on the lines that he would speak to them here or not at all, but the demeanour of his two visitors dissuaded him. He indicated a nearby interview room.

'What is it?' he asked peevishly when they were inside with the door closed.

'We wish to see Mr Miller,' said Kelsey. 'We believe he has information regarding a property at the end of a track leading westward off the Hopetoun-Patchewollock road.'

'What?' Preston experienced more unease. 'What property?'

'We understand it's known locally as the Walters property.'

'Mr Miller is in custody as a suspected sexual predator and Peeping Tom. What information is Mr Miller likely to possess?'

'That's what we're here to find out!'

'What about the Walters' property?'

'We understand it's on a long track off the road to Patchewollock,' Kelsey continued. 'Do you know the track in question?'

'Of course I know it.'

'We want to know what's going on up there. Where is Miller?'

'He's being interviewed. Who the bloody hell are you?'

Kelsey sighed, reached into his pocket and produced a badge, Melanie did the same.

'Australian Security and Intelligence...!' The unease circulating through Preston's bloodstream became more acute. 'What is this?'

'I've told you. This relates to internal national security and we want to see Mr Miller please, as soon as possible.'

'Just get it over and done with, Miller,' Lonsdale was saying, not for the first time. 'Stop wasting our time and yours.'

The door opened and Preston re-entered, accompanied by a man and a woman. Lonsdale reached across to re-start the tape recorder, but Preston forestalled him.

'Why not?' asked Lonsdale. 'Who's this?'

'ASIO,' said Preston. 'They want to ask Mr Miller some questions.'

That moment ranked as one of Miller's most pleasurable, one he treasured for the rest of his days. As soon as those three syllables consisting of four initial letters hit the ether the expression on Lonsdale's face was wondrous to behold. He looked like an expiring fish as his mouth opened and shut. He looked at Miller, who stared fixedly back at him, then at Kelsey.

'ASI ...O?' the last syllable trailed off to a whisper.

'I think that's what he said,' Miller said acidly.

'We have to interview Mr Miller,' said the woman. 'As a

matter of urgency.'

'What...what about?' Lonsdale was still in shock.

'That's for us to know,' said Kelsey. 'Could you leave us for a few minutes, we need to speak to Mr Miller alone, although we'll need to talk with you later. We'd also like to see Mrs Lindsay's statement if that's possible.'

Lonsdale was not the only one in a state of shock, Miller was much the same but at least he had a sense of euphoria allied with it. This sensation emanated not so much because his present situation was alleviated, but that somebody, plainly in authority, believed him and was interested in what he had to say.

Kelsey occupied Lonsdale's chair and Melanie occupied the other. Kelsey produced his file and a pen.

'You've proved very elusive, Mr Miller,' said Kelsey.

'You can thank the police and those bastards at Agnarat Wen for that,' Miller said bitterly. 'I've spent the last few days locked up in farmhouses or police cells and nobody would listen to me!'

'Well...we're listening now,' said Kelsey. 'We understand you followed a man to this area from Melbourne, you and your colleague Peter Hallam. Now, exactly what happened?'

Miller went through the sequence of events, the tailing by Peter Hallam and the subsequent takeover by Miller himself at Litchfield. He described how he had stayed overnight in the area and investigated the track the following day, his foray into the property, his observations of the house and the immediate vicinity.

'What did it look like, what do you think was going on?'

'I wasn't sure at first, I thought it was one of those paint ball shooting ranges, where blokes go for a week end and ...!'

'I know what a paint ball range is,' Kelsey interrupted impatiently. 'Go on!'

'It looked like a military training camp, they were shinning up and over obstacles, crawling through pipes, snaking around on their stomachs and elbows, there was also target practice with something that looked like a dummy on a raised platform.'

'Bloody hell! Yes, go on!'

'I took video footage of it; this was after I'd gone a bit further in and was able to zoom in on them. My main object was to concentrate on filming Hammoud...the bloke I had been following. This was a Workers Compensation case that ...!'

'We know all about that, Bill Clucas at your Melbourne office filled us in,' Kelsey broke in again. 'Never mind the detail, what happened next?'

'I got Hammoud on tape, enough for him to be recognisable, the camera had a good zoom on it. Then I realised two men were approaching, they wore battle fatigues and carried repeater rifles. They didn't see me at first; they didn't know I was there until they got closer. I didn't like the look of things so I wrapped up the video camera and stuffed it in a rabbit hole, I didn't have time to hide anything else, then they...!'

'A video camera?' exclaimed Melanie Cassidy. 'Hold on! You've got video footage?'

'Yes.'

'And you hid the camera where...?' asked Kelsey.

'In a rabbit hole.'

'A rabbit hole?'

'Yes. the bank I was on was part of a rabbit warren with rabbits hopping around. I bundled the camera into the nearest hole before those two bastards saw me. Then they did and I heard them shout.'

'So...the video camera could still be where you left it?'

'Very likely. They were pretty rough when they reached me. I had a rifle barrel jammed in my gut while the other searched me. They collected all my gear and dumped me in a four-wheel drive that came up from the farmhouse.'

'But they didn't find the video camera?'

'Not at the time, whether they've been back and found it since I couldn't say, but it hadn't been discovered when they took me to the farmhouse.'

'Hmm!' Kelsey rubbed his chin. 'We'll need you to show us where that camera is, Mr Miller. You'll have to come with us up that track. I'll have words with the custody sergeant.'

Kelsey turned to Melanie.

'I'll leave Constable Lonsdale to your tender mercies, Mel. I'll sit in on that one. We'll have to leave you for the time being, Mr Miller, but it won't be for long. OK?'

'All right,' Miller treated them to a broad smile. 'I'll say this. I've never been so relieved as when you arrived. I've been trying to tell people about this sodding Agnarat business for two or three days and nobody would listen.'

'Well...we're listening now. We're also dealing with the other aspect. We want to know *why* nobody would listen to you. We'll see you shortly, Mr Miller,' Kelsey made for the door. 'OK Mel, let's go.'

CHAPTER 16

Kelsey and Melanie Cassidy utilised another interview room with Constable Lonsdale and Detective Sergeant Preston. Melanie Cassidy opened the proceedings.

'Constable Lonsdale, we're enquiring into the property at the end of the track off the Patchewollock and Hopetoun Road, what do you know of this property?'

Lonsdale looked puzzled, then shook his head.

'I don't know anything about it.'

Melanie Cassidy leant forward.

'You must know something about it. I understand you answered a 000 call and called on Mrs Lindsay.'

'Yes, I did. We had a report that an intruder was hanging around the house peering through windows.'

'It wasn't quite like that was it, Constable? However, let's return to Mr Miller. When you subsequently arrested him, he mentioned the property further up the track from Mrs Lindsay's house. He said he'd been held captive there for three days.'

'He may have said something like that.'

'Well, did he...or didn't he?'

Lonsdale muttered something and Melanie inclined her head.

'I didn't quite catch that.'

'He may have done.'

'I'll take that as a yes, I can confirm that he did,' Melanie consulted the pad before her. 'Also, Mrs Lindsay told us she informed you that Miller also gave her this information to her when he first contacted her that morning, before you attended the 000 call. But there's no mention of this on Mrs Lindsay's statement, taken by you. Can you explain that?'

'I don't recall her telling me that'

'Oh!' Melanie consulted her pad again. 'Then why should Mrs Lindsay tell us she did mention it to you when we questioned her?'

There was silence, Lonsdale shifted uncomfortably on his chair. Preston said nothing, his facial expression difficult to analyse, but from occasional glances he made in Lonsdale's direction Kelsey assumed he wasn't pleased.

'Very well, let's move onto events after you arrested Miller. He gave you the same information he mentioned to Mrs Lindsay, that he'd been imprisoned for several days at the Agnarat Wen or Walters property at the end of the track. What investigations did you make of that property as a result of what Mr Miller told you?'

Lonsdale bit his lip, then shook his head.

'None,' he said. 'From past experience I considered he was inventing it.'

'What past experience?' Melanie asked coldly.

'At Bacchus Marsh, I caught him outside a kindergarten taking photographs.'

'That's been checked, he didn't take any photographs that day, and if he had they would have been of a suspected fraudulent workers compensation claimant,' said Melanie. 'You confiscated his camera equipment that day and found nothing.'

'The second time I caught him we suspected he'd been taking photographs through the window of a teenage girl's bedroom.'

'We understand the photographs were of the inside of a transport café,' Melanie corrected him acidly. 'Are you married, Constable?'

'No.'

'You have a fiancée?'

'Yes, what's that got to do with it?'

'Probably nothing,' Melanie said and added sarcastically. 'Life must be difficult for your girl-friend when she's with somebody who can't tell the difference between a teenager's bedroom and a transport café full of truckies!'

Both Preston and Kelsey turned away to hide smiles as Lonsdale angrily flushed and started to his feet.

'What the hell do you mean by that?' he stormed. 'I had reason to believe …!'

'*Sit down!*' thundered Kelsey as he too stood up. 'We are asking the questions here. Your omission to follow up this possible lead may have severe repercussions and prejudice our country's security. Surely to God if anyone reports a private army training camp on your patch, I'd have thought the first thing you'd do was to investigate.'

'I didn't consider it likely.'

'What about you?' Melanie turned to Preston.

'I wasn't sure,' admitted Preston. 'But Reg here...that is... Constable Lonsdale said he knew this man and had arrested him twice before. Having been told that, I thought Miller's story was farfetched.'

'It may well be,' said Melanie coolly. 'Maybe he *is* talking a load of bollocks to distract us all from something else, perhaps being a Peeping Tom. We don't know any more than you do, but having heard the story and considered the possibilities, especially with today's international climate, the current court case in Sydney, and past events in Mumbai, Madrid and London together with a foreign dignitary visiting Sydney within coming weeks, it surely should have been deemed worthy of investigation. We came all the way from Canberra because we thought so. This is something you, being on the spot, could and should have done immediately and saved a lot of time.'

'Guess we should,' Preston cast a sidelong look at Lonsdale; his look boded ill for that young man. Clearly, he was not pleased. Lonsdale said nothing, but his expression indicated he was still not convinced.

'We must now look at the whole picture,' said Kelsey. 'We must investigate that property at the end of the track, perhaps you will be vindicated, Constable Lonsdale, perhaps not. Secondly, it appears Mrs Lindsay's statement needs to be revised, and all relevant detail added. If anything is going on there, it will be necessary to add it to her statement. Have you interviewed the local farmer, Mr Parmenter, up there?'

'No.'

'So you have no statement from him regarding possible disturbances up there.' Kelsey sniffed disdainfully. 'We may have something on that shortly. Two of my men are up there now and intend to call on Parmenter, if they haven't already done so.'

'Two of your men?' asked Preston.

'Yes, they went up there this morning, two or three hours ago.'

'Shit!' Preston's eyes again flickered in Lonsdale's direction.

'We need to investigate that track and for Miller to

accompany us. He says he hid a video camera up there when he was apprehended by two armed men; we need him to show us where it is.'

'If there's anything there,' Lonsdale muttered under his breath.

'Indeed,' Kelsey replied. 'That's what we have to ascertain, constable. I assume it will be in order for Mr Miller to accompany us?'

His tone made it clear he wouldn't brook any other course of action. Preston nodded.

'Presumably you and Constable Lonsdale will accompany us, since Mr Miller is still technically under arrest, assuming you can be spared from the station,' added Kelsey. 'In any case, this is your patch, if anything is going on up there, police should be represented.'

They all rose, Lonsdale and Preston departed while Kelsey and Melanie Cassidy gathered up their papers. Kelsey looked at Melanie and smiled.

'I must commend you on the way you handled that,' he said. 'Bramble should have been here. He is a great admirer of your sarcasm.'

*

Miller couldn't believe it when Preston re-entered the interview room and told him he was to accompany Melanie Cassidy and Kelsey to the track. He had had so many false dawns he had few expectations this one would be any different. He also drew great comfort from Lonsdale's facial expression as they all trooped out of the police station and headed towards the cars. Miller accompanied Kelsey and Cassidy while Preston and Lonsdale led the way to the track.

'How are you, Mr Miller?' asked Kelsey as they followed the police car.

'Bloody ecstatic!'

'Nice to be at liberty again?' Melanie steered the car to join the Patchewollock road.

'That's not the main issue,' said Miller. 'Seeing the two of you has been a boost, not only because I'm free of that damned police cell, but because you're taking me seriously. That bloody prat Lonsdale wouldn't believe anything I said.'

'How many did you see at that farmhouse?' Kelsey asked.

'Difficult to say, I only saw the house and grounds at a distance, but at a rough guess I'd say ten. When I was held inside the house, there was much coming and going, with heavy feet tramping in the hallway morning and night. They spent evenings in a conference room near where they held me.'

'How did you get out?'

'There was no lock on the door, but they usually posted someone outside, I had regular toilet breaks to a bathroom down the passageway. One night they were in conference. Their routine was upset and nobody was on guard. I got into the hall but was nearly sprung when two men arrived, obviously newcomers because they didn't know where the hall light switch was. I hid between two items of hall furniture and they missed me in the half light.'

'Would you recognise anyone again?'

'The two who caught me and the head man who interviewed me, plus two who acted as guards outside my door. I'd recognise one of the newcomers, I saw him as he crossed the light shining from the conference room door. The boss man greeted them, the one who interviewed me, he called him Juan.'

'Juan!' Kelsey mused. 'Juan. Hmmm! Was he Asian as well?'

'I couldn't be sure,' Miller then perked up. 'Oh... hang on, he did say one word that puzzled me, at the time I was hiding in the hallway. He said the word 'si'; he was agreeing and nodding at the time. I assume it meant 'yes', he could have been Italian... or Spanish?'

'Either,' said Melanie. 'I took a Spanish language course three years ago, but it could be either.'

'A Spaniard or Italian,' mused Kelsey. 'It's a clue, we'll have to think about that.'

Privately he thought it more than just a clue. He had a shrewd suspicion who the later arrival could have been. The car in front reached and entered the track and Melanie followed. Preston wasn't sure what Kelsey had in mind so allowed them to pass. He fell into line behind as they reached and passed Mrs Lindsay's gate.

'We'll have to see her again,' said Kelsey. 'That can wait. Keep going, Mel, we'll probably meet up with the others.'

They rounded a bend in the track and saw a parked car and utility. Shackleton was propped against the car while Bramble was talking to a man leaning on the open door of the utility. He looked about sixty; wore a battered old hat; denims, canvas boots and a highly coloured shirt.

'I'd say that's Parmenter,' said Kelsey.

'Alan, I never cease to be amazed at your deductive powers,' said Melanie. 'It's a privilege to be working with such a master sleuth.'

Kelsey was grinning as he climbed out. Miller followed suit. They approached Bramble and the farmer. Bramble saw them coming and indicated Kelsey to Parmenter, carried out a hasty introduction and Parmenter solemnly extended his hand.

'I've been asking Mr Parmenter about the property at the end of the track,' said Bramble. 'He's seen a lot of traffic to-ing and fro-ing.'

'That farm used to belong to Joe Walters,' said Parmenter. 'He was my neighbour, and my father's neighbour, for about forty years or more. He promised me last year he'd sell me that paddock over there...' he jerked his thumb towards an adjoining paddock '...he never used it 'cause the creek was in the way and he had trouble getting his tractor across it. Then the old bloke went and died. His son owns it now...' he wrinkled his nose and shook his head: '...nothing like the old man.'

'Who's using it now?' asked Kelsey.

'Dunno!' Parmenter shook his head. 'A lot of vehicles bin going in and out, dunno what sort of farming they're doin'. Weird mob if you ask me, hear a lot of shootin' comin' from it, can't see much, the land rises up over there and I can't see anythin'.'

Kelsey studied him for a few seconds, Parmenter's face was creased and lined from years spent in the open air. His hat was old and battered, Kelsey was mildly surprised not to see corks dangling from it to keep the flies away. He looked a tough customer, brought about by years of toil on the land. He also looked honest, it seemed to shine through.

'What do you farm?' Kelsey asked conversationally.

'Bit of this...bit of that,' answered Parmenter. 'I've been running some sheep and a few Angorra goats. I got some grain on the south paddock.'

'Are you on your own?'

'My son works with me, the missus runs the house. Who are you blokes?'

'We're looking at the old Walters property, do you know who's in there?'

'Bin leased out, some mob called Anorack When or summat like that, they bin there over six months. Don't think they're doin' much farmin'. Criminal waste o' good land if you ask me.'

'You've heard shots coming from over there?'

'My Oath, and a few loud bangs. Reckoned they were trying to frighten the cockies, bloody nuisance they are, took the lead off my roof a few months back.'

'Who did?'

'The bloody cockies, I've shot a few myself,' snorted Parmenter and turned as Detective Sergeant Preston approached.

'Hallo Roger, hope you didn't hear that! How's that son o' yours these days?'

Preston shook hands with Parmenter.

'He's doing fine Norm. How's the wife?'

'OK! Bit of 'flu last week but she's all right now.'

'We're after information regarding the people renting old man Walters' place, Norm. Something ain't right!'

'Like what?'

Preston looked uneasily at Kelsey, wondering if he'd spoken out of turn and pre-empted him, but Kelsey nodded and took a couple of steps back.

'Some funny goings on, have you seen anything?'

'No more than I've told these fellahs,' said Parmenter. 'Plenty of shootin' goin' on, but old man Walters did a fair amount of that, he liked pigeons in the pot.'

'Seen many vehicles coming up the track?'

'Plenty,' Parmenter nodded. 'Mainly four-wheel drives, occasional sedans.'

'Had any contact with them?'

'Nah!' Parmenter shook his head. 'I was up here a few weeks back when four vehicles came out o' there. I gave 'em a wave but got nothin' in response, snooty bastards! Looked like a crowd of wogs to me.'

'And that's all?'

'About it,' sniffed Parmenter. 'One of 'em parked his car

outside my gate last week, where I usually park the tractor. It was there two days but someone shifted it yesterday.'

'That was my car,' interjected Miller.

'Well, it wan't you driving it, that's for sure. Some bloody fool dressed like a bloody marine, lousy driver an' all! He had it in the ditch when he did a "U" turn and it took him about ten minutes to get it out. Then he drove it towards the Walters place.'

Kelsey turned to Miller.

'Hope your car's insured,' he said.

Miller grimaced.

'Wonder what they've done with it.'

'Probably still on the farm,' said Parmenter. 'I ain't seen it come out again, and I've bin working that paddock over there this week, nearly up to the main road.' He pointed down the track towards Mrs Lindsay's.

'You know Mrs Lindsay?' asked Kelsey.

'Sure do,' Parmenter nodded. 'Nice lady. Good looker too. See her now and again when I'm working down there, once or twice in town.'

'Thank you, Mr Parmenter, we'll go down the track and see what we can find.'

Parmenter pursed his lips.

'Bin a lot of 'em coming out the last day or two, like a procession. Seemed to be one-way traffic, din't see any goin' the other way.'

'OK, thanks again Mr Parmenter.'

'See yer, Norm,' said Preston, Parmenter nodded in response before he clambered into his old utility and drove into his property. Preston moved up behind the vehicle as it went through and secured the gate. Parmenter acknowledged with a wave from the driver's window and drove down the track towards his farmhouse.

'Nice old boy,' commented Kelsey.

'He is,' said Preston. 'One of the best.'

CHAPTER 17

After Parmenter's departure they gathered round Bramble's vehicle.

'OK!' Kelsey said. 'Two items have been accomplished, we've met and spoken with Parmenter. We've also found Mr Miller and got him out of jail!'

There was a ripple of laughter, Lonsdale excepted.

'Time is now of the essence. Days have elapsed since Mr Miller escaped from that farmhouse which could prove fatal. It's possible the birds have already flown, both Parmenter and Mrs Lindsay mentioned an exodus of vehicles. But it isn't certain they've all left; which means when we enter the Walters property we must be prepared. I believe three of us are armed, is that so?'

Shackleton and Bramble indicated they were but Melanie shook her head.

'When I left Sydney, the question didn't arise, nobody appeared clear what was involved,' she said. 'The answer is no.'

Kelsey looked at Preston who indicated the affirmative.

'All right,' Kelsey tapped his forehead with his forefinger while he deliberated. 'That makes four of us. We have things to do. Detective Sergeant Preston...hell I can't keep calling you that...I heard Parmenter call you Roger, all right if I use that?'

'Roger will do fine,' Preston gave a mock salute.

'Right!' Kelsey went on. 'Roger, can you come into the property with us? Constable Lonsdale, I suggest you contact lawyers and real estate agents in town, find out who let this property to Agnarat Wen, we must track the paperwork. If you draw a blank in Hopetoun start phoning around Patchewollock. Secondly, and I repeat — secondly, because it's advisable to give the paper chase priority, you must visit Mrs Lindsay, we need her statement to be modified. We have to know if she's been aware of any further strange goings on, anything she may have heard or been aware of over the last few months relating to the Walters property. Got that?'

'Right!' Constable Lonsdale muttered sulkily.

Kelsey turned to Miller.

'Mr Miller.'

'Call me Geoff,' said Miller and added cynically. 'Every time I've been addressed as Mr Miller during the last week, I've either been kidnapped or placed under arrest.'

There was another ripple of laughter, again with one exception. Kelsey smiled.

'OK, Geoff it is. Come with us, we must find that video camera, assuming it's still there. If it is, can we can play it back on the spot?'

'Should do, it was fully charged when I left the hotel to come here.'

'Mel, if we find it, you get it to Canberra,' said Kelsey. 'We'll sort out the details later. We may need a helicopter flyover to view this property in case there's still a full-scale army here.

Check your mobile phones.'

They did so, and all shook their heads.

'We're in a dead spot,' Kelsey turned to Shackleton. 'You picked me up OK earlier on when I called you?'

'I was nearer the main road, Bob stayed here.'

'OK Mel. It's up to you,' Kelsey turned to Melanie. 'As soon as you get a signal get hold of Canberra, we need a chopper to fly over this property. As for the video camera, after we've found it and you've got it, sort out with them how to get it to Canberra.'

'What do I do now?' asked Melanie. 'Stay here?'

'Come with us, when we find the video camera, head back here and contact Canberra.'

Kelsey watched as Constable Lonsdale drove the police vehicle down the track towards the main road, then turned to Preston.

'Roger,' he said. 'How is it you went along with Lonsdale? That Peeping Tom fiasco cost several days.'

'I've no satisfactory answer,' Preston bit his lip. 'Guess I took the easy way; I have so many cases on my plate I accepted his word about Geoff Miller and put it in the solved basket. Then another incident cropped up that needed urgent attention while Miller was being interviewed, which delayed matters further. Lonsdale was adamant about Miller's guilt, said he'd caught him at it twice before and I accepted it. I'll know better next time.'

'Well, it's water under the bridge now. I hope he does this paper trail work properly,' Kelsey turned to the others. 'Any questions? None, OK let's go!'

They entered the two remaining cars and ventured up the track. Miller checked where he'd previously parked his car to see if anything had been left behind, but there were only tyre marks. They reached the gate; Shackleton disembarked and opened it. Both cars drove in but Kelsey directed both be driven out again and placed facing towards the main road.

'You mean we walk?' asked Bramble.

'You could do with the exercise,' Melanie remarked acidly.

'Yes, we walk,' Kelsey pointedly ignored the verbal exchange. 'It decreases any chance of being observed. And we may need to make a quick getaway so it's best the cars are facing outwards.'

He turned to Shackleton.

'Leave the gate open and stay with the cars,' he directed. 'From what Geoff saw when he was here before there are no farm animals likely to escape. We'll head up the track, I'll take the left side with Roger and Geoff, Bob and Melanie take the other,' he turned to Bramble. 'OK Bob? I know how much you enjoy Melanie's company.'

Bramble muttered something which to Kelsey's attuned ear sounded like 'Pigs arse!'

'Lead on Geoff. Take us where you went last time. Eyes peeled, everyone. Geoff was jumped last time he was here, it mustn't happen to us.'

Kelsey checked his hand gun and handed his mobile phone to Miller.

'I want my hands free,' he said. 'Let me know if we get a signal.'

Miller nodded, then pointed.

'I reached there, where the track veered to the right. I was on a ridge with several rabbit holes, rabbits were all around me. I stuffed the camera into one of the holes when those two blokes showed up.'

'OK, let me know when we get there.'

Miller led the way, Kelsey called a halt now and again to sniff the air and listen, pronounce himself satisfied and move on. They reached the point where the trees thinned, Miller indicated to Kelsey and Preston they were near where he had been apprehended. Kelsey called another halt and peered around as did Melanie and Bramble on the other side.

'I lay on that bank over there and did some videoing,' Miller said. 'Over there where the rabbits are, I started filming and also used binoculars. I identified Hammoud so I videoed again on full zoom.'

He started forward but Kelsey restrained him.

'Wait!' he said. 'You were sprung here once and we don't want a recurrence. Check around, Roger, that goes for you too Geoff. Then we move.'

Melanie and Bramble had also paused, Bramble indicated more rabbit holes. Kelsey acknowledged then turned to Miller.

'Move ahead, Geoff, slowly. We must locate that camera,' he turned to the others and placed his hand over his eyes as though checking for intruders. Everyone got the message and moved slowly forward, checking in all directions.

Miller pinpointed his previous vantage point. He surveyed the holes, lay down, reached his hand into one of them and drew out a video camera case. He opened it, turned to Kelsey and gave the thumbs up sign. Kelsey signalled to Preston to stay where he was, went over to Miller and also flung himself flat.

'Can you play it back?' he asked.

'I'm doing that now,' said Miller. 'It's all there.'

'I can see why you stopped here,' said Kelsey. 'It's a damned good vantage point. I can't see any obstacle course or a dais. No crawling pipes either.'

'They've cleared everything,' said Miller. 'But look...they're on film, there you are, this is what I saw.'

Kelsey applied his eye to the viewer and looked grim. It was the type of obstacle course he had often negotiated during his days in the Royal Australian Navy and later in the security services.

When filming Miller had panned around, the platform at the one end came into focus as did the straw stuffed figure on it. This in particular alarmed Kelsey. A raised dais with a dummy on it indicated eventual shooting intentions at a real figure on a real platform. If a private army was practising this, assassination was on the cards and the likely target would be a politician or visiting dignitary. He took his eye from the eyepiece, squinted at the scene below then viewed the video tape again.

'Bloody hell!' he exclaimed. He switched off the camera and backed away from the edge of the ridge. Back on the track he beckoned Melanie.

'There's the camera,' he said. 'The filming was done from that rabbit warren area over there. Get that to Canberra, Mel. That area down there is now clear, but the video shows a full-scale obstacle course with armed riflemen crawling all over it.'

He handed Melanie the camera.

'Get Francis Burton on your mobile, we want a flyover. They need to check the terrain thoroughly apart from checking for signs of life. We'll head down there and take a look. Tell Shackleton we need him down here. Now go, Mel, go!'

He indicated to Preston and Miller to cross the track and they all joined Bramble.

'Shack will be with us shortly,' he said crisply. 'Now, I fancy a look at that house.'

'Somebody's still there,' Miller pointed. 'There's smoke rising behind the house.'

'You're right,' said Kelsey. 'That smoke is definitely behind the house, not from the house chimney. Something is being burnt. We must see what's going on. Anyone see any vehicles?'

'There's one on the right-hand side of the house, probably mine,' exclaimed Miller. 'Just there, behind that gum tree, looks like the front end of a car.'

'There's certainly a vehicle there,' said Bramble. 'Not sure whether it's a sedan or a four-wheel drive.'

'There's plenty of cover if we keep off the track, 'said Kelsey. 'If we double down behind those trees on the left, they should shield us from the house. There's a clear patch further on, but we'll make the decision whether to cross it when we come to it.'

'I'm all for that,' said Bramble. 'Do we go now?'

'Hang on for Shackleton...oh...here he is,' Kelsey gave Shackleton a wave, then turned to Miller. 'Any signal on that phone yet?'

'Not here, but there could be lower down,' said Miller. 'They were communicating with each other when I was down there, but it could have been short wave radio.'

'OK! Try not to show yourselves,' Kelsey turned as Shackleton arrived. 'Did Mel get off OK?'

'She's away,' replied Shackleton. 'We're off, are we?'

'We are,' Kelsey responded grimly. 'Let's go!'

They moved alongside the track, Bramble and Shackleton on one side and everyone else on the other. Cover was limited, Kelsey called occasional halts to examine the property, but they saw no movement. The thin pall of smoke still rose behind the house and drifted slowly in a westerly direction.

'That means somebody is still there,' Kelsey commented during one halt. 'Keep your eyes peeled, if anyone's there, they may shoot first and ask questions afterwards. Can anyone make that vehicle out?'

As they approached closer it looked more like a sedan. Miller reckoned it was his.

'That could mean they've found out who I am,' Miller said.

'Which may have blown our friend Hammoud, I doubt if any of his mates knew he was claiming compo.'

'Possible,' agreed Kelsey. 'If they were picking him up on a Sunday night or Monday morning, as far as they were concerned, he just wasn't working, they may not have known he was claiming compo. I wonder if any more of them have jobs, or are they all rorting the system.'

'Guess that's academic,' Preston put in. 'With people like this their main preoccupation is to cause trouble. But it prompts one question. If the majority of them don't have jobs, who's paying them?'

'Us, mugs that we are. Probably all on bloody welfare,' Kelsey said grimly. 'Some come in as refugees, go on welfare then attack us. Makes you wonder how the hell they get in the country in the first place? Any joy with that phone?'

'Nothing,' replied Miller.

They eased forward and soon made out the curtains in the windows. When Kelsey considered they were near enough, he called another halt. They scrutinised the house, the smoke was still rising. There was a clear space before them where the protective trees ceased, some flowering shrubs were roughly 100 metres further on. The track and approaches to the house must have been an impressive sight in past years but now looked neglected. The front garden was unkempt and flowering shrubs ahead looked straggly.

'When old man Walters was alive...' commented Preston. '...I didn't come here often, way off my beat and off the beaten track for crims...but from occasional visits, I remember the house and garden were a picture, but when Walters hadn't been seen for weeks, we paid a visit and found the old man had died. When we got here the place was really run down. The old man probably lost the will to work in later years. His son didn't live here. I don't think they got on too well. They were often at loggerheads because the son showed no enthusiasm for farming. He was a law student for some years, he's now a lawyer in Sydney'

Kelsey eyed the pall of smoke and turned to Preston.

'What do you reckon, Roger? Make a run for those shrubs?'

'Not much else we can do,' Preston said. 'We have a choice, either that or stay here all day until the cavalry arrives.'

'Assuming Mel made contact,' mused Kelsey. 'Any joy on that phone?'

'Briefly,' said Miller. 'I copped a signal about 10 metres back, then it went again ...hang on, here it is again.'

He stood still, then moved aside two metres. The signal failed again.

'OK! We run for it,' Kelsey decided. 'Let's go!'

They broke cover and ran down the slight downhill slope towards the flowering shrubs, with the track on their right. Bramble and Shackleton ran down the other side of the track when they saw Kelsey and Preston break and they all sprinted for the bushes.

They were nearly at the shrubs when a man appeared round the side of the house, he looked in their direction and they heard a shout borne on the slight breeze. He moved quickly to the house, disappeared inside and re-emerged carrying a rifle.

'Bloody hell! Get down!'

Two shots hit the ether as they reached the bushes and dived headlong into them. They heard a bullet thrash through the undergrowth, the other passed over the top.

'Keep your heads down,' Kelsey shouted as a third shot passed overhead. 'These bastards mean business.'

'Mr Kelsey, I've got a signal,' Miller called out. 'Hang on, yes, I've still got it.'

'Give it here,' commanded Kelsey. 'And the name's Alan! No point being formal when we're knee deep in mud and being shot at...hell...that was close!'

Miller handed over the phone and Kelsey squinted at it.

'You're right, we have a signal,' he commenced pressing buttons.

Melanie was in Hopetoun when her phone rang. She recognised the number on her screen as she answered it.

'Yes Alan?'

'We're in trouble Mel, we're under fire,' he said hoarsely. 'Did you get onto Francis?'

'Under fire? What from?'

'Rifles. Could be worse but we're pinned down. What about Francis?'

'I told him you'd asked for a flyover, but he'd already decided on armed back up before I gave him the situation. He said if there was a training camp they could be armed to the teeth. We were only surmising then, now we know. Francis was way ahead of us. I'll get onto him again and check where the backup squad is.'

'Do that. If these bastards come out and have a go at us, we're in trouble. They'll probably keep out of pistol range. Tell Francis to take his finger out!'

'It may carry more weight if you do it.'

'I can't guarantee reception, our signal comes and goes. If I ring Francis direct, I could fade out halfway through the conversation. Just confirm the backup pronto!'

'Will do!' Melanie rang off and dialled Canberra.

When she eventually rang back; Kelsey was still in a receptive area.

'On their way, a helicopter left Canberra half an hour ago with six men aboard.'

'Good.' Kelsey began to calculate. 'How far is it? About 700 kilometres, how fast do those bloody things fly, Mel, any idea?'

'Don't know, Alan.'

'OK. We'll hang on and pray. Any news on that prat Lonsdale?'

'Nothing! He's in town somewhere.'

'Raise him on his mobile, see where he is, where he's been, and see if you can cover places he hasn't tried yet! I'll have to go! The buggers are trying to rush us.'

The four-wheel drive came around the front of the house, passed through the gate and onto the track.

'Aim for the tyres,' roared Kelsey.

Shots rang out, the four-wheel drive continued on up the track, and there were a couple of shots from the vehicle.

'Aim for the tyres,' Kelsey shouted.

They repeated the process, the four-wheel drive swerved to one side, ground to a halt, backed away, described a reverse three-point turn and headed back to the house.

'Run forward to that next clump of bushes, quick, while they're driving away from us. There's a slight rise there as well, come on, you bastards. *Run!*'

They ran forward for about 60-70 metres, all made the distance without attracting further fire as the vehicle returned to the house. It weaved around a little when it took a curve in the drive, and Bramble gave Kelsey a call.

'Alan, I'd say we hit the windscreen,' he shouted. 'And one tyre seems to have gone.'

'That was bloody lucky,' commented Kelsey. 'How many were aboard?'

'I counted three for certain, maybe four,' said Miller.

'Are you sure about that?'

'Not 100%.' Miller admitted. 'I was trying to check the

occupants while you lot were shooting. On reflection I'd say four.'

'Is that phone still working?'

'Yes.'

'Ring Mel and tell her to pass that onto Francis Burton ... hell!' Kelsey ducked involuntarily as a rifle shot screamed off a nearby tree. 'Tell her we need a phone number to communicate with the troops when they arrive.'

Nearly an hour elapsed, with no further movement from the house or vehicle. Kelsey ordered everyone to fan out, keep under cover, and observe the house from a wide angle.

Shackleton heard it first, whistled to attract Kelsey's attention and pointed skywards. Kelsey saw it approaching behind them. It must have locked onto the track from the Patchewollock-Hopetoun road, then followed it.

'Keep your eyes on those bastards in the house,' he ordered. 'They must have heard the chopper by now.'

It passed over them and swooped on the paddock where Miller had initially seen the obstacle courses and dais. Six figures emerged from it at the crouch and spread out. As they watched, the combat troops converged on the house and moved towards it, taking advantage of any cover as they approached it from front and rear.

'Fan out to the right,' ordered Kelsey. 'Head for that next clump of bushes, there's a rise there that will cover us. They won't be worrying about us now. Let's go!'

When they reached their new destination, they were within 200 metres of the house. Kelsey eyed the sky as they settled into their new position. The sun was low, it would be dusk soon.

He could see soldiers at the front of the house. One had a radio to his ear, he waved to those with him, they approached the building and charged the front door. Kelsey heard gunfire from the rear of the house, and concentrated on the men at the front of the house as they filed in through the front door.

The helicopter was still in the paddock, its props turning, occupied only by the pilot. Kelsey saw occasional flashes, then there was a bright flash and concussion from the back of the house.

'Stun grenades! They're in, front and back,' he said. 'Give me that phone, Geoff.'

He dialled the number supplied by Melanie and received a response.

'Kelsey!' he announced. 'Who am I speaking to?'

He received an answer.

'OK, we're on the south side of the property, in two groups. We're on each side of the long drive, about 200 metres from the house. Are you inside yet?'

There was another response from the other end.

'Certainly three and possibly four we reckoned, they tried to break out in the four-wheel drive an hour or so ago. We think we shot one of their tyres out because they went back pretty quick when we fired on them. What's that? Good. OK, we'll come down now, we'll come down the driveway. There are five of us.'

He waved to the others and shouted.

'Down to the house, put your guns away, keep your hands in plain sight and well away from your sides in case anyone's trigger happy. Go slowly!'

CHAPTER 18

They were met at the front door by a man wearing a bullet proof vest, battle denims, helmet and visor and armed with a repeater rifle

'Captain Bartlett,' he raised his visor as he admitted them. 'Which one is Alan Kelsey?'

'That's me,' and they solemnly shook hands.

'A pleasure,' Bartlett waved his hand at the empty hallway. 'We found two of them, they didn't cause much trouble. We disarmed them and they're in the room at the back.'

Kelsey turned to Miller.

'Where were you held?'

'In here,' Miller indicated his former prison.

'Where's the conference room you mentioned?'

'Along here...not that one, that's the toilet...the one on the other side. That's it. Another room leads off it, through a door at the end, with a table and chairs. That's where their leader questioned me and one of the bastards king hit me.'

Miller entered the conference room occupied by another armed soldier. He entered the room where he had been interviewed and assaulted; the table and chair were still there. The desk drawers were open and their contents on the desk top. Two more soldiers were present while two men were sitting on the floor in the corner, hands behind their heads. Miller recognised them, the man on the left had apprehended him on the ridge; the other had been posted outside his door as a sentry.

'Know them?' asked Kelsey.

'Yes, him!' Miller pointed to one of them. 'That bastard caught me on the ridge. He's also wearing my watch.'

Bartlett seized hold of the man's wrist.

'What make of watch is it?'

'Seiko,' answered Miller. 'The serial number on the back is 535424.'

Kelsey showed his amusement as Bartlett slipped it from the man's wrist, held it up to the light and nodded.

'That's it, 535424,' he handed it to Miller. 'How the hell did you know that?'

'I'm an insurance man,' replied Miller. 'I deal with many claims and we always need proof of ownership for burglary or theft cases. I know every serial number of my equipment at home, stereo, televisions, computers...the lot!'

'I'll remember that when I get home,' commented Captain Bartlett. 'My neighbour was done over last week.'

'What do we do with these bastards?'

'Ship them to Canberra in the chopper, Francis Burton wants them interrogated.'

'Bloody hell!' Miller indicated the contents of the drawers lying on the desk. 'Those are my binoculars, and my mobile phone.'

Captain Bartlett picked them up and pushed them over to Miller.

'What are the serial numbers?'

As Miller gave a double take, he smiled and added. 'I presume you're going to claim on your insurers for them!'

Miller's affirmative response brought smiles from those present, apart from the two on the floor. Kelsey turned to Miller.

'You said something about a chart on the wall.'

'It was in here,' Miller returned to the conference room. 'On that wall over there.'

'They're burning something out back,' said Bramble as they examined the empty wall.

'Let's have a look,' Kelsey said.

The fire was still smouldering in a cut down drum in the small garden at the rear. Kelsey grabbed a couple of sticks, began extracting still smouldering papers from the fire and laid them on the ground. They carefully extinguished the burning edges, most of the papers were too far gone to be any use but some fragments could still be useful. Miller fished out part of the wall chart, it was a fragment showing part of the Sydney Central Business District, just south of the Sydney Harbour Bridge.

'That was it,' Miller pointed with a stick. 'Not much to go on.'

'Unless you remember what it was.'

'I remember a circle drawn round what looked like Wynyard Station, there was a point to the north of it bisected by two intersecting red lines, one from the south west and the other from the south east.'

'Possibly two riflemen,' prompted Bartlett. 'Just a suggestion. It could indicate two intersecting shots from differing directions.'

'Who's likely to be standing in that area that they'd want to shoot?'

'A politician?' Bramble suggested and added cynically. 'Maybe they have the right idea after all.'

'We need to get a map of that area and go through it when we get to Canberra,' Kelsey ignored the comment. 'What is it, Shack?'

'Geoff said three men in that vehicle when it tried to break out.'

'He revised it to four.'

'That makes it worse! There's only two here, where are the other two?'

'You're sure it was four, Geoff?' asked Kelsey.

'Not absolutely, I reckon I saw three heads, possibly four. I had a better look than you guys, I wasn't concentrating on their tyres.'

Kelsey turned to Bartlett.

'Did you see anyone else?'

'Two of my men are searching the bush, they haven't reported back yet.'

'Can you raise them?'

'Hold on.'

Bartlett walked away a few feet, talking into his radio. He returned shaking his head.

'They reckon someone took off in that direction,' he pointed eastwards. 'So far they've had no joy.'

'Tell them to keep looking.'

'They're doing that,' responded Bartlett.

'Let's see what else is in the house.'

*

Kelsey dialled a number on his phone. Bramble looked at him enquiringly.

'I'm ringing Lonsdale,' said Kelsey and had a brief conversation.

'Any joy in Hopetoun?' asked Bramble.

Kelsey shook his head. He held his hand over the mouthpiece and looked at Bramble.

'No joy with estate agents or lawyers in Hopetoun,' he said. 'Lonsdale insists he's been around them all.'

'Do you have confidence in him?' asked Bramble.

'I've no choice,' Kelsey said. 'In something routine like this, I imagine not even he could fuck things up! When it comes to jumping to conclusions, I have severe doubts.'

He spoke into the phone.

'Get over to Mrs Lindsay, either tonight or first thing in the morning,' he said. 'We've got to get that statement right. We don't want these bastards getting off on technicalities. OK? We'll look around Patchewollock in the morning.'

Bramble smiled as he envisaged Lonsdale's sulky expression. Kelsey turned to Preston.

'We'd best get you back to your station, Roger,' he said. 'Nothing much more you can do here. We'll deal with this place. We have more people coming in from Canberra.'

'Right Alan,' Preston looked relieved. 'My case files are up to the roof so I've heaps to do. How do I get back?'

'We seem to have recovered Geoff Miller's car,' Kelsey turned to Miller. 'Anything missing?'

'No!' Miller shook his head. 'They just removed it from outside Parmenter's gateway and parked it here. The blighters scratched the paintwork on the offside wing.'

'Hope you're insured!' Kelsey turned to Captain Bartlett. 'You'll be taking our two friends back to Canberra, Captain?'

'I'm arranging that, Sergeant Prentice and two armed men will accompany them. I'll stay here and help you sort around. I want to look at that training ground to see what they've been doing. From what you told me about Parmenter he said he heard explosions.'

'He did.'

Bartlett drew Kelsey aside and said quietly, 'That man's hair, the one nearest the window, his hair looks unnaturally fair and I don't think it's been caused by shampoo! I've seen this before, it can be caused by mixing chemicals together to make explosives.'

'Maybe he's homosexual.'

Bartlett chuckled and shook his head.

'No, he's not, we checked!'

This caused some amusement before Bartlett continued.

'If they've been mixing stuff that gives off strong fumes, it can have that effect, particularly hydrogen peroxide. I'll look for any vessels they could have used to mix the stuff.'

'Which means...bloody hell?'

'As you so aptly say...bloody hell!' Bartlett bit his lip. 'That means explosives, that means bombs, which means something planned for, more than likely, Sydney.'

'We'd better warn Canberra. I'll ring Francis Burton.'

'No, I'll do it,' said Bartlett. 'I have to report in now anyway. Leave that with me.'

Kelsey became aware Shackleton was behind him.

'What's happening about Mel?' asked Shackleton.

'Damn! I'd forgotten Mel. Hang on, I'll ring her now.'

He had a brief conversation with Mel Cassidy, he ordered her back to Canberra by road with Miller's video camera. Then he asked Miller to take Preston back to Hopetoun.

'We need you to come with us to Canberra, Geoff,' he said. 'We need to debrief you properly, I'm worried about that map on the wall, they're planning something and clearly been rehearsing it here. We'll check things here, you take Roger to

Hopetoun, stay the night if you like, no doubt the police will find accommodation for you.'

This caused more amusement. Preston grinned and nodded.

'You can have your old cell back,' he said. 'Reduced rental this time; special discounts for regular customers.'

CHAPTER 19

Miller spent the night in a police cell, when he and Preston returned to the police station Miller rang around local motels but none had vacancies. The station sergeant, now aware of Miller's changed status, jerked his thumb at the end cell, which was empty.

'You can have that for the night,' he said. 'We'll leave the door open! We can rustle up some blankets,' he nodded at Miller and smiled. 'We can probably arrange for a cup of tea in the morning!'

'Milk and no sugar,' Miller replied. 'And two chocolate biscuits please.'

This exchange underlined he was no longer persona non-grata. As he and Preston helped themselves from the coffee machine, he marvelled at his change of status from his arrival in the police station a few days before.

'Where's Lonsdale?' he asked.

'Dunno!' said Preston. 'Presumably interviewing estate

agents and lawyers in town. He's off to Mrs Lindsay's in the early morning.'

'He won't like that,' said Miller. 'He didn't like being proved wrong.'

Preston bit his lip.

'Look Geoff, Reg wasn't the only one at fault, I accepted what he said and took the easy way,' he said. 'I should have known better. I had a huge caseload, I still have, but that doesn't excuse being bloody stupid and gullible. After you told Mrs Lindsay about the old Walters farm, which she then recounted to Reg, I should have mounted an investigation immediately. I didn't and I was a prat! I'm sorry.'

He sipped his coffee, grimaced, then stirred it with the plastic spoon.

'We get all sorts of outlandish stories from people we arrest to justify what they've done or what they are accused of, you can guess the sort of thing, aliens made me do it or I thought I heard a cry for help in the ladies' toilets! But after 9/11, 7/7 on the London Underground and Madrid, plus reports in USA and Western Australia of private armies conducting manoeuvres and that bloody court case in Sydney, a quick look wouldn't have come amiss.'

'Forget it!' said Miller. 'If it's any consolation, this man Hammoud has been rorting the welfare system for months. When we received his file from the Compensation Board my boss, Bill Clucas, nearly hit the roof. From what he said someone at the board had been bloody careless and missed it. They'd paid out heaps! He should have been investigated months before.'

Next morning Miller utilised the wash room at the end of the block, dressed and folded the loaned blankets. At 8.30 am he rang Bill Clucas.

'Bill, Geoff Miller,' he announced.

'Good Grief!' was Clucas's reaction. 'What the hell's been happening to you, and where've you been?'

Miller gave a quick account of events and mentioned Kelsey wanted him in Canberra. They talked for over twenty minutes, neither Walker nor Winwood was in, the only staff member present apart from Clucas was Lucy Browning who was manning the switchboard, so Miller had no chance to speak to Jacqueline.

'I'll ring her from Canberra, just tell her I'm a bit bruised but otherwise OK.'

'How are you getting there?'

'I've got the car back,' replied Miller. 'The buggers scratched the offside when they moved it from the track. Reckon they caused $1,000 worth of damage.'

'Don't worry about that, as long as you're all right. Keep in touch, Geoff.'

Miller was checking his car in the yard when Preston emerged from the rear of the police station.

'When are you off?' asked Preston.

'Within the hour, at a guess,' replied Miller. 'I'll be heading for Patchewollock, then across to Speed, Robinvale and then Canberra, he gave me the address of the ASIO building. Alan Kelsey wants me to view mug shots and a map covering the same area I saw on that wall map. He wants me to pinpoint those lines I saw crisscrossing it.'

'I may have to cadge a lift,' said Preston. 'There's been a bad accident on the road from Goyura, a truck came off the road and spilt a load of chemicals. There are two squad cars there, the inspector and sergeant are on their way there, and Lonsdale went off early to see Mrs Lindsay. I've got to track back the route you covered from the house to the point where Reg Lonsdale arrested you. You say you were shot at?'

'Several times,' said Miller. 'A couple of shots hit trees. I've never been so scared in my life.'

'I've been told to recce along that track and work back to the Lindsay house.'

'When do you want to start?'

'Any time that suits you.'

'How will you get back?'

'Reg Lonsdale has a squad car at the Lindsay house, I'll join him there and he'll drive me back.'

'No problem,' said Miller. 'We can start anytime you like.'

*

They set off within half an hour, Preston completed some paperwork, then took a call regarding a current case. All the squad cars were still out, and Lonsdale hadn't returned.

'Ready when you are,' Preston said eventually, Miller collected what gear he had and they walked to his car.

'Will you recognise the spot again?' asked Preston.

'I didn't have time to note all the geographic features, Lonsdale pounced on me before I was able to look around.'

Preston laughed as he climbed into the passenger seat.

'OK, let's go!' Preston grimaced. 'Hell! I'm beginning to sound like Alan Kelsey.'

They reached the point where Miller had been arrested. Now his status had been established, he and Preston had struck a rapport and Miller was quite sorry when they reached the parting of the ways.

'I'll just give Lonsdale a call,' Preston said as Miller drew in to the roadside. 'I don't want to get there after he's gone.'

He placed his phone to his ear. It rang and rang, he looked puzzled.

'No answer, what's he doing? Hang on a sec, I'll ring the station and get them to call him on the radio.'

After speaking to the desk sergeant, looked at Miller and shrugged.

'They can't raise him,' he said.

'Maybe his battery's flat,' suggested Miller.

'Doubt it, he might be a prat but he's not bloody careless.'

'Ring Mrs Lindsay. I assume you've got her phone number at the station. That should attract somebody's attention.'

'Good idea,' Preston nodded. 'We'll make a detective of you yet.'

He rang the desk sergeant again and waited. After a few minutes Miller heard the sergeant's voice crackle in Preston's phone.

'No reply, are you sure? Try again.'

Preston waited and again the sergeant's voice came through.

'It's what? Engaged! It can't be, it was ringing before. Try again.'

He shook his head in bewilderment.

'Still engaged, that's odd! What the hell...!'

Miller looked at him, the same thought occurred to them both simultaneously.

'You don't think...!'

'When I was running from those bastards, that house was the first property I came to, I was heading for the main road and stumbled across it. Those blokes who escaped were heading in that direction.'

'Hmm!' Preston considered. 'Half a minute, I'll try something else.'

He rang the station again.

'Andy, check with the school, see if the Lindsay girl is there.'

They waited ten minutes before the sergeant came through again. She wasn't. The sergeant said he'd spoken with the principal and the girl was not in school. They hadn't received any communication from Mrs Lindsay either.

'Hell!' Preston exclaimed. 'I think we have a problem.'

'We'd better contact Alan Kelsey,' said Miller.

'I don't know his bloody number, you had his phone yesterday checking for signals, any idea what it is?'

'No!' Miller shook his head then had a brainwave. 'Half a minute. There was a land line at that farmhouse. Try that, it's probably still in the name of Walters.'

'Good thinking! Hold on, let's try Andy again.'

After another quick conversation with the sergeant, Preston jotted down a number.

'OK!' he said to Miller. 'Here we go. I presume Kelsey and Bartlett are still there.'

He dialled, listened, then gave a thumbs up signal.

'Who's that?' Preston said. 'Roger Preston. Is Alan Kelsey still there...who's that? Oh Bramble. Hallo Bob. Can I speak to Alan?'

'I said 'who's that?' and then Bramble asked 'Who's that?' 'Preston grinned at Miller. 'We could have gone on all day like... hello Alan. We may have a problem.'

Their conversation lasted about five minutes before Preston rang off.

'What was that?' asked Miller. 'What did Alan say?'

'I won't repeat it.'

'I think I get the gist of it.'

'I'll go to the house from here, Shackleton and Bramble are heading for Mrs Lindsay's drive. Two of Bartlett's men are heading east through the woods, the same way you went. I'd better go.'

'I'll come too,' Miller climbed out and slammed the door. 'I know the way, there's a track that leads to the house.'

'This could be dangerous...' Preston began but Miller was already through the gate.

'No more dangerous than anything else I've been through this week. In any case, I know the way, I covered it the other day. We need to get there quick, if those bastards are in the house the sooner we're there the better.'

Preston saw the futility of arguing.

'Agreed! Let's go!'

Miller led at a good pace, they paused when Miller indicated a gash in a tree trunk.

'That was one of the near misses,' he said. 'I was here when I heard a rifle shot and the bullet hit something. I broke the world record for the 100 metres after that.'

Preston studied the tree for a few seconds.

'I think I'll find it again. Come on!'

They arrived at the boundary hedge of the garden, Miller was about to crawl through the same hole he'd used days before, but Preston restrained him.

'If there's anyone there, no point in advertising our presence,' he said. 'We'll go round the side and approach from there, the garage will give cover.'

They crept around the boundary hedge and approached the garage from the rear. There was a back door to the garage and Preston opened it. It was a coal-house, it didn't open into the garage.

'There's another door round the side,' hissed Miller. 'Try that.'

They approached the garage on the side away from the house. A wheel barrow was outside and the door was ajar. They peered through it, Mrs Lindsay's vehicle was in the garage, facing outwards, the front garage doors were closed.

'Why would the wheelbarrow be out?'

'There's a gardener,' said Miller. 'Alan said he was working out front when he came here last time. But there's no sign of him.'

'Unless he's in the house too. He may be if there's anything wrong.'

They reached the front of the vehicle. Preston laid a hand on the bonnet; it was cold.

'It hasn't been used today.'

'Hold on, someone's coming out.'

They heard a door opening and closing followed by footsteps on the gravel drive outside. They looked for cover, there was an old wardrobe near the door used for storing gardening implements, Preston moved across so it shielded him from anyone opening the main garage doors. Miller dived beside the vehicle and crouched by the driver's door.

The garage doors opened and the first door was secured in the open position by dropping the bottom bolt into a socket. As the man stooped to release the floor bolt of the second door and reached up to free the upper bolt, Miller recognised him, he was the second man who had 'arrested' him on the ridge. He secured the ground bolt into another ground socket, straightened up and started to walk to the driver's door. The driveway in front of the garage was in full view, Miller caught sight of Lonsdale's police vehicle parked by the house.

At that point, the man spotted Miller, uttered an exclamation and produced a gun from his belt. Miller was petrified and rose as the man backed off and waved him out.

He said something in a language Miller didn't understand, he didn't need to, the gestures were plain enough. Miller obeyed, but kept his eyes on him as he walked slowly out. It was all he could do to avoid looking to his left, if he allowed his eyes to dart in that direction it would betray Preston. The man was wearing the same battle fatigues he wore when Miller and he first met. He had a set of ignition keys, presumably Mrs Lindsay's.

Miller's mind raced. They meant to escape using the Lindsay vehicle, which indicated they had taken over Mrs Lindsay's house and everyone in it. Miller had the taste of fear in his mouth, he was staring death in the face.

'Come!' his captor snapped, in English this time. As Miller passed in front of him, he turned to face Miller and turned his back to where Preston was hidden. He pushed Miller with his left hand and his gun hand momentarily wavered off target.

There was the sound of rushing feet and 14 stone of policeman hit him, he fell to the ground with Preston on top of him. Miller 'unfroze' and jumped on the hand holding the gun. There was a grunt and the gun came loose. He seized the man's right arm and hung on, while Preston did the rest. There was the sound of repeated blows and movement in the man's arm subsided. Preston continued hitting until the man gave a grunt and lay still.

'My God! Have you killed him?'

'Hope not, but there wasn't time for niceties,' said Preston. 'These bastards usually carry knives as well and I wasn't prepared to chance it.' He laid his hand against the man's neck and nodded. 'He'll survive, find something to tie him up while I check for weapons.'

'Look!' Miller pointed up the track.

'It's those two ASIO blokes,' said Preston. 'Bramble and Shackleton. Give them a wave, let them know we're here.'

They were coming down the side of the track, creeping along the far side of the hedge that ran alongside it. They must have left the car at the gate and come the rest of the way on foot.

Miller gestured to them to keep under cover of the bushes, they got the message. Then he backed into the garage, hunted around and found an extension cord which he handed to Preston.

'Good,' grunted Preston. 'That'll do. Secure this bugger and then we've got another one to deal with. It looks like a hostage situation, which could be dicey but at least we've halved the odds. Have you fired a gun before?'

'In the school cadets,' said Miller. 'But I've never shot at anyone.'

'There's a first time for everything,' grunted Preston. 'Get hold of it.'

They left their victim in the vehicle and locked it, he was securely lashed up with the extension cord, which Preston cut into lengths using pliers from the bench. They headed for the front door and Miller peered inside. The hallway was empty. Preston gestured to Bramble and Shackleton, who emerged from the bushes, and entered the garage.

'We've got one of them in here, that leaves one in the house,' said Preston.

'We saw you jump him,' Bramble remarked and added with mild interest. 'Did you kill him?'

'I wouldn't have cared if I did, but he's still in the land of the living,' said Preston. 'How do we deal with it now? We've still got one in the house, most likely armed and holding hostages.'

'He'll be expecting the vehicle to be driven out,' said Miller. 'What do you think?'

'Reasonable to assume Mrs Lindsay's Land Rover is to be their means of escape.' commented Shackleton. 'They wouldn't be game to use the police car.'

'Makes sense. Our friend came out with the keys,' said Preston. 'If the other man's in the house he'll be expecting it to be driven round the front.'

'Unlash that bastard in the vehicle, get his jacket off and that forage cap off his head,' Bramble said briskly. 'Then tie him up again, we don't want him running loose. Hurry up!'

They removed the man's jacket then replaced his bonds. He was coming round, muttering in some foreign tongue. Shackleton didn't understand the language but didn't need to, the man's facial expressions spoke volumes. Bramble found an oily cloth and wrapped it around the man's mouth, effectively gagging him.

'That cloth's filthy,' said Preston.

'So?' Bramble answered testily. 'As far as I'm concerned the bastard can taste oil until he pukes.'

'OK, OK!' Preston grinned. 'He'll likely sue you for transgressing his human rights.'

'No doubt some do-gooder lawyer will pursue his case, and some bloody kind magistrate will let him off and accuse us of using undue force and being racist!' Bramble snorted. 'Happy days!'

'Or police brutality!' Preston was bitter. 'Why do we bother!'

Shackleton donned the forage jacket and cap and climbed into the driving seat with the keys. He revved up the engine and with Bramble huddled in the passenger well he slowly exited the garage and drove round the corner of the house. He kept the tinted windows up as he wanted to see into the front room window without being seen. He could see the back of a couch just inside the window, with a woman and a girl sitting with their backs to the window. He could dimly make out a man with his back to the opposite wall armed with a rifle.

Shackleton drove the Land Rover forward until he was out of direct view of the rifleman, then disembarked while Bramble crept out the other door.

'There's one man with what could be an AK 47, he's standing

with his back to the hall wall. There's two on the couch, a girl and a woman, presumably Mrs Lindsay and her daughter. No sign of Lonsdale, but all I managed was a quick look.'

'He'll be expecting his buddy to enter through the front door,' commented Bramble. 'We'll follow you, OK?'

They went round the side of the house. Bramble indicated another door to Shackleton.

'This looks like the kitchen,' he hissed. 'I'll go in here; you circle round the house and garage and use the front door. He'll expect his mate to come back in through there.'

Shackleton continued around the house, passed between the garage and the house and headed for the front door. After a hasty discussion with Preston and Miller he entered and ensured he could be heard walking down the hall. Preston followed him, keeping in step so there were only single footfalls. Miller stood by the front door, three metres from the living room door.

Shackleton entered the first doorway, gun at the ready. That was when matters went awry. Shackleton found himself in a smaller room, two doors opened from the hallway and he'd gone into the first one. As he entered, he was king hit without warning and went down as though poleaxed.

The resultant noise obviously reached the ears of the other terrorist. The door further down the passageway opened and he emerged, rifle at the ready. Preston was halfway down the hall and was instantly covered by the rifleman. Thereafter matters moved fast.

As Bramble materialised in the kitchen doorway behind the gunman, he swivelled the gun towards Bramble. Miller was still by the front door, but before the man completed his turn towards Bramble, Miller recognised him.

'Hammoud!' he shouted. 'Hammoud! We're friends!'

As he heard his name the startled Hammoud swung back to face Miller, momentarily turning his back to Bramble. That was enough, Bramble took off and hit him with a Rugby tackle. Miller advanced to the door of the first room where Shackleton was pinning down another man Miller realised was Lonsdale. Lonsdale's uniform jacket was off, cords were trailing around his wrists and lying on the floor. Another man was tied to a chair, it looked like the gardener. Miller forced the combatants apart.

'Break it up, Lonsdale, it's us!' he panted. 'You're fighting with Shackleton.'

He returned to the hallway to find Bramble and Preston had secured Hammoud. He was face down, hands behind his back, with Preston sitting on him. Miller entered the loungeroom. Mrs Lindsay and her daughter were by the couch, both on their feet and cowering against the wall. As the sounds of conflict in the hallway ceased, he heard the click of handcuffs.

Miller stood by the door, he and Mrs Lindsay looked at each other.

'Good day, Mrs Lindsay. We meet again!' Miller inclined his head, raised an eyebrow, then turned and looked at her teenage daughter. 'I assume this is your daughter. Maybe you'd like to introduce us,' and added pointedly. 'I don't think I've seen or met your daughter before!'

CHAPTER 20

The two erstwhile gaolers were secured, one with electric flex and the other with handcuffs. Bramble took no chances; he found an extension cord and lashed them both to the fireplace fender by their ankles. The gardener had been untied, muttering angrily and flexing his fingers as his circulation returned. Mrs Lindsay was still shocked but gradually regained her senses. She made a pot of tea in the kitchen and the gardener sat at the kitchen table; his temper improving as he clasped a cup. Mrs Lindsay's daughter was in the kitchen and didn't seem anxious to be separated from her mother.

'Still thinks I'm a bloody pervert!' was Miller's bitter comment.

Lonsdale was also in the kitchen, Mrs Lindsay, a nurse in her younger days before moving into journalism and book writing, had attended to his face. He had been badly bruised after being jumped when he entered the house and had a nasty bump on the back of his head.

He had been tied up, gagged and dumped in the room where Shackleton had found him, but had displayed initiative by manipulating a sharp edge on the fireplace fender. He had managed, after an exhaustive hour or so, to saw through his wrist bonds.

Mrs Lindsay explained, being a perennial early riser, that she had seen two men in the garden in the early hours of the morning, about 6.30. They had smashed the kitchen door open with their gun butts, then held her and her daughter captive in the loungeroom. They had demanded her car keys, but then observed Lonsdale's arrival as he drove down the drive from the track. They forced Mrs Lindsay to open the front door to admit him, whereupon Lonsdale had been jumped by both men when he entered the hallway, secured then dumped in the room, later joined by the gardener who had been surprised in his potting shed.

Kelsey and Captain Bartlett arrived after the ambush and capture of the two hostage takers. They were incarcerated where they had previously held Lonsdale and the gardener, guarded by two of Bartlett's men.

Kelsey was composing his report at the living room table. He looked up as Miller entered bearing a cup of tea.

'I understand you played a major role in nobbling these two,' he said. 'Cute dodge shouting out his name, how the hell did you know what it was?'

'He was the one rorting the compensation system,' Miller placed the cup and saucer on the table. 'The reason I was involved in the first place. We had his photograph on file; luckily a damned good one. When he appeared in the hallway, I recognised him.'

'Why was he on compensation?' asked Kelsey.

'Said he had a bad back.'

'Ah!' Kelsey nodded. 'Well, if he didn't have one before Bramble tackled him I'd say he has now! That may give us a lever, his rorting of the system was the reason this group was sprung. If his mates find out this led us to the rest of them, he won't be too popular. We'll put that to him when he's interrogated. Where's Captain Bartlett?'

'In the kitchen.'

'And Roger Preston?'

'He's there as well, chatting up Mrs Lindsay,' said Miller. 'They're both divorcees, maybe they've started a beautiful friendship!'

'Well, if they do that's one positive result,' Kelsey observed wryly. 'That's assuming he likes historical mush! How's Lonsdale?'

'On the mend, the worst aspect seems to be his pride,' Miller was amused at Kelsey's dismissive description of Harriet Lindsay's novels, he would ask Jacqui if she'd read any of them. Kelsey gave a cynical smile.

'That won't do him any harm. How's your relationship with Mrs Lindsay?'

'Better than before,' said Miller. 'Although I got off on the wrong foot. The situation hardly called for sarcasm.'

Kelsey succumbed to a dry chuckle, then shook his head.

'I heard about that, wanting to be introduced to her daughter who you'd never seen before. Cynical bastard, aren't you?'

'It just came out, but I apologised, so did she, we both know where we stand now.'

'Well, maybe you'll score an autographed copy of one of her books,' commented Kelsey. 'That might be worth a fortune in years to come. Where's Shackleton?'

'Nursing his bruises,' replied Miller. 'I managed to stop him and Lonsdale knocking seven bells out of each other.'

'That was a shambles,' commented Kelsey. 'It could have caused complete disaster. As it was, shouting out Hammoud's name distracted him long enough for Bramble to flatten him. Bob used to be a fair Rugby player; he had a couple of seasons for Randwick Seconds. As for Lonsdale, to a degree he redeemed himself in my eyes, to free himself like that then take offensive action displayed initiative and courage.'

'As far as I'm concerned, he's always been offensive,' Miller retorted. Kelsey smiled and made a dismissive gesture.

The two prisoners were removed that afternoon, the front lawn had sufficient clearance for a helicopter to land. Two prisoners apprehended at the Walters farm were already at Canberra HQ, the two prisoners captured at the Lindsay household were despatched there in the custody of two of Bartlett's men.

Mrs Lindsay prepared sandwiches for those remaining, they tucked in with relish, and Kelsey was given an autographed copy of Mrs Lindsay's latest book to hand onto Melanie Cassidy. Preston and Lonsdale departed in the police car, leaving Kelsey, Miller, Shackleton and Bramble. Preston shook hands all round, Lonsdale satisfied himself with handshakes with Kelsey and Bramble, and brief nods at everyone else. He made brief eye contact with Miller, they both nodded, then Lonsdale waited by the police car for Preston.

'How was he?' Preston asked Miller as he paused in the doorway.

'Surly!' answered Miller. 'He hasn't forgiven me.'

'He'll get over it,' Preston replied. 'He's young and full of his own importance, like many of us at his age. I'll try and knock sense into him. Funny thing, I had words with my old mate Pat Caslake down south when Lonsdale was posted here, he said he was a jumped-up little prick who knew it all and he wasn't sorry to see the back of him!'

'I remember Caslake,' Miller nodded. 'He initially went along with Lonsdale that I was a pervert, but Lonsdale was obviously getting on his wick as the interview went on.'

'From what Pat told me, that wouldn't surprise me,' said Preston. 'But Pat's got a rookie policewoman under him now, he reckons she's good.'

'Well, if you're going to knock sense into sodding Lonsdale, make it quick,' pleaded Miller. 'I reckon he'll sense it when I have another investigation up this way and he'll be laying speed traps for me if I get within five kilometres.'

'Don't worry, just ask for me and I'll bail you out,' Preston shook Miller's hand as he departed.

Kelsey elected to travel to Canberra with Miller and the other two travelled in the other vehicle. Captain Bartlett and his remaining two men returned to the Walters farm, they were to prevent anything being moved or touched until ASIO forensic teams arrived. Bartlett was concerned about the possibility of bombs having been manufactured on site, he had found traces in a drum, and in the bath, that suggested chemicals had been mixed, he mentioned ammonium nitrate. The site of the backyard fire had been covered over with tarpaulin to prevent wind and rain scattering the embers, there was hope forensics could make sense of any remaining burnt papers.

Miller phoned Bill Clucas and brought him up to date. Clucas was concerned about their video film being removed to Canberra as the Compensation Board was on his back for a report. Footage of Hammoud cavorting over obstacle courses and crawling through pipes would give the lie to his injured back claim and resolve the case for the Compensation Board. Miller said ASIO needed it which Clucas had to accept, but Miller extracted a promise from Kelsey the film would be returned, probably censored in parts that related to the para-military aspect, with anything identifying Hammoud left undisturbed.

After collecting Miller's car from where he and Preston had left it, they headed for Patchewollock on the way to Canberra. Kelsey again questioned Miller about the wall map. Miller did his best to answer but could say little more than he had already.

'It may be easier with a map in front of me. I can recall for certain Wynyard Station appeared to be marked and there was a point north of it where two red lines converged. I can't say any more than that.'

'Hmm!' Kelsey pondered. 'To me that indicates target lines. You say they were practising shooting at a dummy on that temporary platform?'

'Looked like it to me.'

'I tend to agree, from what I saw on your video camera,' said Kelsey. 'We'll see what interrogation brings.'

'Didn't I see in the press there was a visiting President or Prime Minister in Sydney this month?'

'Yes, there is. The President of Taranga, which is a moderate Muslim state but run on secular lines. The people we caught here are obvious fanatics; they prefer a state run by Sharia law,' Kelsey thought for a moment. 'I don't like this at all.'

*

They had little conversation after that until they reached the hamlet of Speed, they had turned left to head for Ouyen when a thought occurred to Miller. Kelsey had dozed off, while Miller churned over the events of the past week, commencing with his departure from the motel at Warracknabeal when on his way to the rendezvous with Peter Hallam at Litchfield. As his mind mulled over occurrences since, he focused on his scariest moment of all, in the hallway prior to making his escape and when nearly discovered by newcomers who entered the hall from the front porch. That vivid memory caused adrenalin to momentarily run, so much so he nearly drifted onto the wrong side of the road, which he hastily corrected after receiving a blaring horn and two-finger sign from an oncoming motorist.

'What's up?' Kelsey blinked awake. 'Was that Bramble blowing his horn?'

'No, it was my fault,' Miller replied. 'I was deep in thought and started to drift over. I put the wind up someone coming the other way.'

'Deep in thought, eh? What about?'

'When I was in the hallway of that farm, the night I broke out. They passed within a few feet of me and didn't see me, if they had I wouldn't be here now,' he shuddered as he recalled that night. As he did so another thought occurred to him.

'Bloody hell!'

'What?'

'I've just remembered something I heard. I'd got out of that room previously on that same night, they were careless guarding me with all the new arrivals at the time and I got into the hallway. I was nearly caught and got back in the room damned quick, but I did hear something the boss man said in that conference room.'

'Go on.'

'I heard him say, he arrives in three days and meets the Prime Minister in Canberra, after that he goes to Sydney. Then he said something about a diversion at or near Wynyard Station and other city centre stations.'

'A diversion! That can only mean one thing to me.'

'What?'

'Explosions...they've been making bombs!'

CHAPTER 21

Kelsey promptly contacted Francis Burton in Canberra which provoked an immediate reaction. The Taranganese President was visiting Australia and Miller's recollections matched his itinerary. De Souza was going to Canberra first, to The Lodge and Parliament to consult with the Prime Minister and meet the Opposition Leader. The next day he was heading for Sydney where he would meet the NSW Premier, attend State Parliament and possibly the Opera House. Simultaneously members of his entourage were consulting with the New South Wales Railways, the Taranganese Government were building their own metro railway system in the capital, Taranga City, and wanted to look at the Sydney system. Then back to Canberra for more talks on mutual co-operation in the southern Pacific sphere.

'They could do worse,' was Kelsey's comment on the railways subject. Francis said something in reply which amused Kelsey who rang off and turned to Miller.

'You've hit the jackpot, I'd say. We must get there quickly

and interrogate those bastards we arrested at Mrs Lindsay's. Put your foot down and to hell with the speed traps, I'll do the talking if we get picked up.'

'What if it's Lonsdale?'

'In that case you're on your own!'

They avoided the indignity of having to haggle with traffic police, the irony didn't escape Miller who had occasionally attracted the attention of speed traps, but now he had carte blanche to put his foot down, confident the government would pay any fine, there were no police in sight.

Kelsey directed him through Canberra to a large building with an underground carpark. A uniformed custodian greeted Kelsey and waved them through when Kelsey showed his ID. Kelsey directed Miller to a parking spot.

'OK!' he said as they climbed out. 'Apart from a cup of coffee, the first thing is for you to view mug shots, see if you can spot the boss man. I'll ask Francis to supply a map of Sydney, we've no time to waste.'

They took the lift to the fifth floor and emerged into an impressive general office area with numerous computers and work stations, a busy scene with phones ringing and a hubbub of conversation as they walked through. Kelsey acknowledged many greetings as he headed for an office pen occupied by a bald-headed man.

'Hallo, Alan, I hear you've had an exciting few days,' said the bald man.

'Good afternoon, Francis,' Kelsey indicated Miller. 'This is Geoff Miller. He's been very useful to us and is responsible for much of our success so far. Geoff, this is Francis Burton, in charge of operations here.'

'Ah, Mr Miller,' Burton extended his hand. 'I've heard much about you over the past few days. Apart from being imprisoned by the people we are now investigating; I understand you've also been arrested by the police.'

'Several times,' Miller said ironically. The handshake was firm and he was aware of a searching glance. Burton had grey eyes, prominent eyebrows and greying hair around the sides of his head and ears, with a gleaming bald pate on top. Miller momentarily wondered if he polished it, the reflected light of the sun caused him to squint. 'Not a pleasant experience; most frustrating when I tried to tell the police what I'd seen and nobody would listen.'

'Frustrating...yes and infuriating, especially when what you saw was highly relevant to our current investigations,' Burton turned to Kelsey. 'Mel brought that film in just before you arrived, I haven't seen it yet but she gave a brief account of what was on it.'

'Where is it now?'

'Being processed,' said Francis. 'We're having it digitally copied to see if we can pick up peripheral details, then we'll release the original back to Mr Miller.' He turned to Miller. 'You understand, Mr Miller; it may be necessary to allow back only part of the film, but enough to show this man Hammoud giving a Tarzan imitation, shinning up obstacles and clambering up ropes.'

'I understand that,' Miller said. 'But you'll have to explain that to my bosses in Melbourne. That film is their property and the Compensation Board has an interest in it. Hammoud has rorted thousands of dollars for a bad back he hasn't got, it's clear from that footage he's perfectly fit. There's also a firm of lawyers involved on the Board's behalf.'

Burton nodded.

'I understand. I have considerable sympathy with your employers and the Compensation Board, I don't like people who rort the system either, it's taxpayers' money. We'll ensure Mr Hammoud's physical activities are prominent in what we do release back to your people.'

'We still haven't identified the man in charge at the farm,' said Kelsey. 'I thought Geoff could view some mug shots.'

'Good idea,' Francis nodded. 'Plus, we'll see how that footage comes up after we've digitalised it, hopefully Mr Miller can pick out the leader on that.'

'Have we any idea where they went after they left the farm?' asked Kelsey.

'Not yet, but Sydney's a fair bet,' Burton referred to a file on his desk. 'We don't know what vehicles are involved yet, presumably four-wheel drives.'

'Have we run a trace on that vehicle they left at the farm?' asked Kelsey.

'Yes, it's registered to Ahmed el Said,' said Burton. 'We've traced it to an address in Cronulla, but the birds may have flown. When the four we caught fail to turn up everyone else may take fright and lie low.'

'Do the Press know anything yet?' asked Kelsey.

'No, we're keeping it under wraps for now, let these people wonder and wait, uncertainty about the missing men will unsettle them more than knowing their fate. Luckily the action happened at a remote farm so any chance of gunfire being heard by anyone are minimal, although some enterprising journo may have noticed our low flying helicopter.'

'An enterprising journo in that area?' from Kelsey which caused some amusement.

'We'll clear that one if it arises,' said Burton. 'We could always say it was a crop duster.'

A thought occurred to Miller and he spoke up.

'We know one of the vehicles that left that farm,' he said.

'What?' Burton swung around. 'Which one?'

'The one Peter Hallam chased from Melbourne; we know its rego.'

'That was the one left behind at the farm, wasn't it? Didn't that belong to Hammoud?'

'No, the vehicle I'm referring to belonged to the man who picked him up,' insisted Miller. 'We traced it to an address in either Brunswick or Fitzroy, I've forgotten which offhand. But what I'm saying is, that wasn't the vehicle they left at the farm.'

'Which means the one you followed from Melbourne, is heading for Sydney, if it isn't there already,' Kelsey turned to Miller. 'What's the registration?'

'I've forgotten it, but while I don't know what it is, I do know what it isn't. It's not the vehicle we picked up at the farm.'

'How can we find out what it is?'

'Bill Clucas at our Melbourne office will have it on file,' said Miller. 'We always note registration numbers when we're on surveillance. Pete Hallam would have it on his report.'

'I'll find out what it is,' said Burton. 'What's your office number?'

Miller supplied it and Burton commenced dialling.

Miller was taken to another area where he was introduced to David McKay, another ASIO operative. A series of books containing photographs was produced and Miller settled down to examine them. He had a mental picture of the boss man etched in his mind and carefully perused each picture. He spotted one familiar face, one of the four they already had in custody apprehended by Bartlett's men at the farm.

McKay produced another set of photographs after Miller had scanned the first collection and spotted another familiar face, another of the four prisoners.

'We're getting somewhere,' McKay remarked. He was similar

in appearance to Shackleton, about 5' 10' tall and fair-haired. 'But no sign of the man in charge?'

'None,' Miller shook his head. 'I can't see anyone who resembles him.'

'We'll give you a session with one of our face artists,' said McKay. 'He has a box of various facial aspects he juggles around so they resemble...!'

'I know what they do,' Miller said. 'I've seen it all on television.'

McKay grimaced.

'All these television series...and bang go all our secret methods. Mundane, isn't it? Check this last lot but if there's nothing there, I'll take you down to see Andrew Guildford. You've no idea of his name? Was anything mentioned at the time, any form of address?'

'No,' Miller shook his head. 'I never heard any names mentioned...except for one, one of the later arrivals was called Juan, I remember that.'

'Juan?' McKay looked thoughtful. 'Juan? What did he look like?'

'Medium height, from what I could see in the half light of the hallway. He had a moustache but there was one aspect about him, he used the word 'si' and was nodding as he uttered it.'

'Did he by God?' McKay looked even more thoughtful. 'Maybe a Spaniard?'

'Well...maybe or possibly Italian or Portuguese.'

'OK!' McKay pushed more files in his direction. 'Just try these.'

Miller perused the last sequence, saw nothing of interest so McKay packed up all the books and photographs, apart from the two Miller had picked out, and they went to another office pen to see Andrew Guildford. He was much younger, probably early twenties, with black hair and spectacles. He looked very studious, which seemed to be in keeping with his status as an artist. Guildford's general appearance and demeanour surprised Miller, he had assumed in his mind all ASIO operatives were James Bond-like, expert in fisticuffs and armed to the teeth. Andrew Guildford resembled a bank or insurance clerk.

Guildford had a plastic covered frame, and asked Miller questions as he slotted in various facial features. It was a long process; Guildford inserted various pieces in response to Miller's answers. Eventually a picture emerged. Miller eyed it quizzically and suggested adjustments until it bore some resemblance to the man in question. Miller puzzled over it.

'It's not quite, I'm not sure why it isn't,' he closed his eyes to picture the man's face. 'Make the nose narrower.'

Guildford slid out one nose and inserted another; Miller looked at the result and nodded.

'That's getting near it,' he held it up. 'Hold on, maybe the eyes a little narrower, try that.'

Guildford made more adjustments.

'That's it,' Miller pronounced. 'That's about as close as we'll get.'

Guildford picked up his phone. McKay entered to examine the result.

'OK!' he said. 'We'll circulate this to the NSW Police, the Feds and Immigration.'

Kelsey was awaiting Miller when he re-surfaced on the fifth floor.

'We got that registration number from Bill Clucas and circulated it,' he said. 'Being a Victorian registration, it should be more obvious to the police.'

'What about my video camera and tape?'

'That's been digitalised and placed on disc,' said Kelsey. 'One of our boffins is working on the disc now, enhancing various figures and faces you filmed when you were on that ridge. Lucky for you Hammoud was on the side of their obstacle course nearest the camera. He's recognisable, although whether his union advocate or his lawyer, if he's got either, would accept it as being him is another matter. Anyway, that's not our worry, the Board will have to fight that out, but they should have the whip hand now he's been identified as part of a terror group.'

'I hope so. I'd hate to think that bastard will get any more benefit from the system,' Miller turned to Kelsey. 'How long do you want me here? I have a job to do, and Jack Winwood can't afford to pay me indefinitely while I'm doing nothing.'

'We need you here and possibly later in Sydney,' said Kelsey. 'But I appreciate Jack Winwood's problem. I'll speak with him. Your presence here is vital. You've seen this man at close quarters and have the best chance of recognising him. It's a case of national security and saving lives, against a few weeks' salary.'

'Agreed,' Miller replied. 'But that won't make him feel any better.'

'I agree, from Winwood's point of view, he's paying money for someone who isn't there. I'll have words with Francis Burton, we may be able to take you on as a temporary, he'll have to clear it with our Finance Department first.'

'OK!' Miller nodded glumly. He was thinking of Jacqueline, although their liaison was brief, he was thinking longingly of her. Another thought struck him as Kelsey turned away. 'How's Shackleton?'

'Shack?' Kelsey smiled. 'Oh, he's fine, if you want words with him, he's licking his wounds at the far end of the floor...that desk there, see him? He's been cleared by the medics, bruised ribs, possible black eye and a bump on the back of the head. He'll live.'

'I'll go and pay my respects,' Miller moved in Shackleton's direction. 'I want to know how many punches he landed on Lonsdale. I'll treasure that!'

*

Kelsey phoned Mike Duval.

'Any joy on Rivera?'

'No chief, we've been in touch with the Feds and Victorian Police but so far nothing.'

'We've found a lead, he possibly turned up at a farm building near Hopetoun in Victoria,' said Kelsey. 'Geoff Miller reckons he saw him when he was held there, he seemed to fit the description for Rivera and the name 'Juan' was mentioned. It's likely he'll turn up in Sydney. I've advised Stan Ellison of the Federal Police and also the State police in Sydney.'

Shackleton's phone rang whilst he was chatting with Miller. He answered it, said 'Got it!' and turned to Miller as he put it down.

'That was Alan,' he said. 'That motor vehicle you chased from Melbourne has been spotted by police in Cronulla.'

'Have they arrested anybody?'

Shackleton shook his head.

'Right now, it's parked in a supermarket car park. A patrol car was called to apprehend a shop lifter, while they were there, they caught sight of it in the car park. When they locked onto it, the engine was warm, so we don't reckon it was dumped. They may be buying groceries, guess even terrorists have to eat.'

'What happens now?'

'They'll keep it under observation, see where it goes,' said Shackleton. 'They'll track it in an unmarked police car, a patrol wagon would stick out like a sore thumb. Alan has called a meeting in ten minutes. We may be on our way to Sydney, Alan won't want to duck shove this onto anyone else now he's got the bit between his teeth.'

CHAPTER 22

No developments yet, the vehicle is still where the police spotted it. The patrol car left the area and an unmarked police car is standing by,' Kelsey was penning a note onto the file as he addressed Bramble, Shackleton, McKay and Miller. 'We're heading for Sydney, by then we may know where the rest of these bastards are, assuming the police can track them. We also have a lead to Rivera who entered Australia through Avalon airport in Melbourne. We've good reason to believe he's part of a plan to assassinate President De Souza of Taranga who's here on a state visit.'

Kelsey held up his hand to silence the buzz of conversation.

'We need to interview Maxwell Walters, the son of the farmer who used to own that farm, he's a lawyer in Sydney. We also need to isolate the lease on that property, Constable Lonsdale apparently drew a blank in the Hopetoun and Patchewollock areas, so if Maxwell Walters was involved in the leasing it may have been transacted in Sydney.'

'When do we start?'

'We'll have a quick bite then we'll go,' Kelsey checked his watch. 'I've asked for Marcus Templeton to be allocated to us for computer work, he'll come with us. As for me, I'll contact Max Walters. Bob, phone Melanie, she's presently in Sydney, tell her we still want her to be available. I know that'll please you!'

'I'm ecstatic,' was Bramble's reply. 'It makes my day!'

*

When they arrived in Sydney Kelsey contacted Sam Holmes, head of the Sydney field office, located in a high-rise city centre building. The next morning, Kelsey and Sam Holmes summoned all personnel to a meeting room, dominated by the Harbour Bridge on the skyline.

Holmes indicated to Kelsey to lead off. Holmes was slim and thin faced with a pronounced chin, and high cheek bones. He wore half-moon spectacles which gave him a school-masterly appearance. He was a good operator and ran a tight ship.

'This is your baby so far, Alan,' he said. 'No point in me being briefed and then briefing others. Take the chair.'

'Thanks Sam,' Kelsey regarded the others. 'I suggest Bob and Dave McKay join the stake-out. The police followed that four-wheel drive to a house in Cronulla, not the one traced from the vehicle left at the farm, but near it. The terrorist trip out seemed to be purely for groceries. We had a lucky break when the police spotted it in a supermarket carpark.'

'Who's watching the premises?' asked Bramble.

'The New South Wales Police set up an observation post last night from a nearby warehouse, after following the vehicle there yesterday. They're expecting us and will brief you. The position's not ideal, but beggars can't be choosers,' said Sam Holmes and gestured to Kelsey to continue.

'Mel, you come with me to see Max Walters, we need details of that lease, it may give us a lead,' Kelsey said crisply. 'Geoff, we have more mug shots for you to go through. Shackleton will stay here, to lick his wounds.'

He paused as a ripple of laughter ran through the group.

'Any questions?'

There were none. Kelsey gathered his files and stashed them into his brief case.

'OK!' he said. 'Any points, Sam?'

'Yes,' Holmes nodded assent.'We have to investigate where they got the stuff they were using in Hopetoun. One of the constituents is ammonium nitrate; we need to know who bought it, when and where. It was likely obtained in New South Wales, but we mustn't forget Hopetoun and Patchewollock.'

'Will you handle that, Sam?'

'I'll put Phil Jackson on it; we'll need police co-operation. Leave that with me.'

*

The lawyers Stewart, Phillips & Walters occupied the sixth floor of a building in Castlereagh Street.

'Impressive address,' commented Melanie as they stood outside.

'Looks like a large firm,' replied Kelsey. 'What time was the appointment?'

'10.45,' responded Melanie.

'OK! Let's go.'

They took the lift to the sixth floor and entered reception. Kelsey asked for Max Walters and they were promptly taken to his room. Walters rose and indicated a couple of vacant chairs.

His office was well appointed and the decor tasteful. The view from the window was impressive; overlooking the Sydney Harbour Bridge and several smaller buildings. Walters was aged about 40 to 45 with black hair, slim and athletic. He came around the desk to greet them, his handshake firm.

'Please sit down, Mr Kelsey, and you, Ms Cassidy,' he said. 'How can I assist you? Something about my father's old property near Hopetoun, you said.'

'That's correct,' said Kelsey.

'Is there a problem?'

'Yes, there is,' Kelsey unzipped his document case, extracted his file and laid it on the desk. 'What exactly happened to that property after your father died?'

Walters looked puzzled.

'Nothing out of the ordinary. My father lived alone, we believe he had been dead for two days before his housekeeper found him, she went in twice a week to clean, do shopping and prepare his meals. Immediately I was notified I went down there.'

'Yes, and then?'

Walters looked at Kelsey, who was obviously expecting him to go on.

'I'm sorry, what is this?'

'I'm also sorry,' said Kelsey. 'You are aware who we are and where we are from?'

'Not exactly,' Walters shook his head. 'Your colleague here said you were investigators. Is there a problem with taxation, or to do with my father's death? As far as we knew from the Coroner's Office it was natural causes, has that changed?'

'No,' Kelsey shook his head. 'There was nothing untoward regarding your father's death as far as we are aware, if there's a taxation problem that's certainly not why we are here. Are you prepared to be discreet, Mr Walters?'

'Discreet? What the hell is all this about?'

Kelsey produced his ID and indicated to Melanie Cassidy to do the same.

'That is who we are; we are nothing to do with taxation, the coroner or the police. We need information. We're dealing with a matter of national security and it has to do with the Hopetoun property.'

'National security? At Hopetoun? Now you've really lost me.'

'Mr Walters, if you'll bear with us and answer our questions, we'll try to fill you in as far as we can. Agreed?'

Walters nodded. 'Agreed,' he replied.

'Right!' Kelsey referred to his file. 'Firstly, after your father died, what happened to the property?'

'It was left to me and my sister on a 50-50 basis,' said Walters. 'We decided to sell as we are both Sydneysiders now, but in recent years my father had allowed the property to run down. Partly my fault, he wanted me to carry it on, this caused a rift between us because I wasn't cut out for farming. But I digress. There were other matters to tie up as well, so my sister and I decided to allow the property to remain in limbo until we were ready to place it on the market.'

'But you leased it out.'

'Yes, I was coming to that. That came via my son, he's at university and must have talked about his grandfather's legacy. Nothing to be overexcited about, but I suppose it qualified as a legacy since he was one of the beneficiaries. He mentioned it at university and came home one day to say a contact at university knew someone who could be interested in leasing it on a short tenure, for about 6-10 months.'

'You acted on that?'

'We did, but I placed it in the hands of real estate agents and left them to handle it. These people were prepared to pay a useful rent whilst Helen, my sister, and I were still sorting things out. My father had property in England as well, he emigrated from there in the 1940's and some of his siblings, and our cousins, were involved in joint ownership of property in Gloucestershire. We had to go to England to sort that out, and left the Hopetoun side of things to the managing agents. We intended to deal with it long term when we returned.'

'You let a property that was in dicey condition?'

'No,' Walters shook his head. 'It needed attention, in normal circumstances we probably wouldn't have bothered to rent it out, but it wasn't in a dilapidated state, if that's what you're saying. A few fences needed securing, some painting was needed and the gardens merited attention. It was in good repair, although some minor items needed attention which were carried out.'

'How were circumstances not normal?'

'Well apparently this company...what was the name...hang on a minute, just let me have a look here...' he reached for his desk drawer.

'Agnarat Wen,' Kelsey interjected. 'Yes, go on.'

'That was it. They were seed merchants or something like that, and wanted barns for storage space. They also had experimental mechanical ploughs, and wanted to try them out. That suited me and Helen, quite apart from knowing the property was occupied which prevented squatters or vandalism, one large paddock had gone to seed. If they were going to plough it up, even on an experimental basis, all well and good.'

'For how long a period was the lease arranged?'

'Due to end soon I think,' Walters reached for his drawer again and produced a manila file. 'Here we are, less than a month now.'

'Have you had any reports from the managing agents about the property?'

'Probably, I say probably because Helen and I haven't been back for long, it took longer than we anticipated to sort out the English end. I've been catching up with the backlog here and haven't checked on Hopetoun yet.'

'You said your son was instrumental in finding these people. Did he go to England with you?'

'No, he stayed here. My wife and I have two sons and a daughter, late teens to early twenties. They stayed behind while my wife and I, and Helen and her husband, went to England and we made a holiday of it.'

'Do you know anything of the people who leased it?'

'Not a great deal! What's happened? Are they drug barons or something?'

'No, but they're not innocents either. We need to talk to your son and the managing agents. Can you supply us with addresses or contact numbers, please?'

'I can do that,' Walters made a notation on a pad, tore off the top page and handed it to Kelsey. 'What is all this about?'

'It's a matter of national security.'

'To hell with national bloody security, what the blazes is going on here?'

'I'm sorry Mr Walters. I can't tell you too much at this stage, and I'm not being deliberately mysterious. I'll just give you a hint, and must insist, please, not a word to anybody. It is absolutely vital nothing leaks out to impede our enquiries, and our actions. You must not breathe a word to anyone, not your wife, your family, your partners, nor the managing agents, nor at this stage, your son, particularly your son. Is that understood?'

'Yes, I understand,' Walters nodded. 'I give you my word.'

'All right, Mr Walters. Write down Agnarat Wen, I suggest in block capitals.'

'What?' Walters looked quizzical. 'What are you...? Hmm! Now what?'

He scribbled the names down and sat with pencil poised.

'Now spell the two names backwards.'

'Agnarat Wen ...that makes it...New ...Taranga ...Jesus Christ!' he dropped the pencil. 'It's so damned obvious why didn't I lock onto it before? Are we talking revolution?'

'I never said that,' Kelsey put his file back together and slotted it into his document case. 'Take care you don't either. Thank you for your assistance, Mr Walters, we'll be in touch. Can you give me one of your cards please...and your son's phone number?'

They paused in the foyer of the building; Kelsey sat on a seat that looked out onto the street. He produced the note Walters had supplied and took out his mobile phone.

'Next stop, Richards & Blair,' he announced. 'Let's see what they know about this.'

He was on the phone for five minutes, snapped it shut then stood up.

'They'll see us as soon as we can reach them,' he said. 'They hang out in Canterbury. Let's hail a cab, Mel.'

Outside they tried without success, in the end Kelsey had to ring for one. The cab driver was Fijian, which caused Kelsey some misgivings as to whether he'd know the location of a particular suburban street, but to his astonishment the cabbie took off like a rocket and deposited them outside the real estate agency in good time.

'Not like you to give a tip,' Melanie commented as they made for the main entrance.

'With a man that size you don't take liberties!' Kelsey

retorted. 'ASIO pays anyway!'

'Ah, now I see your reasoning.'

They entered the agency and Kelsey asked for Malcolm Richards. They were asked to wait, but Richards left his office and greeted them before they had time to admire the view. He escorted them to his office.

'How can I assist?' he asked when they were seated. 'Max phoned and said it was about Hopetoun.'

He was tall, with a receding hairline and dark rimmed spectacles. He was about the same age as Max Walters, dressed in a dark suit, red tie and white shirt. He had an easy smile and a cultured accent.

'You handled the leasing of the Walters property at Hopetoun?' asked Kelsey.

'We did, and still do,' Richards responded. 'It was made easy for us as it turned out.'

'Why do you say that?'

'We received instructions from Max. He was going overseas to deal with matters arising from his father's estate. There was property in England and he and his sister had to deal with it.'

'You do much business with Max Walters?'

'Some, he passes business our way and vice versa.'

'Why does he use you and not anyone in Sydney itself?'

'Is that relevant?'

Kelsey shook his head.

'No, just curious, that's all, since he's in the city and you're out here. Don't answer if you don't want to, but clearly you know each other well.'

'There's no mystery, we were at school together, that was six years of our lives, and then we were both at university. We also played cricket for the same club for some years, and we're both members of Canterbury Rugby League club.'

Kelsey nodded.

'OK! When Max Walters went abroad, what happened with Hopetoun?'

'It was my idea to lease the property out until he returned. He made it into a long vacation, a case of killing two birds. Then he could decide when he returned what to do with it. There wasn't any point hanging onto it, after his father died there was nothing to draw him or Helen back to Hopetoun.'

He opened a file on the side of his desk.

'We had to ask a local managing agent to deal with it for us, I've never been to Hopetoun or Patchewollock in my life, but Roy Walters came to us just after Max left for England, and said he'd found somebody who was interested.'

'Roy Walters?'

'Max's younger son, he's at university. He casually mentioned the property at the university, so he said. Within a day or two someone contacted him and said he knew of someone else who was interested in a short-term lease on a country property, something to do with tractors and a new ploughing machine. We followed it up, to cut a long story short, the deal was done.'

'Agnarat Wen.'

'You're ahead of me. That's correct. We checked them out but saw nothing untoward. They paid up front, so that was that.'

'Did you meet any of their executives?'

'Two men came here to finalise matters,' Richards flicked over a few pages. 'Here we are, Hassan Qassim and Marid Jaafar. Apparently, they had new agricultural equipment they wanted to try out before placing it on the market, I'm not clear on the detail but as long as they weren't growing marijuana or altering the property, I wasn't that bothered.'

'Describe them.'

'Let me think...mid-thirties at a guess, well dressed, they seemed normal business types. Asian in origin, but otherwise dressed like you and me and their English was good. We did a check on the company, as I told you. They were described as general dealers and seed merchants.'

'We've had that description already from elsewhere,' commented Kelsey. 'Anything else about them that struck you?'

'No.' Richards shook his head. 'They had an office address and phone number in the city, we never had occasion to call on them.'

'Has anyone called at the property to check it since they took it over?'

'We haven't ourselves, we hived it off to agents in Hopetoun,' said Richards. 'We've had one report from them, they called by appointment after three months to check all was well, we heard of nothing untoward.'

'Who were the Hopetoun agents?'

'Jackson & Antrobus.'

'Address?'

'Hold on, we have some of their cards here.' Richards flipped one across the desk.

'Thank you,' Kelsey and Melanie rose. 'I'll have one of your cards too if I may, we may need to contact you again.'

When they reached the street, Kelsey turned to Melanie, his face contorted with fury.

'That bloody prat Lonsdale!' he raged. 'He was supposed to check every estate agent in the town. We should have found this out a couple of days ago.'

'What now?' asked Melanie. 'Should we see Roy Walters.'

'My oath!' snapped Kelsey. He rummaged in his wallet and produced Max Walters's card with Roy's number on it, turned it over and handed it to Melanie. 'Read that number out while I dial it.'

CHAPTER 23

Kelsey arranged to meet Roy Walters in a restaurant near the centre of Sydney, where Walters worked as a waiter during the university vacation. Kelsey also rang for a taxi.

'We might score a free coffee,' Melanie commented as they waited for the cab.

'And claim for it anyway,' grunted Kelsey. 'Good idea! But what the hell was bloody Lonsdale doing? I asked him to check every estate agent in the town, and the silly sod slipped up.'

'Maybe he was checking Miller's file for loopholes,' said Melanie. 'Shack told me he wasn't pleasant to Geoff afterwards; it was almost as if he resented him not being a sex offender.'

'I'd agree with that. He thought he'd made his mark by finding a paedophile and couldn't have been more wrong.'

Kelsey was still smarting with anger as their cab arrived.

They were greeted by a young, dark-haired receptionist and asked for Roy Walters, saying they were expected. She led them to a table by the window and said he wouldn't be long.

Other waiting staff were laying tables and re-arranging bottles behind the bar. Within minutes a young man, wearing dark trousers, a blue shirt with a bow tie, and a black waistcoat...the restaurant uniform...headed towards them. He was a thinner and younger version of his father.

'Mr Kelsey?' he asked as they shook hands. 'My father said you wanted to see me, something about Hopetoun.'

'Yes, indeed,' responded Kelsey. 'How long have you been working here?'

'A year or two, on and off, mostly off,' Roy replied. 'I work here during the university recess. Not a long-term career, but it keeps the wolf from the door. Would you like a coffee?'

'For sure!'

He sat down, turned and waved to the young receptionist

'Alison,' he called. 'Could you rustle up three coffees? How do you like them?'

He ascertained that and relayed it to Alison.

'Dad said you were connected with the police. What's up?'

'We're making enquiries about the tenants of your grandfather's farm between Hopetoun and Patchewollock,' said Kelsey. 'We've spoken with your father, as you know, and Richards & Blair. Apparently, you have a connection with these tenants.'

'Me! No,' Walters shook his head. 'Why should you think that?'

'We understand you told the estate agent, Mr Richards, you knew of a prospect who might be willing to lease the farm for several months. Is that correct?'

'Well, I...' Roy Walters hesitated. 'Am I in any trouble?'

'No, you're not. But you introduced the subsequent lessees to Richards & Blair. Can you help us? We have to trace them.'

'There wasn't much to it. After Grandad died, I mentioned at university we had a Victorian property in the bush, miles from anywhere, and were considering leasing it for a short period. It was a bit of a joke at the time, country estate, landed gentry and all that.'

'Then what?'

'Some days after that another student who I know fairly well approached me. He asked about the property, was it isolated, how far from the main road, and stuff like that, so I described its general geographical position. I've often been there in the past, my grandfather taught me to ride a horse there. This chap said he knew someone who'd be interested in leasing it for about twelve months.'

'Who was this student?'

'Abbas Kamiza, he's Asian.'

'Where from?'

'Taranga, I think, his parents were originally from Pakistan.'

'You know him well?'

'Fairly well yes, I see him around. He's taking an engineering degree and I see quite a lot of him. We're in the same cricket team. He's not a bad off spinner.'

So were two of the London Underground bombers, Kelsey thought grimly. He recalled two of them played cricket with relatives the night before they bombed Underground trains in 2005. He dismissed the thought, maybe he was being paranoid.

'Who were the people he represented?'

'He didn't exactly represent them, I think it just came up in conversation with someone he knew, like it did with him and me.'

Kelsey heard Melanie give an almost indiscernible 'Hmmph!'

'Do you know who they were?'

'Not a clue, I gave Abbas Malcolm Richards' number and as far as I was concerned that was the end of it. I called Malcolm later and was told it came off.'

'Has he mentioned it since, this Abbas Kamiza?'

'No, I haven't seen much of him since. I see him frequently during semester and when we attend meetings of various groupings, refugee groups, immigration and civil liberties, stuff like that. Then the semester ended and I spend most of my time here, I usually work here during the recess...oh thanks Alison ...white and no sugar over here for us two and black for Mr Kelsey.'

Alison, the receptionist, served the coffees. Kelsey eyed her appreciatively as she served them. He had paid some attention to her when he and Melanie had entered the restaurant, initially because she greeted them both with a flashing smile that caused her entire face to light up. It would certainly have a welcoming effect upon any arriving patrons. In addition, she had a good figure and walked with an easy grace; she had short dark hair and dark blue eyes. He realised Melanie was watching him, with a cynically raised eyebrow. He smiled at Melanie and concentrated on the coffee.

But Melanie herself was also eyeing Alison with interest, this young woman's demeanour and bearing aroused strong emotions she had not experienced for some time,

It was common knowledge in ASIO that Melanie was divorced, but what was not generally known were the details of that divorce. Melanie's marriage had not gone well, she and her husband over time had realised their personalities were incompatible, they remained co-habiting but their relationship and sex life had not been good, consequently their quality of life had suffered as a result. Melanie, naturally promiscuous, had, in addition, a tendency to being bisexual, which had manifested itself in her teenage years. As she and her husband had drifted apart, to offset her sexual frustrations, she had commenced an affair, but with the wife of a neighbour who lived in an apartment in the same block. When, inevitably, it had been exposed it triggered divorce between Melanie and her husband, the other woman and her husband had promptly moved elsewhere, Melanie had never seen her again.

It later transpired that Melanie's husband had also been playing away, in a more orthodox fashion, this being the grounds for the divorce. Both parties had preferred it that way, no husband would relish admitting his wife had preferred the embraces of another woman to his.

Melanie had not remarried, but had continued with casual affairs, some heterosexual and others not. She was currently unattached, but never averse to another liaison, when it came to sexual gratification, she was open minded.

Occasionally there were women who attracted her attention and interest and warranted a second, or third, look, as she had now with Alison, but usually that was as far as it went. She was no predator, but today she experienced a stirring of interest and appreciation as she watched Alison walk away, with her carriage and trim figure. Further, Melanie's more than sidelong glances were sufficiently unguarded for Alison to become aware of them, as she reached the counter she swung around, caught Melanie's eye, briefly smiled, then busied herself with the cash register. Erotic images arose in Melanie's mind, which she suppressed with difficulty. She became aware Kelsey was speaking to Roy and forcibly switched her attention.

''So Abbas hasn't mentioned it since?' Kelsey was saying to Roy Walters.

'No, but I understand from Dad the lease was about twelve months.'

Kelsey asked more questions, ascertained which university Roy, and thus Abbas, attended, which was about as far as they could get. Melanie interjected at one point and asked if Roy knew any of Kamiza's family or friends outside university, but he shook his head.

'Do you know where he lives?' again Roy shook his head.

'How can we contact him?'

'I don't know where he is, I'm afraid.'

'Do you have his mobile phone number?' but again Roy shook his head.

'I'm not that friendly with him.'

'Pity,' said Kelsey. 'We may need that. OK, thanks Roy.'

He rose to go and Melanie followed suit. As they passed by the counter Kelsey exchanged a few words with Alison. Alison seemed to like Kelsey; she gave him the benefit of her engaging smile as they conversed. Melanie took advantage of their mutual attention to cast an approving eye over her, but Alison became aware of it, turned and Melanie was caught in the act. Alison again turned to Kelsey as he said his final farewell and Melanie followed suit. Alison eyed Melanie curiously as they made their way out.

They left the restaurant and paused further down the street. There were a few flower pots and a small patch of lawn at the intersection, plus a seat which they occupied.

'What do you reckon?' asked Kelsey.

'Not sure,' Melanie's mind was still distracted, she struggled to apply herself to his question. 'He seems straight enough, but I just had a feeling.'

Kelsey eyed her quizzically.

'Intuitive?'

'Maybe,' Melanie shrugged. Kelsey scratched his cheek and considered. He had been prepared to take Roy Walters at face value, but if Melanie had doubts, that was good enough for him. He knew her too well to dismiss it.

'Point taken; we'll bear that in mind. Nevertheless, we've

made progress,' he said. 'Now we've got to contact this friend of his.'

'The university may be the best bet.'

'Yes, I agree. We'll make that our next port of call.'

At the university offices they were greeted by a middle-aged woman with horn rimmed glasses and a severe expression. She looked askance when they asked for the address of a student, until they produced their identification, but was still reticent about producing addresses herself and referred them to the Dean, a tall grey-haired man who responded to her telephoned summons. He examined their identification, nodded and led them to his room.

'Harold Simpson,' he proffered his hand to Kelsey.

Kelsey explained what they wanted, Simpson operated the keyboard on his desk, wrote down an address and handed it to Kelsey.

'Where is this young man from?' asked Kelsey.

'His origins, you mean? Not too sure...hold on!' Simpson consulted the screen. 'He and his family came from Taranga, but they are Pakistani in origin.'

'Does he belong to any clubs or interest groups?'

Simpson eyed the screen.

'Can't answer that, no doubt he does. Most of them do.'

'Do you have a mobile phone number for him?'

Simpson shook his head.

'We don't keep that information on computer, I'm afraid. Sorry!'

They thanked him and departed.

When they returned to the ASIO field office Kelsey called Bramble, Shackleton, Melanie Cassidy and Geoff Miller together. McKay was still on surveillance at the Cronulla address. Sam Holmes, manager of the field office, had been called to the airport as a recent arrival had been detained, the Federal Police had also been summoned.

Kelsey commenced proceedings.

'We've seen Max Walters, nothing sinister there, he seems straight,' he said. 'The property leasing came via his son Roy, who, on the face of it, appeared to be an innocent party, but ...' he indicated Melanie: '...having said that, Mel has reservations. He says he merely mentioned the farm at university. This is where it becomes interesting. Another student, Abbas Kamiza, quizzed Roy Walters about the property and it led on from there.'

'Who is Abbas Kamiza?' Bramble asked. 'Or rather, what is he? Where's he from?'

Melanie Cassidy took up the story.

'According to the university dean, he is an immigrant from Taranga, or his parents were, but they are all Pakistani in origin. The family lives in Caringbah. He's studying engineering which could be anything to do with oil, water, road building, you name it, it covers a host of things. We haven't contacted him yet, but intend to.'

'Is he a member of any political societies?' Bramble queried.

'We don't know, the dean wasn't forthcoming,' replied Kelsey. 'We're not sure whether he knew or not. Melanie will return to make more enquiries. While there we noted various discussion groups on a notice board. How did you make out at Cronulla, Bob?'

'Some comings and goings,' said Bramble. 'We took some camera shots; they're being analysed now. Dave McKay is still there.'

'OK! Melanie, go to the university, see if you can dig up more about Kamiza. Bob, go back to Cronulla. Denis, ring Roger Preston, ask him to contact Jackson & Antrobus and do it himself, not that silly sod Lonsdale who wants his arse kicking.'

'What are they?'

'Real estate and management agents in Hopetoun, for the Walters farm. We asked that bloody idiot Lonsdale to check all managing and real estate agencies, he either missed this one or asked the wrong questions, probably whether they had teenage daughters! Apparently, they've done one routine inspection of the property during the tenure of Agnarat Wen. Get Roger to ask if they noticed anything peculiar.'

'Will do, is Roger's number on that file?'

'No, but you should be able to find him quick enough. All report back here at 1800 hours, so inform all wives, girl and men friends, mistresses and gigolos we're working tonight. We need to see Roy Walters again to finger Abbas Kamiza. Geoff, come with me, we may be getting close to your boss man at the Walters farm, having seen him close to you're more likely to recognise him.'

'What do we tell Roy Walters?' asked Melanie. 'Getting him to point this student out means him taking time off from the restaurant. I'm not sure he'll want to identify him; a case of schoolboy loyalties against authority.'

'Loyalties to the oppressed, more like, I don't know about schoolboy,' grunted Kelsey. 'Having thought about it, Mel, I think you're right about him.'

'How do we justify him taking time off without telling him too much?'

'A good point,' Kelsey rubbed his nose. 'He won't be fobbed off with any airy-fairy story for sure. I'll have to think about that, but we need him for information. Any questions?'

There were none.

CHAPTER 24

Kelsey phoned Max Walters before contacting his son Roy again. Max Walters was still disturbed at the reverse spelling of the Hopetoun lessees, and was willing to assist. He offered to ring his son at the restaurant before Kelsey and Miller arrived, to prepare the soil, as he put it. Kelsey agreed, but insisted he say nothing about possible terrorist connotations.

When they arrived, Alison greeted Kelsey enthusiastically.

'You want to see Roy again?' she asked.

'Yes, he knows we're coming.'

'You can have the same table,' said Alison. 'Coffee again?'

'For sure,' replied Kelsey. 'Where is Roy?'

'He's out back in the store-room, shouldn't be long.'

'Good,' Alison led them to the same table. As she pulled back the chairs, he had an inspiration, based on Melanie's reticence about Roy.

'You're also a university student, are you?' he asked Alison.

'Yes, Roy and I fill in here during vacations.'

'Do you know Abbas Kamiza?' he asked.

'Yes, I know him,' she gave a disdainful sniff.

'We have to contact him, you wouldn't have his mobile number, would you?'

'Yes,' she produced her mobile. 'I have it here, not that I ever ring *him*!' she added pointedly. 'I only ever ring it to contact Roy. He spends a lot of time with Abbas.'

Her phone bleeped and made musical notes as she keyed through it.

'Got it,' she picked up a coaster from the table and made a notation with her pen. 'Why didn't you ask Roy? He's bound to have it?'

'We...um...never thought about it last time. But thanks,' responded Kelsey. As she returned to the bar counter, Kelsey turned to Miller.

'Melanie was right'

'About what?' asked Miller.

'Never mind, she just was. 100%!'

Roy appeared from the doorway at the rear of the restaurant and came over.

'Sorry to trouble you again, Mr Walters,' Kelsey said easily. 'But we have a difficult situation here. Did your father explain anything to you?'

'No, he said you were calling on me again, but not why, but I presume it's about my grandfather's Hopetoun property again.'

'Good!' Kelsey nodded with satisfaction. Max Walters had kept his word and said nothing about the property lessees, even to his son. 'We realise you need some explanation, Mr Walters, but although we can tell you some of the story, we can't tell you all as it involves national security.'

'Call me Roy,' said Roy. 'Did you say national security?'

'I did and Roy, we need an assurance from you of your

absolute discretion if we tell you anything about this affair, can we rely on that?'

'Yes, for sure.'

'I can't tell you everything, but we've reason to believe your grandfather's property was being used by the lessees for illicit activities. They didn't need it for a lengthy period, but they needed a remote property for a specific purpose. We're investigating these activities, but to enable us with this we need to isolate or identify Abbas Kamiza, mainly to eliminate him from our enquiries. We need you to point him out to us.'

'Abbas! What is this? Is he under suspicion by the police? He merely believes in free access to this country by refugees,' Roy Walters became agitated, then indignant. 'I don't like this; he's a friend. Are you going to arrest him?'

'I don't think it will come to that. We don't know whether he's involved or not, he is very likely completely innocent and only remotely connected with the people who leased the property. But we need to contact him to make further progress with or eliminate him from our enquiries. This is a very serious business, which can affect innocent lives.'

'But they needed the property to look after refugees, they were using it as a commune. Are you saying there are drugs or something involved?'

'I can't say at this stage, suffice to say it involves many lives. It's a very serious matter.'

'Bloody hell! Who exactly are you? You're not police so my father said.'

'No, we're not,' Kelsey replied. 'But we are involved with the security of this country. That may sound melodramatic; but I assure you it is so.'

'You're CIA...I don't like this.'

'CIA! What on earth...!' Kelsey was taken aback. 'Look! We

are not, repeat *not*, CIA. We are as Australian as you are. We are the Australian equivalent of the FBI or MI5. I repeat; we are responsible for internal security.'

'You're saying Abbas is doing something wrong?'

'We don't know that, he's probably as innocent in this affair as you are, it's possible all he's done is direct these people to what they wanted, an isolated country property.'

'Why shouldn't they want that? Surely there's no harm if they're merely using it as a commune.'

'I can't tell why they wanted it…yet!' Kelsey leant forward, his forearms on the table. He was becoming increasingly irritated by Roy Walters, and his conclusions, and was trying hard not to show it. Surely, he couldn't believe anyone wanted a property for a commune when they only leased it for a matter of months. 'We need your help, by assisting us you may also be helping Abbas. We believe he may be in danger; we need to find him.'

Roy Walters looked indecisive. Kelsey was about to add something but desisted. Maybe it would be better if Roy's thought processes worked their way through, then he seemed to reach a decision.

'I want to ring my father.'

'Do that,' said Kelsey. 'But I need your word on one point if you leave this table, will you give me that?'

'What's that?'

'That you ring your father and nobody else. Will you guarantee that?'

Roy hesitated, nodded and left the table. Miller turned to Kelsey.

'Do you think he'll warn Abbas?'

'No, he won't,' answered Kelsey.

'How can you be so sure?'

'I'm not! But nearly so.'

Kelsey took out his mobile phone, read off the number Alison had written on the coaster and began to dial.

'What are you doing?' Miller asked.

'Hang on a minute.' Kelsey said. 'Just ignore what I say... Hallo, how are you today? Your number has been selected at random; you are in line to win a prize. My name is Jason Smith, I am from Readers Digest, if you apply for this prize then your name goes forward for another bigger prize due to be drawn in a few months...' Kelsey took the phone from his ear and grinned at Miller. '...he's gone!'

Miller looked perplexed, then light dawned.

'You rang Abbas!'

'I did, hold on, I'll ring him again.'

Kelsey went through the same procedure, this time assuming the role of a financial adviser conducting a survey. This call lasted longer, the person at the other end did answer a few questions before he obviously tired of it and rang off. Miller did the next call, he was selling water purifiers, at this point Roy Walters returned, looking perplexed. Kelsey saw him coming and signalled to Miller who hastily snapped Kelsey's mobile phone shut and pocketed it.

'Er...Dad said it's... er...probably all right. What do you want me to do?'

'We need to speak to Abbas, so we need you to point him out to us. Have you any idea where he's likely to be?'

'No, I don't know where he lives, so I can't help you.'

'Don't worry about that, we do,' responded Kelsey. 'He lives in Caringbah. We'll head for his home address first. Is that all right with you?'

Miller looked at Roy Walters, it clearly wasn't all right, but Kelsey was already rising to his feet, as was Miller, so Roy Walters could do little but follow suit.

They arrived outside the house in Caringbah and parked a few doors up the street. Kelsey indicated a house with a car outside.

'According to university records, that's where he lives. Number 22,' he said cheerfully. 'We need to ascertain whether he's at home.'

He turned to Roy Walters.

'Can you do that?'

'What?'

'You can either knock on the door, or ring him on his mobile.'

'I don't like this. I feel like a Judas. All they wanted the farm for was…!'

'Yes, I know…for a commune,' Kelsey interrupted sharply. 'If he's an innocent party, I can assure you he'll be thanking you afterwards.'

Geoff Miller, having been recently imprisoned and badly treated at the property in question, was equally irritated at Roy's suppositions.

'Just ascertain where he is, Roy. That's all you need do,' Kelsey added.

Walters hesitated, produced his mobile, dialled and placed it to his ear, forgetting he'd previously said he didn't know the number.

'Hallo Abbas?' he said. 'I'm ringing you to…what's that? No listen, I'm not trying to sell you anything…no, it's not a survey either…you've what? Oh I see, you thought I was another one. No, it's me…Roy,' Kelsey and Miller exchanged wry glances. 'How are you these days? Just touching base again before the next semester…you're where?' They could hear a buzz of conversation from the other end, Walters nodded and pursed his lips.

'Whereabouts are you then? Oh. I see. OK, we'll catch up again.' Walters looked at Kelsey, shrugged and rang off.

'Where is he?'

'On a train.'

'On a train? Where?'

'He's heading home from Sydney, says he's been in the city. The train has just reached Kogara. So, he's not at home. We can't do much then, can we?'

'What station will he get off?' Kelsey ignored Walters' question.

'Dunno…oh…Caringbah I guess, is there a station there?' Walters said. 'Look here, are you sure about Abbas, I know him fairly well, I'm sure he's all right. What's he supposed to have done?'

'We don't know that he has, but he's a link to someone who *has* done something,' responded Kelsey. 'Where's Kogara? Hand me that street directory, Geoff.'

'Well, I don't know. I don't like the idea of ratting on him,' Walters shook his head. 'Just because he's not white Anglo-Saxon doesn't mean he's not loyal, all he was doing was finding a home for refugees and asylum seekers.'

Kelsey ignored him, continued checking the Sydney directory, reached the rail network page and located Kogara.

'Caringbah station is twelve stations from Kogara. How long do you reckon, Geoff?'

'Say forty minutes, maybe longer.'

'Right, let's get moving.'

They arrived at Caringbah station, found a parking spot, entered the station complex and wandered onto the platform. Kelsey excused himself, saying he wanted to visit the gents' toilet, so Miller and Roy waited by the ticket barrier. When Kelsey re-joined them, he indicated the exit turnstile.

'We'll stand here,' he said. 'We'll allow him to exit the station platform first, we'll need Roy to point him out.' He looked keenly at Roy, then Miller, before his eyes roved over to Roy again. It wasn't hard to interpret Kelsey's thought processes.

'Should be the next train,' said Kelsey. 'We'll stay here and wait.'

They waited about ten minutes, during which time a train came through from Cronulla, stopped briefly then headed towards Sydney. A police car passed by the station on the roadway; did a U turn and parked in Kingsway. Two police got out and began checking parked vehicles, one of them ambled up to the station building and idly looked around while his companion continued checking registrations.

Miller heard a train in the distance, as it approached Kelsey wandered a few feet away and leant casually against a wall, his arms folded but holding his phone in his hand.

The train halted with a squeal of brakes and disgorged several passengers who passed through the barrier, into the station concourse and main street. Miller scanned them for Asian faces, of which there were a few, and glanced at Roy Walters, who was standing unhappily, hands in pockets. He looked at Miller, then Kelsey, and shook his head.

'Well?' Kelsey asked. 'Any sign of him?'

'No, I don't see him,' said Roy Walters. 'Maybe he's on the next train.'

Miller heard a phone ring. One of the passengers, a young Asian, dressed in jeans and 'T' shirt, carrying a back pack, paused, reached in his pocket, drew to one side and placed his phone to his ear. Roy Walters realised what was happening, took off, ran over to him and grasped him by the shoulder.

'Abbas,' Miller heard him say. 'I think there's a problem but I don't think you're in any trouble, the police are here and want to ask ...!'

He got no further, Abbas looked up, saw a policeman and

Kelsey moving towards him and his expression abruptly changed. He gave Walters a violent push, sent him reeling and ran for the station exit and street with Kelsey and the constable in pursuit. The other constable, still in the carpark, ran to intercept. Abbas changed direction and ran up the street but the second constable was ahead of him, Abbas hesitated; reached into his belt, and his hand emerged holding a knife.

'Drop it!' one of the police reached for his gun. 'Drop that knife, drop it...now!'

Abbas looked around desperately, ran back but realised Kelsey and the other constable were in his way. He backed off, his backpack hard against a car parked in the street, still brandishing the knife.

'Abbas,' Roy Walters passed Miller and headed for Abbas, his hands held out in a placatory fashion. 'Abbas, it's me, Roy. There's some mistake, there's nothing to worry about. I tried to warn you, there's no need to be frightened. Put the knife down and ...!'

'Infidel! You betrayed me!' Abbas snarled and lunged at Roy; the knife aimed at his chest. Miller promptly reacted, an automatic reflex as he flung himself at Walters and hit him with his shoulder. Walters crashed to the pavement with a cry of pain as his right hip and shoulder hit the tarmac with Miller on top of him. Abbas continued with his lunge, but merely hit thin air, he stumbled forward, his knife hit the side of another parked car and made a deep scratch in its paintwork. In the process, he presented his back to one of the police, who reached under the backpack, seized him from behind and pinioned his arms. The other constable joined the fray and they forced him over the car's bonnet. Miller heard the click of handcuffs.

'OK! He's secure,' said one of them while Kelsey kicked the knife away.

'My God! What's happened? Why did he attack me? He's my friend!' Roy cried in anguish as Miller helped him to his feet.

'Some friend,' Miller heard Kelsey mutter.

They undid the securing straps, the struggling Abbas was relieved of his backpack and hustled to the police car, still spitting invective. One of the constables picked up the knife, placed it in a plastic bag, carried it and the backpack to the police car. Kelsey drew a deep breath and leant against another parked car.

'Funny thing,' he said. 'I was almost prepared to give him the benefit of the doubt, I was beginning to believe he could be an innocent party. He answered that for us quite emphatically, didn't he? Everyone OK?'

Miller nodded, but indicated Roy.

'He's a bit bruised and I'm not talking about his shoulder,' he said cynically. 'How did the police get here? That was damned lucky.'

'Lucky my arse!' retorted Kelsey. 'I suspected Walters might try again to tip him off, plus I had reservations about Abbas. I rang the police when I went to the gents' toilet.'

'Well...you were right on both counts,' said Miller.

'Wasn't I just?' said Kelsey eyed the scratch on the bodywork of the parked car. 'That'll cost a few quid, some poor bugger could lose his no claims bonus for that.'

CHAPTER 25

Kelsey had a brief discussion with the police. He didn't want Abbas out of his sight or jurisdiction. The police considered Abbas was theirs but a call to Francis Burton in Canberra resulted in a compromise, Abbas was taken to the ASIO field office under police escort and placed in an interview room with a constable guarding him. Roy Walters sat in the waiting area, like a stunned mullet. Miller stayed with him while Kelsey called Melanie Cassidy and Shackleton on his mobile phone. He snapped it shut, came over and addressed Walters.

'What did you mean when you said you tried to warn him?' Kelsey asked acidly.

Walters flushed and looked uneasy.

'I didn't know what was going on, I thought it was just an anti-Muslim exercise,' he said slowly. 'The CIA have no right to...!'

'Great God in Heaven!' Kelsey looked ceilingward in despair. 'What the hell are you talking about? By what stretch of imagination and lack of bloody intelligence can you bring the CIA into this. We are operatives of ASIO, which deals with security in Australia for Australians by Australians. Presumably you've heard of events in London, Madrid, Mumbai and the bomb explosion in Bali years back?'

'What has that to do with...?'

'It has every bloody thing to do with it!' Kelsey said angrily. 'These bastards are planning a terror attack; we're trying to stop them...and you try to warn the swine! You must be off your fucking rocker!'

'What?' Roy Walters looked flustered. 'Look here, I object to...!'

'I don't give a damn what you object to! I told you it was a case of national security,' Kelsey ignored the interruption and raged on. 'I couldn't tell you what, it's still classified. But now I have to, because you've been so damned stupid. That man Abbas is no more a friend of yours than Attila the Hun or Adolf Hitler, assuming you know who *they* were with the garbage that's pumped into your generation these days. Abbas is involved in a plot to kill people, people who could easily include yourself, your father, your fellow students, your friend Alison at the restaurant, any poor bastard who gets in the way when they explode their bombs in Sydney,' Kelsey paced up and down to relieve his feelings. 'You tried to ring him on your mobile, didn't you?'

'Yes.' Walters' reply was sulky and defiant.

'Then it's a bloody good job I rang him at the same time and blocked his line, wasn't it?' Kelsey snapped furiously. 'Otherwise, we'd never have detained him. Now wise up. Can you tell us anything, anything at all, that could give us useful information? That man in there, your so-called friend, who tried to stab you...if you remember...has information that could save hundreds of lives if we can prise it out of him. Now if you know anything for God's Sake give it to us, and no more of this anti-American CIA bullshit!'

*

The interview with Abbas was inconclusive, he refused to say anything, merely looked defiantly at Kelsey and Detective Senior Sergeant Ken Parslow, present as police had been involved in the arrest. Kelsey finally indicated the interview was to be suspended. Parslow switched off the tape and they left Abbas in the room with a constable.

'You have something in mind?' asked Parslow, a thick set man in his mid-thirties. He was fully aware of the security implications regarding Abbas and had left the interrogation to Kelsey, threatening a police officer with a knife was temporarily on the back burner.

'A gamble,' said Kelsey. 'Do we know anything about his parents?'

'Nothing.'

'All right, I've thought of another tack. We must get this young man to open up,' he dialled a number on his mobile. 'Hallo, Mel! I've got a job for you and Denis.'

*

Parslow had just finished a cup of coffee when Kelsey approached him.

'OK!' Kelsey said. 'We're ready to try again. But we have another interview first.'

Parslow ditched the plastic cup in a nearby bin and followed Kelsey to another interview room. Shackleton stood outside it; an Asian man was sitting inside with Melanie Cassidy. He stood as Kelsey and Parslow entered, Kelsey gestured to him to be seated.

'Mr Kamiza?' he asked.

The other nodded. He looked Indian or Pakistani, dark hair turning grey, with a military style moustache. He looked as if he had kept himself fit in the past but was now adding a little weight. He was uneasy and registered concern, but there was no fear or hostility.

'My name is Alan Kelsey,' Kelsey extended his hand to put him at ease. Kamiza rose momentarily and returned the handshake.

'I work for the Australian Government,' continued Kelsey. 'I am concerned with internal security. You have a son named Abbas?'

'Yes, what is wrong? Is my son all right?' Kamiza looked alarmed.

'He has come to no harm, but he *is* in some trouble. We've brought you here because we need your help. We're dealing with a serious matter.'

'Where is my son?'

'In this building, you can see him shortly, but first, we need to talk to you.'

'What is all this about, what has my son done?'

Kelsey sat opposite Kamiza, and rested his elbows on the table. He nodded to Parslow who activated a tape recorder.

'Mr Kamiza, how well do you know your son, what do you know of his activities over the last few months?'

Kamiza frowned.

'Why do you ask?'

'Mr Kamiza, we don't have much time, if you answer my questions with questions of your own, we are wasting more time. Do you understand me?'

Kamiza looked surprised, then nodded.

'Be assured there is relevance in the questions we ask. Afterwards, you can ask as many questions as you like and I will answer them if I can. Agreed?'

Kamiza digested that in silence, then nodded again.

'So I repeat, how well do you know your son?'

Kamiza looked at Kelsey, obviously thinking hard, then leant forward and rested his forearms on the table.

'In recent months he has been very difficult to understand, he is more withdrawn, and we have difficulty communicating,' he said. 'He seems preoccupied and uncommunicative.'

'I see!' said Kelsey. 'Well let me tell you what's been happening.'

He informed Kamiza of recent events and how his son was involved. He skated over Hopetoun, he didn't want to give too much away, nor did he elaborate overmuch on the possible Wynyard aspect, but said enough to indicate national security was at stake.

Throughout Kelsey's oration Kamiza sat in silence, digesting everything. Finally, Kelsey reached the incident at Caringbah Station and pulled no punches, he described the situation exactly as it happened, where Abbas had not only run from and assaulted police, but pulled a knife and tried to stab a fellow university student.

Kelsey finished the saga, then waited. He watched Kamiza as he processed all that Kelsey had imparted. Kamiza finally spoke.

'What do you want me to do?'

'You don't sound surprised,' queried Kelsey.

'Shaken yes! Surprised...no!' Kamiza pressed his fingers together. 'I have been aware of a change in my son's behaviour over the last year, he has, as I said, become withdrawn and uncommunicative. He stopped attending the local mosque, which has upset me and his mother.'

'How long have you been in Australia, Mr Kamiza?'

'Nine years, my papers are in order, I have been fully processed and accepted by Immigration and I have been ...!'

'Hold on! I wasn't inferring anything like that, nor was I questioning your status,' said Kelsey. 'What I really meant was, do you consider this country to be your home?'

'Yes, I do, I've been an Australian citizen for eight years now. I have been fully employed all that time and pay my taxes.'

'You consider yourself an Australian?'

'I do, I have an Australian passport, am proud to be a citizen of this country and loyal to it ...!' a brief smile passed his features: '...except perhaps, when Australia is playing Test cricket against Pakistan!'

'There's one solid argument for deportation,' grunted Parslow which caused laughter all round. From that moment Kelsey decided Kamiza senior was to be trusted.

'That I can understand,' he said with a smile. 'One of my colleagues left England thirty years ago, and still supports the Poms when they tour,' he leant forward and rested his elbows on the table. 'But we are presented here with something much more serious than cricket allegiance. We believe your son is involved with people who mean this country harm, real harm. We need him to talk to us, and believe you may be the best means we have to get him to do that.'

Kamiza shook his head.

'No,' he said. 'I say that, not because I won't, but because I can't and he won't. Over the past year our relationship has deteriorated badly, I cannot talk to him and he won't talk to me. He has become reclusive and feels more strongly about

Islam, outside influences have had an effect on him that are making him fanatical and extreme. I know who's influencing him, but don't know where this person is.'

'Who's that?'

'My wife's brother, Abbas's uncle. He left Pakistan many years ago and went to work in Indonesia and then Taranga. I don't know much about it, but he became involved with a dissident group, a man named Lebak, an insurgent trying to overthrow their government.'

'We know all about Julius Lebak,' said Kelsey. 'An ambitious coup that failed.'

'Her brother escaped and reached Australia, I don't know how, he just turned up.'

'Why does that not surprise me?' said Kelsey. 'I'm sorry, please go on.'

'He came to Australia and saw a lot of us and my son until about a year ago. He holds strict and extreme Islamic views, and persisted in haranguing and trying to influence us, eventually I forbade him the house. All I want to do is work and support my family, but I fear Abbas looked up to him and listened to his views, he may have continued seeing him.'

'Where is your brother-in-law now?'

'I don't know, somewhere in Sydney or New South Wales, I did ask my son a month or so ago but he refused to discuss him or tell me where he was.'

'Damn!' Kelsey said. 'So we're stuck.'

'Not necessarily,' Kamiza said. 'One man may be able to counter this influence, or at least be able to communicate with my son. I am his father and he will not listen to me. Do you have children, Mr Kelsey?'

Kelsey nodded. 'Yes, I do.'

'How old?'

'Teenagers!'

'Then you know what I mean.'

'Yes, I do, they know everything and we know nothing. I understand what you are saying,' said Kelsey. 'But you know somebody who may be able to talk to your son. Who?'

'Our imam from the local mosque. A good man and a true Muslim, he preaches peace and tolerance. When my son began to change, he stopped going to our local mosque, the moderate teachings of this imam were at variance to what I fear my son now believes. His religious and political views have been distorted by his uncle.'

'What about your wife, does she have contact with her brother?'

'No, she is even more opposed to his views. Her brother took her to task for wearing clothes he insisted were inappropriate. She always wears the headscarf, but he believes she should wear the burka and cover her face, she will not. I told him that how we observe our religion and culture is our business, not his! We had many arguments and during this time he insulted my wife, declared she was a whore and that her mode of dress was shaming her family. After this I told him never to come to our house again, and he has not.'

'What is his name, your brother-in-law?'

'Javid Sattar.'

'What? Did you say Javid Sattar?'

'Why yes, do you know…!'

'Er…no…I…was wondering how to spell it.'

Kamiza obliged and Kelsey wrote it down.

'OK! We'll follow that up. Do you have any photographs of Javid Sattar in your house…anywhere?'

'Yes.' Kamiza nodded. 'We have somewhere; you want me to find them?'

'Yes, we'll send someone back with you, but first of all – who's this imam or sheik from your mosque?'

'I will contact him, if you allow it,' said Kamiza. 'I can ring him now. If anyone can instil sense into my son, he can. My son hasn't been to his mosque for many, many months, but he may still be able to exert influence.'

'Then we'll do that,' Kelsey said. 'Do you want to see your son now?'

Kamiza shook his head.

'My presence may have the reverse effect, I will see him after the imam has spoken with him, assuming you agree to contact him.'

'I do,' Kelsey passed his mobile phone across. 'Ring him now.'

Kelsey went outside the room as Kamiza used the phone, he handed Shackleton the note with Javid Sattar's name on it.

'I think we're getting somewhere; this is the guy Gary Phillips mentioned when I saw him at ASIS. Get onto Immigration, check him out. He probably entered Australia from Taranga, maybe illegally, maybe not. Get the police to check him out as well.'

Kelsey was on the phone as Shackleton entered, he finished the conversation and put the phone down.

'That was the police,' he announced. 'They've traced a large purchase of ammonium nitrate from an agricultural dealer near Camden. It's one of many they've investigated, most are genuine, but this was purchased in the name of Marid Jaafar.'

'One of the Agnarat Wen mob?'

'He is. It was bought six months ago; things are slotting into place.'

'Now we have to find it!' said Shackleton. 'But why didn't the agricultural dealer report it? Aren't they supposed to inform authorities about sales of this stuff?'

'They are!' Kelsey said grimly. 'Sometimes they slip up, or else they don't believe anything like the London Underground or Madrid could possibly happen here.'

'I hope the cops sling the book at them.'

'They probably will,' Kelsey eyed the note on his pad. 'But

the horse has bolted! This purchase was probably round about the time they confirmed the lease at Hopetoun.'

'Maybe, they could have made other purchases elsewhere. Anything in the Patchewollock vicinity?' said Shackleton.

'Not yet. I put Roger Preston onto it and told him not to trust bloody Lonsdale!' Kelsey grimaced. 'How is Abbas progressing?'

'He's praying,' remarked Shackleton. 'But I reckon I've seen him before, possibly one of the people entering that house at Cronulla where that four-wheel drive led us.'

'Very likely,' Kelsey nodded. 'But where had he been when we arrested him. Certainly not Cronulla?'

'We could ask the imam to pose that question,' Shackleton suggested as he departed.

An hour later Shackleton poked his head again around Kelsey's door.

'He's here.'

Kelsey arrived at the reception area where a man, formally dressed in a dark suit, sat facing the window. He stood as Kelsey entered. Kelsey was mildly surprised; he had been expecting someone dressed in Arabic robes.

'Alan Kelsey,' said Kelsey.

'Khalil Rafit,' the visitor shook Kelsey's proffered hand.

'Thank you for coming in,' said Kelsey. 'I'd like a quick word with you first, if that's all right with you.'

The other nodded. He was aged mid-forties, dark hair and complexion, about 5'8' tall. He had a trace of beard around his jaw and chin, his eyes were brown and alert. Kelsey eyed him keenly, after expecting to see a man with head-dress and dressed in robes he was still digesting what he was seeing. He realised he was being regarded equally keenly; he smiled and received one in return.

'We have asked you here at the request of Mr Kamiza. You know him?'

'Of course,' replied Rafit.

'We have a problem and he has asked you to assist. He considers he has personal relationship limitations with regard to his son,' Kelsey said. 'You are aware of events of 7th July 2005 on the London Underground system and similar events in Mumbai and Madrid?'

'Regrettably, yes.'

'Good!' Kelsey nodded. 'What I have to tell you is strictly confidential at this stage, and I'll need an undertaking from you.'

'It depends on what it is.'

'We suspect we have a London Underground bombing situation threatened here, possibly at Wynyard Station, we don't know for certain but that's why we are asking for your help.'

'If that is so, I will certainly assist.'

'Thank you!' Kelsey said. 'But what we also need from you is complete discretion. No inkling of this is to leak out, especially to the press. If that happens it would tell the prospective bombers we know their intentions, they may then change plans and targets and leave us completely in the dark.'

'You have my word on that.'

'Well, this is it,' Kelsey related events of the past few weeks. Rafit listened intently and looked grim as Kelsey elaborated on the saga. He nodded occasionally, steepled his hands and drummed the ends of his fingers together.

'So?' he said as Kelsey ended. 'How can I assist?'

'The reason for your presence here is twofold,' said Kelsey. 'The father, Mr Kamiza, is concerned as he believes his son has been corrupted by fanatics. We consider the son could be involved with these events, we don't know for sure. The father requires guidance and requested we contact you. He is here in this building; we asked him to come here in the same capacity we've asked you, for assistance. He is *not* under arrest.'

He paused; the imam inclined his head to show he understood.

'Secondly, we require information about a possible impending attack, nothing is certain but various incidents have indicated this could be planned. We believe the boy's uncle, Javid Sattar, is a major player and the young man knows details of the plan.'

'Javid Sattar?'

'You know him?'

'I do indeed. He has caused us...hmm...many difficulties in the past at the mosque. There was an attempt by an extreme group to seize control and impose alternative interpretations of the Koran. Happily, we prevented it. Yes, I know him.'

'What we need to know is whether there is a proposed attack, we believe there could be, and if so, when, how and where. He won't talk to us and his father considers he won't talk to him either. We need to know. People's lives are at stake.'

'I understand,' said Rafit. 'May I see Mr Kamiza first?'

'By all means. Thank you for being willing to assist us.'

'I frequently travel by train and use Wynyard station myself,' said Khalil. 'As do many members from our mosque. I cannot make any promises, but will do what I can.'

*

Kelsey fretted impatiently as time progressed. The imam had been closeted with Mr Kamiza for about fifteen minutes before he entered the holding room where Abbas Kamiza was seated. Observation was maintained through the glass screen. The imam was warned they would be observed, but not overheard. Kelsey insisted on it and explained in view of Abbas's demeanour and the attempted stabbing of Roy Walters he didn't want another assault on his hands.

The boy's father returned home accompanied by Shackleton and Melanie Cassidy to search for photographs of Javid Sattar. Shackleton was also asked to check for computers and anything else of possible use.

Kelsey also awaited the arrival of Max Walters; they were still holding Roy Walters, sitting in sullen silence, but couldn't hold him much longer. Kelsey had felt like literally kicking him forcibly out of the main door into the street. He was furious, with such serious matters at stake, that anybody could be so gullible as to believe and act on the almost routine anti-American and anti-Australian themes prevalent amongst some of the young, which could have prejudiced the capture and questioning of Abbas.

He still considered Roy Walters might try to warn somebody else, either out of misplaced loyalty or to take a tilt at authority. Despite the stabbing attempt upon himself by Abbas, Roy was still trying hard to justify it. Kelsey had asked Max Walters to come in and collect his son, but wanted words with him before he did.

'Bloody young fool!' Kelsey muttered angrily to Bramble who appeared by his desk. 'Yes Bob, what is it?'

'Just been talking to Geoff Miller,' said Bramble. 'He's been checking Abbas through the glass screen and reckons he looks familiar.'

'What's he mean…familiar?'

'He's been looking at the Identikit picture he had made up, reckons he looks a bit like it, I've had a look too, there is a resemblance.'

'Does he say it's the same man or not?'

'No he doesn't but says there's a similarity.'

Kelsey nearly made another irritable response then stopped to think. A resemblance? Javid Sattar? He was the boy's uncle. Could he have been the man Miller saw whilst incarcerated at the farm? He picked up his phone and dialled Shackleton.

'Shack, found any photographs yet?'

'A few,' was the response. 'Nearly ready to leave here and bring them in. I'll be bringing in the lad's computer too.'

'Good man. Make it snappy.'

Kelsey had a quick conversation with Max Walters when he arrived and explained recent events.

'The young fool tried to warn him,' Kelsey said. 'I made it clear security was involved, but obviously failed to get through. This anti-Americanism in our universities and the young is rife; maybe as they get older, they'll be thankful the Yanks were allies in World War II, they could be in labour camps and talking Japanese now if the Japs had won!'

'I reckon they did,' Walters remarked cynically. 'I've given up counting Japanese cars and consumer goods.'

'Amen to that!' Kelsey replied. 'As for Roy, you can take him home. He's probably shaken up after that knife attack, but still doesn't accept Abbas is a fanatic and a potential jihadist or terrorist. He's convinced Abbas is much maligned and we're all part of a racist plot. He's convinced I'm CIA and therefore the enemy.'

'I'll try and sort him out, we've had arguments about this at home,' Walters said grimly. 'Regrettably I used to believe stuff like this in my young days when I was at uni, mainly Marxism in those days. Surprising how your views change when you buy a home, have a family, run a business and pay off a mortgage.'

'You weren't alone,' Kelsey agreed. 'But please convince him not to warn anyone else he thinks is being persecuted by us and the CIA. If he causes anyone to do a runner or have a change of plan, he could be responsible for deaths of hundreds of people, which could include people he knows or cares about.'

'I realise that,' Max Walters nodded soberly. 'When bombs go off, they kill everyone in range, Marxists, Muslims, Buddhists, Christians, Hindus, white, black, young and old!'

'And ...' Kelsey looked hard at Walters. '...if he remembers and mentions anything relating to Abbas or anyone else who could be involved in this, give us a call immediately.'

*

Kelsey was still occupying Sam Holmes's office and desk when Bramble entered. He shook his head as Bramble eyed him questioningly.

'No joy so far,' he said regretfully. 'The imam is still talking to Abbas, quietly, probably the only way to get through to the stupid bastard. Any joy your end?'

Bramble shook his head.

'McKay's seen comings and goings, but mainly food or cigarette trips. But I did spot someone going in earlier on who looked familiar, just wanted to check it with a mug shot, but it looked like him.'

'Who?'

'Do you remember that trouble about a year ago with that businessman who was kidnapped at Sydney airport when he flew in from Taranga.'

'I remember, Douglas Van Ekeren.'

'That was him. A coup was imminent to topple De Souza and Van Ekeren was mistaken for one of the plotters. They invited him to a coup meeting where they discussed details without realising who he was…or wasn't! When they cottoned on Taranganese ex-pats at this end abducted him from Sydney airport to stop him blowing it to us.'

'I remember,' Kelsey nodded. 'They held him in a house in remote country Victoria until the coup took place, or that was the intention, but Van Ekeren escaped.'

'And they chased him all over Victoria to try and prevent him betraying them.'

'Van Ekeren contacted us, remember?'

'Yes, we sent Dave McKay to bring him in,' Bramble nodded. 'At the time the Taranganese had recruited that professional hit man, Juan Rivera. But I digress, I reckon he was the man I saw.'

'Rivera?' Kelsey sat upright. 'Hells bells! He entered Melbourne last week through Avalon airport, then vanished. Miller said a man named Juan turned up at that Hopetoun farmhouse. He reckoned he was Italian or a Spaniard. That must have been him.'

'Now he could be in Sydney. Didn't Miller say he'd seen red lines intersecting on a Sydney map?'

'Damn!' Kelsey banged his hand on the desk. 'I meant to get Miller to check a map of Sydney, it slipped my mind. Where is he?'

'No idea, I've just got back in.'

'I'll check,' Kelsey dialled a number. 'Send Miller in…where is he? I don't give a …well get him here, now!'

The phone rang again after he put it down.

'Well have you found him? Get him here…oh! Sorry Roger, thought it was someone else. How are things in Victoria?'

Kelsey listened as the earpiece crackled away, Bramble could vaguely hear Preston at the other end.

'They saw frameworks in one of the barns, you say? Hmm… yes, go on.'

He listened intently, gave the occasional 'Hmmph! Yes... then what?' and 'Bloody hell!' Bramble listened to the array of exclamations with curiosity and some amusement.

'You say they noted all this damned gymnastic stuff, ropes and crawling tubes, and one of them uncovered a gun rack in the barn when he dislodged a length of sacking! Ye Gods! Didn't he think it worthy of mention in his report or tell the police?' Kelsey was incredulous. 'Hell and damnation! We deserve to have our installations blown up. First some stupid agricultural merchants in Camden sell enough ammonium nitrate to blow up a battleship and now this! Are people really that bloody careless?'

It appeared they were, Bramble listened with a wry smile at Kelsey's exclamations as Roger Preston described his visit to Jackson & Antrobus.

'Thanks Roger, we'll be in touch. And give that bloody idiot Lonsdale a blast from me will you,' Kelsey put down the phone and looked at Bramble. 'Unbelievable!'

'I assume that was Roger Preston,' said Bramble. 'I also assume the managing agents found items at Walters farm that shouldn't have been there and did bugger all.'

'You're ahead of me,' Kelsey held his head in his hands. 'Didn't a recent Prime Minister utter a mantra during an election campaign about being alert but not alarmed? Well that one fell on deaf ears!'

'I gathered they found a gun rack in one of the barns.'

'With quite sophisticated guns according to one of the real estate staff who wants his bloody arse kicking. They also observed frameworks in the barns they described to Roger as component parts of obstacle equipment, which sounded like the gear Miller filmed with his video camera. In addition, large quantities of fertiliser were present.'

'Well...it is a farm.'

'They're only there for a nine-month lease,' Kelsey's voice rose an octave and nearly cracked on the last syllable. 'Bloody hell! By the time they ploughed the stuff in the ground the lease would have expired and it would be time to move out.'

'Weren't they trying out new equipment, according to Max Walters, or did we get that from the estate agent?'

'There wasn't any new equipment there, certainly no farming equipment. All that was in there were old, rusting items dating from old man Walters' time. All the silly buggers checked on was that the farm facilities were not being prejudiced or damaged.'

Kelsey was still fuming when Miller poked his head around the door.

'Alan?'

'Go with Bob,' commanded Kelsey. 'You've got to look at some mug shots.'

As Miller turned to leave with Bramble, Kelsey called him back.

'Geoff, Bob said you mentioned something about Abbas, what was it?'

'Abbas?' Miller looked puzzled. 'No, I...yes! That's right I did. I just said he looked familiar, odd moments when I looked at him and then it passed.'

'Well, think about this. Could his appearance, or his features, look like that boss man or anyone else at Walters' farm?'

Miller scratched his head thoughtfully.

'It could be, now you mention it. I'd been trying to work it out, it was like trying to capture last night's dream, you get near and it goes. Yet now I think specifically of Boss Man at the farm, yes...could be.'

'Lock onto Shackleton when he gets back, he's got

photographs from Mr Kamiza that relate to Javid Sattar. Can you arrange for that, Bob?'

'Will do!' Bramble headed for the door. 'He's due in shortly.'

They were halfway out when Kelsey called Miller back yet again.

'Map!' he said. 'Sydney …have you had a look at that central map of Sydney?'

'I was about to when you sent for me,' said Miller. 'Which do you want me to do first?'

'Look at the map, until Shack arrives with those photographs and then give them priority. The photos shouldn't take long anyway. Case of yes, it is or no it isn't!'

Miller still hovered by the door.

'You have another question?'

'Well…' Miller hesitated. 'Just a thought. How long do you want me here?'

'How long indeed?' Kelsey considered. 'Yes — sorry, you have a right to ask, you've got a job to do. But I'll be blunt, we want you here as long as you are of use to us. For the present, you're needed. We need you to identify that man, and this man Juan you saw briefly. We need you in the field, purely for recognition purposes, we haven't caught all those bastards from the Walters farm yet.'

He swung his chair around and faced Miller.

'You may lock onto them more quickly than the rest of us. Shall I ring Bill Clucas?'

'It would help.'

'OK, I'll do that.'

There was a tap on the door, the imam stood on the threshold. Kelsey waved him to a chair. Rafit smiled but shook his head.

'I can't tell you much, but am making headway. The boy's father was right about the uncle. Abbas is considerably under his influence and admires him. He's been schooling him in texts from the Koran that deal with killing non-believers and exacting vengeance.'

'Vengeance? On whom?'

The imam spread out his hands.

'Vengeance on anyone who doesn't believe as he does. He's a very confused and aggressive young man.'

'The Koran isn't alone with texts like that,' Kelsey said grimly. 'The Bible has similar passages; fanatics took them literally which resulted in the Crusades. Splinter groups take various texts out of context and apply them rigidly.'

'Agreed. But with him this has become obsessive. I had difficulty getting him to open up at all. But he did say one thing, that within three days we shall strike.'

'Three days,' Kelsey mused. 'Three days...that was all he said?'

'So far, yes. I need more time with him. This could be significant to you, so I have called a temporary halt, but will go back to him.'

'Good, thank you,' Kelsey sighed. 'Can we offer you any refreshment?'

'I'd appreciate green tea if you have it,' Rafit smiled. 'Then I'll see him again.'

*

'What's the latest on comings and goings at Cronulla?' asked Burton. 'Do we still have surveillance there?'

'We do, Bramble has just replaced McKay, who'll be in shortly.'

'You say Abbas stated there will be 'retribution' in three days. We have a presidential visit taking place, is that connected?'

'I fear so,' Kelsey said grimly. 'Miller said as much when we let him out of jail. He heard something to that effect in the same time slot when he was at Walters' farm.'

'Keep me posted,' Burton said and rang off.

*

McKay was waiting for Kelsey when he returned.

'Anything?' Kelsey asked tersely.

'Yes, we logged three men who arrived on foot at the house at 3.30 pm, they all toted backpacks, standard for university students these days.'

'Backpacks and all walking?' Kelsey mused. 'Where would they have been?'

'Possibly the main shopping centre in Cronulla, it's not far away. Maybe they were buying groceries again.'

'And maybe not ...if they were walking, and didn't take a cab, they hadn't come far. Perhaps from a bus stop?'

'Possible, not sure about any bus services around there, but the suburb centre is within spitting distance.'

'What time of day did you say?'

McKay consulted his notebook.

'3.26 in the afternoon.'

'That was shortly after we arrested Abbas Kamiza outside Caringbah station,' Kelsey sat back. 'Hang on! They could have come from Cronulla railway station, from the same train as Abbas Kamiza, if they got off a train about that time.' Kelsey leapt to his feet 'Christ! Abbas was carrying a bloody backpack as well! Remember the CCTV footage the Brits isolated after the London Underground bombing?'

'Yes I do. Cameras picked up those four bombers at a railway station boarding a London train, all carrying backpacks.'

'It was Luton. They caught a train from there and headed for London! It looked so commonplace and mundane, but they killed over 50 people. We've got to move fast, Dave. They've just carried out a rehearsal!'

'That's him.' Miller perused photographs Shackleton had obtained from the Kamiza household. 'I'm fairly sure, shortly after my interview I was king hit, but yes...yes!' He picked up another full-face photograph and added: 'That *is* him! Yes, I'm sure now, it's him.'

Miller was in a conference room with Shackleton, Kelsey, David McKay. Melanie Cassidy was a late arrival, and attracted considerable comment and repartee because of a very brightly coloured and jazzy shirt she was wearing, to which she responded in kind.

Bramble was stationed at the police observation post opposite the house in Cronulla. Kelsey had convened the session after a lengthy phone call to Burton in Canberra, who in turn had had equally long phone consultations with the New South Wales Police Authority and railways. Burton had requested access to surveillance tapes at the Wynyard Station complex and Cronulla, the police were chasing up the tapes.

'What can Immigration tell us of Javid Sattar?' Kelsey asked Shackleton.

'Nothing yet: they're still looking.'

'Call them again and wake the buggers up. We need to see Mr Kamiza again,' said Kelsey. 'He may know something.'

'He's here, he came back with us,' said Melanie.

'Good… ask him about Javid Sattar; when did he arrive here, how and by what means? Was it by air or a damned fishing boat?'

Melanie departed.

'Geoff, have you checked that map of central Sydney?'

'Yes,' Miller answered. 'I had a couple of glimpses of the one at the farm, the second time after being slugged from behind. But recalling the map in relation to Wynyard Station, which was clearly marked, I'd say it's in the vicinity of Bligh Street.'

'Where there are large and prestigious hotels. Where is the Taranganese President staying?' Kelsey looked around, nobody ventured to answer.

'We have to find out. I'll leave that to you, Dave.'

'What's happening about Cronulla?' asked Shackleton.

'We're going to move in with the New South Wales Police,' said Kelsey. 'I've had words with Francis, in view of what we now believe to be true we can't delay much longer. If this was a rehearsal, they are nearly ready to go.'

'When's the raid scheduled?'

'Tomorrow morning, small hours. If anyone comes out, we'll wait until they're clear then jump them. In the meantime, with the possibility of explosives in the area we'll clear nearby houses of occupants as unobtrusively as possible. The police can use the excuse of a gas leak.' He turned as Melanie returned from the other interview room.' Yes, Mel?'

'He doesn't know a great deal, Sattar just arrived out of the blue. He told him he'd arrived by air from Taranga, which Kamiza never bothered to check, he had no reason to and probably didn't care. He could have got here by rowing boat as far as he knows.'

'Maybe he did, like many others,' Kelsey commented. 'We'll have to wait for Immigration,' he turned to Shackleton. 'Did you find a computer at the Kamiza household?'

'Yes. Marcus Templeton is checking it.'

'Tell him to hurry up. What else did you find, Mel?'

'I obtained details of university clubs earlier today,' said Melanie. 'The usual left wing sprinkling of Marxists, Labor, Greens, Students Union and an active group pushing for unlimited immigration, plus a Liberal Club.'

'Marxists?' queried Kelsey. 'Is anyone still pushing that bandwagon?'

'Quite a few, presumably people who never lived under the type of regime they are advocating and are never likely to.'

'Like Karl Marx himself,' grunted Kelsey. 'How many names have we got?'

'Hundreds,' said Melanie. 'Walters is in most of them; except the Liberal club.'

'No surprise,' said Kelsey. 'How does he find time to do any studying. Max isn't too happy about Roy's leanings at present, but feels it's best to let Roy work things out. The question is, how much leeway do you give a prat like that?'

He jumped as his phone rang.

'Damn! Can you answer that, Mel?'

Melanie picked up the phone.

'Put him through,' she turned to Kelsey. 'Speak of the devil, it's Max Walters.'

'Right, I'll take it...hallo Max.'

Melanie could hear Max Walters' voice at the other end but

couldn't make out the words. Kelsey listened intently, nodded occasionally and uttered the occasional 'Aye', 'what?' and 'OK', followed by: 'What did she do then?' There was more from the other end over several minutes. Kelsey wrote on his pad then rang off.

'Mel, is there an Alison Furnell on any of those lists?'

He reached over to pour himself a tumbler of water from the water jug on his cabinet. Melanie perused the various lists and nodded.

'Here she is,' she handed Kelsey a couple of lists. 'She's in the Labor club, Students Union...but most of them are in those. Anti-discrimination, Immigration for All, and the Multicultural Club, in short...the 'Be nice to everyone' clubs!'

'She is, or was, also Roy Walters' girl-friend.'

'She'd be the receptionist in the restaurant. What do you mean? Was his girl-friend?' Melanie asked.

'Max Walters said she came to the house tonight, late afternoon anyway, not an unusual occurrence. They were in Roy's room but suddenly there was a huge altercation with raised voices, Max described it as a screaming match. Initially Max was alarmed; he was up the stairs three at a time, thinking it was a physical or sexual altercation, but heard some of the words being exchanged whilst still on the landing.'

'What was it about?' asked Melanie.

'Max heard Alison shouting something on the lines of 'You shouldn't warn them, you should tell your father or those people who came to the restaurant. If *you* don't tell them then I will!' Max beat a hasty retreat when he heard footsteps approaching the door, but the altercation continued after she'd opened it. Max had reached the hall by the time she flounced down the stairs.'

'Did he find what it was about?'

'Max asked if anything was wrong, probably the understatement of the year. Roy was chasing after her, but Max said she reached the front door, let herself out and departed at a fast rate of knots.'

'She didn't tell Max what it was?'

'No, she'd gone, and neither did Roy. He followed her out and to date hasn't returned. But Max was concerned because of what he did hear, references to us, knowing the direction of Roy's loyalties, and that Alison was obviously alarmed by something he intended to do. Max said Roy is still making excuses for Abbas, convinced he's a compassionate, oppressed young innocent being hounded by reactionary forces and the CIA. There could be something here for us.'

'Do we know how to find her?'

'Max supplied her mobile number and address; he found them in an address book in Roy's bedroom. Roy is involved with something with which she plainly disagrees. We need to contact her tonight if possible, bring her in for interview and find out what it is.'

Melanie picked up the note from Kelsey's desk.

'I'll go and find her,' she said.

Kelsey waved his hands in acquiescence as Melanie departed and turned to Shackleton and McKay.

'Go to Max Walters' house and pick up Roy, if he's there. He knows something, or someone, and still believes they are being hounded by the CIA as part of a sinister Right-Wing plot. Max said he'd gone out, but he may have returned. I'll get onto Marcus Templeton see if he can track his mobile phone.'

Melanie was subject to conflicting emotions as she commenced her quest to contact Alison, wondering if she had been wise to volunteer. Her reaction at their previous meeting still disturbed her. Since her indiscreet sapphic affair with her neighbour, Melanie had had several similar relationships, being highly sexed and naturally promiscuous, but none were permanent. The liaison with Isabel, her neighbour, had evolved because they lived in the same block of units, her marriage was not the best either and she obviously had tendencies similar to Melanie. Her husband was away a lot, her sex life had been sparse and one thing led to another.

Melanie called at the restaurant first but neither Alison nor Roy was working that evening. She phoned Alison's mobile and Alison answered immediately, she angrily barked: 'Hallo! What do *you* want?' before Melanie had a chance to say anything, obviously assuming it was Roy.

'Alison?'

'Oh! Who's this?'

'Melanie Cassidy, we met at the restaurant. You supplied us with coffee.'

'Oh...I remember. I'm sorry. I thought it was someone else.'

'How did I guess?' Melanie said cynically. 'Alison, I must see you, where are you?'

'I don't want to see anybody!'

'Are you at home?' Melanie ignored the statement.

'I'm busy,' she replied after a brief silence.

'So am I, my boss and I need to see you again. Where do you live?'

There was another slight delay and Melanie feared she was going to hang up, then the information came.

'Benton Street? I know it,' replied Melanie. 'I'm just around the corner, a matter of minutes.'

'Very well,' was the eventual reluctant concession. 'I'm in the top flat.'

It took Melanie nearly twenty minutes to reach it, strictly speaking she hadn't been 'just round the corner'. She parked under a street light outside and rang the bell marked: 'A. Furnell'. Alison's voice came over a speaker, Melanie announced herself and the front door clicked open. Before she mounted the stairs, she ensured the front door had locked behind her. There had been too many cases where astute intruders gained access to residential apartment blocks before an entry door closed behind legitimate visitors.

Alison admitted her, more welcoming than she'd been on the phone, giving Melanie a brief smile. She was wearing a tight mini skirt and an equally tight, red nylon top, with the word "Swans", the local football team, in large white lettering emblazoned across the front. It also possessed a low neckline which Melanie could not fail to register. She must have dressed anticipating or hoping for an intimate night with Roy, now disrupted by their recent violent altercation.

'Nice to see you again, what is it?'

'Nice to see you too,' Melanie took her eyes off her with an effort. 'You support the Swans do you?'

'Why do you say that?'

'Well I...Just a guess!' Melanie said ruefully which broke the ice and Alison smiled. 'You live here alone?'

'No, I share with another girl, she's away at present. My home is in Albury. What is this?'

'This isn't entirely a social call.'

'No, you're FBI aren't you...sorry, I mean ASIO.'

'Same thing, different acronym,' Melanie ruminated that FBI made a change from CIA, and being counter intelligence was nearer the mark. 'We want to speak to you about Roy. My colleague Alan wants to talk to you, can you come with me to our offices, it's very important.'

'I thought that was on the cards. You mean now, at this time of day?'

'It would be advisable, we need to talk with you, but this may also be for your own protection…sorry if I sound melodramatic.'

'Protection? How? Who from?'

'Trust me please, I know what I'm saying.'

'Are you arresting me?'

'No! We have no reason to,' Melanie shook her head. 'But we know you had a violent argument with Roy about something he intended to do. You felt sufficiently strongly about it to leave his house in a huff. We have an idea what it was about. You were heard to say if *he* didn't tell the authorities, about the intentions and plans of people you both knew, *you* would. If Roy has contacted them, and we think he has, it's likely he'll mention your intention to inform on them.'

'You know about me and Roy? How? Oh! Mr. Walters told you.'

'Yes, he knows what's at stake here. We've taken him into our confidence. That's why he contacted us. What was your argument with Roy about?'

'Things.'

'What things, please answer and don't be evasive, this could be important.'

'It's about a society we belong to.'

'And?'

'Roy says they're planning to do something, it involves Wynyard Station, something about creating a diversion to divert attention from something else they intend to do, he said they were going to put matters right.'

'What matters?'

'I think it's to do with Taranga. He said they were righting a wrong and it would be soon. What's all this about?'

'I'd sooner Alan told you. Have you reported this to anyone?'

'No, I didn't know what to do, I'm still…maybe I should.'

'That's why I'm here, we are the people you should tell. Please...come with me, you could be in danger if you stay here.'

'How can I be in danger?'

'Because this affects Australia's security, it could now affect yours. We've already had an attempted stabbing today connected with this, we don't want another,' Melanie decided to give her facts. She explained that if Roy had contacted his friends in Cronulla, they could consider silencing anyone they thought could betray their intentions, Abbas had already illustrated that. Alison went pale.

'They'll what?'

'I think you heard me and know what I'm talking about. I'm serious.'

Alison stared at Melanie.

'You know something is going to happen, roughly when and where and who's going to do it, don't you?' said Melanie.

'I...I...yes, of a sort,' Alison said hesitantly. 'I know they're organising something to happen soon and some of the people involved, but I'm not sure what, I'm only on the outer fringes. I told Roy I didn't like the sound of it, something to cause disruption could be dangerous and cause damage. I've told him it's wrong, he should either tell them to forget it, or warn the authorities, and if he didn't I would. It's to attract attention to one of our causes, refugees, and to cause distraction and disruption, a demonstration...!'

'You're half right, but it's more than that,' said Melanie. 'You've heard of 7/7 have you? The bomb attacks in London?'

'What?' Are you saying ...?'

Yes.'

Alison hesitated briefly then reached for her shoulder bag.

'Oh God! I never thought...! Alright, I'll come.'

Melanie experienced a flow of relief. They left the apartment and Alison locked up. They descended the stairs but as they reached the ground floor hallway, Melanie laid a restraining hand on Alison's shoulder.

'Wait,' she said. 'I'll look outside first!'

Alison acquiesced; uneasy now. Melanie extracted a capsicum spray from her bag and held it firmly in her left hand as she opened the door.

'Dammit!' she thought. 'I've even put the wind up myself now!'

Yet within minutes her reticence and precautions were justified. Melanie's car was parked, illegally, with the driver's door adjacent to the pavement. As they approached it, she unlocked the doors remotely, opened the driver's door and inserted the key in the ignition. At this point a car drove up fast, parked in a vacant spot some distance behind and three men emerged. They had opened the front gate of the apartment block and entered it, when one of them looked back and spotted Melanie and Alison under the streetlight roughly twenty metres away, about to enter Melanie's car.

The streetlight overhead showed them both up in sharp relief, he stopped in his tracks, shouted something in a foreign tongue, the others swung round and Melanie saw a flash of what appeared to be a knife blade

She needed no translation. She yanked open the rear door, bundled Alison onto the back seat and slammed the door. The foremost man ran towards them, but she used the capsicum spray and he stumbled back cursing and holding his eyes. She flung herself into the driver's seat, hurled the capsicum into the passenger well, seized the ignition key and turned it. The engine fired immediately and the car took off like a drag racer, the driver's door still open. Luckily the road was devoid of traffic.

Two other men had rushed for the car, one on each side. The

rear left side attacker managed to open the rear passenger door but such was the speed of Melanie's departure the attempted intruder was left sprawling. The other failed to make any purchase at all, the knife in his hand scarred the inside panel of the open driver's door and fell into the seat well at Melanie's feet. He too landed heavily in the road in their wake.

'Shut that door!' Melanie shouted as she slammed her own, Alison pulled it to.

'What do we do now?'

'Just hold on!' Melanie shouted as she accelerated. 'We've got to lose them.'

She had to halt before turning right at the intersection, uncomfortably aware their attackers were already in pursuit, they gained but lost ground after Melanie pulled out as they had to allow a truck to pass. Melanie couldn't phone for assistance as she had to concentrate on evading the car behind, if Alison had a mobile phone she was best placed to call "000".

'Ring Treble "0"' Melanie shouted as she put her foot down.

'My phone's still in the flat, it was charging.'

'Damn!' Melanie's phone was in her bag on the floor on the passenger side so she couldn't get at it nor could Alison from the back seat.

Melanie raced through the streets, why was it when she wanted to be picked up for speeding there wasn't a police car in sight? Then her heart went cold as a second car tried to cut her off, two vehicles were chasing them. She swung to the left, made a sudden brake and turn, scorched round an island and made off to the right. Their pursuers lost ground but followed, Melanie knew it was only a matter of time before they caught up.

She outran them for ten minutes, was nearly run off the road, managed to evade disaster, overtook a truck on the inside, caught up with another and overtook it on the other side. As she did so the second vehicle cut in ahead of them but she spotted a notice ahead on the left indicating a nearby entrance to a drive-in cinema. This meant people, which also meant, hopefully, sanctuary. She cut in front of another truck, turned left and drove up the access road, to be confronted by four kiosks, each with three or four cars in a queue waiting to enter. Melanie had no time for niceties, she cut in front of a Toyota as it eased up behind a stationery car awaiting its turn. It jammed on its brakes as Melanie scraped in front of it, ignoring the horn blaring and angry shouts.

'Pay the man,' she shouted as she reached the kiosk and Alison opened her window.

'What's the hurry?' shouted the kiosk man but Melanie merely gave an embarrassed wave, ignored the shouting from behind, snatched the tickets and drove into the complex.

She had no illusions they had permanently evaded their pursuers, she switched off the lights, headed for the far side, found a vacant parking spot, parked between a white sedan and a van with about four young people and switched off. The neighbouring van's back door was open, teenagers were clambering into the van's rear that seemed liberally endowed with mattresses, then pulled the door shut.

'How can they see the film from there?' Alison asked from the back.

'They can't, their object is group sex, away from prying parents,' said Melanie. 'Those vans are called Bonking Chariots or Sin Bins! Any sign of those bastards?'

'Not yet.'

'Keep your eyes peeled, they won't give up.'

'Why are they after us?'

'Because they have terrorism in mind and, thanks to Roy, they think you know too much of their intentions.'

'But what do I know?'

'What Roy has told you, Alison. He put you in danger by telling them what he'd told you...that they intend to do something drastic to advance their cause and when.'

They waited in trepidation for nearly ten minutes, nothing untoward happened. By now the drive-in was filling up, the entrance still busy with cars streaming in. Then all the lights dimmed, the screen lit up and a stream of advertisements began to play. Melanie spotted distant movement behind them in the mirror, shadows moving around on foot, and the occasional flash of torches.

'They're checking round the cars to locate us, now it's dark they're using torches.'

'What about security, won't they stop them?'

'They're probably not doing anything wrong...yet...hold on, I'll call it in.' Melanie reached for her bag and opened up her phone.

'*Battery flat.*'

'Shit!' she exclaimed. 'We're stuck.'

'Can't we drive off?'

'If we do that, it will tell them where and who we are, the exit gate will be shut and they'll catch up with us there.'

'We could get out on foot,' suggested Alison.

But this immediately proved impracticable. Melanie spotted more torchlights ahead of them, the second car must have parked at the other end of the cinema. If they ran from one group, they'd run into another, walking around would be asking for trouble.

She looked to the right. The Sin Bin van next door was starting to move on its springs, the teen occupants were commencing activities. Similarly, the occupants of the sedan on their other side, a youth and a young girl, had vacated the front seats and entered the rear.

This gave Melanie an inspiration. She picked up the capsicum spray, got out of the car, hooked the speaker onto the front window, clambered into the rear seat with Alison and locked the doors with the remote control.

'We've got to merge in.'

'Merge in?'

'Behave like the hoi polloi,' snapped Melanie. 'Like those kids in the Sin Bin and that car next door. They've come here for is sex. That van is a bonking chariot.'

'I don't quite…Oh!'

'If we behave like the others, we may get out of here alive. They only caught a brief glimpse of us, but your Swans 'T' shirt really would have stood out under that street light,' snapped Melanie. 'I've locked all the doors, but get that damned 'T' shirt off and stuff it under the front seat.'

'What?'

'Don't argue…do it.! That Swans logo stands out and will give us both away.'

Alison hesitated, then appreciated the logic. She stripped it off and pushed it under the front seat, then turned to Melanie.

'So will your jazzy top? That would have stood out like a beacon as well under that street lamp. They'd recognise that again.'

'Hell!' Melanie looked down at her shirt and could only agree. 'You're right.'

She undid the shirt buttons, removed it and also pushed it under the front seat.

'Now pull your skirt up to your hips.'

'What!'

'Just do it. They'll be looking for two petrified women probably sitting in the front seats,' snapped Melanie. 'If they spot us canoodling in the back seat, like teenagers, we may pass muster.'

'Oh!' Alison caught on and hitched up her skirt, although being a mini it didn't have far to go. Melanie did the same and peered through the rear window, the searchers were close, two or three cars away. A glance through the windscreen indicated the frontal assault squad was also nearby. Alison had drawn up her skirt so she was exposed to her hips. A light flashed outside, only two cars away. Melanie pulled Alison towards her, wrapped her arms around her and tilted her head back.

'We've got to make this good,' she said,' Kiss me and look as if you mean it. '

'But won't they see we're two women?' protested Alison.

'Maybe, maybe not, but teenagers, gays and lesbians all want privacy, from parents and society. That's one reason they come to drive-ins. Now do it, our lives could depend on it.'

Melanie moved over to Alison and clasped her to her. Despite her tension and fear of what was outside, she experienced a thrill as she did. They were in a tight embrace when a shadow appeared outside, a light flashed onto the side of the combo van, then onto and into their car. Melanie suspended the kiss and managed to look indignant, as would any interrupted lover. The light played across them, paused, then passed on to the neighbouring sedan, but another shadow, waving a flashlight, appeared on the other side of their car. She felt Alison wriggle beside her, so Melanie turned and kissed her again. When the newcomer's light also played across the front seat and then the rear, for good measure she ran her hand over Alison's legs and thighs and hoped this would register with the outside observer.

The torchlight flickered over them, hesitated then moved on. Alison and Melanie stayed as they were as the two shadows moved away. Melanie watched them go and hastily removed her hand.

'I think we're safe for now,' she said.

'But they'll know we're around here somewhere,' said Alison. 'We'd better stay as we are, if we're fully dressed when they come back that'll be a giveaway. There may be more of them checking around.'

She was right, there were more flickering torchlights and another shadowy figure briefly examined the sin bin next door before moving across to illuminate their own front seats.

'We'll need to...er...get close again...' Melanie faltered, she found it difficult to put it into words but Alison was ahead of her.

'If it saves our lives, let's do it,' she said.

Melanie hesitated, surprisingly she experienced some embarrassment, but realised Alison's comment was relevant. If they were in a drive-in for sex, they would have to *look* as if they were. These men meant business, the recent knife attack and the wayward knife under the driver's seat proved that.

She smiled ruefully, ironically sex *was* the best alibi? She pulled Alison towards her, they hastily embraced again as the torch light flickered from the front seat to the back. Melanie felt an acute rush of adrenalin as the light lingered longer this time, it seemed an eternity before the figure moved away.

'We passed muster,' she said consolingly. 'Maybe we can leave soon.'

'We can't, we'll have to wait until the film finishes,' said Alison. 'If we leave prematurely, it'll give us away, they'll be onto us and in any case the gates will still be shut to stop gatecrashers so we can't get out We have to leave when everyone else does, merge in with the crowd.'

'That means we could be here for another two hours,' objected Melanie.

'Not much we can do about it,' said Alison.

There was more movement outside and more flashes of torchlight. Alison moved up and hugged Melanie, stretched up, kissed her and ran her hand over Melanie's bare midriff.

'There's another one out there, we'll have to put on a show.'

That was the point when all Melanie's reservations and inhibitions evaporated, despite the severity of the situation her frustrated sex drive took over. The proximity of this young woman, nearly naked, together with the effect on her of intimacies already enacted, was too much. She seized her roughly and kissed her, she half-anticipated resistance and to be pushed away, but after a brief hesitation, Alison acquiesced. The torchlight wavered and passed on.

*

'Marcus, any joy with Abbas's computer yet?'

'No, nothing, chief. It's password protected, I'm trying for a back door but I'm making headway.'

'Let me know when you find anything.' Kelsey put down the phone and turned to Shackleton.

'That was Marcus Templeton. You've brought Roy Walters in?'

'He wasn't there but I collected his lap top, Max Walters was most helpful. Marcus is arranging a trace on Roy's mobile phone.'

'What about Mel, has she brought that young woman in yet?'

'Not yet, we haven't heard from her. We're trying to make contact.'

'She was to pick her up from her apartment, maybe she wasn't there,' Kelsey pondered then shrugged. 'Keep trying, not like her to be out of contact. When they get here put the girl in an interview room and arrange for coffee to be taken in, I don't want her antagonized or frightened. Tell Mel to treat her with kid gloves until I get there.'

*

After further torchlight investigations by shadowy figures, Melanie had been startled by Alison's responses as they cohabited on the rear seat. Alison seemed to be developing her own agenda, which alleviated any guilt engendered by Melanie about being a seducer, at least for now. They were almost oblivious to the outside world when the interior was flooded with light, which caused them considerable alarm.

Melanie peered through the rear window. A car well behind and away to one side of them had switched on its headlights, bathing the area in light and causing the movie picture on the screen to fade. She heard a car horn sounding, and through the steamed up side and rear windows could just make out activity well away to the left as running figures, many bearing torches, made for the headlights. They heard shouting.

'What is it?' Alison asked.

'I think security has woken up, our friends must have overstepped the mark. Someone's raised the alarm.'

'What should we do?'

'Stay as we are,' responded Melanie. 'The same applies as before, we can't do anything, and the exit gate may still be closed. We're safe here for now, and anonymous, if we try to move Security may jump on us as suspects.'

The activity persisted, men with torches, this time security, milled around, the headlights were eventually switched off and patrons were able to concentrate again on the film, or whatever else they had been doing.

'What should we do now?'

'Wait for at least another hour. What do you suggest?'

When they did finally leave, they joined the queue of cars slowly crawling out. Security guards were superintending the line of vehicles and there was a police presence. Melanie wound down the window.

'What was all the excitement?' she asked.

'Some nutters tried to break into a car holding two women, a young woman was slashed on her arm.'

'God! Is she all right?'

'Paramedics dealt with her; she seemed OK. They're taking her to hospital.'

'Who did it?'

'We don't know yet, the police are investigating.'

'It sounds as if someone was mistaken for you,' Melanie turned to Alison as they drove out. 'We were damned lucky.'

They left the drive-in, without any signs of pursuit, after leaving their details as possible witnesses. Melanie plugged in her phone to charge it during the journey. She reported in, gave a quick synopsis and mentioned the stabbing incident before her phone gave out again.

That was the only conversation that took place, Melanie and Alison didn't speak again until they reached the ASIO underground car park and Melanie slotted into a parking space. There was an awkward silence, Melanie's mind was racing, as it had been since they left the drive-in. She stared at the wall in front of the car and dared not look at Alison.

Possible consequences of the last three hours dominated her thoughts. She had been dispatched to bring in a young woman to headquarters, a member of the public, for questioning as a witness and/or for her protection. Whilst so doing she had sexually compromised her.

If this escapade ever became common knowledge, it could instigate an enquiry hosted by bureaucrats. Whatever justification she pleaded, even fear for their lives, her days as an ASIO operative could be over. Bureaucrats who rarely left their desks, and unaware of tensions encountered in the security field, would treat her explanation with scorn and disbelief, judge her reaction and actions beyond the pale and likely sling the book at her. This would be devastating as she loved her job. Further, with an incident such as this on her CV she could find herself unemployable, even in these enlightened days. In addition, although circumstances had justified it, Melanie knew in her heart, she was not guiltless. As the situation had developed, her own sapphic desires and leanings had taken over and dictated her behaviour and reactions. She knew a 'Guilty' verdict would have some justification

After what seemed an eternity gazing at the wall before her, she fearfully cast a sidelong glance at Alison. Since leaving Alison's apartment, this was the first time they had been in any sort of definitive light and able to communicate visually. Alison's eyes met hers levelly, then...to Melanie's overwhelming surprise and relief...she smiled.

'Are you...are you...all right?' Melanie asked tentatively.

'Yes...why?'

'Because...well...that should never have...I don't know what...I'm really sorry...!'

'Don't be, I'm not about to complain.'

Melanie found herself struggling for words, but finally asked the question.

'Have you...have you...ever done...considered...anything like that before?'

'No, never. But you have, haven't you?'

'I...well...yes. What made you say that?'

'It didn't take much to work that out,' commented Alison. 'We've met a couple of times now and I had a feeling...about you. The way you looked at me in the restaurant, I caught you several times, you looked at me the same way a lot of men do.'

'God! Was I that obvious?'

'To me you were, but I didn't mind, it was nice to be regarded as a sex object by someone...anyone! Anyway, I liked you.'

'I don't follow, what about Roy?'

'Don't talk to me about bloody Roy, I'm finished with him, he's a prat.'

'I wouldn't argue with that,' commented Melanie.

'We've been going steady for months, but he treats me like an ornament to take around with him while he traipses around to political meetings, pursues idealistic causes and discusses policy with his firebrand friends...and Heaven knows what else after what you've just told me. I'm his girl-friend, more fool me, I thought it was the thing to do to be loyal and accept things, but I've had enough. I don't claim to be promiscuous but I've had no sex or anything approaching it for months...in fact...ever! He pays me so little attention at those meetings that Doug Fenway, another student, has taken me home more than once.'

'But your mode of dress tonight was...is enough to turn any young buck's head! It certainly turned mine.'

'I'm dressing more and more provocatively these days, to spark some reaction from Roy, fat chance!'

'Even dressed like that?'

'Nothing,' Alison said bitterly. 'I got more from you than I ever get from him.'

'Yes, I'm sorry,' said Melanie.

'Don't be. When you phoned and said you were calling, I wondered if by seeing you I was tempting Providence.'

'You mean you thought something...?'

'I had nothing in mind,' Alison shook her head. 'Nothing like what happened, although I did think it would be nice to be looked at appreciatively by somebody...anybody.'

'Well, it worked. When we were at the restaurant Alan, my colleague, gave you the once over many times.'

'I know, I saw that. I liked him too,' said Alison. 'But I'm not sorry we had this romp, affair, frolic, caper, call it what you will. I guess I finally snapped in that drive-in, I'm tired of a life of celibacy, it's like being a nun.'

'You didn't behave like one tonight!'

'Maybe, who knows what goes on in those nunneries? But I've had nothing from Roy, while Doug Fenway is frightened to touch me, probably thinks it would be disloyal to Roy,' Alison said with exasperation. 'And if you're feeling guilty...don't! It takes two to tango, it was a one off, we both know that, but once we started, I couldn't stop myself. In any case that girl being stabbed proved you were right...they *were* after me. What gave you the idea...the sex I mean?'

'That sin bin alongside,' explained Melanie. 'Drive-ins have a reputation for romps like that, if we did the same, we'd merge in, it could be an alibi, and was.'

'That's one word for it,' commented Alison.

'Yes, leave it at that,' said Melanie. 'It saved our lives, but we'll keep this off the record. Strictly between us ...OK?'

'I'll say nothing,' Alison said. 'Let's say it never happened.'

'But it did, I hope you benefit from it,' Melanie commented. 'Get a decent man instead of that prat Roy.'

'I intend to,' Alison replied, then added. 'Anyway, it's been an eventful night.'

'Not really, in our line of business it happens all the time,' was Melanie's response which caused them both much amusement as they walked to the lifts. 'We'd better get moving, Alan will be getting worried.'

*

As the lift bore them upwards Melanie fixated on Alison's "T" shirt.

"Your "T" shirt, it's inside out.'

'What…oh bloody hell.!'

When they reached the fifth floor Alison was still replacing her top, pulling it down from under her armpits when the doors opened to reveal Bramble, delegated by Kelsey to ascertain details of the stabbing incident phoned in by Melanie. He stood in the corridor waiting to enter, and eyed the blushing Alison as she finished re-adjusting her top before he switched his gaze to Melanie.

'Hi Mel, hear you've been having problems,' he stood aside to allow them to exit but his eyes narrowed as he surveyed them closely and stepped into the lift. 'Did you enjoy the movie?'

'We didn't see much of it,' confessed Melanie. 'There was too much going on.'

'I bet there was,' was his response, and as the lift doors were closing, he added. 'Hot night was it, or a hot film?'

Alison eyed Melanie as they headed down the corridor.

'What did he mean by that?' she asked.

'I've given up trying to understand anything Bob Bramble says,' Melanie stretched out her hand for the door knob as they reached their destination. 'He's a devious bastard at the best of times.'

She was about to open the door when Alison seized her arm.

'Your buttons, they're out of kilter.'

'What?' Melanie glanced down. 'Bloody hell!'

As she undid her frontage and re-aligned it, the import of Bramble's parting aside as he left them hit home.

*

Kelsey and the others greeted them with relief, Melanie explained about her mobile, now partially re-charged, and gave a further rundown of the attack outside the apartment and expanded on their evasion of their pursuers by entering the drive-in cinema.

'Bob's gone to see if he can ascertain details about the stabbing!' Kelsey turned to pick up his file from the nearby table. 'If you'd like to go in here...'he indicated an interview room to Alison '...we'll be with you in a minute. You'd better write up what happened, Mel, the police will need it for their incident report.'

*

Two floors below, Bramble arrived in his room and switched on his computer. His mind was working overtime since he had caught sight of Melanie's shirt in its disordered state, with Alison frantically pulling down and re-adjusting her top. What the hell...?

He knew Melanie well as a feisty woman who was not averse to giving and receiving sexual favours, and being an observant type, over time he had concluded there was within her a tendency to be oblivious of gender.

Further, there seemed to be something about those two when he had accosted them, a rapport, exchanges of glances, almost secretive. The witness had been brought in safe and sound but...curious nevertheless! At some time during their journey in, during which they had been delayed and confined together at a drive-in cinema for nearly three two hours, Melanie's shirt had been unbuttoned from top to bottom. Why was that? And that younger woman too, frantically pulling on her "T" shirt that must have been recently removed. He grinned to himself as he reached for his phone to ring the police about the stabbing incident. Maybe he'd keep an eye on Melanie!

CHAPTER 29

Meanwhile Alison was in a ferment. Kelsey didn't enter the room for some time which left Alison to her own devices and thoughts.

During that time, she thought hard, not just about the same sex episode with Melanie but events before and leading up to it. What she had told Melanie was true, Roy treated her as his personal property, an ornament to trail either with or after him, while he pursued political agendas and endeavoured to impress individuals that he very much admired, which she certainly did *not*. Being young, virile and nearly out of her teens, Alison's hormones were active and demanding but with Roy she wasn't getting anywhere, merely a diet of extreme politics, being ignored and taken for granted. She was developing feelings for another student, another member of various organisations, who more than once had taken her home after meetings because Roy was "too busy with on-going policy discussions" to accompany her, saying he'd 'be along later!'

She had now, belatedly, reached the conclusion that a young man who left an attractive and nubile young woman to make her own way home late at night was hardly a desirable prospect. Doug Fenway, who did escort her home, was too shy, too ethical, and too much of a gentleman to do anything behind Roy's back, something Alison now ardently desired.

As for the escapade with Melanie, although Alison could be termed innocent, she wasn't ignorant, she was fully aware people existed with sexual tastes other than hetero. Consequently, when Melanie's eyes had repeatedly swivelled in her direction during her visit to the restaurant, Alison had been cognisant of this and suspected an agenda.

When Melanie had joined her on the rear seat, after the attempted knife assault outside her apartment and the subsequent car chase, Alison's demeanour had been one of fear and panic. Melanie's suggestion, or plan, for an alibi, to look from the outside as lovers taking advantage of the facilities of a drive-in, made sense. After momentary hesitation and misgivings, Alison had acquiesced. Once they had both reached a stage of undress, Alison's fear and panic had been sublimated by an urge for sex. After the attempted attack outside the flat and subsequent car chase, she'd even considered the night may be her last so why not experience life before it ended. Thus, when Melanie had initiated physical contact, it had awoken in Alison an urge to go in boots and all, she craved sexual gratification, it being the lesbian version had been irrelevant.

Her thoughts were interrupted as Kelsey and Melanie entered and sat opposite her, as they did so she again thought of her recent sexual experience and her thoughts turned to Doug Fenway, if only Doug wasn't so shy, considerate and so bloody principled. Many others would have cut across Roy and snapped her up. Doug was too ethical. Now her sexual libido had been aroused she wanted more and determined to do something about it.

Melanie was looking at her which sent adrenalin through her as she recalled the events of the past few hours. They exchanged smiles, clearly the same thoughts were occurring to them both. Alison blushed and looked down into her lap.

Kelsey gave what he thought was a pleasant and friendly smile to instil confidence and received one in response, albeit a tentative one.

'Miss Furnell, my name is Alan Kelsey. May I call you Alison?'

Alison sat twisting her hands nervously. She nodded briefly.

'We've met before briefly and Melanie you already know. Our apologies for dragging you here at such short notice, but we're in the middle of a security crisis and need information. We think you could fill in a few blanks.'

'What do you want, Mr Kelsey?'

'My name is Alan. I stress you're not being held here, you're not under any form of arrest. You can leave anytime, when you do Melanie will take you home.'

He momentarily looked down at the file before him and missed the glances and rueful smiles exchanged between the two women. When he looked up again the moment was over.

'We need information you may possess, information you may be unaware of that could be vital. Alternatively, you may have nothing you can tell us. If you can't, then we've lost nothing. But I repeat, there's a situation here that could be serious, any peripheral information could be critical.'

'I don't follow?'

'No, I realise that, but it'll become clearer as we progress. What was the cause of the argument between you and Roy Walters tonight?'

'It was personal.'

'I realise that, but during the argument you said Roy should contact either myself or Melanie and not warn someone.'

'Was Mr Walters eavesdropping?'

'Did he overhear? Yes. Was he eavesdropping...no he was not!' Kelsey shook his head. 'When you overhear someone using a loud hailer, you're not eavesdropping!'

Despite her unease Alison smiled ruefully.

'I did raise my voice, I concede that,' she said. 'Roy told me about the knife attack at the station and that Abbas accused him of betraying him. He was still finding excuses for Abbas. I've never liked that man and what happened didn't surprise me.'

'Why not?'

'He's strange; he has the air and manner of a fanatic. He seems to disapprove of women generally. Whenever we coincided at meetings of various groups he obviously resented me being there, I could see it. Not only me, he treated my friend Simone the same way. I'd say he disagreed with women being at meetings and universities in general.'

'What meetings were these?'

'Immigration for one, there were others dealing with Racial Discrimination, detention centres, and the Labor Party group. In the Immigration group, we disapproved of the government's attitude to refugees. It was originally formed years ago after the Tampa incident, when it picked up those refugees who weren't allowed to land in Australia.'

'Why did Abbas disapprove of you?'

'His culture, I'd say, Roy told me not to be offended by it, he insisted Abbas was all right really, it wasn't personal and we didn't understand. I didn't agree, at times Abbas said things that seemed very personal, and hostile to women generally. He obviously objected to me and Simone participating in these groups, and at times made hostile comments about Australia and the way we live, which I found offensive.'

'What sort of comments?'

'Oh, general remarks really. Simone upset him during one of the meetings, I thought he was going to hit her.'

'How did she upset him?'

'Once he made derogatory remarks about Australia and our way of life, so she asked, if he felt like that, what he was doing here, and that if he wanted to live in a country run on religious lines then he should go to one where he'd feel more comfortable, instead of trying to change things here.'

Kelsey gave a brief smile.

'Is that *exactly* what she said, word for word?'

'No, she did express herself more forcefully,' Alison's tension evaporated as she recalled the incident, she giggled and shook her head. 'Abbas jumped from his chair and headed in her direction, he looked very angry. Two of the guys intervened.'

'Who were they?'

'Two members of the group, Doug Fenway and Godfrey Thomas, they didn't like him either, and neither of them like Roy.'

'So, tell me more about Abbas.'

'He was, is, very anti-American and anti-Israel. He didn't like Australia following America's lead. He often said we were CIA lackeys.'

'I seem to have heard that one before. Did you agree with that?'

'I think the CIA has more influence here than it should, but I don't like terrorism either. Abbas always appeared to argue points and make allowances for suicide bombers who set off bombs in market places and on school buses.'

'What else did he say, or infer?'

'He disapproved of society here generally, how women dressed in Australia and how we were opinionated, he obviously disapproved of us speaking out at meetings and offering opinions. A friend of mine, another girl, came to one meeting, when she greeted him, he refused to shake her hand, ignored her, turned his back and wouldn't even speak to her.'

'I see. Tell me, where were these meetings held?'

'In the university campus usually, although we held some in office blocks in the city. They also held meetings elsewhere in private houses but Simone and I weren't invited to those. In fact, we haven't been invited to any meetings since Simone said what she did, not that we wanted to. One member of the group runs an agency of some sort in Sydney, something to do with immigration I think, nothing to do with the university. He has an office in a building near the centre. When we attended meetings there, some of us would leave early as we don't like being late in the city. Four of us usually left in a group, two of the guys, Doug and Godfrey, escorted me and Simone home.'

'Did Roy and Abbas leave at the same time?'

'No. They always stayed behind with other group members who had access to the offices.'

'Why didn't Roy escort you home?'

'He usually stayed behind to discuss things, he was always late back.'

'Who rented these offices?'

'His name was Kasim or something like that. He's not from university, Roy said his father was a leader in his community and he was a good friend of Abbas,' she paused and added bitterly. 'Being a friend of Abbas seemed to make it OK for Roy. Well, it didn't for me. This man Kasim was as bad as Abbas for being anti-women and pro-terrorism.'

'Why did you tell Roy he should talk to us?'

'He was going to contact this man Kasim, to tell him Abbas had been arrested. He was going to meet him and wanted me to go with him.'

'Where and why was he going to meet him?'

'Roy says he is a community leader. Are you going to arrest him?'

'I didn't say that,' Kelsey became irritable. 'But I can assure you of this, he's no community leader. The leader of the local Muslim community is a man named Khalil Rafit, he's with us now, trying to assist us with Abbas.'

'Isn't he the preacher at the local mosque?'

'He is. Where was Roy going to meet with this man Kasim?'

'I don't know, he rang him while I was there, that was what caused the argument.'

'Why did you feel so strongly about it?'

'I don't like Kasim, he told him Abbas was under arrest and from what Roy said I think Kasim must have said something about bringing their plan forward by a day. I was worried about that knife business too, we were clearly involved with something bad and out of our depth,' Alison clasped and unclasped her hands. 'I said we should get out; I was getting scared. I think something's going on that's not right.'

'My oath there is! And Roy thought it was all right?'

'Yes, he laughed it off and said Kasim and Abbas were really nice guys, I disagreed and thought we should have nothing to do with them.'

'You were right,' commented Kelsey dryly. 'You were out of your depth and there *is* something going on. Now we have to find Roy.'

There was a knock at the door and Shackleton entered. He beckoned to Kelsey who excused himself, and went outside.

'What is it?'

'We've just had a call from Bramble. The birds are leaving the roost at Cronulla. Vehicles arrived and there was a mass exodus. By the time the police back up arrived they'd gone, but we do have some vehicle registrations. Bramble and two of the unmarked police cars are following them, but the house has been vacated.'

'Shit!' Kelsey exploded. 'Roy bloody Walters has tipped them off. That damned young fool could have signed the death warrants of hundreds of people. Bugger it!'

He walked back to the interview room, Alison and Melanie looked up as he stormed in and slapped his file on the table.

'That bloody fool Roy has warned them,' he snapped angrily. 'They've pulled out, and we may lose them. Alison, we certainly need your assistance now. We need you to phone Roy Walters, and arrange to meet him tonight.'

He rummaged around in the sheaf of papers.

'Next! Can you tell us where that office block is?'

'I can do that,' Alison responded. 'Can someone lend me a pen?'

CHAPTER 30

There was an urgent call from Bramble, they had lost the vehicles in heavy traffic, but he reported they were heading in the Marrickville direction. Further interrogation of Abbas was essential, and Kelsey decided Roy Walters should be brought in again. One or both may know where the group was heading.

Marcus Templeton was working on Abbas's computer. He had no password and was looking for a back door. Another member of the computer staff, Mike Duval, was working on Roy Walters' computer, brought in by Shackleton.

Shackleton and Cassidy arrived outside the restaurant. They parked the car and waited. Alison had been persuaded to arrange a rendezvous with Roy Walters, the call was prolonged as long as possible while Marcus Templeton tracked Roy's mobile to a point near Canterbury. His response to Alison's overtures had been encouraging, he arranged to meet her at 8 o'clock that night.

Roy knew Melanie Cassidy by sight, so they agreed Shackleton would enter the restaurant posing as a customer before Roy arrived and position himself to block the rear exit when Cassidy entered the front. Kelsey didn't care whether they used force or not.

'If we cuff him, we'll humiliate the silly sod in front of his friends and colleagues at the restaurant. I couldn't give a damn if we do, if it helps us find where these other bastards are,' Kelsey had said pointedly. 'He reckons we arrest people just for the sake of it, so we've nothing to lose.'

'But we have no powers of arrest...!' Shackleton began but Kelsey interjected

'I know that...and you know that. I'll bet he doesn't,' Kelsey had responded. 'This is too serious now to split hairs.'

*

They hadn't been waiting long before their quarry appeared.

'There he is!' Cassidy indicated Roy approaching 50 or 60 metres away, hands in his pockets.

'Action stations!' grinned Shackleton. 'Away I go.'

He disembarked, crossed the road and entered the restaurant. He evaded the reception area and strolled to the rear bar. After Roy entered, Cassidy followed him in.

'Hallo Roy,' she said.

Roy turned with a welcoming smile, which evaporated when he saw who it was.

'What are you doing here?'

'I've come to see you, Roy. Alison couldn't make it, but I'll take you to her.'

Roy looked around desperately, contemplating flight but it

was too late. Shackleton materialised behind him and seized his elbow.

'Nice to meet you, Roy,' he said. 'My name is Denis. Alison wants to see you, which is why we're here.'

Roy looked around wildly, but they stayed close. He seemed to resign himself to the inevitable and nodded.

'All right.'

They escorted him to the door, on guard in case he tried to bolt, they took no chances. When they reached the car, Melanie drove with Roy and Shackleton in the back seat. Both rear doors were locked, she could never face Kelsey if Roy escaped through the rear door at a traffic light.

'They're bringing Roy Walters in,' McKay advised Kelsey as he put down the phone. 'They should be about 20 minutes.'

'Take him straight into Interview Room 2. I want to see him immediately. Keep him away from Alison. Contact Max Walters, tell him we have Roy for questioning and ask him to come in.'

When they arrived, Roy Walters was escorted into the interview room by Shackleton and Melanie Cassidy. As Kelsey entered and regarded him, he expected the worst. Absolute hostility and defiance were etched all over his features. Kelsey sighed.

'I sorry to bring you in again, Mr Walters,' he tried a placatory tone, but Roy merely glared.

'This is disgraceful, why are you hounding these people, all they want is a decent life here. I can understand why Abbas became frightened and aggressive when we treat them like criminals. You don't understand what these people go through in their homelands.'

'Really? Then why is he trying to introduce lifestyle aspects of that homeland here?' Kelsey responded. 'Did you warn your friend Kasim we were investigating him and his group?'

'Warn him? I merely told him his group was being investigated by the CIA and ...!'

'The CIA...here we go again...what the hell are you talking about?'

'We all know the CIA is ...!'

'Hells bells!' Kelsey hit his palm on the table. 'What the blazes are they teaching young people in our universities these days?'

'Well, somebody has to tell the public what the CIA...!'

'Shut up!' Kelsey snapped. 'Just shut up and bloody listen. We didn't tell you this before, and it's as well we didn't, otherwise you'd have shot your mouth off and caused the deaths of hundreds of innocent people.'

He drew a deep breath and controlled his anger with an effort.

'Your friend Abbas is a member of a militant terror group planning to assassinate a visiting President and organise a coup d'état in Taranga. This is the same group who leased your family property at Hopetoun, a remote area to practice guerrilla warfare, which they plan to unleash in Sydney within the next few days. We raided that farm, found literature they failed to destroy, and evidence explosive devices had been manufactured there.'

'You expect me to believe...!'

'Those explosive materials are now in Sydney...' Kelsey ignored the interruption, '...we've discovered they intend to detonate bombs in the metropolitan area on trains in a similar manner to events in London, Mumbai and Madrid. This will be a diversion to the main game which is to assassinate the President of Taranga currently visiting Sydney.'

He leant over the table and his eyes bored into Roy's.

'By tipping off these people you enabled them to disperse all over Sydney, we had them under observation but now we don't know where they are. We believe Wynyard Station is one of their targets. If we are unable to prevent it, you'll have the deaths of hundreds of your own countrymen on your conscience plus the possible assassination of a foreign leader which could spark hundreds of deaths in his country.'

'I don't believe you,' said Roy Walters. 'I've never heard such bullshit.'

'I didn't expect you would,' Kelsey said wearily. 'I can't believe someone as intelligent as you purport to be could be so stupid. Do you remember Geoff Miller?'

'Miller?' Roy Walters shook his head. 'No, I don't think I...!'

'Geoff Miller saved your life at Caringbah Railway Station, I challenge you to disbelieve *that*! He brought you down with a Rugby tackle just before you were knifed through the heart by your so-called friend Abbas, risking his own life in the process. Geoff Miller isn't one of our men; he has no connection with ASIO.'

'I don't believe...!'

'Shut up and just bloody listen! Geoff Miller is an insurance investigator from a firm of loss adjusters in Melbourne. While investigating a dodgy claimant who was rorting the workers compensation system in Victoria, Miller accidently discovered the training camp at Hopetoun. He was assaulted and held captive by these people, who intended to silence him permanently. He used his initiative and escaped, that's how we got onto this whole business.'

'I still don't believe...!'

'My God! How bloody stupid can...!"

Kelsey raised his eyes ceilingward, for a moment Shackleton

thought he was going to give Roy a backhander. Roy thought so too, he rocked back on his chair but Kelsey controlled himself. There was a knock at the door and Mike Duval, who was assisting Marcus Templeton, appeared in the doorway.

'Mr Walters is here,' he announced.

'Good, thanks Mike,' Kelsey said wearily and stood up. Roy looked triumphant.

'Now you're in trouble,' he said. 'My father's a solicitor, you can't hold me here.'

'We'll see,' Kelsey walked out to where Max Walters was waiting.

'You've arrested my son?' asked Max Walters.

'No, not yet, but it may come to that. We're trying to ascertain certain facts from him, but he refuses to believe us. This man Abbas seems to exert some hypnotic hold over him. We've tried to tell him about the impending terror attack but he won't believe us.'

Kelsey indicated a chair on the other side of the desk.

'I have a problem,' he said heavily. 'Despite nearly being stabbed by this man Abbas, Roy has, since he left your house, tipped off this man Kasim, another member of the terror group. We had tracked them to a house in Cronulla where they were under surveillance. It was going to be raided tonight; we had reason to believe explosives were there.'

'You've raided the property?'

'No, before we could do it your son tipped them off. A few hours ago, there was a mass exodus from the house, our men watching the house followed them but lost them in traffic. This group is now somewhere in Sydney like a battery of loose cannons. We hoped Roy would tell us where they might be, but...' he shook his head in resignation: '...we can't get through to him. He is obsessed with the CIA and anti-Americanism.'

Max Walters pursed his lips.

'This information you have, it is genuine...factual?'

'As near as we can judge, yes,' said Kelsey. 'All the arrows point in that direction. But Roy won't tell us anything. Frankly, I don't know what to do with him. I've now told him more than I should have done about the suspected impending terror raid involving Wynyard Station or trains leaving from it. I thought that would jerk him into reality, but it hasn't, any more than when he was nearly stabbed. I've even told him De Souza, the visiting President of Taranga, is under threat, but he won't believe that either. He still thinks we're perpetrating a racist CIA plot to stop immigration of Middle Eastern and Asian refugees. But we've compounded our problem.'

'How?'

'By telling him what we know, or suspect, this group has in mind. If I release him, I fear he'll tell them. Right now, it's unlikely they realise what we *do* know. It's imperative we apprehend these people before they carry out their intentions. If he warns them again and tells them what we know, the plan will change and they could hit somewhere else. In fact, there's no might about it, they *will* change it. They'll know if they stick to the original plan they could be walking into a trap.'

'I see,' Max Walters compressed his lips. 'They'll adopt Plan B, if they have one!'

'Precisely! If they have a contingency plan, and I'm sure they will, they'll select an alternative target and we'll have no idea where, or when it is.'

'Hmm!!' Walters was deep in thought. 'Does Roy know I'm here?'

'Yes. He's cock-a-hoop because he thinks you'll get him released.'

'Hmm!' Walters bit his lip. 'You are absolutely sure of this information?'

'Absolutely.'

'Have you contacted Alison?'

'Yes, she's here.'

'Have you asked her if she has any idea of any further addresses?'

'She's given us one, a serviced office block in the city,' said Kelsey. 'She said other places were used for meetings, possibly private houses, but she and a girl named Simone were excluded. Sex was a problem...I'll rephrase that...the problem is they are women.'

'Simone eh?' Max Walters rubbed his jaw. 'I know her, a very feisty young woman, she certainly wouldn't go down well with fundamentalists. Tell me, have you come across a young man named Doug Fenway?'

'Alison has mentioned him.'

'You should try him. He struck me as someone who's going off the boil. He is, or was, involved like all the others with left wing and do-gooder groups as most young students are these days, at least initially. I've met Fenway occasionally when he's come to the house, he's made the odd comment in passing that indicated to me he's questioning certain aspects.'

'Do you know where we can find him?'

'Apart from the university, no! Alison may have an address or phone number.'

'Right! We'll do that,' said Kelsey. 'But we still have this problem with Roy. If he warns these people again and tells them what we know...!'

'Let me see him, after what you've told me, I share your concern. I can't guarantee to sway him, I'm only his father, all said and done, a stupid old stick-in-the-mud living in the past who knows bugger all!'

Kelsey nodded sympathetically.

'That's the second time that's been said to me today,' he said. 'I spoke to the father of this young man Abbas this afternoon. He is horrified at what his son is doing. He reckoned he was the worst person to speak to his son as he wouldn't listen to him. He suggested we get the local priest, imam or sheik, to speak with him.'

'A good idea, although in our case that would be a non-starter. Our family has never been involved with the church. But it might be necessary, in light of what you've told me, for him to kick his heels for a night or two in here. His mother will never forgive me, but I don't want him, or me, to have the deaths of hundreds of fellow citizens on our consciences.'

CHAPTER 31

'Who owns that building, Denis?' asked Kelsey.

'Smith, Wheeler & Associates. We have their registered address and a phone number,' replied Shackleton.

'We need to look inside those offices, tonight,' Kelsey responded. 'We're applying for a warrant but it may take more time than we have. Go with McKay and contact their keyholder, see if Detective Sergeant Parslow can go with you and a constable, uniforms will work wonders. If we gain entry, look around but don't start ransacking the place. Has Marcus Templeton unravelled Abbas's computer yet?'

'He's found a back door and is searching files,' said Shackleton. 'Mainly uni courses, engineering data.'

'Good. Have we traced Doug Fenway?'

'Alison Furnell gave us his address. Melanie went with Phil Jackson to pick him up.'

'We're making progress,' said Kelsey. 'Where's Bramble?'

'On his way to Smith & Wheeler's serviced office block. I've arranged to meet him there with the keyholder.'

Bramble was outside the building when Shackleton and McKay arrived with Peter Wheeler, the keyholder, who wasn't happy. He'd been about to commence his evening meal, but the presence of a uniformed constable and Detective Sergeant Parslow persuaded him to endure the pangs of hunger a little longer.

The building was seven storeys and fairly old, dwarfed by other more modern buildings in the vicinity. Wheeler unlocked the main door and admitted them.

'Where's the office occupied by ...' Shackleton checked a wall directory and consulted his notebook, '...Kasim?'

He proffered his notebook to Wheeler who shook his head.

'No Kasim here,' he said. 'Not spelt like that, anyway. Maybe you mean Qassim... beginning with a 'Q'?'

'Ah, could be,' agreed Shackleton. 'Which floor?'

'Look, is this all kosher?' asked Wheeler. 'Shouldn't you have a warrant?'

'It's on its way,' said Parslow. Kelsey had set the wheels in motion, but there was no accounting how long it would take. As they entered the lift Shackleton rang Kelsey on his mobile phone.

'Alan, we have a connection here. The offices are in the name of Qassim,' he spelt it out. 'Isn't this the man who was ...?'

'Agnarat Wen!' Kelsey was ahead of him. 'Bloody hell! Why didn't I think of that spelling before? I must be bloody senile!'

'If you are, we all were, I didn't consider it either,' responded Shackleton. 'On our way to the 7th floor. We'll be in touch.'

*

Mike Duval appeared in the doorway as Kelsey put down his phone.

'Mel and Phil Jackson are back, with Doug Fenway.'

'Good! Thanks Mike,' said Kelsey. 'Take him into the same room as Alison Furnell and tell Mel to come in here.'

Duval acknowledged and disappeared; Melanie arrived within minutes.

'I've asked Mike Duval to place Fenway in with Alison Furnell,' said Kelsey. 'She spoke about him before as a kindred spirit. Together, they may give us information.'

'I'd say it's more than that,' said Melanie. 'I have a feeling about him, when I said Alison was with us, he wasn't sure what was happening or what we wanted him for, but his concern was all for her. He asked how she was, was she all right etc. The way he speaks of her I'd say there's strong feeling there, from him, even if she isn't fully aware of it.'

'What's your opinion of him?'

'Nice lad, from what I've seen of him, I like him,' said Melanie. 'If he knows anything, I think he'll try to help.'

'If he does it'll be the first assistance from the younger male species tonight!' Kelsey said grimly. 'We'll see how we go...oh... incidentally Mel, that business at the drive-in. Something has arisen from that.'

"What!' adrenalin ran through Melanie's system and sweat formed on her brow. '...the drive-in...what...!'

Had Alison had second thoughts? After she'd had some hours to think about it had Alison decided she had been violated, and reported it as an assault? If this was so then Melanie was in trouble.

'Yes, we've received an incident report...!'

'An incident...report!' Melanie's knees began to feel weak;

visions of a day in court arose, dismissal, unemployment and the dole queue reared up in her mind. 'What did it…what…?'

'Bramble's been in touch with the police. It was a mother and daughter, apparently. Characters with torches were wandering around peering into cars, which is what you told us. They tried to enter this particular vehicle and slashed the arm and shoulder of the young woman in the passenger seat, but security arrived just in time.'

'Oh…oh I see,' Melanie began to feel lightheaded with relief.

'According to the cops she was wearing a red Swans football club top. Funny thing, according to the report…here…are you all right, Mel?'

'Yes, yes I'm fine,' Melanie was almost fainting with relief.' Yes Alan, I'm fine.'

'Ah…OK good. Well apparently, the car had some football insignia, Sydney Swans stickers and the like, on the rear and side windows. Wasn't Alison wearing a Swans top?'

'Er…yes, I believe she was…I didn't really notice.'

*

Shackleton closed the blinds and switched on the lights, with Peter Wheeler present, wandering around the offices in torchlight would have looked furtive and covert. Parslow and the uniformed constable stayed by the door with Wheeler and engaged him in conversation.

There was a desk, two filing cabinets, a computer and a bookcase. There were chairs in the room arranged in the centre of the office all facing the same way, as if for a meeting. Bramble examined desk drawers, and riffled through papers he had extracted. Shackleton examined the bookshelves. Some books had a militant flavour which caused him to pause and snap them with his mobile phone. He had been half expecting to find books on bomb making, but was disappointed. He turned his attention to the phone and began unscrewing the mouthpiece, Bramble wandered across and stood between Shackleton and the door as he inserted a small bug into the instrument and re-assembled it.

'We'll see what we glean from that!' Bramble commented.

McKay had switched on the computer, but it was subject to a password. He tried one or two random words, two he tried were Agnarat and Wen, but it didn't react.

'Any suggestions?' he grunted but Bramble shook his head.

'No can do, unfortunately, we haven't got a …' then realising Wheeler was within earshot, amended it: '…until the search warrant arrives.'

He indicated a box of CDs on top of a cabinet. McKay checked it, there were five unused CDs in it.

'We'll anticipate it then,' he slotted in one of the virgin CDs.

'You know what you're doing do you?' Bramble asked acidly. 'Anything we get from it could be disallowed in court.'

'You're too bloody cautious,' snapped McKay. 'If these bastards are planning to set off explosive devices, they'll have exploded them long before we're involved with legal technicalities. Just look busy and stand between me and the door,' he inclined his head at Wheeler, still chatting to Parslow.

'You'll never get in without a pass …!'

'Just shut up and leave me to it, Marcus showed me a few tricks, I hope it will be enough.'

Bramble shrugged and muttered under his breath. He and McKay were not the best of friends, but he knew McKay had spent time with Marcus Templeton over the years when they had been to-ing and fro-ing between Sydney and Canberra. Consequently, McKay had a measure of computer knowledge, so Bramble left him to it.

Bramble flicked through a desk diary but saw nothing of note. It included entries with 'Meeting' written in, which could refer to meetings in which Alison, Roy and the other two young men had been involved, together with Abbas and others.

McKay did some key manipulations and managed to download something, but finally conceded defeat. Bramble motioned to McKay to turn off the light. McKay extracted the disc from the computer and switched it off.

Shackleton opened the blinds to ensure they left the room as they found it. The light from the moon and street lamps down below filtered into the room, the moon cast a pale sheen on the desk and floor, while street lamps lit up the ceiling. As he was turning away, his attention was drawn to the view below. Some 100 metres or so away and almost facing him as the street curved away to the left, was the frontage of the Worthington Hotel, brilliantly lit with floodlights.

'Not a bad vista,' he murmured.

'What isn't?' asked McKay.

'Our friend Qassim has a good view from here,' observed Shackleton. 'It's a damn sight better than the view from my desk in Canberra.'

McKay walked to the window, and uttered an exclamation.

'Do these windows open?' he asked Wheeler.

'Yes,' Wheeler answered. 'They used to open outwards, but since we've been here, we've installed sliding windows. They only open about four inches, enough to admit fresh air and not enough for anyone to fall out. There's flywire to keep the flies out.'

'Look at this, Bob,' said McKay.

Bramble looked at McKay and raised an eyebrow, but McKay shook his head, they left the room and Wheeler locked up. They thanked him and went down in the lift. They had a brief conversation with Wheeler in the foyer then trooped outside. As they gathered by their two cars, Bramble looked at McKay.

'What were you showing me?'

'Remember Geoff Miller mentioned two red lines converging on a point, he thought it could be in this area, probably Bligh Street.'

'Yes, I recall something about that.'

'That window overlooked the hotel over there. Look, there's the main entrance,' McKay pointed up the street. 'You saw the steps through the window, didn't you?'

'I get it!' Shackleton pointed up. 'If there was a marksman up there with a rifle …!'

'Anyone on those steps would be an easy target,' said McKay grimly. 'Shades of Lee Harvey Oswald in Dallas. A gunman could take out anyone emerging from the hotel and down those steps, a gunman who had a perfect right to be in the building!'

'With a readymade escape route,' added Bramble and McKay nodded.

'I'd say we've found one of Geoff Miller's red lines.'

CHAPTER 32

When Melanie Cassidy escorted Doug Fenway into the interview room, he bounded across to Alison and seized her hands.

'How are you, Allie? They said you were here, it's a relief to see you.' Alison gave him a hug; then he turned to Melanie. 'What's all this about?'.

'We are investigating a possible terrorist attack, we believe you can assist us,' replied Melanie.

Kelsey had asked Melanie to undertake the interview and interrogation; as he was completing arrangements for the coming raid at Cronulla. Forensics had extracted information from burnt papers at the Walters farm so Kelsey deemed they would lose nothing by raiding the Cronulla address despite the terror gang having abandoned it.

'Terrorism?' Fenway sat up with alarm. 'You think I'm a terrorist?'

'No, we don't! Not you,' Melanie shook her head. 'But some

of the people you've been associating with probably are. Do you know anybody named Abbas, and Qassim?'

Melanie studied him closely, as did Phil Jackson. Fenway was tall, slim and athletic with dark curly hair. He was also very conscious of Alison's presence, as he persistently glanced in her direction. Alison was aware of the tacit attention and seemed to like it.

'Yes, Abbas belonged to a couple of groups we were involved with, immigration was one and the other was racial discrimination. We were also in another group against detention of illegal immigrants.'

'We need to know where these meetings took place, we know about the serviced office block in Bligh Street, but meetings were held elsewhere. Can you tell us where?'

'In various places,' Fenway was pensive. 'Why do you want this? What's going on? Are you investigating these groups?'

'Not specifically, but we're investigating some of its members and want to know their whereabouts. We believe Abbas is involved with an extremist group planning an attack within central Sydney. You've heard of the London Underground bombings, Mumbai and Madrid? It could be our turn next,' Melanie decided there was no point in half measures.

'An attack?' Fenway was startled. 'My God! You mean, bombings, shootings?'

'Possibly both,' Melanie said dryly.

Fenway looked at Alison; she nodded. Fenway shook his head, not as a negative gesture but as if clearing his head.

'Why does that not surprise me?' this was directed more at himself than Melanie. 'Nothing about that bastard Abbas surprises me and this certainly doesn't.'

'Clearly you don't like him?'

'Clearly...you're right and clearly...I don't,' retorted Fenway.

'Bloody oath I don't! I was getting more and more pissed off with his views and how he treated Alison and Simone. He treated another friend of ours, Evelyn Jacobs, even more rudely. He refused to shake her hand and wouldn't speak to her, just turned his back on her. She's a bit outspoken like Simone, but there was more to it than that. It was her surname. He thought she was Jewish, which obviously upset him, but she isn't. Her father is an Anglican minister from England. She was born there and is as English as the Queen.'

'Can you identify any houses or venues where these meetings took place?'

'Some yes, I don't know them all. Thommo and I stopped going when they became more intense and spouted a lot of extreme Left Wing and militant stuff. They were proposing demonstrations outside the US and Israeli embassies and planning violence. You know the sort of thing, missiles, ball bearings under horses' hooves, baseball bats etcetera. Apart from that, we considered they were demonstrating outside the wrong places.'

'Who's Thommo?'

'Thommo? Oh, sorry, Godfrey Thomas. He says the name Godfrey makes him sound like a pansy so we all call him Thommo.'

'Oh!' Melanie smiled. 'Now! These addresses, what can you give us?'

'Hasn't Roy given them to you, I thought he was here too.'

'Roy won't give us anything, he considers it's none of our business and Abbas is his friend, even after he tried to stab him. He's also convinced we're a branch of the CIA'.

'He thinks what? What an idiot.' Fenway pursed his lips. 'Oh! Sorry Allie!'

'Don't worry, I think so too ...now,' said Alison.

'So, what have you got?' Melanie persisted.

'Give me a pad and a pen,' replied Fenway.

*

Kelsey was in a conference room when Mike Duval ushered in Khalil Rafit. Kelsey indicated a chair and the drinks machine in the corner.

'Can I offer you anything?' but Rafit smiled and shook his head.

'How is our friend Abbas?' Kelsey asked.

'Praying, and, I hope, thinking hard,' responded Khalil. 'He's very confused and involved with a very radical group. There are many people in this world, not only Muslims, who worship their religion with more intensity than they worship the God it represents.'

'I'd agree with that,' responded Kelsey. 'I was stationed in London when the IRA exploded a bomb in the Docklands. What astonished me was the division and hatred in Ireland between two branches of Christianity, they didn't hesitate to kill and maim each other and anyone who got in the way. That Dockland bomb killed two Hindu Indians while a bomb in a Birmingham pub killed two West Indians.'

The imam sadly shook his head.

'Regrettably this is happening within our own faith, Shi'ite and Sunni are not only opposed to the infidel, worshippers of other religions, but fighting each other. Many of both beliefs were killed in the war between Iran and Iraq, all Muslims. Admittedly, nationalism was involved but sectarianism played a large part.'

'Where do we stand with Abbas?'

'He hasn't said so in as many words, but I believe he is

prepared to die for the distorted faith implanted by his uncle. He's antagonistic towards his parents, they don't observe the faith as he believes they should. I know them well, they are good, hardworking people and regular attendees at our mosque. During our talk, the young man even eyed me with suspicion, but made possible significant references. I believe the event is timed to take place the day after tomorrow, he mentioned the date twice.'

He paused while Kelsey noted it.

'Further, the intention doesn't seem to be suicide attacks, although I can't guarantee it, but more on the lines of Madrid and Mumbai. Bags to be left in certain places, say commuter trains, and detonated remotely or by timer.'

'Do you know where?'

'There I can't assist...yet!' said Khalil. 'I have left him to seek his God; I pray he will receive guidance. I'll see him again; I suggest half an hour. He may talk to me, or may not.'

'You have done well. Thank you for what you *have* done.'

'I too would like to seek guidance, is there a place where I can ...'

'Certainly, yes,' Kelsey rose to his feet. 'There is an empty office across the corridor. Please use it. I will see you are not disturbed.'

As he escorted Khalil out, Mike Duval re-appeared at the doorway.

'Boss,' he said. 'This is a list of addresses from Melanie compiled by Doug Fenway, and Marcus wants to see you.'

Templeton was peering at his computer screen when Kelsey materialised at his elbow with Fenway's list in his hand.

'What have you got?'

'I got in through a back door, boss, and isolated some files,' explained Templeton. 'I've accessed his address book, and printed some of them out.'

'How did you get in?'

'With great difficulty,' replied Templeton. 'I still haven't reached some areas, but I've extracted these so far.'

Kelsey examined the print-out and compared it with Doug Fenway's list. He grunted and looked at Duval.

'Where's Bramble?' he asked.

'Dunno!' Duval shrugged. 'Last I heard he was coming back from Bligh Street with Shackleton and McKay.'

'Phone him,' ordered Kelsey. 'Get him in here pronto. These lists don't correspond exactly, but some addresses appear on both. We must investigate these now and prioritise any on both lists. Take a photocopy of this list, or print out another, and give it to Doug Fenway. See if he recognises any of them.'

Kelsey's mobile rang; it was Francis Burton from Canberra. Kelsey wrote down details, snapped his phone shut and turned to Templeton.

'That was Francis Burton,' he said. 'He's just given us the date of the proposed attacks. It coincides with what we got from Khalil. They intend to fan out from Wynyard. Captain Bartlett has interrogated our friend Hammoud and persuaded him to talk. Hammoud's nearly crapping himself with fright, Bartlett emphasised we traced the Hopetoun training ground through his Workers Compensation rort. Bartlett's offered to keep it from his fellow conspirators if he talks to us and threatened to broadcast it if he doesn't! Hammoud is talking, he fears for the safety of his wife and children if it gets out how we traced it.'

'Bit late to worry about his wife and kids,' commented Templeton. 'They'd be a damned sight better off if he'd stuck to his job and earned a wage instead of taking time off planning to kill people.'

'I know that, and you know that!' Kelsey said resignedly.

'There's no accounting for how some people's minds work.'

Kelsey was with Mike Duval, Bramble and other returnees from the serviced office block, when Melanie Cassidy entered with a copy of Templeton's print out.

'Anything new?' he asked.

'Doug Fenway recognises some addresses, he's not sure whether they're significant. One of them is his own, another is Alison's, another belongs to Godfrey Thomas. It seems they're addresses of group members who may be peripheral hangers on or, like Doug and Alison, perennial joiners of clubs and societies. There are several of them.'

'We'll give priority to the common addresses, those supplied by Doug Fenway and Abbas's computer,' said Kelsey. 'Bob, have a good look at these and see what, if any, vehicles are outside them,' he turned to Melanie. 'What about Fenway and Alison Furnell?'

'I'd say we've got all we can from them,' said Melanie. 'But like Geoff Miller, we may still need them for recognition purposes.'

'I agree. Most of the people we're looking for don't appear in police mug shots, or ours. Can we put them up anywhere for the night? We'll need them close by.'

'There's a hotel over the road, we could put them up there, at government expense,' suggested Melanie.

'Good idea. Can you arrange it?'

'Yes,' said Melanie. 'Leave that with me.'

'Mike, give this CD to Marcus Templeton,' Kelsey said to Duval as Bramble and the others departed. 'He might make something of it. McKay tried to download something onto it. Where's Geoff Miller? We must check if he can recall any detail about this other red line he saw. That could indicate the position of a possible second sniper.'

*

Shackleton left the car and wandered towards one of the addresses isolated via Marcus Templeton's computer and by Doug Fenway. He walked slowly; it was an older neighbourhood with cars parked in the street. He had a list of registrations of all vehicles formerly parked outside the Cronulla address and checked them off against it. He looked across the street where McKay was similarly engaged.

'Bingo!'

He spotted one familiar number plate and noted it.

'Number three on the list,' he muttered but it was the only vehicle of interest.

He crossed the street and returned, McKay did the same and they re-checked all number plates. They arrived where Bramble was sitting moodily in the driver's seat.

'Any joy?' he asked.

'One, third on the list,' replied Shackleton and McKay agreed. 'A grey Holden Commodore.'

'I'll call it in, where's the next address?'

*

They arrived at the next address on the list. This time McKay and Bramble did the checking while Shackleton waited. This time they drew a blank, they examined the target house to see if there was anything unusual or significant. There wasn't.

'They need a carpenter,' McKay commented as they returned. 'The front gate was falling apart.'

'I'll put that in the report,' Shackleton responded gravely then reported in. The next address they checked, they struck gold as two of the ex-Cronulla vehicles were parked nearby, one being the Victorian vehicle followed from Melbourne by Hallam and Miller.

Bramble called it in, and Kelsey replied at length. He advised that Roger Preston had received a call from Jackson & Antrobus, who had checked their Agnarat Wen file and found a Sydney phone number which was the initial contact number; any subsequent contact had been via the Walters farm landline. Templeton had traced it to a building near the serviced office block, on the other side of the Worthington Hotel. He suggested it could be Geoff Miller's other red line.

'Another thing,' Bramble said to Shackleton. 'They're raiding Cronulla, they're on their way. Alan said he'd done enough pussyfooting around. It's happening now.'

CHAPTER 33

Whilst en route to the city Bramble's phone rang. It was Marcus Templeton, Bramble exchanged a few words with him then turned to Shackleton, dictated a name and address, then rang off.

'That's the phone number Roger Preston obtained from Hopetoun, it's that other serviced office block,' he said. 'It's near the Worthington Hotel.'

'We're going there now, are we?'

'We've got a search warrant this time,' said Bramble. 'The manager, Robert Colbeck, has alerted the supervisor, Barry Rawlings, but we have to roust him out first. Any more coffee in that flask, Dave?' he brusquely asked McKay. 'Or have you had the lot?'

'You finished it off, remember?' was McKay's acid reply.

They found the address in Paddington, Bramble hammered on the door. It was opened by a bald-headed man, aged about 45, wearing a dark blue uniform with a badge on the left-hand breast pocket.

'Mr Bramble?'

'You'll be Mr Rawlings?' replied Bramble. 'Has Robert Colbeck given you a call?'

'He has,' Rawlings turned and shouted: 'See you later Joanne,' closed the door and turned to Bramble.

'The name's Barry, let's go. Shall I lead the way?'

'Good idea, Barry,' grunted Bramble.

'What's this all about?'

'Can't tell you, sorry,' responded Bramble. 'But we have to check the office used by Agnarat Wen.'

'Agnarat Wen?' Rawlings shrugged. 'They're on the 6th floor.'

They followed Rawlings to the building and drew up outside. Rawlings left his vehicle and unlocked the main door.

'Hang on,' he said. 'I'll switch the alarm off.'

It was a modern office block. Bramble looked up at the frontage, the building was 8 storeys and the frontage 90 or 100 metres. To the right he could see the Worthington Hotel frontage on the same side of the street, with an intersection in between. The hotel was about 100 metres away, quite visible as the street curved around.

'Do you know much about them?' asked Bramble.

'Agnarat Wen?' Rawlings shook his head. 'Nah! I don't have much to do with tenants, I maintain offices, organise office cleaners and take care of general maintenance. You'll need to speak to Rob Colbeck, he deals with tenants.'

They took a lift to the sixth floor, the corridor floor was carpeted, although the carpet showed signs of wear in places. Rawlings led the way to an office and unlocked the door.

'What sort of clientele do you have in these offices?' asked Bramble.

Rawlings shrugged.

'Anybody who wants a city address and can't afford their own building, or street frontage. It's small businesses; mainly single individual enterprises. There's a life insurance broker on one floor, a personnel agency, a small secretarial agency on the floor below, and a private detective on the second floor.'

They entered the room.

'Two men and a woman conduct public speaking training in that office down the corridor,' Rawlings continued. 'Some nights they run evening courses, and use the kitchen area at the end for refreshments. I've got to know a few of the businesses when I'm doing maintenance and repairs.'

'But you don't know anything about this Agnarat mob?'

Rawlings shook his head.

'Nope. Nothing. I occasionally see them coming in or going out, there's quite a few of them, they use it mornings and afternoons and hold meetings at night.'

'They're not listed in the phone book,' commented Shackleton.

'Wouldn't know about that, but there's a phone here,' Rawlings pointed to the desk. 'Now I'm here there's a small repair job in the foyer which I may as well do now. Call me on my mobile when you're through. Here's my card, the number's on it.'

His footsteps faded away as he went down the corridor.

'There's also a computer,' added Bramble dryly. 'Have a look at that, Shack.'

Shackleton tried to switch it on. It didn't react.

'It's switched off at the wall,' commented McKay, he flicked the wall switch, the computer hummed and the screen lit up. Shackleton worked on it briefly then shook his head.

'Password entry,' he said.

Bramble pulled out his mobile and dialled.

'Marcus, get over here pronto,' he gave the address. 'Or send one of your minions. We've got a computer here and can't get into it. You know the address. Bring a phone bug with you.'

Bramble snapped his mobile shut.

'He's sending someone down, with a disk or flash drive and spare bugs,' he said. 'He'll have a go at it.'

'I hope he takes his finger out, we don't want to be hanging around here for too long if Qassim decides on a night in the office.'

They closed the blinds and searched the room. They found a screen in one of the cupboards which indicated Qassim held occasional instructional sessions with either videos or overhead projector. McKay checked the window; he took several shots of the Worthington Hotel frontage with his phone. He was grim as he viewed some of the photographs on his phone and turned to Bramble.

'This is like the other office building, having a clear shot onto the hotel steps but from the opposite direction.'

'If there's a diversion with explosions on trains, police would be diverted elsewhere. If the President exits out front, he'd be a sitting duck.'

'How would he get a clear shot, this window is fixed glass, it doesn't open.'

'No problem, it's easy enough these days to cut a circular hole with either a diamond glass cutter or a chemical agent,' grunted Bramble. 'Let's face it, we've used them ourselves. If there's simultaneous sabotage on the rail system, a sniper shooting from here could make a clean getaway.'

'With assassination the main aim,' said Shackleton.

'What else?' Bramble pursed his lips. 'We have a moderate leader of a predominantly Muslim state, not only would this throw Taranga into chaos, it would also prejudice Australia because it took place here. The rail system destruction would be a diversion, the Madrid bombings caused the Spanish government to fall, the new government panicked and withdrew troops from Iraq, which is another factor. It could be an attempt to influence our foreign policy,' he turned to McKay. 'Anything in the paperwork?'

'Correspondence with a firm of accountants, but I think Alan knew about them. They registered their business name.'

'Well, keep looking. We can't leave until Marcus gets here.'

'It wouldn't be a clear shot from here,' said Shackleton. 'There's a horizontal flagpole sticking out from the wall of the building next door.'

'You're right,' Bramble squinted through the glass and lined up with the front steps of the hotel. 'We'll check on other offices or windows on floors below. When they were planning, this may have been the only office available.'

'Which got them into the building,' commented McKay. 'We'll check with building management.'

Bramble called Rawlings on his mobile, and told him to be ready to admit Marcus Templeton or whoever he sent. They carried on searching, but found little of interest. After twenty minutes Mike Duval emerged from the lift and entered the office.

'Where's the computer?' he asked and McKay jerked his thumb at it.

'Where's the phone bug?' asked Shackleton.

Duval handed a small package to Shackleton who commenced work on the telephone. Duval started hitting the keyboard, he started, stopped, paused deep in thought, then tried other tacks. He picked up his mobile and called Templeton. McKay and Shackleton moved up behind to see what was going on, Duval grunted and nodded in response to Templeton, hit a sequence of keys. the monitor came alive and a list of formulae cascaded down the screen.

'OK!' said Duval. 'I'm in, inserting the CD, keep your fingers crossed.'

It wasn't clear who he was addressing, Templeton at the other end or his two watchers. A light glowed on the computer's CD slot and there was a buzzing noise.

'I think we're in business.'

Bramble's phone rang.

'What? Damnation! How long have we got?'

He turned to the others.

'A group of men have just arrived outside. They're using their key on the front door. Rawlings says he'll hold them up, he thinks they are from Agnarat. How long, Mike?'

'Just minutes; it's copied 38% already.'

'Matter of minutes, Barry!' he said. 'How do we get out ... where? The corridor to the rear of the building, internal staircase. Right, got it!'

He closed his phone and turned to Duval.

'Well?'

'47%' answered Duval. 'Moving all the time, 53% ...now 58%'

'Shit!' Bramble grumbled. 'I wish the bloody thing would hurry up.'

'62%' commented Duval.

'Everybody out!' Bramble ordered. 'All barring me and Mike. Go to the right, there's a staircase at the end of the corridor.'

'What about you?'

'Last minute stuff I'm afraid,' said Bramble. 'But the more who get out now, the less obvious we are.'

The others left the room, after tidying up and removing traces of their occupation.

'How far now?' he asked Duval.

'70%'

'Bloody hell!' Bramble peered anxiously through the door up the corridor. He jumped when his phone rang again.

'Yes?'

'Barry Rawlings,' a voice said. 'I told them the lifts were out of action because they're being serviced tomorrow. They're taking the stairs at the front of the building, not the back stairs. You'll have about five minutes. Don't worry about the office door. It's self-locking.'

'78%,' from Duval.

'Thanks Barry,' said Bramble. 'We should be well out of here.'

He checked the computer, it had reached 85%. He watched the blue line slowly cover the last 15% and then bleep. Duval extracted the CD and shut the computer down. He placed the CD in its jacket.

'Everything looks OK,' said Bramble. 'Let's get the hell out.'

He had a last look around as Duval entered the corridor, he was about to close the door when he realised the light was still on. He hastily switched it off, then recalled McKay had turned the computer on at the wall. He reached out and flicked off the wall switch. Then they scuttled to the end of the corridor. He heard the rumble of voices at the far end as the Agnarat men reached the sixth level, while he and Duval passed through the door of the back stairs and began to descend. The others were waiting in the foyer, with Barry Rawlings.

'Thought you'd left it too late,' commented Shackleton.

'Damned nearly did, but I think we got what we wanted,' said Bramble. 'Somebody tell Alan Kelsey the phone bug is operative,' he turned to Rawlings. 'How did they get here, is that their car outside?'

'Nah!' Rawlings shook his head. 'They came from the rear of the building. I'd suggest you check around there. They do use the offices at night, although it's irregular. They're not the only ones, a computer tuition organisation carries out evening courses occasionally. That car outside the front door has been there for about an hour, it probably belongs to someone from an office over the street.'

'We'll have a look round the back,' said Bramble. 'What will you do now, Barry? Wait until they come down again?'

'I don't have to, but I will,' Rawlings replied. 'I've disabled the lifts, having told them that I thought I'd better be consistent. I'll ring them in a few minutes and tell them I've re-activated them…out of the goodness of my heart! I've got my own office here, I've a few things to do. I'll see them out, then head for home. I'll be right.'

Several vehicles were parked at the rear of the building, their registration numbers noted and reported to Kelsey on return.

'Marcus will ask for these to be run through the system,' said Kelsey. 'Check this CCTV footage received from the police. It relates to Wynyard Station a few hours before we picked up Abbas. Geoff Miller, Doug Fenway and Alison are viewing it but they haven't spotted anyone yet. I'll be down after I've spoken with Francis Burton.'

Melanie Cassidy was operating the remote control while Fenway, Furnell and Miller viewed the screen. The new arrivals gathered behind them to check the images.

'Hang on Mel, freeze it there,' McKay said. 'That guy with the rucksack!'

The rucksack was unmistakeable, two more were on screen with backs to the camera.

'That's Abbas.' Fenway pointed at the screen. 'I'd know that bastard anywhere.'

'What's he looking at?' asked Shackleton.

'The other tape may show that, there's a camera ahead of this one pointing in the opposite direction,' Templeton riffled through the tapes.

'Good job he turned to look at someone, or something, otherwise all we'd have got was the back of his head.'

'Probably conversing with someone off screen,' suggested Bramble. 'At least we've isolated him. That leaves at least three others, the three who got off that train at Cronulla.'

Templeton re-started the tape and ran it forward. The two backpackers, already in view, moved forward, a third appeared in the right-hand corner of the screen, the one Abbas had turned to. The quartet moved forward and disappeared in the throng of passengers.

'Whereabouts is this?' asked McKay. 'This isn't the main entrance section, is it? This is a lower level, as I recall from occasional trips from Wynyard.'

'Yes,' Templeton agreed. 'But we haven't picked them up entering the station, this is the first tape we've viewed where they've appeared.'

'That's it for that tape, have we got one from the entrance hall?'

'Not yet, but we do have one from that camera situated further on,' said Templeton. 'Hang on while I load it.'

He ran the next tape to the right time slot, and located the same scene from a different angle. Instead of moving away from the camera the quartet was moving right to left, so when Abbas turned to address a companion behind him, he was readily identifiable,

'Anything?' Bramble turned to Miller.

'That one ahead of Abbas, he may have been at Hopetoun. The picture quality doesn't help, but it could be him.'

'Any sign of Qassim?' Bramble asked but Fenway and Furnell shook their heads.

They viewed several tapes, which added nothing. Templeton ran through one covering the station main entrance but there was no trace of the quartet. Bramble halted the tapes several times to make notes. Templeton extracted the last tape and turned to Doug Fenway, Alison Furnell and Miller.

'Thanks for your assistance, much appreciated,' he said, but Fenway remained seated and gestured to Templeton.

'Put that one on again,' he indicated a tape and Templeton re-inserted it. The familiar scene of Wynyard Station re-appeared; the two forward backpackers were on screen, but Abbas and his companion were not. Fenway leant forward, hand under chin, studied the screen, then pointed.

'Him!' he said. 'He attended meetings in Bligh Street. I'm sure of it now, that's him.'

'Who's he?'

'They called him Shehzad, he gave me the creeps the way he looked at the girls. He treated them as chattels, second-class citizens, like Abbas did, but his eyes were all over them,' said Fenway. 'Allie asked me to take her home early one night, she didn't like the way he was looking at her. That was the last meeting we attended, same with Simone, she never went back either. It wasn't just about the girls being uncomfortable: they were spouting a lot of rubbish too. That was when we wondered what we'd got into.'

'Was that right?' Bramble asked and Alison nodded.

'I remember that; it caused trouble when we decided to leave. Roy was incensed, he was comfortable enough there but when we upped and left, he followed us out and accused us of being insulting.'

'Why doesn't that surprise me?' Alan Kelsey had just entered.

'That young man is so politically correct he can't think straight. He's very taken with these people and very impressionable...' he turned to Bramble '...are we finished here?'

'Just about,' replied Bramble. 'Incidentally, what *is* happening with Roy Walters?'

'He's staying here, screaming habeas corpus, but he became subdued when his father agreed it was for the best. He's in a comfortable room, with canteen access if he wants it, but no phone.'

'And Max Walters agrees?'

'He's a realist, he also said something we've known for some time. University campuses have long been recruiting grounds for extremists, he remembered his own university days when students were seduced by extremists, but it was Marxism then. He's also shattered their family property was used for terrorist purposes and was bloody furious when Roy tipped off Qassim. Max certainly wouldn't like it if Roy was in a police cell, but compared with a cell, our room on the 5th is more like a five-star hotel.'

'Five star my arse,' Bramble gave a discernible double take. 'But I need to discuss some notes with you, Alan.'

'Good. You can all go. What is it, Bob?'

'I took notes as we scanned those tapes,' said Bramble. 'Those four backpackers were in a group then parted company. One headed for the Hornsby line, possibly heading over the Harbour Bridge, another headed for Circular Quay, and the other two headed south, for Town Hall Station and beyond, possibly for Town Hall Station, Central Station, or both.'

'The London Underground syndrome all over again, fan out in all directions,' mused Kelsey. 'Christ! The sooner we get these jokers under restraint the better.'

'We could still be looking for four, Abbas may be replaced.'

'If they stick to their original plan, it could be an afternoon operation, to catch the afternoon commuter traffic. Bloody hell!' Kelsey made for the door. 'Where's Marcus, we need to get something from those computer files.'

CHAPTER 35

Police vans were randomly parked along the street of the house they intended to raid. The officer in charge checked everyone was in position via radio before he gave the order. With personnel positioned around the back of the house, a small contingent approached the front door.

'Go! Go! Go!'

There was a crash and rending of woodwork as the front door caved in, and the squad poured in, bellowing 'Police!' The lower floor rooms were invaded and declared clear before heavy feet clumped on the stairs.

'All clear up here!' came from upstairs and the same call was repeated below. Simultaneously, armed police flooded the rear garden, and approached a shed in the south-east corner. They shone torches through the two windows, alert for booby traps. The door was secured with a padlock, which was promptly despatched.

'Bloody hell!' said one of the raiding police. 'They've been busy in here.'

*

'We've raided the house at Cronulla,' Kelsey reported to Francis Burton. 'Nobody there, we knew they'd flown, but we found bomb making equipment and materials in a large shed at the rear. We're checking it now.'

'That's good news,' Burton replied. 'What's next?'

'We have other addresses. We'll go for those. I'll be in touch.'

Phil Jackson entered as he put down the phone.

'What is it, Phil?'

'The imam is here boss. He wants a word.'

'Ask him to come in,' Kelsey advanced to greet Khalil and indicated a chair. The imam looked weary and Kelsey commented on it.

'Yes,' Khalil admitted. 'It hasn't been easy, my loyalty and dedication to my faith has been questioned, not a pleasant experience to be so accused by one so young. Regrettably this young man has been indoctrinated to believe violence is the only recourse and it's his duty to destroy anything in this country which doesn't conform to his beliefs.'

'He's not alone, there are many like him,' replied Kelsey.

'I agree, he is not,' Khalil sadly shook his head. 'But I've made progress, I have countered some of his arguments and statements and, I think, supplied food for thought. He unbent a little and talked, he's confirmed the attacks are planned for the day after tomorrow to take place at 4.30 — 5.00 pm, peak commuter time.'

He paused momentarily then continued.

'Regrettably, he assumes I do not disapprove of what is to take place, which is why, to a degree, he opened up to me. I didn't disabuse him in case he clammed up, nevertheless I am uncomfortable. I feel guilty of lying to him, by implication if nothing else. I must make my own stance clear eventually, but plainly now is not the time.'

'I understand your dilemma. What have you discovered?'

'The attackers intend to enter Wynyard Station and fan out in various directions, his target was to be Kings Cross while one of his associates was to leave a device to detonate at Circular Quay station. The others he doesn't know.'

'That confirms some pointers we've already deduced from CCTV, but we didn't know about Kings Cross,' said Kelsey. 'With Abbas in custody we must assume he's been replaced.'

'A man named Shehzad is tasked with Circular Quay; a friend of Abbas. I understand he was a member of one of the discussion groups, he attends the university.'

'That's useful to know, we have two people who could identify him. You have done well. Australia is in your debt.'

'I am pleased to have been of service, to my country and my faith. These people are a blight on both, their activities affect the well-being of 99% of good Muslims in this country, of which his father is one, who merely wish to support their families. Every time there's an incident like this, we are all tarred with the same brush.'

'Which causes prejudice, oppression, violence and in turn more extremist converts,' Kelsey was sympathetic. 'It rests with people like you and me to combat reactions that cause yet further reactions. Who was it who said 'Life wasn't meant to be easy?'

Khalil smiled.

'One of our past Prime Ministers,' he said. 'He may not have been right all the time but on that particular occasion he was!'

*

'Those addresses you looked at are also being raided tonight,' Kelsey faced Bramble and Shackleton. 'We're not pussyfooting around anymore. The attacks are apparently timed for the day after tomorrow.'

'Do we have warrants for this lot?'

'We got them about an hour ago.'

*

'What is it, Marcus?'

'Can you come down here, chief,' Templeton's voice came over the phone. 'I've managed to crack this computer from the serviced office block, the first disc we got hold of.'

When Kelsey and Bramble arrived Templeton and Mike Duval were seated at their work stations. Templeton had a list of addresses on his screen, which he scrolled down.

'These addresses are worldwide,' said Templeton. 'Some in USA and others in Europe. There are Australian addresses, we know most of those already, although there's a few we didn't.'

'Print them out. I'll check them. Anything on the impending attack?'

'Not yet. There's a file that may refer to it. I'll check that next.'

'Make it priority. It's possibly set for the day after tomorrow, which will soon be tomorrow, during the afternoon rush hour period.'

'Leave it with me.' Templeton activated the printer.

'Anything on Roy Walters' computer?'

'Nothing of interest,' said Mike Duval. 'Mainly newspaper articles.'

'What sort of articles?'

'Anti-American stuff, justifying what bombers and terrorists do because we've been nasty to them.'

'What newspapers?'

'Predominantly New York Times and The Guardian, with oddments from Australian newspapers, namely The...!'

'I can guess, why did I bother to ask?'

*

Francis Burton was dozing in his office at Canberra when Kelsey came through. It was 3 o'clock in the morning, Burton jolted awake when the phone rang.

'Yes,' he said irritably, as the veils of sleep slowly evaporated. 'Who is it?'

'Kelsey.'

'What have we got, Alan?'

'Not a lot,' was the reply. 'We've raided four houses identified from information received or via vehicle registrations. We arrested seven people from various houses; we found forensic indications of explosive chemicals or materials, but no devices. There may be further houses they're using we don't know about.'

'Shit!' Burton exploded. 'Are you saying we don't know where the buggers are?'

'Afraid so, but we have an idea where they'll turn up,' Kelsey explained. 'Which isn't much consolation right now.'

'How much time do we have?'

'Tomorrow, as far as we know, at about 4.30 pm.' Kelsey replied. 'We've salvaged paperwork and two more computers.'

'Very well, keep me informed,' said Burton. 'I have to report to Cabinet this morning. We'll have to arrange for entry to that station to be limited, we cannot risk large numbers of commuters being injured. Leave that with me. As for the Taranganese

President, he arrives at the Worthington tomorrow…no sorry …' he glanced at the clock: '…I should say today, at about noon. Later he has a meeting with the State Premier about 4.30 in the afternoon.'

'What's on at 4.30 the next day?'

'Something at the Opera House, it's a performance of Sleeping Beauty, or is it the Nutcracker? It's ballet anyway.'

'Well, that's the day we have to worry about.'

*

But it wasn't! Kelsey and the rest of the group, barring Marcus Templeton who was still at his computer, managed to snatch a few hours' sleep before the sun's rays percolated through half-closed blinds. Shackleton shook Kelsey's shoulder as he slept in a plush office chair in a conference room.

'Yes…what is it?'

'We've intercepted a phone call from the office block.'

'Which one?'

'Where Barry Rawlings is, the second one we searched. It was short and to the point, today is now the day, not tomorrow. The raids must have panicked them, they've advanced 24 hours.'

'Won't that affect their main plan? The sniper shots…Shit! No, it bloody won't. The President is scheduled to leave at the same time of day, today that is, for State Parliament. Get Francis Burton on the line in Canberra, he's seeing Cabinet today. The President's itinerary must be changed.'

*

Burton negotiated with New South Wales Police and Railways, then came back to Kelsey who was in the canteen having a hurried breakfast. This had opened up an hour earlier, causing grumbling from canteen staff who had been called in.

Kelsey promptly assembled his troops, Bramble and Shackleton were unshaven, while Templeton was red-eyed and weary, having worked all night. Sam Holmes was still involved at the airport.

Miller, Furnell and Fenway had been accommodated at the hotel across the street, while Roy Walters had been allocated a bed on the top floor with a security gyard outside the door. Max Walters, the imam and Mr Kamiza had gone home at about 1.00 am, while Abbas had been removed to the nearby police station in the custody of Detective Sergeant Parslow. Miller, Alison Furnell and Doug Fenway arrived from the hotel.

'We're moving out of here,' announced Kelsey. 'Burton has been negotiating with the Premier and the Police Commissioner. We're needed at the Railways Operations and Communications Centre, temporary control will be handled by a senior military officer. Grab some breakfast and we'll get over there.'

He seized some toast and marmalade and bit off a mouthful.

'That includes you, Geoff, and you, Alison and Doug. You people have had personal contact with some of the bastards we're tracking and may spot them more quickly. Go and sort out your breakfast, we've called canteen staff in early and they should be able to serve up something.'

*

When they arrived at the State Government Operations Centre there were military vehicles outside, men in battle fatigues in the foyer. A couple of Army officers were leaning over the reception desk talking to the man behind it. They turned as Kelsey and his group entered, followed by a high-ranking police officer who had arrived simultaneously.

'Commissioner Phillips,' the last arrival walked up to the Army officers. 'You'll be Major Collins?'

The senior officer nodded and extended his hand. He was 6 feet in height, had a moustache and was straight as a ramrod.

'Where is Mr Kelsey?' asked the Commissioner.

'Here,' Kelsey advanced from the entrance. 'I've just arrived.'

The Commissioner and Major Collins shook Kelsey's hand.

'Good to see you again, Alan,' said Major Collins. 'Nasty business, this!'

Kelsey introduced Bramble and Shackleton, McKay was outside parking the car. Kelsey waved his hand around the others, Miller, Fenway, Alison Furnell, Phil Jackson and Melanie Cassidy in a general introduction. Their names were probably forgotten as soon as introductions were complete. Kelsey shook hands with a captain and a civilian introduced as Tony Mariner, in charge of the Operations room.

'We need a quick briefing to sort out protocol and procedures before we start,' said Major Collins. 'The advancement of their plan by 24 hours means that plans we had to reduce passenger numbers have been prejudiced.'

Mariner indicated a ground floor conference room. Major Collins installed himself at the head of the table to establish his authority.

'I have direct lines to the Premier of New South Wales and the Prime Minister. From this point I am in command. This must be made clear to everyone in the operations room upstairs. All matters requiring a decision relating to passenger control are to be channelled through me and/or Captain Roberts,' he indicated the officer by his side, a tall man who had pronounced sunburn, also with a military moustache. 'As you'll appreciate, we have several organisations represented here, but with the seriousness of the situation we can't afford clashes of authority. Is that understood?' he looked around, everyone nodded or mumbled assent.

'Having said that, we have with us Alan Kelsey, with whom I've worked before on Internal Security matters, his colleague Sam Holmes is detained at the airport where he's involved in another matter that could have a bearing on what's happening here,' Collins continued. 'Alan knows more of the background of this operation than I do so if you have a question, don't hesitate to approach Alan. Are there any questions?'

Major Collins swung around as McKay entered.

'Who are you? And why are you adrift…ah…David McKay,' Collins extended his hand. 'Good to see you again, but I still want an answer to my second question.'

'I had to park the car ready for a quick getaway,' explained McKay as he shook Collins' hand. 'We shall be heading for Wynyard Station very shortly.'

'Right! Good! Everyone clear so far?'

It seemed everybody was.

'Then let's go upstairs. The Commissioner and Tony Mariner will explain matters to those upstairs when we arrive.'

Major Collins marched into the Operations & Communications Centre with the Police Commissioner and Tony Mariner following. They fanned out and Tony Mariner, normally in charge of the centre, attracted everyone's attention.

'Attention everyone!' he called and the hubbub of background noise ceased. There were roughly twenty in the room, mostly sitting before computers and some wearing headsets. Three large wraparound screens were on the wall which showed the full railway system, plus a patchwork of monitor screens depicting station scenes, passageways and platforms, in an array before which sat various operators, the scenes flicked and changed constantly.

'This is Commissioner Phillips of the New South Wales Police, and Major Collins of the SAS,' announced Tony Mariner. 'Major Collins is assuming temporary command of this complex insofar as it relates to passenger control until further notice.'

Collins advanced to the centre of the room to face all the operators.

'All of you; give me your attention.'

There was a rumble of voices, heads popped up and turned in Collins' direction.

'Can you hear me?' he bellowed.

Most of them did. Some of his men went amongst the operators, tapping shoulders of those still on phones.

'We're dealing with a Category Red emergency which takes absolute priority,' said Collins. 'We're dealing with a situation where we suspect at least four men, possibly more, will attempt to enter the system with explosives which they intend to detonate in the rail system. Did everyone hear that?'

They did, there was a buzz of voices.

'Silence!' Major Collins thundered. 'If you talk amongst yourselves, you may miss what I have to say. Now, we don't know if they are suicide bombers as per the London Underground, or whether they will leave packages, bags or whatever on trains or in stations à la Madrid or Mumbai. We believe, from information received; they plan to enter the system via Wynyard Station, then spread out in four or more directions, as they did in London.'

'Is this for real?' A hand was raised. 'In Sydney?'

'Regrettably yes, it is…and in Sydney!' replied Collins. 'We want every CCTV camera in the system checked, particularly those in Wynyard, Town Hall, Central, Museum, St James and Circular Quay railway stations. Those are likely targets. For these people...better a target in the city centre if you are making a point, no point hitting a station in the outer suburbs, although I'm not denying it could happen. All clear so far?'

There was a rumble of assent.

'We are looking for men of Asian appearance, call them what you will. They will probably be carrying bags or backpacks.'

A girl at one of the consoles spread her hands in a protesting motion.

'Are we assuming that because they're Asian in appearance that they're ...?'

'Yes, we bloody well are,' Collins snapped. 'What's your name?'

'Wendy Adamson.'

'Very well, Wendy, do you have friends or relatives using the system today?'

'Yes, I do, but ...!'

'Then you could be responsible for their death or injury if you have reservations about fingering people of a particular appearance. If anyone has any politically correct emotions or reactions that will affect their judgement and possibly cause death and disaster, I suggest you get out now. We're facing a serious situation here and we don't have the time or inclination to horse around with political correctness. Anybody have a problem with that?'

He looked around belligerently but nobody moved, Wendy Adamson pouted and looked down at her console.

'Good! We've been pursuing this situation full-time for the last few days, and some months overall. We know the types we're looking for and what motivates them. I will qualify what I'm saying, look for anyone behaving suspiciously, but pay attention to anyone of Asian appearance;' he turned and gave a grim smile. 'That is; a complexion similar to Captain Roberts here.'

There was a ripple of laughter and Captain Roberts grinned.

'Is that clear?' Major Collins glared around, clearly it was.

'Remember, if these people carry out their intentions, people close to you or people you know could be maimed or killed. We believe the time they have in mind is the afternoon rush hour, 4.30 to 5.30,' he turned to Tony Mariner. 'Contact every station master on the underground system, plus Circular Quay and in addition, Chatswood. They must be on the alert for anyone behaving suspiciously and report in here. That includes the main railway stations and probably Redfern.'

Mariner nodded and went to one of the consoles. Major Collins turned to Kelsey.

'I've arranged for troops to be on call at all those stations. We may have a situation where we have to clear a station completely, not an easy task. We'll have another problem if we frighten them off, they'll change plan and go elsewhere, any station will do if they can't reach their planned targets. We need people, police and...' he turned to Kelsey: '... your chaps, to be within these stations and, hopefully, unobtrusive. Will they be able to recognise any of these bastards?'

'Some,' Kelsey responded. 'We've had some positive ID's, Geoff Miller here will recognise one of the ring leaders if he spots him, and Doug Fenway and Alison Furnell here could recognise others. If Wynyard is their focal point, I suggest these three be stationed in the main concourse of the Wynyard Station.'

'Are they likely to be recognised themselves?'

Kelsey pursed his lips.

'They all could be recognised, Miller in particular, he was imprisoned at Hopetoun for four days, while Doug Fenway and Alison have attended meetings with others.'

'I'll ask Tony Mariner if we can fix them up with railway uniforms,' said Collins.

'No,' said Kelsey. 'I have a better idea, if they're in uniform people might approach them asking for directions. Not only will this distract them, it will attract attention if they can't answer simple questions. Dress them up as cleaners and give them a bucket and broom apiece. Give them baseball caps as well, that should complete their disguise.'

'Good idea,' mused Collins. 'The Commissioner has already suggested some of his railway police dress as itinerants and ordinary passengers.'

'Good!' Kelsey nodded. 'Get Tony to warn his staff some of our fellows will be on the spot. Ensure they all have a good look at these three here, Geoff, Doug and Alison, and warn them what they'll be doing. I suggest we place them all at Wynyard.'

'Yes, and get them wired up. We need instant warning if they spot anyone!'

CHAPTER 36

t was agreed to position Miller at Wynyard Station and Alison Furnell at Circular Quay, where it was calculated Shehzad could show up. Doug Fenway didn't like that but Kelsey was adamant. Alison would be more likely to pick out Shehzad.

To allay Fenway's protective instinct, Kelsey stressed that Phil Jackson would accompany Alison armed with a handgun, plus a broom and bucket as a disguise, plus two plain clothes police officers, while Alison posed as a passenger. Kelsey decreed she wear sunglasses and a baseball cap or some other headgear to prevent recognition.

Kelsey needed Fenway at Wynyard, if the bombers stuck to their original plan despite altering the time schedule, Kelsey needed someone at Wynyard capable of pointing the finger. Bramble was situated at a lower level with ASIO personnel. Police were stationed in the bookstall and a florist's shop; all pointed out to Miller and Fenway and vice versa so they knew who was who and where they were.

Undercover police were at the main city stations with army detachments within closed vehicles awaiting the call.

Shackleton was to take station in the serviced office block in Barry Rawlings' office on the ground floor. Melanie Cassidy was to be on reception, with McKay outside the building across the street. The Agnarat Wen offices were unoccupied and undercover police were watching the rear door of the building. Police were also in the other office block, where an office was rented in the name of Qassim, posing as cleaners. Kelsey thought it unlikely that office would be utilised by the terrorists, Roy Walters' tip off would have intimated it was compromised, but it would have been unwise to ignore it.

Down below numerous police and ASIO operatives were occupying platforms and travelling on trains, the plan was for them to travel to and from Chatswood in the north to Redfern in the south, departing from and alighting at city stations. Station staff had been placed alongside communication ports in case radios were ineffective down below or in dead spots, if anyone suspicious was spotted an operative would pass the message to a railway employee who would use a line phone to report.

Kelsey advised all arrangements to Francis Burton in Canberra. Burton took details and said he would be at a Cabinet meeting within the hour.

'Are you happy with Major Collins?' he asked.

'Very!' Kelsey responded. 'I've worked with him before on similar exercises, he's no fool and knows what he's doing. My only complaint is, he treats me as if I'm one of his bloody foot soldiers.'

'About time somebody did!' Burton gave a dry chuckle. 'Keep me posted, Alan.'

*

It was five hours before the afternoon rush hour. It had been decided no obvious public warnings should be issued as this would have tipped their hand to the bombers who could then postpone the operation, move it elsewhere, or both. Major Collins carefully weighed this up and consulted with Canberra before making the decision. His political masters had reservations, fearing the possible media and electoral repercussions if people were killed or injured, but Major Collins pointed out if the operation was postponed because it was clearly blown, the bombers were then free to pick their time for another attack and could strike anywhere without warning.

Waiting time was employed checking communication procedures and equipment. Sam Holmes had returned from the main airport, where an incoming arrival had been detained by Customs. This was another potential terrorist situation which, after action by Customs, Federal Police and ASIO, was now downgraded. Holmes was given control of two dummy runs whereby a police operative posing as a passenger was tracked by personnel on the spot and by those watching monitors in the Operations Centre. Blind spots were found where cameras didn't cover particular areas and personnel positions were adjusted.

Miller and Doug Fenway were given a bucket of soapy water, a mop and squeegee and allocated an area to clean up. Markers were placed to prevent passengers walking across this area, and Miller set about cleaning his patch. Major Collins and Kelsey had stressed they must genuinely work. The bombers would be alert when they entered stations, men armed with buckets and mops standing around and peering in all directions would arouse suspicion. Genuine activity was the key, act like a floor cleaner and merge in.

'You missed a bit there,' Bramble called on his way down

below as Miller began swabbing down.

'Get stuffed!' was Miller's response, Bramble made an appropriate gesture as he continued down the escalator.

*

The afternoon was otherwise uneventful, Sam Holmes ran another drill at 2.30 pm, this time an undercover policeman dressed in jeans and 'T' shirt. He was checked to the lower levels and picked up by all outposts on the way down, the cameras also monitored his progress until he boarded a train for Circular Quay. The reporting in also functioned well, at Circular Quay he was picked up and reported in by Phil Jackson, also by police observers. He caught a train back to St James where he was picked up again. Holmes and Major Collins pronounced themselves satisfied.

'Everyone maintain full alert,' Collins broadcast on all personal radios. 'These buggers could appear any time now. Stay alert.'

He clicked off his radio and turned to his Army radio operator.

'Tell Fenway and Miller to keep their eyes peeled, Ramage, check with Jackson at Circular Quay that Furnell is also alert and he doesn't stray too far from her.'

Kelsey had decided to station Melanie Cassidy at the reception desk in the serviced office block superintended by Barry Rawlings, to work alongside Angela Parish, a bubbly 19-year-old blonde.

Melanie had been given a lift there by Bramble, as he was driving to Winyard Station it was on his way. As they arrived Angela was tidying up a table top just inside the glass frontage. As Melanie prepared to disembark, Bramble had indicated Angela.

'Is that who you'll be working with?' he asked.

'That's her,' Melanie swung her legs out onto the pavement.

'Nice looking bird, could be your lucky day! Nearly your type, eh Mel?' he said cheerfully and Melanie froze in the act of closing the door.

'What?'

'Thought you preferred brunettes!'

Bramble gave her a thumbs up sign and pulled the door to. He pushed his right arm out of the driver's window and gave a cheery wave to Melanie as he drove off, leaving her staring after him. As the implications of his comment sank in, she had a rush of adrenalin.

'Bastard!' she said with a rueful smile. Trust Bob to work things out. As she walked into the building to be greeted by Angela, her emotions were moving back onto an even keel. She knew Bramble as well as he knew her, discerning he may be, but he was no gossip, and no grass. Despite their many differences of opinion, she knew her indiscretion would be safe with him.

Angela Parish was to handle incoming calls and people, while Melanie was to sit and look busy. She was connected to the main operations centre via an earpiece in her left ear; tuned into Corporal Ramage, Major Collins' radio operator.

Nobody had entered the Agnarat offices, Barry Rawlings made a couple of trips there armed with his tool-kit and reported the room was empty.

Melanie often ruminated that although ASIO was a good means of earning a living, it had its moments of sheer boredom. One of her great grandfathers had been in the trenches during the 1914-18 war, he was reported to have said it was 90% sheer boredom, 8% alertness and anticipation, and 2% wild excitement and sheer fright. To Melanie life in ASIO ran on the same lines.

Communications in her ear indicated nothing to report, the clock indicated 3.00 pm, if the raid was intended for 4.30 onwards there was still time to go. But what would the bombers be doing and would they necessarily stick to their timetable? They must be preparing themselves, wherever they were, maybe they were already on the move.

She thought over the past few days, and briefly smiled as she recalled Constable Lonsdale's facial expression when she and Kelsey arrived at the police station and identified themselves. Lonsdale's part in this affair had been erratic. He had demonstrated blinkered single mindedness when he refused to listen to or believe Geoff Miller about the happenings at Walters' farm. Then he demonstrated initiative and courage, after being hog-tied in the room by Hammoud and his accomplice, by breaking free and going on the offensive when someone entered the room, although the object of his aggression had been the hapless Shackleton.

Then he had demonstrated more sloppiness when he called on Jackson & Antrobus, if indeed he had visited them at all.

'Probably too busy booking motorists!' had been Kelsey's bitter comment.

'Or checking if they had teenage daughters!' was Miller's equally bitter aside

Lonsdale's assumptions about Geoff Miller, and his refusal to listen to him, could have prejudiced the entire investigation. He had a penchant for missing the obvious, as had the surveyor from Jackson & Antrobus who failed to report the presence of enough artillery to start a small war when he inspected the property. History was full of campaigns lost through missing the obvious.

Melanie 's thoughts also strayed into the episode with Alison. Despite her sexual ambivalence, what had happened had taken her completely by surprise, and in retrospect caused her considerable mind searching and concern. Immediately after the event she really thought she had prejudiced her career with ASIO, a job she loved. Yet Alison seemed unperturbed by the event, which aside from the sexual aspect had certainly saved their lives. Melanie wondered if, ironically, she had done Alison a favour by arousing realisation that being loyal to Roy was a waste of time, when she had an alternative prospect in Doug Fenway. But if, in the cold light of day, Alison reacted adversely and reported what had happened (Melanie instigating a sexual liaison with a young woman who was a Crown witness) Melanie realised she could be out of a job. So far there had been no signs of such a reaction by Alison, Melanie could only hope.

'Like some coffee?' Angela broke into her reverie.

'I'll get it,' Melanie indicated the door to the left. 'It's over there, isn't it?'

'That's it,' Angela replied then answered an incoming call. As Melanie entered the small kitchen area, she was aware of a jarring in her mind. Something in her various thought processes had raised a query as she reached for the kettle.

She took two coffees to the desk. They drank in silence. Angela wasn't aware of Melanie's exact status. She knew she was connected with law enforcement and something was afoot which affected one of their clients but little else. The phone rang again and Angela answered it, while Melanie sat, deep in thought, still wondering what had jarred her mind.

Was it something to do with the viewing of CCTV tapes? Every time she considered the puzzle it transported her to CCTV viewing. She shook her head, then realised she was being addressed by Barry Rawlings.

'Penny for 'em,' he said and smiled.

'I'm sorry,' answered Melanie. 'Just a train of thought.'

The thought occurred to her again, something to do with... what was it? Train...what was that? Her mind nearly grasped what had been worrying her, before it evaporated. What was it?

'Check with Angela whether office 8 on the fourth is occupied,' Barry Rawlings said. 'Someone is in there. Ask if it's been rented out in the last few days. If it has, I knew nothing about it. Room 8 on the fourth, it was used by Hill & Berrett who pulled out a week ago.'

'What?' Melanie came back to reality. 'Sorry, I missed that.'

Barry repeated it and added. 'Room 8 on the fourth, ask her to check it.'

As he turned to go Angela finished the call and called him back.

'What was that, Barry?'

'Room 8 on the fourth. Who's in there?'

Angela activated her computer, consulted the screen, and shook her head.

'Hill & Berrett,' she replied. 'Hang on ...they've gone, haven't they? They left last week. There shouldn't be anyone in there. It's vacant.'

'That's what I thought. There's someone in there now.'

'Well, I don't know who,' said Angela.' It's been vacant since Eddie Hill and Jack Berrett moved out.'

'Are you sure?'

'Positive,' replied Angela. 'I'd know if it had been rented out again,' she checked a keyboard behind her. 'The keys are still here.'

'Odd!' Rawlings rubbed his chin. 'Somebody's definitely in there. I'll check it out.'

He headed for the lift but Melanie catapulted out of her chair and called after him.

'Barry, wait!'

'What?'

'Which side of the building is that office...office 8?'

'Which side?' Rawlings scratched his head. 'Um! Let me think...it'll be on this side, the south.'

'The same side as the Agnarat office?'

'Yes, that's south as well, two floors further up.'

'So the Hill & Berrett office is two floors lower down on the same side as the Agnarat Wen offices?'

'That's right!'

'Tell Shackleton!'

'Why?' Rawlings looked puzzled then enlightenment dawned. 'Christ, you don't think...!'

'It's a possibility,' snapped Melanie. 'Tell Shackleton. Call him, now! Whatever you do, don't go near that office until Shackleton and McKay are with you. I mean that!'

'Very well,' Rawlings shrugged. 'If you say so...!'

'I do say so,' Melanie said tersely, then the jarring came again. This time it broke through. 'Give them a ring now. Do it! I've got to ring someone else.'

She seized her mobile phone and rang Kelsey who answered immediately.

'Hello Mel,' he said. 'What is it?'

'Two things, there's an unauthorised occupant in one of the rooms on the fourth floor, I'm getting Shackleton and McKay to check it out. But something else just occurred to me. That CCTV we viewed.'

'What about it?'

'We never saw them enter Wynyard Station's upper level from the street.'

'Well, maybe Marcus hadn't got to that tape when you...!'

'Yes, he did, he had them all. We never saw them come in

from the street. We first caught them on the lower level.'

'Meaning what …? Hell!' Kelsey was ahead of her. 'They came in by train from elsewhere and met in the station, then caught another train out. They'll probably do the same today, fan out and leave at the same time.'

'So they'll synchronise their departure. When they come in, they won't use the street entrance at all, unless someone goes out that way.'

'I'll inform Major Collins and Sam Holmes. On the other matter, I'll contact Shackleton, he may need back up. Thanks, Mel.'

CHAPTER 37

Shackleton, having reached the sixth floor, had just finished speaking with Barry Rawlings and took the call.

'Yes Alan, got it! I've just been told the same thing by Barry Rawlings. Will do!'

He contacted McKay, still across the street. McKay entered the building, nodded to Melanie, entered the lift and emerged on the fourth floor; Shackleton was already there.

'Which office is it?'

'Down that corridor,' Shackleton pointed. 'Last but one on the left. The window of that office overlooks the Worthington, it's two floors lower down than the office upstairs and commands the front door and steps.'

'So that office has a clear view of the front steps?'

'Which means, if it's them, they're in there for two reasons. Firstly: they may consider the office upstairs has been compromised.'

'Because of Roy bloody Walters singing loud and clear!

Makes sense, they'll know he's in custody. And the second?' asked McKay.

'There isn't a flagpole to affect a clear shot.'

They approached cautiously. McKay checked his watch.

'Time?' queried Shackleton.

'Nearly 3.30 pm,' said McKay.

'When is the Taranganese President due out?'

'About four, it's been brought forward.'

'But he's been diverted through the rear door,' said Shackleton. 'It was changed within the last half hour.'

'Maybe this fellow doesn't know that...hold on...' McKay caught Shackleton's sleeve '...someone's coming out.'

The office door opened slowly, a man peered out and looked up and down the corridor as they backed into a doorway for cover. An Asian man emerged, closed the door and walked down the corridor away from them, carrying a case. To Shackleton it looked capable of carrying a dissembled rifle.

'I'd say he's been informed of the plan change. What now?' asked McKay.

'Jump the bastard! He's no right to be in there...bugger it... he's spotted us!'

The man had looked back, then turned and ran. Shackleton and McKay took off in pursuit. He reached the corridor's end and turned the corner. They followed into another corridor with a bank of office doors. He rounded the next corner, but obviously hit an obstacle as there was a disturbance and raised voices. When they turned the corner they found their quarry had collided with a document trolley and was on his knees. A young man was slowly rising to his feet.

'Why the hell were you running like that ...?' he was shouting.

He got no further. The Asian regained his feet but lost seconds reaching for his case, which was his undoing. McKay launched into a Rugby tackle, hit him above the knees and they both hit the deck. Shackleton entered the fray, floored the Asian as he struggled to his feet and slipped handcuffs over his wrists.

Doors along the corridor opened, heads appeared and there was a buzz of voices, all asking the same question, what was going on? McKay turned to a young girl from the nearest office, presumably the one the document trolley had just left. She shrank away from him as he moved towards her.

Shackleton reached for the suspected gun case and pulled it towards him. McKay dialled a number: 'Barry, get up onto the fourth.'

The young girl remained standing still, eyes wide with fright. McKay seized her arm and shook her.

'Ring the police...*now!*' he bellowed at her, but she stood as if paralysed. 'Police...ring them...go!' he snapped. She finally got the message, nodded and re-entered the office doorway. McKay dialled again and spoke to Melanie.

'Tell Alan I think we've arrested one of them,' he said tersely. 'We've asked someone to send for the police but I'm not sure if she registered it, can *you* do it? This bloke had a gun case...' and added as a qualification '...we think!'

'Have you got him?' he asked Shackleton.

Shackleton nodded. The Asian man was struggling and protesting furiously.

'This is a disgrace, release me at once. Who are you? I rent offices in this building.'

'Not that one you don't,' commented McKay dryly. 'That office has been vacant for two weeks.'

'I have just rented them, get these handcuffs off me or you'll be in trouble. Release me at once.'

Shackleton began to experience misgivings, the man sounded

convincing. Was it possible they'd overreacted, arrested and manhandled a legitimate office occupant? The man displayed no emotion other than fury and indignation. That case could contain surveying equipment, a terrifying thought

'Bloody hell,' he eyed McKay who obviously had similar doubts.

'If that's so,' McKay asked. 'Why did you run?'

'You were chasing me. I thought you were thieves, of course I ran.'

'But when you starting running, we hadn't moved,' said Shackleton.

There was silence, what their captive would have come up with next they never discovered as there was the sound of lift doors opening and Barry Rawlings arrived.

'All right everyone, everything is under control, I know who these men are!' he shouted to placate various onlookers as he ran towards them. 'Who have you got there …My God! Mr Qassim'

'Rawlings, tell these men who I am,' the Asian snarled angrily.

'We know who you are. He's just told us,' Shackleton said. 'Your office is on the sixth floor, what were you doing in that one?'

'I had permission to view it, we were thinking of renting it instead.'

But Barry Rawlings shook his head.

'That's news to me!' he said. 'I have no knowledge of that, we've just checked our listings. That office is still vacant and hasn't been advertised, we've had no enquiries.'

'You'll have no objection if we look in your case, Mr Qassim?' Shackleton asked pleasantly.

'You have no right…!'

Shackleton snapped the case open, still entertaining considerable unease. It was still possible they'd manhandled someone who could give a logical reason for being in that office, and that Colbeck, the building manager, knew something Barry Rawlings, the building superintendent, didn't. Or maybe Angela had missed something when she checked it. But this was not the time to entertain reservations. Shackleton opened the case, as he did so his fears dissipated and overwhelming relief flooded through him. There was an expulsion of air from Qassim's lungs when the case's contents were exposed. The contents were not surveying equipment, as Shackleton had feared, but component parts of a sophisticated rifle, with a telescopic sight.

'Going grouse shooting, were you?' he dialled Melanie's number. 'We've hit the jackpot, Mel, we have a rifle, we also have Mr Qassim. Advise Alan, quickly.'

McKay approached the protesting Qassim and began searching his pockets.

'This is an outrage!' spluttered Qassim. 'You have no right…!'

'Shut up!' Shackleton snapped the case shut. 'Why are you carrying a rifle with a telescopic sight?'

There was no answer, Shackleton turned to McKay as the latter continued emptying Qassim's pockets and laid the contents on a nearby table, a mobile phone, a clip of bullets, a hand gun and a wallet. There was also a small note book and a ball point pen.

A bell pinged from the direction of the lift shaft and two police, a sergeant and a constable, emerged. Shackleton recognised them as members of the guard on the front of building. They came down the corridor, hands on holsters.

Shackleton flashed his ID, they peered at it closely and the sergeant nodded. They looked at McKay.

'He's with me!' snapped Shackleton. 'Dave, show your ID for God's sake, before we have any misunderstandings.' McKay reached slowly into his pocket and complied. The sergeant, turned to Shackleton.

'Who's he?' he indicated the office junior who had set his trolley upright and was collecting scattered mail.

'He works here!'

'And him?' he jerked his thumb at Qassim.

'Suspected terrorist, we've just caught him with that,' Shackleton indicated the case. 'There's a dissembled rifle in there with a telescopic sight. He was in an office overlooking the Worthington Hotel where the Taranganese President is staying. I don't think he meant to keep the mice down!'

The sergeant permitted himself a thin smile, then indicated the items on the table.

'What are these?'

'His. My colleague is just checking,' Shackleton indicated McKay who was pressing buttons on the mobile phone. 'He's all yours, you can take him and the rifle.'

'We should take all this stuff as well,' said the policeman.

'Go ahead,' McKay was still pressing buttons and examining the small screen. 'But we'll keep the phone...Bloody hell, Shack, come down below, quick!'

He headed for the lift and Shackleton followed, as he did so he turned to the sergeant. 'Whatever you do, don't lose him! Major Collins will want words with him.'

'I think we know what to do!' the sergeant replied with a trace of sarcasm.

*

At the control centre Major Collins was checking all monitor screens.

'Watch those two lower platforms,' he commanded. 'We

believe that's where they'll come in and congregate, they will synchronise their departures to wherever they're going and then split up.'

He turned to two operators on the end of the console.

'Keep watching the upper level, I don't trust these bastards to do what we expect them to do,' he turned to Commissioner Phillips. 'Make sure your boys are concentrated on that lower level. We suspect they'll be carrying bags or rucksacks. I want your blokes to jump them when they are all together. Our bomb squad will be on hand.'

'We're ready,' the Commissioner eyed his watch. 'They should be appearing soon if they stick to their schedule.'

'The time is …' Collins consulted his wrist watch: '…3.43 pm. OK everybody! Keep your eyes peeled!'

*

'What's up?' asked Shackleton.

'Look at this message,' McKay indicated the mobile phone. 'He received a text message, that's why he left that office when he did.'

Shackleton peered at the screen.

'DS shortly cmg out rear of WH. 4.00 pm. Van in position Get out now.'

'How the hell did they find that out?'

'Inside knowledge, somebody is tipping them off, maybe a mole on the President's staff,' said McKay. 'There's an earlier message on there, have a look.'

'Off bg watched. Do not enter, go straight to HB office 8 — 4th.'

'That came through last night, so they knew we'd been in there.'

'Doubt if we left any traces,' said Shackleton. 'It's always possible, but I reckon that prat Roy Walters tipped them off. We'll have words with Mel on the way out.'

They exited the lift on the ground floor, Shackleton diverted to speak to Melanie.

'We're going to the street that runs along the rear of the hotel. They know the President is going to exit from the rear and have repositioned themselves. Tell Alan somebody has ratted on us about their sixth-floor office, they knew we'd been in there.'

'Got it!' Melanie promptly dialled Kelsey.

'The police are bringing Qassim out?' Shackleton shouted from the door as they passed through it. Melanie nodded in reply then began speaking to Kelsey.

*

'I think I've got something, sir.'

'What? Let me see — where?'

'Lower level, two Asian men with back packs.'

Kelsey signalled to Major Collins and Sam Holmes who both came over.

'Put it on main screen.' Collins commanded. The image of the lower-level platform at Wynyard appeared above them, a train was pulling out. Two men bearing backpacks stood in the middle of the platform. They didn't communicate, but stood still two metres apart, seemingly waiting for someone.

Collins turned to Captain Roberts.

'Likely candidates, Captain, alert everybody on the two levels we have isolated two males, lower level. Watch the other arrival platforms, others may appear.'

Captain Roberts spoke into a microphone, alerting those already on the platform. Kelsey watched as the camera panned around, he recognised some operatives already down there. One was a scruffy looking type dressed like a tramp, ostensibly asleep on a bench. A railwayman walked up to him and roughly shook him awake, there appeared to be an altercation. Kelsey smiled; they were very convincing. The official was one of Sam Holmes' men passing on the message received via landline.

A young woman wearing a short skirt sat on another bench further along. She had a shoulder bag and was showing plenty of leg, which caused many sidelong glances from passers-by. She was Catherine Parkinson, a colleague of Melanie Cassidy's and an experienced ASIO operative. In addition to her provocative appearance, she was also a karate expert and a dead shot with a hand gun, well able to take care of herself. She observed the performance between the apparent railway official and the tramp, the former paused by her, seemingly uttered some comment about the tramp and moved on. She looked straight into the nearest surveillance camera, gazed at it for some seconds and briefly raised one hand.

'She's got the message,' Kelsey said to Major Collins.

'Another one's appeared, he's just come from that Southern Line train. He's hovering five or six metres from the other two. That one there...see him? He's checking time tables.'

'Pass it on,' Collins turned to Captain Roberts. 'That female operative has already locked onto him.'

'Abbas must have been replaced; they're still expecting someone.'

'There's another!' the dark-haired girl operating a nearby monitor turned to Kelsey. 'He's just got off the Bankstown train. There...he's approaching the other three, they've seen him, look...see there.'

'But they don't seem to be grouping together.' Kelsey commented.

'They're breaking up and heading in various directions,' said the girl operator. 'Two going to lower-level platforms and two to the upper level.'

'They're splitting up,' Kelsey beckoned to Major Collins.'There they go, Major, two down below and two going above.'

Collins came over to check the screen.

'Opinion?' he asked.

'They're off, I'd say.'

'Agreed! Then so are we. Captain Roberts! Execute!'

Roberts picked up his hand receiver.

'All units! Go! Go! Go!'

CHAPTER 38

Melanie passed on the message from Shackleton to Kelsey via mobile as he watched units spring into action on the monitor screen. Kelsey turned to Major Collins.

'We need security units at the rear of the Worthington Hotel, Major...now! They've got wind of the changed Presidential itinerary. Shackleton and McKay are already down there.'

'How the hell did they lock onto the changes?' rapped Collins.

'There could be a mole in the President's entourage,' Kelsey replied. Another thought occurred to him and he spoke again to Cassidy. 'Mel, check with HQ that Roy Walters has been under constant surveillance, and is Abbas still locked up?'

*

McKay and Shackleton crossed the street outside and entered a side street. McKay looked towards the next intersection; the back entrance to the Worthington was about 100 metres away. Vehicles were parked on both sides.

'The text message said it was a van.' Shackleton looked right and left.

'I can see three vans. We'll have to check them all.'

'What about the other side of the hotel?'

'We can't be everywhere. Check these three first.'

They cautiously approached a white Hi-Ace. McKay checked the passenger window; the cabin was empty. He tried the door but it was locked. Shackleton went to the rear and craned his neck to look through the back window, acutely aware he could be risking a shot through the head. It was empty. Gear was scattered throughout the van's rear but it looked innocuous.

'Try the next!'

They approached a blue Ford. It wasn't parked well; its front end was against the kerb and its rear end angling outwards. But that small detail was forgotten as a police vehicle approached, with flashing red and blue lights, another appeared at the opposite end of the street. There was sudden activity in the third van, a red one, further down the street. It abruptly pulled from the kerb, described a 'U' turn and roared in their direction.

'Dave, somebody jumped out before it took off,' Shackleton shouted. 'He's running down that street…there! Come on! The police will deal with the van.'

The running figure was dressed in a leather jacket and blue denims. He crossed the street and vanished between two buildings.

When they reached there, the runner had disappeared, they ran down the alleyway, looking left and right as they passed doorways and rubbish skips. They reached the street at the far end but the runner had vanished.

'Shit!' Shackleton checked all directions, McKay phoned in the fugitive's description, last known position and the direction he was heading.

'What's down there?' asked McKay.

'Martin Place station,' said Shackleton. 'If he boards a train, he goes either to Kings Cross or Town Hall.'

'I'll call it in,' McKay spoke again into his phone. 'Guess we're through here.'

They returned to the rear of the Worthington Hotel. The fugitive red van had been blocked by a police car, which it had tried to circumvent, and in doing so rammed the white Hi Ace van. The driver had been arrested and placed in the rear of a police car. Several police surrounded the two crashed vehicles. As McKay and Shackleton arrived, brandishing IDs, the police were inside the rear of the red van.

'Could have been nasty!' Shackleton commented. As they approached, he saw Parslow by the rear of the van. 'Hallo Ken, so you caught someone. More than we did.'

Parslow smiled and gave a wave of acknowledgment.

'They knew we were coming, that's why they took off. There's a scanner inside the van, they were picking up our messages. We found a couple of high-powered rifles inside and the back window was removed, they were ideally placed for a sniper attack. You lost the other guy?''

'Last seen heading for Martin Place,' said McKay. 'We alerted the Major. If he catches a train he'll head for Kings Cross. Going through Town Hall he'd run into trouble.'

'Who was he, any idea?'

McKay pondered.

'It could have been Juan Rivera, a mercenary, we've come across him before, a hired gunman and a crack shot. Geoff Miller saw him arrive at Hopetoun. He's a loner and no mug, he took off when he saw how things were going.' He indicated the man in the police car. 'Do we know who *he* is?'

'Not yet,' said Parslow. 'We'll find out when we take him in. What's happening at Wynyard?'

'No idea. We're hoping for the best. Who owns the white van?'

'Don't know yet,' commented Parslow. 'We're running it through the system. The poor bastard's in for a nasty shock! Hope he's insured!'

'If he is, he's lost his No Claims Bonus!' said McKay. 'What about the red van?'

'Hired or stolen, we're still checking.'

*

Bramble received the signal by relay via land line and shouted 'GO!' The men on the lower-level platform simultaneously sprang into action. One of the two backpackers on the lower level was overwhelmed and his bag removed. The other evaded capture and headed for the South Line platform, where a train was about to leave. He leapt through the open doors just as they closed, and the train moved out.

Bramble swore angrily as they lost him and shouted to the man relaying messages. 'That train is going to Circular Quay. Alert Major Collins! Got that?'

He received an affirmative and hared up the stairs, knocking into people who protested angrily as he bowled them aside.

'Let me through...Police!' he shouted as he bounded upwards.

A third man they were chasing reached the upper level, dodged behind a pillar and pulled out his mobile phone. He became aware he had crossed a line of red witches' hats and looked curiously around as he prepared to dial.

CHAPTER 39

At Wynyard Station Geoff Miller was cleaning a stretch of tiled floor for the fifth time and was beginning to take pride in his work. Fenway was on the other side of the concourse; they exchanged nods as Fenway likewise applied himself. Miller continued working, then became aware of activity near one of the escalators. He leant on his plastic mop and saw someone emerge from the scrum.

Miller froze...it was Javid Sattar, familiar to him as 'The Boss Man'. Sattar separated from the gaggle of people and dodged behind a pillar; in full view of Miller but hidden from the centre of the concourse. Bramble and others materialised at the top of the escalator, Bramble spotted Miller and shouted.

'Where did he go?'

As Miller indicated Javid Sattar standing by the pillar, Bramble screamed at Miller.

'Don't let him use his phone!'

Miller's paralysis evaporated, he seized and swung the half

full bucket by the handle, shouted as he sprang forward, hurled the bucket and covered himself with soapy water in the process. The bucket struck Sattar on his right wrist, knocked the phone in his hand out of alignment and caused him to stumble. By the time he'd recovered himself Miller had launched himself in a Rugby tackle, meaning to strike Sattar at knee level, but instead his left shoulder hit Sattar's rib cage.

They fell in a tangled heap on the concourse, Sattar tried to rise but Miller struck him across the side of the jaw with the outside of his left hand. As Sattar went down again his head struck the side of a drinks machine. Miller landed on top of him, kicking and punching like a man possessed, completely out of control as accumulated anger and frustration of the two previous weeks erupted within him. The weight of unjust accusations, arrests by police, incarceration at the Walters farm including the blow he had received there that had nearly knocked him senseless, and the refusal of Mrs Lindsay and Lonsdale to believe him when he had been telling the truth, finally struck home.

He momentarily lost his grip on Sattar who, despite the punishment being administered, regained his phone. Miller knew he'd lost as Sattar's hand gripped it, then Sattar screamed with pain as a heel crunched down on the back of his hand. The phone slid across the tiled floor and hit the wall as Bramble joined the fray, from that point Sattar's resistance ended. The constables from the newsstand and florist pounded up and Miller heard the click of handcuffs. As Miller was assisted to his feet, Doug Fenway was sprawled on the floor nearby.

'Was that you?' he asked Fenway as one of the police picked up Sattar's mobile phone. 'Did you stamp on Sattar's hand?'

'Yes,' Fenway nodded. 'Just a reflex action!'

'Bloody good reflex action,' grunted Bramble who overheard. 'I reckon his pack was to be detonated by his phone.'

'I thought they weren't suicide bombers.'

'I don't think that bothered *him*,' Bramble replied as Sattar was hustled away. 'That was his Plan 'B', probably known to him and nobody else! It nearly came off.'

'Have we got them all?'

'One got away. He got on a train to Circular Quay.'

'Oh God!' Fenway covered his face with his hands. 'Alison'.

'Don't worry,' said Bramble. 'We've got it covered.'

*

As the train drew in at Circular Quay Alison walked along the platform as if intending to board. No passengers were awaiting the train, police and the military had sealed off the stairways leading to it. A few passengers alighted and Alison scanned them all, turned and headed back again. Then she saw him, her heart thumped as she saw the face she loathed. She experienced a thrill of fear when she realised he'd seen and recognised her. Alison turned to Phil Jackson, right behind her.

'There!' she shouted. 'Brown jacket.'

The man stopped, looked around desperately then turned to run. He made about four paces before two undercover police intercepted him. He was borne down onto the platform by sheer weight of numbers, hands secured behind him. Shehzad glowered furiously at Alison as he was dragged to his feet.

'Whore! Slut!' he screamed. He was still abusing her as the police escorted him away. Phil Jackson ran forward as two men from the Army bomb squad arrived. Station staff shepherded disembarked passengers away and down the steps.

'He's left a bag on the train, that carriage,' Jackson shouted and the two Army men boarded the train.

Alison's eyes filled with tears, she covered her face with her hands and sobbed as an avalanche of invective directed solely at her continued from Shehzad as he disappeared from sight; Phil Jackson put a consoling arm around her shoulders.

'Time to go,' he said. 'If somebody like that thinks that badly of you, there can't be much wrong with you...eh?'

But Alison still stood, hands over her face and wept, Jackson led her to the stairwell.

'Come on,' he stood before her and seized both her shoulders. 'Remember, you've helped save hundreds of lives today.'

He pressed a button on his phone.

'All secure at Circular Quay,' he reported. 'Bomber under arrest, Alison fingered him. He left the bomb on the train, the army is handling it.'

*

Kelsey snapped shut his mobile phone and turned to Major Collins.

'That was Phil Jackson, Major. The man who escaped from Wynyard has been arrested. They jumped him at Circular Quay.'

'Have we got them all?'

'The bombers, yes. One of the snipers got away but left his rifle behind. We know who he is, Juan Rivera, Geoff Miller saw him at Hopetoun. Rivera is different from the others; they are political agitators and religious fanatics; Rivera is a mercenary.'

'Why hire anyone?' Captain Roberts asked the inevitable question. 'They seemed to have enough homegrown resources when you look at people like Abbas.'

'They needed a marksman,' said Kelsey. 'Rivera has done work for them before, and he's a dead shot. Further, all the others with a motive for killing De Souza were Taranganese, a nationality we were looking for. Rivera is a Spaniard, a European, who could slip through the net. Also, if their assassination attempt failed, and Rivera was caught in the act, it could be blamed on a nutter, a criminal or mercenary Western element, not a faction in Taranga.'

'That makes sense,' grunted Collins. 'It leaves them to fight another day and say it was nothing to do with them.'

'Rivera could shoot the wings off a fly at 100 metres,' continued Kelsey. 'That was what they needed in the situation they planned. The first shot counts, there may only be time for one.'

'Like Lee Harvey Oswald,' Major Collins said grimly. 'If the Dallas rifleman had been an average shot Kennedy may have survived. But why wasn't he shooting from the window, why in that back street?'

'The window was the original plan,' Kelsey replied. 'But the Presidential entourage and our Federal Police agreed to vary the routine and use the back door instead of the front.'

'Then why was Qassim in the building?'

'As I see it, when Rivera entered the building, Qassim accompanied him to establish authenticity. He stayed in the Agnarat Wen office, while Rivera occupied the old Hill & Berrett office where he had a clear shot,' said Kelsey. 'The original plan was for shooters in two buildings but the other building was compromised and they had to abandon it.'

'Which just left the one?' commented Captain Roberts

'When it was decided De Souza would exit via the hotel's rear door, Rivera was needed there and switched to the van outside it, but couldn't take the rifle with him.'

'Why Rivera? Why not the redundant shooter from the other building?'

'Presumably he was Taranganese and would have been

spotted immediately, Rivera is European. Then Qassim assumed Rivera's position in the vacant Hill & Berrett office to remove the gun. He had a right to be in the building and could legitimately walk out carrying a valise,' said Kelsey. 'If the assassination was successful, it was vital to get anything associated with the plot out of the building, Qassim was told to get out.'

'Is Rivera still armed and liable to shoot people?' asked Major Collins.

'I doubt it,' answered Kelsey. 'There were rifles in the van, but when he was running from Shackleton and McKay, he carried nothing. Rivera works for cash. He wouldn't shoot people at random...no payment therefore no point. He was hired to shoot De Souza. Escape would be his priority now.'

'From what you've said about Rivera, how the hell did he get into Australia?'

'Good question. He entered through Avalon Airport using the name Alvarez.'

'Nobody recognised him?'

'Obviously not, Major,' said Kelsey. 'We're investigating it now.'

'If he got in, how will he get out?'

'Another good question!'

'Bloody hell! Incidentally, where's President De Souza now?'

'Safely out of his hotel, Major, on his way to Parliament House to meet the Premier. They've changed the vehicle and the route. But although this aspect is over, there's definitely a leakage from the President's entourage.'

'My bloody oath there is, with a gunman on the loose I hope that's sorted and damned quick.'

Kelsey and Sam Holmes later convened the operatives at the ASIO station in Sydney.

'I've seen all the paperwork now,' said Holmes. 'But one thing bugs me. How did Qassim and Rivera get into that office of Hill & Berrett?'

'I can answer that,' said Melanie. 'I spoke with Barry Rawlings and Robert Colbeck. Hill & Berrett imported and sold French spectacle frames and serviced optometrists in New South Wales and Victoria, they were mainly on the road. When Agnarat Wen were negotiating for the upper floor office, they asked if they could view the Hill & Berrett offices, which were being vacated two weeks later.'

'Why did they do that?' queried Holmes.

'The office they rented established a base within the building, but had a flaw, a flag pole prevented a clear shot. The Hill & Berrett office was similarly placed, a few floors down. Colbeck reckons, when viewing it, they nicked one of Hill's business cards and made up their own using similar fonts and format, easy with computers these days. Somebody, not the two Agnarat partners who were known, entered the building when they knew Hill and Berrett were up country, claimed to be reps or associates, said they needed entry to the office and could they please have the key.'

'With business cards that identified them as such,' Kelsey added. 'Easy when you know how. When they got the key, they made an impression of it.'

'It was probably that prat Roy Walters, they might have queried a Taranganese,' said Shackleton. 'How did Colbeck and Rawlings lock onto that?'

'The receptionist, Angela Parish, checked the Hill Berrett file and found a forged business card,' said Melanie. 'She was on duty at the time and remembered it. Robert Colbeck has contacted Jack Berrett since then who confirmed the business card was fake, a good reproduction but Jack spotted discrepancies, the font was slightly different.'

'Does that answer your question?' Kelsey asked and Holmes nodded. Kelsey hammered the table to quell the buzz of conversation.

'Let's have some quiet and get on with the business, we have work to do.' Kelsey gave a brief resumé of events as they stood. 'For some of you, your part is finished. You can go back to your own occupations and studies with the thanks of the Australian government. Without you our task would have been immeasurably more difficult,' he turned to Miller. 'Your Rugby tackle was a classic, have you ever played?'

'Second grade in Victoria, and at school. The headmaster was a Welshman.'

'Say no more, you can go back to work now, we've had your car checked over, at government expense. A few scratches incurred at Hopetoun have been rectified.' Kelsey then added with a smile. 'But whatever you do, don't get caught speeding through northern Victoria. I blasted Lonsdale yesterday, as did Roger Preston, Lonsdale will be after blood, especially yours.'

He turned to Fenway and Alison.

'We appreciate you put your lives on the line, your presence was essential to point out these people as we had no record of some of them,' he looked around. 'We also owe much to Mr Kamiza, the father of Abbas. He could have gone the other way, but didn't. He put consideration for his fellow men above family when he knew what was at stake. And Khalil Rafit, the true face of the Muslim community whose assistance was vital.'

'Alan...one point?' said Miller.

'What's that?'

'If they're planning a terror attack, why invite people like Roy Walters, Alison, Doug Fenway, Godfrey Thomas and others into their organisation?'

'I can answer that,' Sam Holmes intervened. 'The reverse was the case. They infiltrated an existing organisation. Those you mentioned, being of European origin, acted as a front to divert attention from their fundamentalist theme, but they weren't introduced into the terror aspect. Communists used this tactic, find fellow travellers, people like Burgess and MacLean, as do Islamist fundamentalists. Infiltrate groups and contaminate minds of young people, in some cases even persuading them to become active fighters.'

'Young converts become useful to them, when they've reached that status they are introduced more and more into the centre of things,' added Kelsey. 'Where security organisations like ours keep an eye on possible Taranganese terrorists, in the main we check people of Asian origin. Young Westerners, co-opted or corrupted, can slip under our radar. Regrettably converts are often the most volatile.'

'But with Fenway and Furnell, they obviously failed.'

'They succeeded with one, Roy Walters' said Sam Holmes. 'It's a numbers game. Roy Walters was gullible, but Doug Fenway, Godfrey Thomas, Alison and that young lady Simone did not. One out of five is a fair return for these people, Communists are adept at it.'

'Those who prove useless to them, not persuadable, are just cast adrift,' explained Kelsey. 'Or, like Godfrey Thomas, Alison, Doug and Simone, they cast themselves adrift.'

'Were all these groups connected?' asked Miller. 'Were they involved with that group who've been in court over the past month?'

Holmes shook his head.

'Separate group altogether but similar aims,' he said. 'Those in court are Islamic terrorists, pure and simple, this group we've just broken up were Taranganese nationalists, or regime changers, call them what you will.'

'Who was the ASIO man the defence counsel was trying to identify in court?'

'That's classified,' Kelsey commented. 'But you know him, just leave it at that!'

'What will happen to Abbas?' asked Miller.

'Difficult to say,' Sam Holmes shrugged. 'A young, misguided fool in my opinion, in the same category as those who flew aircraft into the Twin Towers. The imam made headway and extracted some information, but whether Khalil can restore him to the true faith...!'

'Will he finish up in jail?' asked Doug Fenway.

'Good question,' said Sam Holmes. 'If the courts let him off, I wouldn't like him living next door or in the same street as my family!'

'Especially if he has a garden shed,' Kelsey added grimly.

*

As they broke up Melanie found herself facing Alison across the table, who was accompanied by Doug Fenway. Melanie's eyes strayed across to Fenway, then to Alison, their eyes met and they exchanged brief nods. Melanie eyed Fenway meaningly. Alison smiled, Melanie collected her papers, smiled again at Alison, then left the room.

'Ships that pass in the night,' she thought. 'But if she drops that prat Roy, some good will come out of it.'

Kelsey and Bramble escorted Doug Fenway and Alison Furnell to the foyer, and briefly conversed by the main door.

'I've arranged for Phil Jackson to drive you home,' Kelsey said to Alison and pointed. 'There he is, by the kerb at the bottom of the steps.'

Kelsey and Bramble shook hands with them both and the two students left the building. As they descended the steps en route to Phil Jackson and the car, Kelsey turned to Bramble.

'Two things really got to me in this whole business, Bob. One is bloody Lonsdale, that stupid prat nearly allowed them to slip under our radar. The other is Roy bloody Walters. What he did was worse, we had strong leads but he nearly destroyed everything by tipping them off and could have caused hundreds of deaths. Despite his father having a go at him I doubt if he's learnt anything. He's got away scot free!'

As Kelsey turned and headed for the lift shaft, Bramble continued looking through the glass frontage. He called Kelsey back.

'Alan, you're wrong,' he said. 'Look!'

Kelsey followed Bramble's pointed finger. Alison Furnell and Doug Fenway had descended the steps and were approaching the car. Roy Walters had emerged from behind the mounted pedestals at the foot of the flight, advanced towards Alison and reached for her hand in a proprietary manner, but she snatched it away. A heated discussion ensued, then Alison turned around, seized Fenway's hand and they entered the car. The doors closed and Jackson drove off. Roy stood looking after them, then turned, disconsolately, and slouched off in the opposite direction, hands in pockets and shoulders slumped.

'He'll probably blame the CIA for that,' said Kelsey.

*

'Will this do you?' asked Jackson and Alison gave the affirmative. She scrambled out, but Fenway remained in the back seat.

'It's been nice, Allie,' he said uneasily, 'I'll probably see you around...!'

'Come on up, I'll make you coffee,' Alison said sharply.

'Well, no...I 'd better not, but thanks any...!'

But after the events of the past couple of weeks, with her hormones awakened, and screaming for more, Alison was not in the mood for indecision or reticence. She reached over, disconnected his seat belt, seized his hand and pulled him out of the car.

'Shut up! Just come on.'

Fenway found himself on the pavement, shuffling his feet awkwardly, Alison kept hold of his hand and pushed him towards the gate. She became aware that Phil Jackson was grinning as he sat with his elbow propped on the open window.

'Thanks,' she said. 'See you later.'

Jackson nodded, waved and wound up the window.

'Lucky bastard,' he said to himself as he drove off.

CHAPTER 40

Miller stayed overnight in Sydney, there was no point leaving late afternoon as Shackleton and McKay brought in slabs of beer which they demolished in the conference room. The session relieved the accumulated tension of past weeks. All were aware, had anything gone radically wrong, hundreds of people, including themselves, could have been killed or severely injured.

During the evening, Miller buttonholed Sam Holmes and Kelsey.

'Who tipped off those snipers?'

'Well, it wasn't Roy Walters or Abbas,' said Kelsey. 'Both were in custody and incommunicado. They're looking into the possibility of a mole on the President's entourage.'

'What will happen to the ones we caught?' Miller asked.

'What indeed?' Sam Holmes said with a trace of bitterness. 'We catch the bastards and the judiciary will probably let them off. The last time we nabbed bastards like this we had civil libertarians accusing us of racism and being a Police State.'

'They talk of human rights,' Kelsey added with the same degree of acidity. 'But not a word for human rights of commuters passing through Wynyard and other city stations, or their rights to use the railway system without being killed or maimed.'

'You reckon they'll get off?'

'Not if we have anything to do with it,' said Holmes grimly. 'We have the bombs they were going to detonate, with their finger prints on cases that held the explosives.'

'Just watch the newspapers,' said Kelsey.

'What about Roy Walters?'

'Don't talk to me about Roy fucking Walters,' Kelsey said angrily. 'That silly sod nearly cost us the whole operation. But one good thing came out of it, he lost the girl.'

'Girl?' Miller cocked his head to one side. 'Ah...you mean Alison?'

'I do!' Kelsey said with a smile. 'She gave him the old heave ho when he tried to claim her outside and she went off with Doug Fenway.'

'Good!' said Miller. 'A vast improvement. He stopped Sattar dialling on his mobile, that bastard could have blown us all up.'

'He broke two of Sattar's fingers so I heard.' added Kelsey.

'Good!'

Miller thought of Roy losing Alison, then wondered if he could have lost Jacqueline Jameson. He realised in all the excitement he hadn't phoned her for several days. 'I've got to make a phone call; is there a phone I can use?'

'Feel free,' said Holmes and turned to Alan Kelsey. 'How has Max Walters taken it?'

'Very well, Max is a realist,' Kelsey replied. 'He's told me he used to be a radical himself when he was Roy's age and modified his views when he got married and took on a mortgage, as we all did. I did mention one thing to him, indirectly connected with what we've been through,' he turned to Miller. 'Do you remember Parmenter?'

'Parmenter?' Miller's brow knotted then light dawned. 'Oh, the farmer up that track, nice old boy.'

'When we were talking to him, Parmenter mentioned Max's father had promised he'd sell him some land that bordered Parmenter's land, a paddock he couldn't get a tractor into because of a deep creek and a rocky outcrop. I mentioned it to Max, he's going to Hopetoun next week and said he'd look into that. He's going to sell the property anyway now, so hiving off that paddock separately won't bother him unduly.'

Miller stayed the night in the motel, was it only that morning he had left it? He collected his car from the ASIO car pool and after handshakes all round departed with instructions for reaching the South Eastern Distributor. Kelsey and his colleagues were heading for Canberra later, while Melanie Cassidy, as one of Sam Holmes's permanent operatives, remained in Sydney.

As he passed through the car park entrance, he wondered if the world would ever seem the same again.

He spent that night at a Hopetoun motel, rang Roger Preston and called on him the next morning on his way out of town. Roger was pleased to see him and they had a cup of coffee in the police station.

'How did it go?' Roger asked. 'We saw reports in the morning papers, did you catch them all?'

'We caught the bastard who was running the Walters farm operation,' said Miller. 'We broke two of his fingers when we got him.'

'Wish you'd broken his bloody neck!' commented Preston.

As they shook hands outside the police station Preston said: 'Watch your speed as you head south, Lonsdale is operating a speed trap down there, he'll be overjoyed to see you again!'

'He'll book me whether I'm over the limit or not. I'll just pray he doesn't recognise my registration,' said Miller. 'Thanks Roger, I'll call you if I have another job around here.'

*

The passengers mustered near the gangway ready for their run ashore on the island of Vanuatu. Before they disembarked, the purser gave a brief run down on what to do and what not to, what to avoid and how not to be taken in by people who would attempt to sell them anything, such as watches guaranteed to work until the ship left harbour. He emphasised duty-free liquor could be purchased aboard ship more cheaply than at any local liquor outlets.

As the shore going passengers reached the quayside one of them, a man in his middle thirties, walked briskly from the harbour area into one of the main streets. He entered a small antique shop.

'I was told you had examples of first edition Shakespeare volumes for sale.'

'They are in short supply,' replied the bearded proprietor. 'But we have very old editions of Daniel Defoe, a copy of Captain Singleton in very good condition.'

'I'd like to see that. Do I have to make an appointment?'

The shop was empty. The shop owner jerked his head to one side and indicated to the customer to follow him to a room at the rear. He jerked his thumb at a vacant chair.

'Our friends in Chile have to confirm, it should not take long, arrangements will be made,' he said. 'I heard things went badly,

Julius Lebak had to leave Jakarta in a hurry, De Souza demanded the Indonesians arrest him and extradite him to Taranga.'

'Where is he now?' asked Rivera.

'In a safe place, leave it at that. As for you, be patient, we cannot rush things but matters are in hand,' responded the bearded man. 'Where's the passport you were using?'

'Here,' Rivera handed it over.

'Senor Plasencia,' the other said cynically. 'This must be destroyed as they will be on the lookout for it after you disappeared from the cruise liner. Make yourself at home, I have to get back to the shop.'

'How long before I move from here?'

'As soon as arrangements can be made, it should not take long, maybe a week, even two. For the present …'the bearded man laughed briefly '…enjoy!'

*

Miller sat at his desk riffling through current files. Don Atkinson was still away and Peter Hallam had handled Miller's work during his absence. Pete had completed some, others awaited responses from insurers. Footsteps headed in his direction, it was Jacqueline. They had had dinner at a restaurant the previous evening and had returned to Miller's place where she had stayed the night. Despite that, he still felt his mouth go dry as he watched her move towards him.

She waggled her rear end as she sat opposite and crossed her legs, fully aware of the effect she was having. She laid a file on the other side of his desk.

'Bill said you were to handle this one,' she said.

'Why?' Miller answered.

'You've seen him before.'

'Oh yes?' Miller raised an eyebrow. 'Who is it?'

Not bloody Hammoud! No, it couldn't be. He was in jail unless the do-gooders had let him out! And please, not that bloody man Smith again! She handed him the file and Miller spotted the name on the top.

'Not him again?'

'Yes, again. Bill said you should see him.' She rose to go. 'Incidentally, the Hawks have a supporters' night on Friday night. Interested?'

'Very!' Miller replied cynically. 'I could do with some excitement!'

She gave one of her trademark smiles that hit him between the eyes.

'Well, I can probably guarantee that,' she walked back to her desk. He watched her go and thought that indeed she would.

*

'What happened this time?'

'Same as last time, they came through from the lane way at the rear and broke in through the laundry door,' said Bert Butler.

'Didn't you install a burglar alarm?'

'Nah! I didn't think it was worth it, not so sure now,' Butler shook his head.

'You said lightning would never strike twice.'

Butler smiled and shrugged.

'Yes, I did!' he admitted. 'You know how to rub it in, don't you?'

'Well, blokes like you keep me in a job,' Miller replied. 'Without you I'd have nothing to do.'

'How many jobs have you done since you were last here?' asked Butler.

'Not many,' admitted Miller. 'About seven all told.'

This was true; he had done some burglaries when Clucas had kept him from surveillance jobs after the second arrest by the police. After that he had had the three subsequent surveillance jobs for workers compensation, the last of which had resulted in his incarceration at the Walters farmhouse and subsequent time in Sydney.

'By God!' Butler said with feeling. 'You blokes have a cushy life! I've done twenty jobs since I last saw you. What have you done since then? Twiddled your thumbs?'

'Something like that,' Miller said gravely.

*

THE END

P8: References to Van Ekeren, a businessman caught up in a previous coup d'état, were the subject of a previous book by the writer entitled *Double Dutch*.

www.ingramcontent.com/pod-product-compliance
Lightning Source LLC
Chambersburg PA
CBHW020250120726

47904CB00001B/150